The Bad Women

The Bad Women

Jennie Ensor

This edition produced in Great Britain in 2025

by Hobeck Books Limited, 24 Brookside Business Park, Stone, Staffordshire
ST15 0RZ

www.hobeck.net

A CIP catalogue for this book is available from the British Library.

ISBN 978-1-915-817-x84-6 (ebook)

ISBN 978-1-915-817-85-3 (pbk)

Cover design by Jayne Mapp Design

https://jaynemapp.wixsite.com

Are you a thriller seeker?

Hobeck Books is an independent publisher of crime, thrillers and suspense fiction and we have one aim – to bring you the books you want to read.

For more details about our books, our authors and our plans, plus the chance to download free novellas, sign up for our newsletter at **www.hobeck.net**.

You can also find us on X/Twitter **@hobeckbooks** or on Facebook **www.facebook.com/hobeckbooks10**.

For all of my friends who struggle with their physical or mental health, yet continue to get up each day

Part One

Part One

Chapter 1
Ashley

Oh God, if only her mother could stop complaining for a moment. Especially anything involving her uncomfortable mattress, cold bedroom, the long list of foods she couldn't eat or the inadequacies of Brampton. Why had she ever suggested that her mother move in, and how could she survive five more months of this?

'I'm going for a walk,' Ashley announced as her mother began to describe her nocturnal journey to refill her hot-water bottle. Diane's intensely groomed eyebrows met beneath her fringe.

'Can you take Brillo, too? You only took him out for half an hour this morning. He'll enjoy seeing some new scenery.'

Ashley grabbed the lead and stomped towards the front door.

'When will you be back?'

She didn't answer. Right now, she didn't feel like coming back.

Outside the village, instead of heading towards higher ground, she took the undulating path that wended between waterlogged fields. The landscape here wasn't at all striking but there would be no flocks of sheep to tempt the dog.

'Let's go!'

Brillo paid no attention. The Welsh terrier had stopped yet again, this time nosing inside a plastic wrapper. Thankful for her fur-lined boots, she jogged on the spot to stay warm.

The path continued past farm buildings and a pile of shredded plastic in a field. Her boots squeaked on frozen mud. Ahead, Brillo criss-crossed the path. It was a weekday afternoon in early January. School and work had re-started; hardly anyone was about. She felt a pang for her work as a book illustrator. If only the pay had been enough to hire a carer... Thank God, they'd agreed for her to return after six months' leave.

The wooded slopes bordering the old quarry loomed. In over five years living here, she'd never come this way. At a frozen puddle, she stopped. A sign guarded a narrow path leading off this one:

QUARRY AHEAD: PRIVATE PROPERTY
KEEP OUT

Her nostrils twitched. Something horrible... it had a foul base note, like rancid food. She checked her watch. Gone three. They ought to head back before the sun sank any lower. She turned to the dog as he scampered onto the other path towards a squirrel.

Blasted dog! Once he caught a scent, there was no stopping him.

'Brillo, come!'

She strode into a thicket of bare trees along the path, pushing past stray branches, peering left and right, occasionally yelling for the dog.

Ahead, the ground rapidly descended. Ashley stopped at the edge. The jagged, roughly circular hole hewn out of the earth was partly filled with rubble and slabs of concrete. She'd never seen the remaining quarry from this close. It was bigger than she'd imagined.

A figure in silhouette on the far side caught her eye – a female, emerging every so often from bushes. Something on her body glinted. She was running, clumsily, as if her feet were landing awkwardly. Without slowing, the woman swung her head to look behind. Moments later, she vanished.

Ashley waited. She half expected to see someone chasing. But there was no sign of anyone else... nor of the dog.

'Brillo!'

No flash of ginger-brown fur, only forlorn echoes and the flap of wings. The first stabs of panic arrived. Carefully, she made her way down towards an ancient wire fence. Its lower section was uneven and gappy; Brillo could have squeezed underneath. Attached to the fence was a flaking sign:

DANGER:
KEEP OUT

She stared into the huge pit beyond. Brillo... Another stab of panic. She scrabbled through the undergrowth, following an over-grown path along the quarry's rim. Sections of the fence lay broken. Beyond it, the ground fell steeply towards uncertain depths.

'Brillo!'

Her cry returned, mocking.

A loud bark from just ahead made her jump. Relief, as Brillo trotted towards her. He stopped, tail down and barked three times.

'What's the matter?'

He let loose a volley of short, high-pitched barks.

She spread her arms. 'Show me.'

To her surprise the dog trotted along in the direction he'd come from. She followed him to the far side. Ahead, a finger-like section of rock protruded over the quarry.

'Brillo, wait!'

Ashley stepped over the broken fence and took several steps

along the overhang – there was nothing to stop her falling thirty feet – and peered down. It took a while to notice what lay there: a body, unmoving. She gasped and hurried after Brillo, fear gnawing as she tried to follow the makeshift path between rocks and debris. Finally, she arrived at a flatter section. The dog stood barking beside the body then began nosing at a protruding arm, whimpering.

'Get away!'

At her shout Brillo lay down, still whimpering. She stepped closer. It was a young woman in a waterproof jacket over a jumper, leggings and trainers – the woman she'd seen running just now, surely. Dark brown hair rippled onto the icy ground. Her jaw was tilted unnaturally backwards, exposing a silver chain in the hollow of her neck. Her upper body was twisted and misshapen. A gold chain circled her right wrist, on the inside of which were marks and scratches, red against her white skin. Her eyes were wide open, as was her mouth.

Ashley dropped to her knees. A cold tremble travelled through her body. Though she knew there was no point, she pressed two fingers to the young woman's wrist. The skin was warm. She waited a while then raised herself unsteadily and stepped backwards, almost losing her footing. Then she sank onto a concrete slab and called 999.

They arrived home in the back of a police car. Ashley flopped onto the sofa and closed her eyes. As instructed by the call handler, she had made her way up to a narrow road behind the quarry, dog at her side, waited for the police and paramedics to turn up and led them to the body. She had told a uniformed police officer how she'd found it, though she'd forgotten to tell him about the running woman, she'd realised in the car afterwards.

While she was mindlessly watching TV – her mother in bed asleep – an officer from Elven Police called. Would Ashley be able to come to the station in the morning to give a statement?

She agreed, thinking that she would mention the missed details.

Reluctantly, she phoned Zac. Though their conversations generally went badly, she ought to update him on the day's events. Her husband didn't interrupt and said nothing when she'd finished.

'Are you still there?'

'What made you do it, Ashley?'

Her heart began to pound. 'Do what?'

'Get yourself involved with the police again. Go hunting after bodies—'

'That was the dog, not me. He ran off—'

'But why did you have to call the police?'

'I'd just found a dead body!'

'Someone else would have found it, sooner or later.'

'Are you serious? I can't believe you're saying this. I always thought you were...' She stopped. A good man? But who was she to judge?

'Ash, listen. By some stroke of luck, you've got away with what you did – so far. I don't think you should be going anywhere near the police unless it's absolutely necessary.'

'It's done. I doubt that telling the police what I saw is going to set off anything.' She hoped this was true. But what if her actions were to stir things up again?

'Goodnight, then.' His tone was curt.

Zac hung up. The distance between them greater than ever. She sat limply, listening to the intermittent scraping from next door. Elspeth had eventually sold number 33 to Ken Dickson, a DIY enthusiast.

It's over between us.

That thought brought sadness but also relief. Zac had separated from her, emotionally as well as physically – and she needed to do the same.

Slow, heavy footsteps from the hall. Her mother, wrapped in a duvet-like garment and clutching her walking frame, appeared in the doorway.

'I heard you talking.' Diane's face gathered into an expression of not-so-stoic suffering. 'I'd just managed to doze off.'

'Sorry to wake you.' Damn, she'd forgotten to keep her voice down. Had her mother heard something she shouldn't have?

'I got your message. You found a body in the quarry?'

'Brillo did, actually. He led me to it. You're right, he's a real terrier.'

Diane blinked sleepily. 'Of course he is. I told you he's a hunter.'

'I'm going to put some soup on. Do you want any?'

'My hip's agony right now. I'm not in the mood for eating.'

'Have you put on Voltarol?'

'What do you think? I'm in pain, I haven't got dementia.'

'God's sake, Mum! I only asked.'

Although barely a month had passed since Diane's arrival with Brillo and her many 'essentials' in tow, it felt like a year. She urged the universe for her mother's hip replacement operation not to be delayed, and for Diane to recover quickly and return to Surrey.

Ashley lay in bed, awake. Every time her eyes closed an image of the dead woman returned: the shocking brokenness of her body, her fixed, terrified expression – and beyond that, the woman's broad face with its arrow-straight nose and downward-sloping blue eyes. There was something familiar.

Of course, Alison. But Alison, if she'd lived, would have been thirty years older than this woman.

Her mind wandered. Who was the dead woman and how had she died? Could she have taken a wrong turn in the failing light, run towards that ledge and been unable to stop? Had she stumbled while trying to evade a pursuer? Or had someone pushed her off that ledge?

Granted, she hadn't seen or heard anyone. But she was quite certain of it: that woman had been fleeing from something, or someone.

The next day

Unlike the former Brampton police station, Elven police station was situated in a shabby building. Ashley signed in at reception and put her ID on. A uniformed officer arrived, looked at Brillo in surprise then took the pair through a turnstile and two sets of secure doors to a room containing a crate full of Lego bricks.

Yawning, Ashley settled into one of the upholstered chairs beside a table. It was only nine thirty and she hadn't slept well. Her mother had persuaded Ashley to take the dog because she had a dentist appointment and she didn't want Brillo 'being left on his own after the stress of yesterday'.

A youngish woman in a long cardigan over leggings entered.

'Ashley Khan? I'm Detective Constable Kate Peters.' The detective spoke assuredly with a London accent. She smiled broadly on seeing the dog, his head resting on his paws. 'And who's this?'

'Brillo. He's always wanted to see inside a police station.'

Clearly pleased to welcome a canine visitor, DC Peters rubbed Brillo's back. She was around thirty and the same height as herself, five feet four, with a more womanly figure. Her jaw was framed by dark blonde hair.

'Could you describe what you saw and heard at the quarry yesterday, please?'

Ashley repeated her story. 'There's something else, something I forgot to mention yesterday. I saw the woman running shortly before she... Shortly before I spotted her body.'

DC Peters looked up sharply from her notebook.

'You saw a woman running? The deceased?'

'That's right.'

'Where exactly was she running?'

'She was across the quarry from me, quite far away. I saw her in silhouette.'

The officer frowned. 'What time was it, do you remember?'

'It must have been close to four. The sun was low.'

'And what time was it when you first caught sight of the body?'

'About ten minutes later.'

DC Peters leaned forward. 'Why do you think that body you found belonged to the woman that you saw running?'

Ashley shifted. 'The body on the ground looked like her,' she replied slowly. 'The same height and build, the same long hair.' It was obvious to her that the woman she'd glimpsed running was the same woman that she'd discovered dead on the ground.

'But you can't be certain, given that the woman you saw running was a considerable distance away?'

'Not one hundred percent, no.'

The detective nodded. 'Have you anything else to add to your statement, Ashley?'

'There was something about the way she was running. It wasn't like someone out for a jog. More like she was being chased.'

'Did you see anyone chasing her?'

'No.' She drank water from the glass, then met the detective's eyes. 'Could someone have pushed her off that ledge?'

'Rest assured, we'll be looking into how exactly she died.' With a thump, DC Peters pushed her notebook shut. 'Thanks so much for your help, Mrs Khan. Do you have any questions?'

'No, but could you let me know if there are any developments?'

A marginal nod. Ashley wasn't sure why she'd asked; she hadn't known the young woman and this officer seemed competent and conscientious.

At the same time, both women stood and looked at Brillo, who was emitting a long, rumbling snore. The detective smiled and bending, ruffled his fur.

'What a cutie.' Abruptly, she straightened and offered her hand to Ashley. 'Thanks again, Mrs Khan. My colleague will give you a lift home once you've checked your statement.'

Chapter 2
Elspeth

That afternoon

Elspeth gathered the last of the dead leaves into the pile. The daylight was without warmth, as brittle as these ghost-thin leaves, more holes than leaf.

Bending down, she transferred another armful of leaves into the garden waste bag. A sharp pain in her hip joined the twinges of arthritis in her lower back and the steady ache in her knees. What a creaky old thing.

Now she had reached her ninth decade, younger friends frequently suggested she ought to be 'slightly more careful'. Slightly more careful when about to enter a crowded bus or busy shop so as not to 'catch something'. Slightly more careful when waiting at a bus stop in case she got mugged. Slightly more careful when walking on a potentially icy pavement. Slightly more careful, full stop. She had tried to take their advice, thought twice now before doing anything vaguely challenging. But how long would she be able to keep up this Slightly More Careful regime? Spring was coming, and with it, an urge to forget her age.

Elspeth tied off the bag and lowered her bottom to the bench.

From here, she had a good view of the semi-detached house next door, helped by the lack of leaves on the lime tree in the garden of Tara's old house, number 33. Automatically, her gaze flicked up to the mezzanine roof terrace beside her own, as if Tara might have popped outside to have a gander.

She tutted. By now, she should have got used to the fact that her former neighbour had departed irretrievably from this world.

She leaned her head back against the shed and closed her eyes, enjoying the temporary absence of pain. Perhaps it wasn't so surprising that after eighteen years of living next door to Tara Sanderson – combined with the abrupt departure of the woman – she hadn't quite got used to the fact that Tara was gone for good.

Gone for good. All things considered, it was apt. The woman had hardly been an asset. The Covid situation must have unhinged her... ll the same, she missed Tara. Despite the woman's pettiness and possessiveness, and her less-than-likeable traits, Tara had been a character.

Elspeth shifted on the bench. Unlike Ashley, she had got on with her life without undue worrying about being held to account for their roles in Tara's death. Fortunately, there was little chance of that now; the murder investigation had long since faded.

She thought again of Ashley's news. As unlikely as it sounded, her friend at number 32 had found a dead body in the old quarry. Was that a good omen, or...? She felt a tiny shiver.

Weak sunshine broke through, catching the window giving onto the roof terrace next door. For a moment she could imagine a woman standing behind the blinds, looking out – one with a substantial, colorfully draped upper half, a swirl of dyed blonde hair and eyes that missed nothing.

But no. Ken Dickson lived at number 33 now. He lived alone and wasn't prone to having visitors, certainly not female ones. She must rid her mind of all this supernatural guff.

Elspeth gave her arms a brisk rub and pushed herself up from the bench. Time to go inside to get warm.

Chapter 3
DC Peters

'Sorry I'm late. The bus went off piste.' Kate shuffled towards the table, where two men were seated beside her boss. Oh, how she wished she'd never joined this Force.

'Kate. I thought you'd decided to stay at home.' DI Lister straightened her back. Her black hair drawn into a tight pony tail. Her harsh lipstick not distracting from a weak chin. 'We're having a look at the quarry death. You've met DS Renn?'

'Not properly.' She met the eyes of the crumpled looking middle-aged man beside DI Lister. She had blundered into Detective Sergeant Renn at the coffee machine on her first day, head fuzzy after getting in atrociously early. Apart from her apologising for making him spill his coffee, they'd not actually spoken.

'Kate, welcome.' Smiling, DS Renn nudged his paper cup further away from her.

'Hello, sar... sarge? Sergeant?'

'Sarge will do, or Rob.'

'OK, sarge.' He had a smattering of grey hairs around his temples and deep brown eyes. If she hadn't been useless at relationships, she might have fancied him.

'And this is Kelvin, our SOCO,' DI Lister said, indicating the younger male and turning to the screen behind, displaying a slide headed *Timeline: Emily Hale*. 'Right, let's not waste any more time. As we know, a female body was found in the old Brampton quarry the day before yesterday, by a local woman walking her dog.'

There were no signs of any third-party involvement, the DI explained; the deceased, identified as 24-year-old Emily Hale of Brampton Wood mobile home site, a beautician in Brampton village, appeared to have fallen from an overhanging ledge. The DI shifted. 'The pathologist found signs he thought might be suspicious – some cuts and developing bruises on the wrists and forearms, basically. A full PM was later carried out. 'DS Renn, the Duty DS, attended the scene with two scene of crime officers. 'Kelvin, do you want to say what you found?'

'We found a tyre mark beside the access road and a footprint near the body,' Kelvin replied, putting aside his egg and bacon roll. He had none-too-clean fingernails. 'The tyre mark is from a Ford panel van, which isn't much help. The footprint was found in an icy patch near the body. We took a cast. It's a Timberland, size 11. There's a ridge on the toe area from gum or something stuck to the sole.'

Kate sat up. That could be useful.

Unimpressed, the DI brushed a piece of dandruff from her blouse.

'Do we know how long it might have been there?'

'A few days, maybe. It's been below freezing at night for nearly a week and not much warmer during the day, down inside that quarry.'

'So the print could have come from anyone.' The DI drummed her fingers on the desk. 'Now, the report from the Home Office pathologist. I've gone over it.' She opened the document in front. 'Death due to massive head and neck trauma, consistent with falling from the height of three storeys, the approximate height of the overhang, and landing head first on a hard surface. There were crushed vertebrae, crushed ribs, broken bones, extensive damage to internal organs.' She shifted to another page. 'Some minor abrasions on her left wrist and developing bruises to her forearms, which he thought could indicate she had been restrained—'

'Restrained?' The sergeant looked up sharply.

'But those marks may have come from the fall, so he says. There was bruising elsewhere, too, and some scratches likely to be from thorns and the like, on the way down. Nothing to justify the cost of a forensic PM, as far as I can see.'

'He didn't find anything else that might be suspicious?' Kate looked at her boss.

'No, Kate, he didn't.' DI Lister gave her a vindictive look. No solidarity among female officers here, then.

'What about that other thing, boss?' The sergeant arched an eyebrow. 'I checked. It wasn't put on the exhibits list.'

'Oh,' DI Lister said, coaxing a white fleck floor-wards. 'You mean that piece of tape?'

DS Renn looked hard at Kelvin. 'It was a piece of gaffer tape about five inches long. Stuck on a bush, near the tyre mark.'

'I didn't see it. Nor did my colleague.' Kelvin shrugged. 'Maybe it blew away, Rob. There was a breeze, remember?'

'That must have been it,' DS Renn replied sotto voce.

'Right.' DI Lister spoke briskly. 'I'm glad that's sorted.'

Kate felt uneasy. The DI had dismissed the sergeant's concern as she might an annoying fly. She switched her attention to DS Renn. Ms Hale had taken a lot of time off work due to ill health, he was saying. The specialist diagnosed her with acute liver disease, cause unclear. Her symptoms worsened a few months ago, and her GP sent her to a kidney specialist. I didn't get to speak to him—'

'I did, Rob.' DI Lister looked at her notes. 'He'd seen Emily on the 8th of January, four days before her death, and had told her she had kidney disease. What was interesting was that he told me that he didn't like to "sugarcoat things for patients" but in retrospect he thought he might have been too blunt. He had warned her that her kidney damage might be irreversible, and dialysis might be needed at some stage. Emily had got upset at this and left.' The DI bent over her notes. 'I also talked to the sister, April. April had talked to Emily later that day. She said Emily's mood had been very low. She hated the idea of being hooked up to a machine for hours.' DI Lister paused. 'April told me she thought Emily's death could well have been suicide.'

'But Emily's mood could have improved once she'd got over the shock of her diagnosis?' It was the sergeant.

'Of course, it *could* have. But no one has said so, to my knowledge.' DI Lister sounded irritated. She scratched the back of her head, more flecks drifted. 'OK, the last person to see Emily alive... Rob, you spoke to her neighbour?'

DS Renn had spoken to Dawn Elms, who had waved to Emily about half past two on the afternoon the body was found, as Emily passed Dawn's window. Dawn thought Emily might have been heading to sit by the river, which runs close to the site; she often went there in the afternoons.

'Kate. You talked to... ah, Ashley Khan. Did you glean anything?'

That supercilious manner again.

'I did, boss. She told me she'd seen Ms Hale on the far side of the quarry just before she died – running as if she was being chased by someone.'

'And you believed her?'

'I did. Mrs Khan was clearly affected by shock but otherwise she seemed a reliable witness. It was far away, granted, so it could have been someone else. But she definitely seems to have seen someone—'

'You think Emily was pushed off that ledge?' DI Lister's frown spread.

Kate opened her mouth to reply, then changed her mind.

'It's possible, isn't it?' DS Renn interjected. 'Emily could have been murdered.'

'But why would anyone want to murder her?'

The sergeant persisted. 'Isn't that what we should be finding out?'

'If we decided to open an investigation. But this one doesn't look like murder to me.' The DI glared at her laptop screen. 'Ashley Khan didn't mention anything about Emily being chased in her first statement, to PC Howe.' She looked accusingly at Kate. 'Isn't that right, Kate?'

'She could have forgotten in the shock of finding the body—'

'Whatever.' The DI let her knuckles contact the table with a stern rap. She doesn't strike *me* as particularly reliable.'

Ignoring the DI, Kate removed her egg-and-cress sandwich from her rucksack. In her efforts to get to the briefing on time, allowing for the vagaries of the 380 bus, she hadn't eaten breakfast.

DS Renn rubbed his jaw before speaking. 'What's the pathologist's estimate for Emily Hale's time of death?'

DI Lister turned to her notes. 'Between 3 and 4 pm.'

'Which doesn't contradict Ashley's belief that she saw Emily running just before she died.'

'No, it doesn't. But it means Emily Hale may have been dead for up to an hour before whoever it was Ashley Khan saw running.'

'No suicide note was found at the scene, or at Emily's home?' DS Renn again.

Kelvin indicated 'no'. Kate bit into her sandwich.

'What about Emily's mobile phone?' The sergeant again. 'Did anyone find it?'

'It wasn't at the quarry,' Kelvin replied. 'And it wasn't at her home when we searched it.'

'So it's possible someone took her phone from her...

'All this is very interesting.' DI Lister drummed her fingers on the table. 'But it doesn't mean Emily Hale didn't take her own life.'

'No, but if you take them all together...' DS Renn fingered his collar. 'Another thing. Emily told Dawn that someone had contacted her about an article, and she was hoping to meet them before flying to America. She couldn't remember the name—'

'That would be Cindra Patel.' DI Lister cut in. 'A would-be journalist, unemployed. Yesterday she gave me a convoluted account about Emily Hale having been poisoned by this, that and the other, then started railing against various heinous local characters who ought to be in prison.' The DI rolled her eyes. 'Apparently Emily had agreed to help with an article she was working on, whatever's that's worth. To be honest, she came across as one of those conspiracy theory types, grasping at straws.'

Kate coughed – a bit of egg was stuck. Her boss's attitude was hardly impartial. Clearly, they did things differently here. Were Elven's detectives in the habit of dropping cases that might prove tricky to solve, or was something else going on?

'Let's finish up shall we, before Kate chokes.' The DI flicked her a cold smile. 'In my view, further investigation isn't going to get us anywhere – I'll inform the DCI. Rob, did you want to say something?'

DS Renn, who had raised a hand, lowered it. DI Lister declared the meeting over and hurried off. Kelvin gave them a curt nod and followed.

'You don't agree with her, do you?'

DS Renn, glanced at the open door then at Kate. 'There are too many things that don't add up.'

She waited but he said no more. *Is it always like this here?* she wanted to ask; there was something disquieting about this place. The silence was broken by her stomach's gurgle. They both laughed. Detective Sergeant Rob Renn was on the right side, she decided, launching into what she was desperate to share.

'I realised last night that Ashley Khan, the woman who found the body, is the same woman suspected of murdering her next-door neighbour back in 2020. I've been looking into some cold cases – when there's nothing else to do, of course.' She hadn't yet been allocated to a current case. Most of her time had been spent trying to make headway with the Force's computer system.

'I remember Ashley.' The sergeant massaged his knee. 'Her goose looked cooked for a while, but the enquiry got sidetracked by a witness report and fizzled out. The other suspect was a feisty old lady who didn't take kindly to DI Lister – DS Lister, as she was then. It was practically my first job as a detective.'

'Could you give me some background on the case, sometime?'

'Sure.' DS Renn gathered up his things again. 'By the way, sorry for being abrupt with you at the coffee machine the other day. I was deep in thought, as usual.' He smiled. 'When did you start here?'

'This is my third day. I was in the Met before. Things didn't work out too well.' That was one way of putting it.

Alone, Kate demolished the remains of her sandwich. Thankfully, the sergeant hadn't asked what had happened at the Met. He'd been friendly, too – the only person in this godforsaken place to show her even a hint of welcome.

Chapter 4
Bird Woman

12 January

In the kitchen drawer I find three silver teaspoons not used since my brother's visit in 2008 and place them on the counter. While I'm at it, I recover three napkins from the lower cupboard. Elspeth and Ashley will appreciate silver and linen with our next afternoon tea, which might compensate for the lack of dusting.

More rummaging reveals an unlovely tea towel, a hideous vase my brother gave me when I moved in and my first pair of binoculars. Then I spy the cylinder of cartridge paper.

The drawing. I lift it from the cupboard, unpick the sellotape and unroll the A2 sheet onto the table. Two men and four women are gathered around a buxom woman in a puff-sleeved top, cropped jeans and flip-flops. She is cowering, hands over her face. Stains are evident on her clothing and the exposed parts of her body.

The scene is drawn in pencil, from memory, including details I observed through my binoculars: the red flashes on the disabled man's electric vehicle, Elspeth's glittering emerald earrings,

Ashley's petite but sturdy frame and the shine of the apple gripped in her hand. I'd only just started drawing people and it took me considerable time to get the figures right, especially the hands.

I turn away. I can't look at the drawing for long. It's as if I am seeing everything for the first time.

Perhaps I shouldn't have drawn such a gruesome subject. But something compelled me – an urge to portray life in extremis or a sudden desire to prolong that short period of drama in my life. Not much happens to me most of the time, which is entirely my fault.

I settle into the armchair. The fire isn't going, due to my lethargy – more logs need to be hauled inside. Beyond the window, jays and magpies hunt for bacon scraps. I pull the blanket over. To ward off the cold, I'm wearing fingerless gloves, two pairs of socks, three pairs of leggings, my two thickest jumpers, my winter boots and a bobble hat, both from the Oxfam shop.

Thanks to my substantial lunch, I nod off quickly. (No bird observations of note.) Plus, this chair that Elspeth bought me with the rest of the money from number 33 is supremely comfortable.

I'm startled awake by a commotion at the front door. It's Liz Peaches, the vicar of Brampton's melancholy little church. A hemp shopping bag is slung over her shoulder. Lately she's in the habit of coming to my door at the most inconvenient times – when I'm about to finish a book or on the toilet. Ever since I attended three of her sparsely attended but gloriously heated Sunday services, I've become the target of her efforts to help me find religion, and, I suspect, bring me into the 21st century. She has started to take an inordinate interest in my wellbeing: how much I am eating, whether I can still afford to cook/heat the cottage and whether I can manage without a computer, mobile phone or microwave.

'Hello vicar,' I say, offputtingly.

'Hello Clare,' she shoots back. Currant eyes gleam inside her sun-worn face. 'Do you mind if I come in for a moment? I have a few things for you.'

I do mind but allow her to step inside. I've been doing my best to be polite to people, as Ashley suggested.

'Ooh, it's chilly in here.' She hauls the shopping bag onto the kitchen worktop, pulls her hood down to expose frizzy greying hair and scrutinises the narrow, cluttered space.

I've been asleep, I tell her. The vicar smiles as if this will excuse her intrusion, upends her bag and tips out a medley of wrinkled root vegetables.

'I wondered if you'd like some veggies. We can't get through them all. There's half a cooked chicken, so you won't have to use the oven.'

At the whiff of roast chicken, I bite back my protest. The vicar unzips her coat to reveal a clerical collar over a jumper and pleated skirt, and wanders towards the table.

'What's this?' She stoops over the drawing, lips parted and eyes roving over it in delight.

One of my old drawings, I reply, nudging her out of the way before she can examine the drawing further. I'm in the process of going through them all, I add, because Ashley and Elspeth suggested I take some to the local gallery. Her expression darkens, her left eye shutting briefly.

'I'd better put it away so it doesn't get marked.' I snatch the picture and return it to the cupboard. The vicar's eyebrows twitch.

After she's gone, I re-stow the drawing at the back of the cupboard. For the rest of the day, I am agitated. What if the vicar recognised the subject of the attack, Tara, and spotted that it doesn't contain the two men I supposedly witnessed, but includes six quite different persons? I've been careless.

To this day, no one has challenged the story I gave to the police. No doubt they still have the photofit pictures I helped them construct, depicting the two men I claimed to see in number 33's kitchen. My lies were to save Ashley and Elspeth from being arrested and charged with murder. Now, these two women, who mean more to me than anyone else in the entire world, are at risk of getting into serious trouble.

Chapter 5
Ashley

The next day

R hianna jogged up behind her French bulldog, which was barking at Brillo. With a sinking sensation, Ashley waved.

'Hello, Ashley!' A toothy, overbright smile. The remains of a Welsh accent loitering. 'You'll have to excuse madam, she's in a foul mood today.'

'Come here, Brillo.' Ashley spoke sternly. 'Sit.'

The terrier came to her side and sat. The bulldog stopped barking. It was ugly with large, droopy bat-like ears. At least Brillo looked like a proper dog.

'Have you got rid of your wi-fi yet, like I suggested?' Rhianna wiped at her perspiring brow.

'No,' she admitted. 'But I've been switching it off at night.'

'You shouldn't take your health for granted, Ashley.'

'I know and I don't. How's the campaign going?'

Rhianna exhaled, pulling her dark curls away from her damp brow with purple-nailed fingers. Her near neighbour lived at 28 Wilton Close, the highest house in the cul-de-sac and the closest to Brampton's mobile phone tower. She, and a handful of local residents, were trying to stop the tower becoming 5G.

'It's dead in the water. The council won't accept our evidence on the harmful effects of transmissions.'

'I'm sorry to hear that.' While Ashley didn't like the thought of a phone mast nearby emitting copious amounts of electromagnetic radiation, it wasn't high on her list of concerns.

'So now we all just have to accept this magnetic gunk continuing to rain down on us, with God knows what consequences. I can't sleep for the buzzing in my head.' Rhianna turned her attention to Bat Ears, barking at a Labradoodle. 'Stop that, Molly!'

'Residents don't seem to have much say in these things. But what else can we do?'

'Bryce helped me put up a Faraday cage around Dylan's bed. It's made of aluminum. It shuts out all the dangerous radiation.'

'I see.' Ashley imagined the boy trapped inside. 'He doesn't mind sleeping in that?'

'No, he loves it. Says it's like being in his own little igloo... Molly! Leave that dog alone.' Rhianna tugged her dog's lead.

Brillo was no longer sitting beside her, she realised, scanning the green.

'Sorry, I have to go. Brillo's gone. I daren't let him run off again.'

'He ran off?'

'I lost him in the quarry the other day,' she explained.

Rhianna inhaled loudly, her eyes wide. 'It was you who found the body in the quarry?'

'Yes, it was. How did you know?'

'It was in the *Herald* this morning. They said a dogwalker found the body. It was Emily Hale, did you know her?'

'No, I didn't.'

'She used to work in Brampton. I recognised her from the photo. I chatted to her a few times at that new clinic – the alternative health place? It's in that big house overlooking the river, near Dinton.'

She didn't know the house. Dinton was a village south of Brampton, in an area she hadn't explored yet.

'It opened last year,' Rhianna continued. 'They're very good. The consulting rooms are impressive. They have all the latest hi-tech equipment. Craig Matthews runs it. He's helping me with my auto-immune condition. I'm on one of his detox programmes.' Rhianna frowned. 'That poor woman. I could see she wasn't well. Her face used to have a horrible grey tinge. But she was always so cheerful. I had no idea her condition was so serious. If she jumped, that is. The paper doesn't say—'

Ashley raised her hand sharply. 'Sorry, I've got to go... Brillo!'

She stepped away, calling the dog while scanning the loop of the road around the grassy oval. A ginger-and-black Welsh terrier scampered over from the thicket of silver birches, ears flapping.

Thank God. Since the incident in the quarry, she'd been afraid to let him out of her sight.

'Good boy for coming back.' She rubbed his back. 'But you're going back on the lead now, mister.'

Dog safely tethered at her side, she took in the view of the village and beyond. To the east, the wooded banks of Brampton's river and the road leading towards Elven, the nearest town of consequence. A round, greyish patch was just visible behind distant woodland – the old quarry, it must be. She stared at it, feeling uneasy suddenly.

BODY IN QUARRY IDENTIFIED AS LOCAL BEAUTICIAN

A body discovered by a dogwalker in a former quarry on the outskirts of Brampton three days ago has been identified as Emily Hale, 24, of Brampton. Her relatives have been informed.

Miss Gale died from injuries believed to have been sustained in a fall from a rocky ledge at the rim of the former quarry.

Elven Police are investigating the incident. Following a post-mortem, they believe the circumstances of the death to be non-suspicious.

Ashley stared at the close-up of the woman's face in the newspaper. The photograph showed a younger, prettier Emily Hale than she expected.

She re-read the short report, lingering over the last sentence and looked up, puzzled. Outside, through the window of her office – once her son's room – leafless branches were stark against a colourless sky. How could they not consider the young woman's death to be suspicious? She had told the detective constable what she'd seen: the woman had been running away from someone. What was going on?

She found the DC's card in her desk drawer and called the number.

'DC Peters, can I help you?'

'Hello, this is Ashley Khan,' she began uncertainly. 'I came in to give a statement a few days ago.'

A beat.

'Yes, you came in with your dog... You found the body in the quarry.'

'That's right. I've just read the report in the *Herald*. The woman's name was Emily Hale, I understand. The report said that the police don't believe her death to be suspicious.' She paused. 'I was wondering how that could be, given what I told you.'

At the other end, breathing.

'OK, Mrs Khan. We have investigated the circumstances surrounding Emily Hale's death. I can't tell you the details. But after looking into all the available evidence, we believe Miss Hale jumped into the quarry of her own volition. There was no evidence to indicate that anyone else was involved in her death—'

'But I told you, I saw her running away from someone,' she interrupted, the hot mass of frustration building in her voice. 'Doesn't that count as evidence?'

'You caught sight of a woman that could have been Emily Hale – from a considerable distance, in poor light.' The voice was less confident, apologetic even. 'I'm afraid that what you witnessed wasn't considered strong enough to counter the other evidence.'

'What other evidence?'

Another hesitation.

'Miss Hale's medical reports, I believe, and her state of mind in the days before her death. We believe the most likely scenario is that she took her own life. I'm sorry, I can't tell you anymore. I assure you, we've done all we can to investigate the matter.'

'I see.' She deflated.

'I'm sorry, Mrs Khan.'

Later, Ashley replayed the conversation in her head. Something felt wrong. In one way, what she had heard sort of made sense. If the woman had recently been told she was seriously ill... Depressed and unwilling to face the prospect of her decline, had she decided to end her life?

But there must be more to it. She recalled the DC's hesitations and use of the passive voice: ...*what you witnessed wasn't considered strong enough to counter the other evidence.* The woman's state of mind, and what else? More than likely, someone other than DC Peters had decided how much weight to attach to Ashley's statement. For whatever reason, a higher-ranking officer must have decided not to open a murder investigation.

What did it matter though, that the police had decided there was nothing untoward about Emily Hale's death? It was no business of hers, and there was nothing she could do about it. She pressed the heel of her hand against her brow and groaned.

A call from downstairs interrupted her.

'Are you alright, Ashley? You've been up there a long time.'

'Down in ten!'

She walked to the window. The wind was picking up. Flakes of snow weaved across the yellowish glow of streetlights.

The image of the dead woman's face returned, and those awful, staring eyes. Suddenly, she remembered. Her heart began to pound. Emily Hale had appeared in her dreams last night. The young woman had been trying to escape from something, running for her life. Then, bizarrely, Emily had morphed into her university friend, Alison. Alison had walked slowly towards Ashley, her gaze direct, insistent.

Alison. How strange that she should dream of her friend again, after all these years.

She pictured Alison's gentle eyes and expressive face, as mobile as water, so often laughing or smiling, rarely hinting at the pain and darkness inside. Like Emily, Alison had died young. Her death, ruled as misadventure, had also been caused by a fall, from the steps of the overpass on her walk home, probably the result of drinking large amounts of alcohol .

From outside, a rattle of branches and the soft moan of wind. Ashley stepped away from the window. Was Alison trying to tell her something? No, that was the sort of thing Elspeth would believe. But maybe she could find out how Emily had really died.

Chapter 6
Elspeth

Two days later

E lspeth lowered the watering can and turned to Wilton Close.

The odd-looking woman was back, mooching around the cul-de-sac and peering into its semi-detached houses. She seemed particularly interested in the houses at this end. In particular, her own, Ken Dickson's and Ashley's at numbers 32, 33 and 34. Was she a debt collector, or a government official? Or – the most likely, Elspeth decided – a policewoman in plain clothes?

Not so plain, in this case. The woman wore narrow-legged trousers or leggings with low-heeled black boots. She also wore a trench coat, very 1970s, opened at the neck to reveal a bright orange scarf. Wavy dark blonde hair escaped from under a yellow beanie.

Potential Policewoman approached number 32, her eyes darting. Turning back to the planter, Elspeth resumed watering from on top of the chair. A bolt of nervousness made her miss the bulbs, spilling water onto the ground.

Oh, dear.

The unknown woman had passed safely by on her way around Wilton Close's central green island, or so Elspeth thought, risking a snatched glance towards the pavement. Instead, she met Potential Policewoman's eyes. The woman was standing outside the drive looking up at Elspeth with interest.

'Morning,' she said with a strong, pleasantly low-pitched voice. 'Lovely day, isn't it?'

She didn't have a local accent, but one from of the nicer parts of London. As she spoke, the woman pulled a strand of blonde hair from her face. She wasn't just here for a nice stroll, Elspeth was certain.

'Good morning, dear,' Elspeth replied, smiling. 'Yes, it's glorious.' That was exaggerating a little. The pallid January sunshine was a nice change.

Potential Policewoman smiled back. 'You must be Elspeth Chambers?'

'That's right. Who are you?'

'I'm Detective Constable Peters from Elven Police. I'm following up some matters to do with our enquiry into the death of Tara Sanderson.'

Elspeth blinked, just managing to stop her mouth from gaping. The police hadn't contacted any of them since shortly after Tara's funeral. The murder enquiry had faded month by month, year by year before dying a natural death, so she and everyone from Tara's now-disbanded community group had assumed.

'There's nothing to worry about, it's just routine,' the detective said. 'I'm taking a look at some old cases.'

'Right, um, I see.' In her discombobulated state, her usual facility with words had departed. 'Is there anything else you need to know?'

'I don't think so.' The detective smiled again. 'Not at the moment, anyway.'

Elspeth stepped off the chair, watching the figure recede as it rounded Wilton Close. Oh, hell and damnation. She needed to tell Ashley – though that would risk provoking an anxiety attack in her friend.

'Hello, there.'

The 'new' neighbour, as Elspeth still thought of him, appeared on his front garden path, hands in pockets. He dipped his head. As usual, Ken Dickson was wearing an awful grey anorak. In the eighteen or so months since he'd moved into number 33, they had communicated little beyond the exchange of semi-friendly glances. She hadn't minded. Their lack of closeness had been a contrast to her relationship with Tara.

'I meant to ask,' he said suddenly, 'if my DIY disturbs you at all. I've been at it quite a lot lately, I know.' His lips twitched into an awkward smile. Ken was a good decade younger than her, at a guess, but made little effort with his appearance. He had thinning hair and a slight stoop, making him look older. Annoyingly, the lenses of his spectacles were always smeared.

'No, not at all.' She went up to the low fence between their gardens. 'Oh, Ken, while you're here, did you notice that woman who stopped outside my gate just now? The one in the yellow beanie?'

Ken glanced at his front gate and shifted from one foot to the other.

'She was the woman who knocked on my door yesterday. She said she was with the local police. She asked about you. You and Mrs Khan.'

'What did she ask?'

Ken's brow furrowed. 'She wanted to know if you were both still living here. I think that's all.' He sounded defensive. 'I confirmed that you were.'

'Why did she ask *you* that?'

'I don't know. You were probably both out at the time.' He scratched the back of his head. 'She said it was a routine follow-up... Something about an enquiry into the death of the woman who used to live here.'

'Did she say anything else?'

A deep wrinkle formed above Ken's nose.

'I don't think so.'

She stared at Ken. Was he telling the truth? You never knew who you were living next to. Tara had proved that well enough. Ken didn't seem to have the gumption required for deception, though.

'I probably should have mentioned it before,' he said. 'But she said she was going to come back.' Another frown. 'I didn't realise it was so important.'

'Well, it is to me.' She'd had no end of questions from the police after she found Tara's body.

As she turned to pick up the watering can, Ken made a remark she couldn't quite hear. Surprised, she turned back to him. This could be the most they'd spoken since he'd moved in.

'Sorry, what did you say?'

'It's quite strange, you know.'

'What's strange?'

'I don't know if you're the type of lady who's interested in inexplicable phenomena. I wasn't myself, until recently.'

'You've seen a ghost?'

'I imagine it must have been.'

The colour was draining from Ken's cheeks. Elspeth let go of the watering can, which toppled onto its side.

'What did it look like?'

He gestured towards his house. 'When I came into the kitchen, I saw someone leaning on the sink, looking out of the kitchen window. It was a woman. When I come closer, it disappears.'

The hairs at the back of her neck lifted. She stared at Ken, who was making no move to leave.

'How very odd,' she said. 'How long ago was this?'

'The day before yesterday. That was the third time.' Ken stepped up to the fence, grasped it with both hands and peered at her. 'She's the woman who died in my house, isn't she?'

Elspeth had begun to nod but quickly turned it into a sideways movement. She didn't want to alarm the chap any more than he was already, or alert him to anything that he might not be pleased to find out. When selling number 33, as she'd been obliged to as the executor of Tara's will, she had admitted to the estate agent that the previous occupant of the house, in her fifties, had died there unexpectedly in mysterious circumstances. By then of course, everyone local knew that the house on sale was the house that Tara had died inside. They also knew that the police had initially treated Tara's death as murder and that for a short time, Elspeth and Ashley had been prime suspects. However, in the interest of finally getting the house sold, she had been a little economical with the truth with Ken, an outsider from Bristol. She had mentioned the mysterious circumstances to him, but that was all.

'I don't know about that,' she replied. 'It's possible, I suppose... If you believe in ghosts and such, that is,' she added.

'Of course. It must seem very far-fetched.' Ken frowned at the fallen watering can. 'I'd better leave you to it. I'm sure you don't want to be hearing all this.'

'Not at all, it's fascinating.' And very alarming. Just the thought of Tara haunting the house next door made her feel ten years older. 'Do you think you're getting enough sleep? People can hallucinate from lack of sleep, I've read.'

Ken gave a sad smile and moved his hands back into his pockets. Before he had a chance to say anything else, Elspeth scooped up the watering can and hurried indoors.

Chapter 7
Ashley

The same day

'Off you go!'

Ashley released Brillo from the lead. She set off at a good pace along the path, which more or less followed the river.

The forecast had been for occasional showers in the afternoon. It wasn't even midday though, and already thick grey clouds covered the sky. It was bitterly cold. But no way was she going back home. After days of washing copious sheets and towels, preparing diet-friendly meals and ferrying Diane to the doctor, dentist and hairdresser, she was desperate for a long walk. With luck, there'd be time to explore Dinton village.

Her phone was turned off in case Diane called. Zac was unlikely to call; since his relocation to Edinburgh, he had hardly contacted her.

With each step the clutter in her mind fell away, replaced by clarity. There was someone else in his life now, Zac had virtually admitted. There was no way back for them, she knew in her heart. It seemed their life together had ended on the day of Tara's death

– *that day*. Not telling anyone the truth for so long, not even their two teenagers, had taken its toll.

Her spirits began to lift. This landscape was unexpectedly beautiful, despite the starkness of winter. Occasional wan sunlight picked out the bronze in bluffs of rock. Beyond the river's churn, a near silence permeated the valley. Brillo bounded on ahead, not looking back.

Nearly two hours later, the sun had disappeared. It was too cold to stop. As Ashley paused to feed the last of her sandwich to Brillo, snowflakes drifted down. So much for the weather forecast. She got out the Ordnance Survey map. Dinton was only a mile and a half away. She walked faster, imagining a warm café, her hands around a steaming mug of tea.

She followed a sign up to Dinton. The path arrived at a twisting minor road. A tall hedge bordered the road, interrupted by a wide gravel track. Ivy House, according to the sign poking from the hedge. There was no sign of the house from here. Curious, she called Brillo to heel and followed the curving driveway.

Abruptly, the house came into view. She paused to admire the property. A glass section had been added to the original building. Cradled by a nest of woodland just under the crown of the hill, the house took full advantage of its position.

A loud squawk – a fowl of some kind? Before she could react, Brillo charged off. She sprinted after him. Ahead, the gates across the driveway were open.

'Brillo!'

In response, excited barking from the other side of the gates. She sprinted through them towards low buildings. The barking stopped, replaced with a cascade of alarmed sounding clucks and squawks. Oh, no...

She peeped inside the first. Rakes, brooms, power tools. No birds. She hastily withdrew, coming face to face with a slim, lightly tanned middle aged man in jeans and trainers, tugging Brillo along by the collar. He held out his other hand, revealing several brown and cream feathers.

'Is that...? He didn't...?' She stared up at the man, heart pounding. Had Brillo killed one of his chickens?

The man's lips pressed tightly together. Wordlessly, he stepped forward and let her take the dog. Ashley grabbed Brillo's collar and attached his lead.

'He had Flo's tail in his mouth,' the man said, voice tight. 'She was wandering outside her cage. You're lucky, she managed to get away without too much damage.' He let go of the feathers. 'But she's going to be jittery for a while.'

'I'm really sorry. I saw the sign to your house, and I couldn't resist having a look. Brillo heard your hens and shot off.'

'I suggest you keep him on a lead– and maybe avoid going into private property uninvited.'

The man stepped back. His anger seemed to be waning.

'I'll be off, then.' She shivered. Now the panic was over, she realised how cold she was. If only she'd carried on to the village, rather than venture anywhere near this man and his blasted hens.

'You're frozen, aren't you?' His voice was gentler now. He had an accent that was hard to pin down.

'I am, a bit. I've been walking for two hours.'

'Have you got far to go?'

'The same distance again – we started at Brampton. I was on my way to Dinton.' She glanced up. The snow continued.

'I'm Craig Matthews, by the way.' He offered his hand. She took it. She knew his name but from where?

'I'm Ashley Khan.' She didn't introduce Brillo.

'You live in Brampton?'

'For the last five years. London before that.'

'I moved here last year, from New Zealand.' He gestured towards the house. 'I run the Dolphin Clinic. I thought this would be the perfect spot for it.'

It registered. Rhianna had visited his clinic. So had Emily Hale, the dead woman.

'I've heard your name,' Ashley said. 'A neighbour mentioned your clinic.'

Craig brushed some flakes off his jumper, a chunky cable-knit crew neck. He looked well put together, whereas she felt as damp and bedraggled as the dog.

'Why don't you come in for a hot drink? You look like you need one.'

'Thanks, but I should head back. The weather's getting worse—'

'It won't take five minutes. You can use the bathroom, too.'

He seemed trustworthy. Keeping Brillo on an ultra-short lead, she followed Craig through a small area of coats and boots, into a traditional kitchen. It was deliciously warm. Timber beams ran across the ceiling.

'You can let him off here, if you like. Tea, coffee?'

'Tea please. Milk, no sugar.'

Brillo trotted around the kitchen, nose to the flagstone floor, while Craig put the kettle on.

'There's a toilet down the corridor.' He pointed. 'Third door on the left.'

'Thanks.' She felt herself thawing towards Craig Matthews's easy, self-assured manner.

In the bathroom, dried flowers had been arranged in a vase and hand towels were stacked on a shelf. A woman's touch, it looked like. A housekeeper, or...?

On her way back, she glanced along the corridor. The three

doors on either side were all shut. At the end, a spiral staircase. Beyond it, an open area bounded by a floor-to-ceiling expanse of glass.

'Here you go.' On her return, Craig handed her a mug and leaned back against the Aga. He had a dimple on his chin. His eyes were striking, their irises a soft grey tinged with blue, like a spring sky.

'You have quite a place here.' She tried to stop looking into his eyes. 'Was it a lot of work to get it how you wanted it?'

'The extension was already built when I moved in. A friend of mine bought the house. It was perfect for the clinic. We put in consulting rooms and extra facilities.'

'Do you live here by yourself?'

'I like it that way. The clinic has taken a lot of hard work to set up. There's not much time for anything else. Fortunately, we're getting repeat business and word is spreading.' He watched her face. 'Sorry I was sharp with you earlier. It was bad luck the gates were open.'

She felt her eyebrows arch.

'I was about to go out in the car again,' he explained. 'We don't get many casual visitors –people tend to make appointments.'

Was he having a go at her, or teasing?

'I hope your hen will be OK,' she said. 'Brillo is a handful. He's my mother's dog – we're still getting used to each other.' She was about to mention that last week he had led her to a dead body, when Craig reached into his pocket and retrieved a key fob.

'I'll drop you home, if you like. You shouldn't be walking so far in this weather.'

'Thanks, but I'll enjoy the walk back now I've warmed up.'

One side of his mouth turned up. 'Really?'

'I'll be fine, don't worry.'

He shrugged. 'Whatever.'

'Thanks for the tea, and for the use of your bathroom.' She felt awkward suddenly and gulped down the rest of her tea.

'No worries. I'll see you out.'

She bent down to put the dog on the lead and hurried after Craig towards the front of the house. A new looking Range Rover sat on the gravel driveway. It was just as well she hadn't accepted a lift; Brillo would have left hairs all over the seat.

'Bye, Craig.' She lifted a hand. 'See you around.'

'See you, Ashley. Enjoy your walk home.'

She walked as fast as she could to ward off the cold, keeping a close eye on Brillo. The sprinkling of snow made the landscape even more beautiful. Her thoughts returned to Craig. It had seemed like the right thing to do, not to accept a lift – and she hadn't wanted to put him to any trouble, especially after Brillo's attack. However, a ridiculous sense of regret lingered.

She pulled a chocolate bar from her pocket.

Three days later

Ashley picked up the glass beetle brooch and pinned it to her jacket. She hadn't worn it for years. After giving her wrists a blast of perfume she hurried downstairs, excited suddenly at the prospect of going out.

'Nearly ready,' she greeted Elspeth, who arrived on time looking effortlessly glamourous, a black dress and a gold rope necklace showing underneath her coat. It was hard to believe she would be 83 in October. 'You look stunning.'

'Thanks, darling.' Elspeth touched the brooch. 'I love that. I've not seen it before, have I?'

'Probably not. A friend gave it to me years ago for my 20th birthday.' It was the last gift Alison had given her.

She called out goodbye to Diane but got no response. She had invited her mother to join them; Diane had insisted that her hip was hurting too much for her to enjoy an evening out.

Elspeth peered at the menu through her reading glasses. 'What do you fancy?'

'I don't know,' Ashley replied. 'I can't read this print.'

A candle flickered on the table between them. At the next table, young women with gigantic lashes were talking loudly over each other. Going to The Anglers, Brampton's riverside pub, had been Elspeth's idea.

'Let's have one of these,' Elspeth said, pointing to what was described as *our signature gin cocktail*.

Ashley looked around. The décor was smart and somewhat old-fashioned, evoking a traditional country pub: rose velvet seating, polished wood everywhere and photos of fishermen in Edwardian apparel beside their catches.

'This is a nice change.' Elspeth said as two cocktail glasses arrived filled with a pale green liquid. She was nervously niggling her rings to and fro.

'What is it?'

'Something happened the other day,' Elspeth said with a sigh.

'What happened?'

'It's a bit worrying, actually. I've noticed a woman nosing around outside our houses. This morning, she came over while I was watering my pot plants. She said she was a police officer based at Elven and she was following up on some old cases. One of them was the investigation into Tara's death.'

'You're joking.' She felt a chill go through her.

'She was here yesterday, too,' Elspeth went on, 'according to Ken. He said she'd arrived when we were both out. She'd knocked on his door and asked if we were still living here.'

'Why would the police be poking into all of that again?'

'I don't know.' Elspeth drained her cocktail.

'Did she give her name?'

'I made a note on my phone. Here it is. DC Peters. She's quite young, blondish, on the heavy side—'

'I know her. That's the woman I talked to after Brillo found the body.'

They looked at each other. Around them, voices and bursts of laughter echoed.

Ashley shifted on the sofa. Had her appearance with Brillo at the police station triggered the detective's interest in Tara's death? Whatever the reason, it was disconcerting. What if this officer were to discover something that the other police officers had missed?

'Are you going to obsess over this all night?' Elspeth sounded annoyed.

'Sorry, Els. But I can't help thinking about that detective turning up, and what it might mean.'

'For goodness' sake, Ash! We're meant to be enjoying ourselves. I'm off to the loo. Do you fancy another one of those cocktails?'

Ashley watched Elspeth wriggle between tables. With her cleavage-revealing dress and bold jewellery, she looked every inch like she belonged here. Even her footwear – up-to-the-minute ankle boots – fitted in. In contrast, her own outfit was unremarkable.

Five minutes later, Elspeth still hadn't returned.

'A lager shandy and a gin cocktail please,' Ashley asked the ruddy faced, balding man behind the bar, the manager, she guessed. A short distance away, two men were seated on stools at the end of the bar: a solidly built man with cropped greying hair, his shirt worn loose, and a tall, slim man with light brown hair. They looked roughly her age, early fifties maybe. They were talking, their heads close.

'We may need to come over to yours later, mate,' she heard the heavier man say. He tipped his head towards the man serving her. 'Nick's gotta close up on time tonight.' His accent wasn't local – from the northeast. He wasn't in the best of shape, and his nose was shorter than it ought to be.

The bar man placed two glasses down. 'Nine pounds twenty please, madam.'

She tapped her debit card on the card reader, glancing at the slim man, drinking from his wine glass. Craig Matthews, she realised with a jolt. He looked different – his hair neat and his stubble gone, a jacket over his chinos. Hoping he hadn't seen her, she snatched up the drinks and headed back to Elspeth.

'You're away with the fairies, this evening. Did you hear what I just said?'

Ashley turned to Elspeth. 'Sorry, I was thinking about something else. What did you say?'

'Didn't you hear any of it?' Elspeth made an exasperated face. 'Ken has seen Tara. In his kitchen.'

'I don't understand. How could he have seen Tara?'

Elspeth explained that their mutual neighbour had been visited by an apparition, whom he believed was Tara's ghost.

'Did he seem concerned about it?'

'I'd say so. Anyone would be, wouldn't they?' Elspeth bit down on her lower lip. 'Especially as he didn't think he was the type to see things.'

She wondered what exactly 'the type' was – not someone sceptical like her, presumably Elspeth meant.

'Don't you think it's strange?' Elspeth pressed.

'Yes, very. But there must be an explanation. He knows Tara died in unusual circumstances and that people have been wondering what really happened to her. He's all alone in the house and his imagination is working overtime...'

Elspeth frowned. 'You don't think it's real, then?'

She paused. Elspeth believed in horoscopes, homeopathy and

all manner of things; she wouldn't appreciate Ashley dismissing the ghost notion.

'I don't know. I try to keep an open mind, but...'

An out-of-sorts expression settled on Elspeth's face.

'Why do you think Ken bought the house in the first place,' Ashley went on quickly, 'knowing someone was killed there?'

'He didn't. The estate agent didn't mention anything about the police investigation or the unlawful killing verdict, and neither did I—' Elspeth stopped abruptly, rolling her eyes to one side. Ashley glanced up to see Craig Matthews standing beside their sofa, a wine glass in his hand.

'Oh, Craig,' she said, casually. 'Hello there. It's good to see you.'

'I saw you come up to the bar.'

Her heart put on a spurt. 'I saw you, too. I didn't like to interrupt. You and the other guy seemed deep in conversation...' She trailed off, feeling awkward.

'That's my mate Steve. He owns this place. We had a few things to sort out.'

Craig smiled at Elspeth. Elspeth, who'd been frowning at Ashley, smiled back at him.

'Why don't you join us, Mr...?'

'Matthews, Craig Matthews.'

'Elspeth Chambers.' Craig offered his hand, which Elspeth immediately clasped. 'Pleased to meet you, Craig. How do you know Ashley?'

'Her dog came after my hens.'

Indignation surged, before she registered the laughter in his eyes.

'So, you're the man with the hens.' Elspeth gave her a look.

'It was my fault for not shutting the gates,' Craig said good naturedly with a glance at Ashley.

Elspeth bestowed him a radiant smile. 'What do you do for a living, Craig?'

'I'm in health and wellbeing – natural alternatives to medicine. I run a clinic in Dinton.'

Elspeth asked a string of questions, which Craig was only too happy to answer. Ashley left them to discuss natural remedies and went to find the toilets.

'Sorry darling, I wasn't letting you get a word in,' Elspeth said on her return.

'Another drink, anyone?' Craig raised his hand and caught the eye of the waitress.

'I'll have a tonic water, please.' Elspeth turned to Ashley and lowered her voice. 'I'm off to the loo. You have a chat to him without me.'

Craig spoke first.

'I hope you had no trouble getting home the other day?'

'None at all.'

'I kept an eye on the weather forecast in case I needed to dash out and rescue you.' He had a smile in his voice. He leaned forwards on his chair, hands pressed between his knees. 'You don't think much of alternative health, do you?'

'I'm not against it, by any means. Whatever helps to make a person better—'

'I saw your face when I was talking about the clinic's treatments. You looked... sceptical.'

Oh, bloody hell. She wasn't in the mood for this.

'I believe in eating well and having a healthy lifestyle and using alternatives to drugs where possible. Actually, I've tried quite a few alternative things over the years.'

'For example?'

'Bach Flower Remedies, lavender oil at night, sound baths, acupuncture... all sorts of things.' After Alison died, she had even gone to a medium. 'I certainly haven't got a closed mind. But nor do I accept everything blindly, without evidence.'

'Ah, evidence. That word.'

She waited for an explanation.

46

'People use it to dismiss what they don't understand.' An edge to his voice. 'The medical industry isn't infallible, you know. Plenty of people don't get the help they need because potential treatments are overlooked or their symptoms are misdiagnosed.' He raked his fingers through his hair, his eyes glistening. 'I lost my daughter when she was eleven. She died because of an incompetent doctor. He didn't recognise that she had encephalitis till it was too late. I'll never forgive him.'

'That must have been horrendous. Was she your only child?'

'I have a son, somewhere. We aren't close.' He focused on her again. 'What makes you anxious, Ashley?'

She couldn't help smiling. Did he expect her to be honest?

'I've always been highly strung, I suppose,' she replied. 'I find it hard to switch off from everything. And lately...' She couldn't tell him the rest. The many times she'd imagined police officers knocking on the door and asking her to come with them, long after the investigation into Tara's death had fizzled out. The countless early morning hours wondering whether the police might unearth something that would send both her and Elspeth to prison, and quite possibly the others, too.

'Lately?'

He was inviting her to come clean, to tell him everything. Maybe it was time. She released a breath.

'Things have been difficult,' she said.

'I can see something is troubling you a great deal. If you ever need to talk about it...' Craig leaned towards her, his eyes drawing her in. Their irises gleamed with shades of dark golden honey.

'I hope I'm not interrupting anything?' Elspeth, freshly lipsticked, hovered at a distance.

Craig sat back. 'I think we've finished for now, haven't we?'

She nodded, feeling both relieved and disappointed. She had been alarmingly close to opening up to this man, whom she hardly knew. Was it his interest in her and what troubled her, or her state of mind, a desire to purge herself of her secrets?

'I have to go.' Craig got to his feet, pulling a business card from his jacket pocket. 'If you're open to trying something different, I might be able to help. The clinic has plenty of treatments on offer, to suit everyone. Some are quite...' he quoted with his fingers '..."mainstream". We've started putting on workshops, too. Why not drop by some time and let me show you round?'

Ashley took the card without looking at it. She wanted to, and she didn't. Craig turned to Elspeth.

'You're both more than welcome to visit.'

'It would be fun to try something new.' Elspeth said without hesitation.

Craig grinned as he stood, the corners of his eyes crinkling. She noticed the smattering of freckles around his nose, and how much younger he suddenly looked.

'Great! Let me know when you're coming.'

'Is there something going on between you two?' Elspeth asked when he'd gone.

'Of course there isn't.'

'He seemed to be paying you a lot of attention.'

She shrugged. 'Because I'm a challenge to him. He knows I don't believe in all that alternative stuff, and maybe he needs new customers for his health business, whatever it's called.' She picked up the business card. A pale grey dolphin shape floated over the lettering:

Dolphin Clinic
21st century health for body and mind

'"Dolphin Clinic". What a cliché. I mean, really.'

'I don't see what's wrong with the name.' Elspeth folded her arms. 'I like Craig. I think he's a natural helper who's passionate about what he does. You could do with being less closed-minded!'

She felt a sting of hurt. Elspeth's expression softened.

'It would help if you gave things the benefit of the doubt more often. People, too.'

Biting back a response, she picked up Craig's business card and placed it in her handbag. Was there a grain of truth in Elspeth's words? She would try to keep an open mind about what the clinic offered, and the man who ran it.

Chapter 8
Bird Woman

20 January

I fetch my paintbrush jar, remove the brushes and fill it with water. Then I insert the stems of early flowering Hellebores that I had spent the morning plucking from the wood and place the jar at the centre of the table. The profusion of dipped heads resembles a violet-grey shawl. As I thought it would, the pale green of my old bedspread perfectly complements the flowers.

A noise at the door. Loud raps are punctuated by excited calls. Elspeth's voice.

'Clare, are you in? It's us!'

It's twenty-five past two in the afternoon. They're on time. I hurry to the door.

Ashley stands beside Elspeth. Both are bright-faced, expectant. Behind them, the wind hurls dead leaves across the Laurel hedge that separates my front garden from the wood.

'Hello, my dear. Are we early?'

Elspeth steps inside, holding out a cake-shaped box. I thank her, even though the cake isn't necessary. The vicar brought me one yesterday when she turned up again with provisions.

'I've made sandwiches,' Ashley says. 'Ham, tomato and chutney, salmon and cucumber.'

They both know by now that I've a substantial appetite and enjoy sandwiches as well as cake with my two mugs of tea. Ashley makes them just as I like, with bread cut in generous chunks from a fresh white bloomer.

Did you walk here, I ask.

'No chance,' Elspeth replies emphatically. 'It's meant to be sleeting later. We parked in that lane you told us to, where the parking wardens don't go.'

Given that I possess no electronic devices, the council's scheme allowing residents to pay for one's visitors to park, which can only be accessed from the internet, is of limited use.

I put on the kettle.

The table is square and not really large enough for two, let alone three. My insides growl loudly. Lunch was sparse, I explain – I was saving myself for afternoon tea.

Ashley smiles. She is the youngest of us, in her middle fifties, still slim and pretty. She's quieter than Elspeth. Like me, she dresses with practicality in mind. Today she wears trainers, jeans and an Arran jumper. In contrast, Elspeth is always sporting a new hairstyle and loves dressing up. Today she wears loose cashmere trousers and a mohair top in a swirl of Battenburg cake colours, and a welter of beads and bracelets. Then there's all five foot ten inches of me – sixty-four years alive with no social graces, too much fat in the wrong places and my hair cut by my own hand.

'That colour suits you dear,' Elspeth says, indicating my lilac jumper, picked up at Oxfam. 'You should wear it more often.'

Nearly everything I wear is either old or recycled. The Casio on my wrist is the only watch I've ever worn. The face bears multiple scratches and the strap has been replaced several times.

'How have you been Clare?' Ashley says after I've finished my first sandwich. Both women look at me steadily.

Such questions are a source of difficulty. I cast my mind back over the past few weeks. How to summarise my state of mind and personal circumstances over this length of time, given the variability of what is being considered?

'Not as clean, possibly,' I reply. I explain that I've stopped taking a bath every day to reduce my gas bill. Now I only run one once a week, unless there is a definite need. 'Don't worry'. I catch the alarm on Ashley's face. 'I had one this morning.'

Both women laugh with gusto. I start to laugh, too.

'This cake is divine,' Elspeth says, cutting another, fractionally thinner slice of the passionfruit and lime cake that came with Liz Peaches' latest delivery. 'Is it from the vicar?'

'She seems to think I need feeding up,' I reply. 'Though I've told her I'm supposed to be on a diet to stop diabetes.'

Elspeth's forehead wrinkles. 'The vicar comes over rather a lot, doesn't she? I mean, I know you're on a pension and you don't have a lot to spend, but is it her place to bring you food?'

'I think she likes to have someone to help.'

To be fair, I've always managed to get through each food delivery, and the vicar's material offerings are of more use than her advice and aphorisms. The other day, she told me that I am loved and I deserve to live in the light, I need not shut myself away from everyone in my dark house in the woods. Furthermore, I need to open my heart to receive the Lord. I avoided telling her the truth, that I am not receptive to religious messages despite attending church services from time to time (mainly for the singing, warmth and fleeting company of others).

Ashley asks how my diet is going. I need to lose more weight, I tell her.

'You'd better not have any more cake,' Elspeth says with a smile.

'I can manage one more slice,' I reply. She passes me the cake plate. I take the largest slice and try to eat it slowly. Elspeth scolded me at our last tea party after I took the last piece of cake dispatched it in a few bites without first asking if anyone else wanted it. I have a hunch that, like the vicar, Ashley and Elspeth are on a mission to repatriate me with the wider world.

Outside, dark grey clouds brood over the treetops. Flurries of sleety drizzle wet the pane. The bird feeder is swinging precariously. Sticks and pieces of branch are being snatched by the wind. I think of the birds and their nests, exposed to the forces of nature. The bird bath on the lawn is still empty.

I've been hearing noises from the wood at night, I tell them. Elspeth lowers the slice of cake she's about to bite into. Ashley scrunches up her face.

'What sort of noises?'

'Cries and shouts,' I reply. 'They often sound muffled. Sometimes there are thuds, too, like someone kicking at a door or hammering it with their fist.'

'How far away?'

'I'm not sure. They sound quite close, sometimes. But my closest neighbour is five hundred yards away.'

'How strange.' Elspeth leans forward, forearms on the table.

Ashley shifts in her chair. 'On cold nights, sound can travel a long way.'

'At two o'clock this morning,' I say. 'I remembered the back door wasn't locked and ran downstairs to lock it.'

Elspeth's green eyes open wide. Ashley bites her lower lip. I don't admit that for the first time ever, I felt scared in my own home.

'I think you need to be more careful, Clare.' Elspeth looks stern. 'Make it a habit to check that the back door is locked when you go to bed.'

'And all the windows,' Ashley adds. 'Whenever you go out.'

I'm tempted to say that I always keep my bedroom window open, even in the winter. But what they say sounds sensible.

Ashley gets up and inspects the nearest window. All the windows and frames were replaced during the renovations organised by Elspeth. The work has made a big difference to my comfort, removing the draughts let in by the old sash windows. Even better, the ladder I used to access the flat roof over the kitchen has been converted into proper stairs, and a wall has been constructed around the roof to make it safe. The roof is an excellent spot for observing birds, and people.

'Do you go out at the same times every day?' she asks.

I tell her my walks are more regular at this time of year. I like to go for a daily walk, usually soon after breakfast or lunch, at either half past nine in the morning or two in the afternoon.

'It might be a good idea to be more flexible with the times. We don't know who might be roaming around. Ever since I found that body, I can't help wondering...'

'What body?'

'Oh, sorry, Clare! I forgot to tell you. I found a woman's body in the disused quarry. Brillo found her, to be accurate. Just over a week ago.'

Ashley saw a woman running along the top of the quarry, Elspeth adds. Her mother's dog led her to the body. Ashley thinks the woman was pushed off a ledge.

'I went to the police station to make a statement.' Ashley continues. 'I told them I saw a woman running away but the police ignored it. They think the woman committed suicide because she'd been told she was seriously ill.'

I ask who the woman was.

'Her name was Emily Hale,' Ashley says. 'She lived in Brampton.'

Elspeth smiles sadly. 'She worked in the beauty salon on the high street until recently. She used to give wonderful facials. A lovely girl, such a sunny nature...'

'I know her,' I say. They both turn to me, startled. I describe Emily. She was a willowy young woman with beautiful hazel eyes who always said hello to me whenever our paths crossed.

'How did you know her?' Ashley asks.

A year or so ago, I explain, she'd moved into the mobile homes across the wood. One day I'd had a letter from my nephew informing me that my brother had died. She'd seen me sitting glumly on a fallen tree and had invited me in for a mug of tea.

I explain that the last time I had seen her, Emily said she wasn't well and she was going to have to give up work. She was intending to visit Texas to be with members of her family. I had knocked on her door when I next passed the mobile homes but there had been no answer, I'd assumed she was away in America.

Silence.

Elspeth's eyes are dewy. Ashley clears her throat before speaking.

'The police didn't ask you anything about this?'

'No,' I tell her.

'Can you remember exactly when you talked to her?' Ashley's voice is urgent.

'You sound like a police officer,' Elspeth tells Ashley with a chortle. 'More tea, anyone?'

I say I might have put something in my bird log.

'Can you have a look?'

I retrieve the notebook and skip back through the pages. What once contained purely bird observations has expanded to include notes on noteworthy happenings in my life. I pass Ashley the brief entry I wrote for the 7th of this month.

7 January

Longish walk after lunch. No birds. Stop off at the mobile homes on the way home and speak to Roger, Emily and Vesna. Roger offers me a cup of tea. We talk of the cost of stamps and the foul smells invading the countryside. On the way out I say hello to Jason, who's sitting on the step of his van, his head of matted hair bent over a fishing rod. He's mending, I assume. He gives me a stern nod, as usual. He is more of a hermit than I am, I think, and just as lonely.

Ashley looks up quickly. 'The seventh of January. That's just three days before Emily died! Was that the last time you spoke to her?'

I confirm this.

'Another odd thing recently,' Elspeth begins, setting the filled teapot on the table, 'the policewoman Ashley spoke to has been nosing around Wilton Close. She's talked to our new neighbour – the elderly chap, you've seen him.'

The neighbour is actually younger than Elspeth, I am fairly certain.

'The police are looking into Tara's death again,' Ashley says. 'But we're not sure what's prompted it.'

At the mention of Tara's death, I feel guilty. I haven't yet told them about the vicar spotting my drawing. But I start off with my good news.

'I've taken some of my drawings to the art gallery on Brampton High Street,' I report. 'The man said he'd like to exhibit some of the bird ones later this year.'

'Oh darling, that's wonderful!' Elspeth claps her hands and takes another bite of cake.

'Congratulations, Clare!' Ashley raises her mug. I lift my mug to hers.

'We told you, didn't we?' Elspeth looks at me with a serious expression. 'You have talent, my dear.'

'There's something else,' I say, foreboding coming over me. 'To do with the police officer coming to Wilton Close.' I tell them about my drawing of Tara being pelted with fruit and how the vicar came to see it.

'You drew me and Elspeth and everyone else in Tara's kitchen, just before she died? Please, tell me you're joking.'

I'm afraid to reply. I've never seen Ashley so upset.

'Why did you draw such a thing in the first place?' Elspeth looks equally shocked.

'I needed to get what I saw out of my head, somehow.' I explain that I didn't draw the scene for anyone but me.

Another long silence. Ashley gets up and stacks the crockery in the sink.

'I'm sorry about the drawing,' I say joining her, meaning both doing the drawing and then leaving it where the vicar could see it. 'I should have been more careful.'

'It's done now,' she says.

'Don't worry about it dear,' Elspeth says, stuffing her arms into her coat sleeves.

But I do. After they've left, I sit in my armchair, drifting down and down into my thoughts. I wish with all my heart I hadn't let the vicar in that day.

When I come to, it is nearly dark. I open the kitchen door and stand looking at the back garden. The sleet and the wind have gone. There are hints of gold in the western sky. In the big oak beyond the back fence, parakeets squawk and fluster.

I'm glad now Elspeth insisted on getting a new fence put up around my garden, in addition to all the work she organised on the cottage; her gifts have been welcome indeed, despite their less than wholesome source. Living away from others has always been important to me. But I'm vulnerable here, on the edge of this woodland. If anyone had a mind to, they could get inside the cottage without anyone finding out. I might not know myself even until it was too late.

Later, in bed

I've just locked the back door and drawn both the bolts, top and bottom. This doesn't put my mind at rest. What if I should need to escape quickly?

The only sounds now are soft nocturnal noises as the cottage settles. Little groans of walls and floors, and from time to time the rough brush of a branch across the roof.

Chapter 9
Ashley

The next day

'Ashley, are you there?' Diane's plaintiff cry arrived from downstairs.

'Coming!'

She had started bringing her laptop and morning coffee up to Sam's old room for a brief respite from her mother. She clicked onto the next *Elven & District Herald* article in her internet search for 'Craig Matthews'.

It was from last May, the week of the clinic's opening, and was positive in tone. She read a quote from the 'director of Dolphin Clinic':

We have worked tirelessly getting ready for the opening. We hope this place will be of value to local people. Our aim is to offer alternative healthcare options to those who are disenchanted with conventional medicine or wish to explore drug-free approaches to healing mind and body.

No shortage of people like that around here, she thought.

The next article on the list was published in a business magazine at around the same time and took a critical perspective.

Matthews's previous ventures in the health field include a startup company, Mind-Lab, which developed an app to teach self-hypnosis and claims to treat a variety of conditions including OCD, stammering and insomnia. In 2020, Matthews founded a company based in Jersey, Mind-Body Enterprises, which appears to have made healthy profits from extensive use of unproven health-related technology

She skimmed past examples of the 'pseudo-science technology' that the company was associated with, such as 'a device that vibrates while you stand on it, claimed to reduce the fat levels in the body', and others that claimed to diagnose and treat various health conditions from several drops of blood. The concluding paragraph began:

Getting reliable information about Matthews has proved difficult. He has built up a considerable following on his You Tube channel and recently on Instagram, referring to himself as a 'health guru for the 21st century'. However, he clearly likes to keep his business affairs private, with a pattern of residing and starting businesses in overseas territories where there is only limited compliance and oversight. In my view, serious questions should be asked about this man's suitability to run a UK-based health sector business. Note: Craig Matthews refused to give any response to the points raised...

Another yell from downstairs.

'Ashley, will you come? I'm stuck!'

She hurried down to Diane's bedroom beside the kitchen, once Zac's office.

'Can you help me get out of these trousers?' Diane sat pink-cheeked on the edge of the bed. 'I can't do them up anymore.'

After sustained tugging, the trousers came off. Her mother's new GP in Brampton had declared her obese and advised her to go on a strict diet.

'What are you going to wear instead?' Ashley picked the jogging bottoms up from the back of the chair.

'Not those old things. I'm going over to Bryce's this afternoon for a cup of tea.'

'Bryce?'

'He lives on the other side of the green.'

'What does he look like?'

'Grey hair, usually in a ponytail, and slightly bulbous eyes. But he's got a strong physique for his age.'

'Oh, the Kiwi chap.' It was Bryce from number 11, she realised, one of the anti-tower movement. 'How are you getting there?'

'On foot, of course. It's only down the road. I'll take the walker. Oh, Ashley, before you go, could you take my case down from the top of the wardrobe, please? I didn't unpack everything. There might be some more suitable clothes in it.'

She stood on a chair to reach the large suitcase, then placed it on the bed.

'Anything else you need?'

'No thanks, I'm good now.'

Her mother began digging through the suitcase. Ashley hurried out of the room.

From the hall, loud, excited barks.

'Brillo, stop that!'

The dog was by the front door, watching the corner of a package being pushed through the letterbox. The object, one of Diane's many clothing catalogues, thudded to the floor. As Brillo was about to sink his teeth into it, Ashley dragged him away by his collar. 'Kitchen!'

Brillo slunk along the hall towards his bed. Ashley girded herself to start on the day's tasks. As usual, she needed to do food shopping, and her mother had an appointment at Curl Up and Dye this afternoon.

First, the laundry. Stuffing a load into the washing machine – Diane's underwear, sleepwear, casualwear, and a collection of sheets, pillow-cases and towels – her frustration returned.

She turned to what had become a regular task since Brillo's arrival: cleaning the downstairs floors and walls. It was alarming how much fur the dog shed, not to mention the amount of dirt that came off him. She got down on her hands and knees and began on the skirting board, considering tonight's meal.

Her thoughts turned to what Clare had said about her conversation with Emily Hale. Making plans to fly several thousand miles was not typical behavior for someone about to commit suicide, surely. It was puzzling. Had something happened to make Emily change her mind about taking that trip. Or had someone stopped her from going?

She wondered if she should tell DC Peters. But doing so wasn't likely to prompt the police to start investigating the matter properly. The coroner had declared the cause of Emily Hale's death to be 'probable suicide', she had read in the local paper. If Elven detectives had decided to ignore the truth, what could *she* do about it? Also, she shouldn't be drawing attention to herself while the detective constable was sniffing around... Whatever DC Peters might have told Ken, she had a hunch it was nothing to do with any 'routine' enquiries.

'Everything OK now?' She popped her head around Diane's door. Her mother was dressed in a pale blue top and matching trousers.

'I'd left them in the case; they wouldn't fit in that little wardrobe. Would you mind if I put some more of my things in your wardrobe, for now?'

She took a deep breath. 'No, Mum, I'd rather you didn't. When I get a chance, I'll move out some of Zac's things to make some space for your stuff.'

A notification from her phone – an email from John. She headed back to the kitchen to read it, glad of the distraction. Her friend was still in Spain, enjoying the hospitality of his friends in their villa. His Spanish had vastly improved, as had his swimming. She visualised his strong arms pulling through the water. Instantly, she was transported back to that fateful evening, and her surprise at the power of John's right arm as he launched an avocado at her neighbour. Had its impact caused Tara to slip? Or had that messy floor been the reason?

She would never know. The coroner had ruled Tara's death an 'unlawful killing'; her death likely from the impact of her head on the worktop corner. The events leading up it were unknown. However, the markings found on the body indicated that a 'deliberate attack' was likely to have led to her death.

Ashley pressed her knuckles into her brow. The horror of that August day still lurked inside her, along with the guilt. It had been her idea to confront Tara; the others would never have been there if she hadn't suggested it. Going by the many digs she'd made since, Ursula blamed Ashley, too.

The brisk ring of the doorbell made her start. She wasn't expecting a delivery and, except for Elspeth, no one called at the house without texting or phoning first. Before she could stop him, Brillo was barking at the front door.

'Brillo, get away!' The dog reluctantly trotted down the hall. 'I'm coming!' she called out.

Cold damp air rushed in as she opened the door, rain was beating down. The woman standing on the doorstep looked back at her with a despondent expression. She was no taller than Ashley. Slung over one shoulder, a black rucksack. Rain-heavy hair escaped the hood of her waterproof jacket. With a speeding heart, Ashley realised who she was.

'Hello again, Mrs Khan. It's me, DC Peters.' The woman unzipped her jacket and raised the ID card that hung around her neck. 'Would you mind if I came in for a few minutes?'

What now? Ashley turned to Brillo, who was letting off another volley of barks from the kitchen doorway. 'Bed!' She turned back to DC Peters.

'Getting them to do what you want isn't easy,' the detective constable said sympathetically. 'I've one of my own.'

'Come into the kitchen.' She glanced at DC Peters's damp trousers. 'I'll turn the heating on so you can dry off.'

Brillo came over to sniff the new arrival. DC Peters, who'd removed her jacket, bent down and patted his rump.

'He's a character, isn't he? How long have you had him?'

She had a surreal sense that she'd just bumped into a fellow dogwalker.

'Just over a month, since my mother moved in. I'm trying to train him not to go into attack mode whenever someone comes to the door.'

'That's not such a bad thing you know.' The DC smiled. 'Barking deters intruders.'

'Can I help you with that?'

DC Peters had also taken off her sweater and was arranging it beside her jacket on a chair she'd pulled up in front of the radiator.

'No worries.'

Damp tendrils of hair stuck to her collar, a vivid yellow. She was the last person you'd expect to be a police officer, Ashley thought.

'Would you like a tea or coffee?'

'That'll be great, thanks. Tea please.'

She rooted around for a clean mug.

'Would you mind if I used the toilet?'

On hearing the click of the lock on the downstairs toilet door, Ashley knocked on her mother's door and went in. Diane was sitting at her makeshift dressing table. Frowning, she turned to Ashley.

'Who's that you're talking to?'

'It's the detective who took my statement about the dead woman.'

'What does she want?'

'I don't know.' She had a strong feeling: this visit must be connected with Tara's death.

'You'll be fine, love. Don't let her rattle you.'

She looked at her mother in surprise. Two minutes later, Ashley and DC Peters were seated at the table with their mugs of tea. The DC had chosen the chair at the head of the table, adjacent to hers.

Ashley waited for the DC to speak. Weren't the police busy with high workloads, the pressure of cases to be solved? She tried to look as if she had nothing on her mind.

'How long have you had your dog?' she asked.

'I got Mitzi as a puppy,' the detective replied. 'Just over four years ago. But she's not with me anymore.'

'You mean she's... passed on?'

The DC chuckled mid-sip, her tea overflowing onto the table.

'She's still very much alive, thank you. I hope so, anyway. I meant she's not living with me anymore. I had to leave her with my friend when I moved to Elven.'

'Oh! So you're new to the area?'

'That's right. I transferred here from the Met.'

'I see. It was a shame you had to leave Mitzi behind.'

'It was one of those things.' DC Peters pursed her lips, looking sad. 'She was used to the flat, the local walks. My friend was staying on. She offered to look after Mitzi.'

'That's a big upheaval,' she said, wondering how to push the conversation on. 'I moved out of London, too. It took me ages to get used to village life.'

'I miss home, I must admit. And my friend – partner, really – didn't want to move all the way out here.' DC Peters seemed even sadder now, and still not in a hurry to ask any questions.

'You didn't choose to work here, then?'

'No, they made me transfer to another Force. It was that or resign.'

'Did you do something wrong?' Ashley felt a surge of sympathy. She ought not to be chatting like this to a detective, she couldn't help thinking, even the most junior-level one. But the woman seemed to have a strong need to talk.

'I made a mistake.'

'Oh?'

From the room next door, the creak of floorboards. The sound seemed to pull the woman to her senses. 'Is your mother in the house?'

'Yes, she's next door. She moved in with us so we could look after her better. Me and my husband, I mean.'

A frown passed over DC Peters's face.

'Why I'm here... I was looking through some of our files on unsolved cases and I came across the enquiry into the murder of Tara Sanderson.'

Ashley's heart put on a spurt. The DC casually brushed a hair off her upper arm.

'Tell me, Ashley. You're on good terms with Clare Titchfield, aren't you? The woman people call Bird Woman?'

'Clare?' She stared at DC Peters. 'Yes, yes, I am. I see her from time to time. Elspeth and I helped repair her cottage. Why?'

A gap before the reply.

'As you probably know, shortly after the murder, Clare came forward to say she'd seen two men in the victim's kitchen at the approximate time that Tara Sanderson is believed to have died. At which point, the focus of the enquiry shifted from you and Elspeth to the men that Clare supposedly saw.' The detective paused, studying her face. 'That was one of the things that struck me as being not quite right.'

The DC was looking intently at her, as if expecting a reply. Ashley tried to breathe normally. Was the detective accusing her and Elspeth of killing Tara? Or was she fishing for information that might result in a breakthrough in a lifeless case?

'What are you saying, exactly? And why are you talking to me about all this? The case is closed, isn't it?'

'Cases are never closed, Ashley.' The detective drank the rest of her tea, got up from the table and strode to the glass doors, where she stood frowning at the back garden. 'The thing is, we've had some new information.'

'Really?'

'A drawing was seen in Clare's cottage.'

'A drawing?' Her heart began to thud. 'Clare draws all the time, that's hardly unusual.'

'It was quite detailed, according to my source. It clearly shows Tara Sanderson defending herself from a group of people who were throwing objects at her – various kinds of fruit. It appeared to represent the scene from an eyewitness stationed outside Ms Sanderson's kitchen window, shortly before she was killed.'

She heard a gasp emerge from her throat and converted it into a cough. That damned drawing.

'What's all this got to do with me?'

DC Peters tucked a damp strand of hair behind her ear.

'You were one of the people depicted in that group, Ashley. You were shown holding an apple, aimed at Ms Sanderson. Also, you must already know that your fingerprints were found on an apple later discovered in Ms Sanderson's kitchen.'

Indeed, she did. Those fingerprints might have had her charged with murder, if Clare hadn't intervened... Ashley shifted in her chair, suppressing a nervous giggle. Quickly, she pulled herself together.

'How do you know the drawing isn't from Clare's imagination? It must be, because nothing like that ever happened.' Ashley pulled at the neckline of her sweat-top and channelled her fear into a huff of breath. 'Why don't you ask Clare about the drawing?'

'I already have. She admitted to doing the drawing shortly after she found out about Tara's murder – only when I asked to see it, she couldn't find it. She told me it was an imaginary scene—'

'Well, then.'

'The thing is, Ashley...' The DC was rubbing her jaw, her brow furrowing. 'Before I asked about this particular drawing, Clare told me she only ever draws from observation. She was quite definite about that.'

The detective's eyes were steady on hers. Was she hoping for a confession? Ashley swallowed the lump in her throat.

'I'm sorry, I don't know what else I can say.' She stood up, nearly knocking her chair over, and poured herself a glass of water. 'I'm quite busy today, I'm afraid. My mother needs looking after.'

'I'll be on my way, then. I wouldn't want you to neglect your mother.' DC Peters stood up too, turning to her clothes on the chair. 'Thank you for the tea.'

Thank God, she was leaving. Ashley watched her preparations from a distance, trying not to look relieved.

'DC Peters, before you go... There's something I need to tell you.' The detective turned on her heel. 'It's about Emily Hale.'

Blue eyes scrutinised her. 'Go on.'

'I told you I didn't think she jumped. I'm even more certain of it now. Just before she died, Emily had been planning to fly to Texas. Did you know?'

DC Peters lowered her backpack to the floor. She hadn't known, as far as Ashley could tell.

'Where did you get this information?'

'From Clare,' Ashley admitted. 'They knew each other. Emily used to live on the mobile home site not far from Clare's cottage.'

'Thanks for letting me know,' the detective said after a pause. 'But I doubt this will change anything. As I said, we've decided not to proceed with our enquiries into Emily Hale's death.'

After DC Peters had gone, Ashley relayed the essence of the conversation to her mother.

'They've got some new evidence to do with the death of your neighbour. What sort of evidence? And why did she want to talk to *you* about it?'

'I was her next-door neighbour, that's why.' She slipped away to her laptop before Diane could ask any more awkward questions and clicked onto the Dolphin Clinic website. Beautiful images and polished prose were displayed in a contemporary page design. On the home page, a large photo showed a smiling, tanned Craig in a designer polo shirt. He looked much younger, without any shading around the eyes and his hair sprouting thickly. Underneath, a bold headline:

Disenchanted by doctors? Fed up with popping pills? In despair at long waiting times?

Here at Dolphin Clinic we offer a haven from the tired, broken system that is conventional medicine with its overworked GPs and over-reliance on pharmaceuticals. Renowned health practitioner Craig Matthews and his team of experienced therapists offer clients an extensive range of therapies in a health-care environment second to none. Our high performance imaging and diagnostic technology delivers unsurpassed health solutions, tailored to the individual. Contact Dolphin Clinic today for a free consultation.

She scanned the list of therapies, from 'Sound Bath with Reiki' to 'Breath and Rebirthing'.

On the *About Us* page was a photo of Craig standing inside a sunlit atrium. Beside him stood the man he had been talking to at The Anglers. Both were smiling, looking into the camera. The caption gave the man's name as Steve Weston, 'a local investor, construction executive and property developer'. The blurb below suggested that Mr Weston had recently bought the property in which the clinic was housed for 'a sum of at least three million pounds'.

Ah, that was interesting. She googled Steve Weston. Aside from The Anglers, he appeared to own much of Brampton and the surrounding area, including an upmarket health club and a boutique hotel. Her mind whirred. How exactly, she wondered, were Craig Matthews and Steve Weston connected? Was it only friendship? They seemed so different on the surface – one an unashamedly rich businessman not exactly brimming with health, the other trim and health conscious who wanted to heal people.

Clicking through the clinic's site, she spotted a workshop taking place later that week: 'Free Yourself From Anxiety'. It cost £35. She clicked the *Book* button. It would be interesting to see Craig in professional mode, and he might even be able to help with her anxiety.

Her phone rang.

'You'll never guess what I just found out about Craig,' Elspeth began.

'Go on.'

'I got into a chat with Rhianna, you know, the woman with the squash-faced dog. She told me he's on Instagram and he's got thousands of followers, Ash. Over five hundred thousand.'

'That is a lot.'

'I had a look at his profile just now. He posts about healthy living, detox diets, cleansing your body, being the best person you can be, et cetera, et cetera. He's practically a guru!'

'I've been digging, too. You'll never guess where I'm going on Tuesday.'

'Tell me.'

'I'm doing a workshop at the Dolphin Clinic. With Craig. It's meant to help with anxiety.'

'Oh, what fun! I'd like to go myself.'

'I'm only going to it because of Emily Hale's connection with Craig.'

'Really? Pull the other one.'

'OK. I like him, I admit. But the clinic's the main reason.'

With a chuckle, she ended the call. Who was she kidding? She and Elspeth were as bad as each other. Both of them were smitten with Craig.

That night as she was trying to fall asleep, her thoughts went back to the detective's visit.

Was she a murder suspect again?

Thoughts arrived, one on top of the other. What if the police found Clare's drawing? She had better speak to Clare. DC Peters was clever and determined. She was bound to find out the truth sooner or later.

Oh, God. She turned over and reached for her phone. It was no good, she'd have to start the Calm app. She needed to forget Emily, then there would be one less thing to worry about. It wasn't as if she had known the woman. What did it matter how she'd died?

But thirty-five years ago, her lack of action had allowed her best friend to die.

The body had been found at 11.15pm on Alison's route home, on the pavement beneath a flight of steps where an overpass crossed a busy road. Before walking home to their shared house, Alison had been seen drinking heavily and slurring her words at the pub they had been drinking in before Ashley had left. The coroner had ruled the cause of death as misadventure. Despite everyone telling her she wasn't to blame, she *had* blamed herself. She had known that Alison was anxious and stressed about her upcoming exams – enough to be drinking far too much and seeing a counsellor – but she hadn't insisted Alison leave the pub with her. Instead, she had spent the last hours of her friend's life revising.

Of course, the situation with Emily was very different. But she couldn't abandon Emily, too.

Ashley settled her head back on the pillow. She would do one last thing before giving up – visit the caravan site where Emily used to live. Someone might know something.

Chapter 10
DC Peters

The lift was stuck again. With grim determination, Kate Peters headed to the stairwell.

The one-bed flat and its location were far from ideal, but it was all she could afford. This particular evening, after a day fruitlessly chasing potential criminals around the Force's convoluted system followed by further fruitless chasing of the 380 bus, the three-flight climb was more of a trudge than usual.

Panting heavily, Kate hurried past the unsightly walls – whoever had thought of bubblegum pink? – and unlocked her front door. No labradoodle... The usual tug on her heart. Lately, she was missing Mitzi far more than her ex – another sign, no doubt. After locating a carton of frozen stew, she plonked herself down on the bony little sofa with a bottle of Heineken Zero and checked her phone. No more messages from Gabby. She replayed the video of Mitzi jumping up for a piece of toast. Then, in her head, she replayed the morning's dressing down, squeezing the cushion beside her from time to time.

The resentment she'd experienced on becoming acquainted with DI Lister's intolerance and sarcasm was morphing into despair. She had a horrible sense that this soulless woman was trying to get her pushed out of the Force.

According to the DI, Kate needed to learn to listen to her superiors.

You know the line DCI Hill is taking on Emily Hale. I don't want to hear any more talk about her being murdered. We can't keep squandering our resources picking away at what in all likelihood was the suicide of a desperate woman.

The DCI, as Kate well knew, was pressing for everyone to focus on catching 'Moped Man', the most visible manifestation of the thuggish violence enveloping this town.

The same goes for following up cases from donkey's years ago that are unlikely ever to be solved – even with a mind as brilliant as yours.

Throughout, Kate had refrained from mentioning that certain facts relating to Emily Hale's death pointed towards murder not suicide. Nor did she mention the fact that Tara Sanderson's death – very possibly at the hands of her next-door neighbours – was one of the most interesting cases she had come across in her three years as a police officer, nor her view that DCI Hill and DI Lister had allowed their common sense to be hijacked by an eccentric birder.

Nor had she spoken at the DI's parting thrust, delivered in a low hiss.

You'd better watch yourself Kate, or you'll be lucky to find a job in the Outer bloody Hebrides.

With a daring loud cry – the walls were thin – Kate punched the cushion. If only she had been able to report good news in the Tara Sanderson case. Her early progress had stalled. As yet, the drawing of the murder scene as described by the vicar of Brampton's St John the Baptist church, remained undiscovered. Ashley Khan, the younger of the two suspects in the original enquiry, was hiding something, Kate was certain. As to the second suspect,

Elspeth... The octogenarian appeared cheerful and harmless – as did some of the worst criminals, she was well aware.

The initial enquiry had strongly pointed to Ashley and Elspeth being responsible for the unlawful killing of Tara Sanderson. Undoubtedly, they should have been charged with murder rather than being let off following the spurious identification of two young men by a birdwatching hermit who had every reason to lie in order to protect her friends.

Ms Sanderson had died from blunt force trauma to back of skull, the pathologist had concluded. But what had led to this was unclear. Evidence gathered from the scene suggested that her head had struck the kitchen worktop, composed of a lovely but compact stone resembling marble. Fruit stain traces had been detected on the floor; bruises and traces of apple, orange and avocado found on the upper body were 'consistent with the victim being pelted with fruit'. The victim's skin cells were found at the edge of the worktop, and also on a dented apple retrieved from the gap between the cabinet and the fridge. Furthermore, this apple had also contained Ashley's fingerprints. Elspeth's fingerprint had been detected on the fruit bowl, which conceivably could have been the murder weapon despite no blood or skin being detected on it. The glass could easily have been wiped, though...

In Kate's view, either the victim had slipped on fruit residue or received a well-timed push – or perhaps a blow to the head with the empty fruit bowl – causing her to fall and strike her head on the worktop. Which of these scenarios was correct, she couldn't wait to find out.

With renewed resolve, she retrieved her notebook from her rucksack and completed the latest entry, begun that morning on the bus.

Summary of new evidence in the Tara Sanderson case (gathered by KP)

Vicar claimed that on 12 January while bringing food supplies, she saw a drawing depicting six people attacking TS on CT's table, and she believed the persons in the drawing to be:

- *TS, wearing a short-sleeved top, cropped jeans and flipflops ('It was definitely Tara. She started looking quite frumpy towards the end.')*
- *AK, holding an apple ('I recognised Ashley straight away. I often see her walking around the village with that scruffy dog of hers. They look a bit like each other, come to think of it.')*
- *EC, wearing an emerald ring ('definitely Elspeth – exactly the same over-the-top clothes and ostentatious jewellery')*
- *JB, on a mobility scooter ('I'd swear it was John. His disabled machine has the same red markings. He tears about on it like a hooligan. I understand he's pally with Ashley.')*
- *UC ('It's definitely Ursula. She's on the church choir committee. She's always asking me to make sure the church is vacated on time'), and*
- *the other two (now deceased) individuals in the community group (now defunct)*

CT stated that she drew the scene purely from her imagination. Earlier however, CT said she only draws people from observation.

Conclusion:
The new evidence suggests to KP that there is every reason to continue the investigation. The alleged drawing, if it can be

located, could provide crucial evidence against AK and EC (also JB and UC) that would allow the four to be charged with murder.

Kate put down her pen and gave the cushion a final squeeze. She felt a lot better.

Chapter 11
Bird Woman

24 January: 3.45pm

Ashley was on my doorstep when I got home from my walk. I was surprised to see her as it wasn't a day when she normally visits.

'It's about your drawing, Clare. It's been on my mind ever since that police officer came over asking questions.' While we stood in the hall, she said she was sorry to ask this of me, but she needed me to destroy my drawing. Specifically, she wanted me to shred it and discard the shreds in several different dustbins, excluding my own.

'Otherwise, we could all be charged with murder,' she added. It appears she has been visited by the same detective who came to talk to me.

After a thorough examination of the lower kitchen cupboard, I explain that as much as I wished to comply with her request, the drawing is no longer where I had placed it three weeks ago, after the vicar's visit.

Ashley gets up from the sofa, her brow furled. 'So where is it?'

The only explanation I can think of, I say, is that the vicar took it last Monday when she came over with her unwanted groceries.

'While I was unpacking it all I had to excuse myself to go to the toilet. There would have been enough time for her to roll up the drawing and put it in her shopping bag, leaving me none the wiser.'

'But how would she have known where you'd put it?'

'She must have cased the joint on her previous visit,' I say, explaining that I had been in the back garden refilling the bird feeders when she arrived. The vicar offered to put the groceries away for me so I could finish. On my return I'd caught her closing the lower cupboard door. I asked her what she was doing and she nonchalantly explained she was trying to find a home for the mint sauce, which I found odd as I'd already told her where the condiments were kept.

'Are you certain it was the vicar who took it? Could someone else have come in and taken it?'

'Only you or Elspeth, or DC Peters,' I retort. 'No one else has set foot inside this cottage since last year.'

A long, miserable silence.

'I'm sorry for causing all this trouble,' I say. Admittedly, though I really don't want to see my friends in trouble, I am secretly glad that my drawing has caused such a stir.

'That's alright,' Ashley says, attempting a smile. 'It's disturbing to think that someone took it, though. You'd better not say anything about Liz Peaches taking the drawing to DC Peters, in case she goes after *her* for it. And in future it might be an idea to keep an eye on the vicar when she comes over.'

'I'm not letting that deceitful cow inside my cottage ever again!'

Ashley laughs. I go to toss out the mound of wilting root veg left by Liz Peaches. How she ever got to be a woman of the cloth, I don't know. She can stuff her roast chicken and leftover parsnips up her jumper.

Chapter 12
Ashley

Four days later

'Well, this has been most pleasant. Almost like old times.'

Ursula put down her mug of coffee. There was a snide tone to her voice.

Ashley broke in.

'Actually, there's something I need to tell you. A police officer came to see me recently. A detective.'

Ursula swallowed the rest of her biscuit.

'She's looking into Tara's death,' she continued. 'She's new to the area. I think she wants to make a good impression on her superiors.'

Ursula looked at her suspiciously. 'Did you tell her anything?'

Ouch. That was uncalled for.

'No, of course not.'

'What did she ask you, then?'

She neatened the assortment of magazines and shopping list-bearing scraps of paper that her mother had left on the kitchen table.

'Someone has told her about a drawing that Clare did.'

Ursula frowned. 'What drawing? I don't know what you're talking about.'

'Clare drew a picture of all of us throwing fruit at Tara. It was quite detailed, I gather.'

'What?' Ursula blinked rapidly. 'Why on earth would she do a thing like that?'

'She said she couldn't get the scene out of her head. Also, she was practicing drawing faces and hands.'

Ursula was clearly having difficulty absorbing this information. Her face flushed and she flung her hands wide as she spoke.

'She kept this drawing all along... and she's only just told you about it?'

'I was taken aback, too, so was Elspeth.'

'Who else knows about it? How did this detective find out?'

'DC Peters didn't tell me who gave her the information. But Clare thinks the vicar saw the drawing when she dropped off some groceries recently.'

'So, the vicar must have spoken to the detective?'

'I should think so.'

'This gets better and better.' Ursula's voice dripped with sarcasm. 'Next you'll be telling me that all of us are clearly identified in this drawing.'

Oh, dear. She made an effort to keep her voice level.

'I think we're all in the drawing, Ursula. As to whether or not anyone could have recognised us—'

With a cluck of irritation, Ursula interrupted. 'What was in the head of that bloody woman, doing something like that?'

Ashley picked up their mugs and rinsed them under the tap. Ursula hadn't been this agitated since Tara's death.

'Where's the drawing now? She's not keeping it at her cottage, is she?'

She was tempted to lie but had vowed to keep her deception to a minimum from now on.

'It's gone missing.'

'It's gone missing?' Ursula looked near apoplectic. Her flush had darkened to a deep red and spread to the base of her neck. She paced up and down the kitchen floor, breathing heavily.

'She thinks someone took it—'

'What, another person?' Ursula made no attempt to curtail the sarcasm, or volume, of her delivery.

'Ursula, will you stop shouting at me!' She made an effort to speak quietly. 'I don't think we need to worry too much. Someone describing a drawing that only they have seen probably doesn't count for much as far as evidence goes.' She didn't know if this was true, but it seemed to calm Ursula.

'Has this police officer talked to anyone else, or just you?'

'She's talked to Clare and she had a word with Elspeth... and she's spoken to our neighbour, Ken.'

'I see. Hopefully she won't want to talk to me. Or John, for that matter. Is he still in Spain?' Ursula pushed her glasses up her nose and directed a piercing stare towards Ashley. 'You're in touch with him, aren't you?'

'He's staying near Seville,' she said curtly.

'You three had better be careful,' Ursula said in a low voice.

'What did you say?'

'Never mind.'

She took a deep breath. 'If you have something to say, I'd like to hear it.'

Ursula blinked twice. 'Thanks for the coffee. No need to see me out.'

When the woman had gone, Ashley let out a sigh. Good riddance to the old bat. As well as infuriated, she felt unsettled. Beneath Ursula's veneer of politeness was something hard and unyielding. It didn't bode well.

Chapter 13
Elspeth

Two days later

It was her Friday afternoon catch-up with Ashley over tea and biscuits.

'Do you think Clare's right, then? The vicar saw this drawing and went to the police about it, then came back and stole it?'

'I honestly don't know.' Ashley broke a biscuit in half and dunked it into her tea. 'It's bizarre. If she went back to Clare's under false pretences to get her hands on the drawing—'

'She ought to be ex-communicated,' Elspeth replied with feeling. 'Or whatever the Anglican church does. She's meant to be a Christian, a messenger of the Lord and all that.'

'Why would anyone go to so much trouble getting their hands on that drawing, though?'

'Maybe she's going to blackmail us with it. Maybe she has a grudge against one of us...'

They looked at each other.

'What should we do?' Ashley stared at the remains of her biscuit. 'If we ask what she's up to, she'll deny it.'

'Let's wait and see what happens.' Elspeth gathered her

courage. 'I wasn't sure whether to tell you this... You know about Ken thinking he's seen Tara's ghost? Well, I've seen her, too.'

Ashley sat up straight. 'What? Where?'

'When I'm in the garden. It's happened a couple of times now. I look up and she's looking out from the roof terrace, or her bedroom window.' This had been a bad idea, she could see from Ashley's deep frown. 'I know I must be imagining things,' she said quickly. 'It can't really be her, can it?'

'It could be delayed grief. I've heard of people who keep seeing loved ones who've died... Their brains conjure up the dead person they can't let go.'

Tara had hardly been a loved one, but still. 'You don't think I should tell my GP?'

'It wouldn't do any harm to mention it. Have you had any other odd symptoms? Confusion? Forgetfulness?'

Elspeth considered. Talking to oneself occasionally was normal, wasn't it? And so was occasionally forgetting which day of the week it was.

'I don't think so.' She hadn't forgotten to go out without her door key or any other essential item for well over a year, which was more than Ashley could say of herself.

'I suppose when you reach your eighties, you can't take anything for granted,' Ashley said, picking up her mug.

She felt a surge of indignation.

'I've still got all my faculties, I'll have you know. I do *The Times* crossword and sudoku every day and my hearing isn't bad for my age, Dr Patel told me. Once I get my cataract sorted and my other knee done, I'll be right as rain.'

Back at number 34, Elspeth settled into her favourite spot in the house, the terrace room with a view of distant hills. Sunlight seeped through the ever-changing clouds. Could her sightings of a dead woman mean there was something wrong with her mind? What if they were the start of dementia, or something equally awful? She put on her glasses, picked up her smartphone and opened Instagram, always a pleasant distraction from tiresome thoughts.

Mere weeks after her godson had helped her to set up an account, checking her Instagram feed had become a daily activity. She'd followed some accounts under dance, health, wellbeing and so on. But the person she was most interested in was @natural-healer21C – the 'handle' printed on the back of Craig's business card.

His feed had plenty of health and nutrition advice, with regular items such as Trouble Sharing Corner, Prove Your Doctor Wrong and Tips for Longevity. Every day a new post appeared, often accompanied by a photo of Craig – sitting cross-legged in his meditation room, feeding his hens, strolling in his garden or whatever – along with photos of healthy-looking food and attractive women drinking smoothies or doing yoga poses. There were videos of Craig, too, musing on topics from letting go of unhelpful habits to the benefits of celery.

Did he have an assistant to help him with all these posts, she wondered. Some had received over a hundred comments and most had been replied to, if briefly. All this was presumably a way to market his services; in the text below there was often a mention of some online offering from his clinic. She scrolled through the comments on Craig's recent posts. They were mostly supportive, often coming from women who seemed disgruntled with their treatment by the medical profession.

Today's 'Health Tip of the Day' popped up on her screen. The photo showed a bowl of green liquid topped with a dollop of cream, or more likely a low-fat dairy alternative. She scrolled down to the words below, headed 'Don't forget your greens'.

Eating spinach, kale, and other such green leafy veg regularly is helpful for maintaining brain and eye health, and for warding off conditions including dementia and macular degeneration.

Goodness, could she and Craig have a telepathic connection? No, of course it was coincidence that she'd just been musing on her own brain health – along with a high proportion of Craig's followers, no doubt. She began typing a comment. It showed up half a second later, the first.

Thanks for cheering me up. I'm going to make spinach soup tonight.

She would get out the food processor and start concocting some of the soups and wotnot that these wellness gurus suggested, rather than idling away her time on Instagram, and ogling Craig Matthews.

Chapter 14
Ashley

The next day

Ashley stepped onto the fenced timber decking adjoining the narrow home and knocked at the purple-painted door. Number 12 was on the corner of the site, nestled in a bend of the river adjoining the woods.

The '1' hung upside down, held by a single screw. Despondency settling, she turned to leave. What was the point of all this? No one here wanted to talk to her. She turned towards the next mobile home, covered in faded white-painted weatherboard.

Give it a chance, she told herself, knocking again, this time more vigorously.

A curtain at the window lifted. Footsteps inside then the harsh scrape of a bolt. The door opened outwards and a woman looked down at Ashley with a chilly expression. Her hair was flame red, roots showing grey. Her lips bore traces of violet lipstick.

'Hello... I wonder if I could trouble you for a glass of water? I've been walking and I stupidly forgot to bring any.'

It was the eleventh mobile home she'd tried and only the third time the door had been opened. By now she really did need one, though from the nervous churning of her insides rather than physical exertion – the site was less than two miles walk from Wilton Close.

'Wait there.' The woman's voice was deep and throaty. She wore loose layers in various shades of purple.

Ashley gazed towards the river. The view was obscured by tall trees lining the riverbank. In their shade sat a handful of campervans.

'Thanks ever so much.' She reached up over the step to take the beer glass offered. After consuming its contents she looked up at the woman, who was holding onto the door. 'My name's Ashley. I live in Brampton.'

The woman looked distinctly unfriendly. Ashley ploughed on.

'A friend told me Emily Hale used to live here.'

No reaction.

'I was hoping to find someone who knew her, who might be able to tell me something about how she seemed in her final days. Before she passed, I mean...'

'Who's your friend?' The woman spoke with uncompromising directness.

'She lives in a cottage over there.' She pointed. 'On the edge of the wood.'

'Oh, Bird Woman you mean.'

'That's right. She used to chat with Emily from time to time. The last time – not long before she died – Emily told her that she was ill.'

'You're not from the police, then?'

She heaved an involuntary sigh. She was dressed in her trademark casual style: jacket, jumper, jeans and trainers with vaguely brushed hair and virtually no makeup.

'Do I look like I'm in the police?'

'No, can't say you do.' The woman had opened the door a

little further, with a frankly appraising look. 'What do you want to know, then? Emily lived in the van next to mine.'

'Er... How well did you know her? Did she say anything to you about not being well – or anything else that was troubling her?'

'You'd better come in,' the woman said with a glance behind Ashley, pushing open the door and stepping away from the entrance.

She stepped into the narrow space, made smaller by a clutter of women's clothing.

''Scuse the mess.' The woman pulled the door shut. 'I keep meaning to clear up, but you know how it is.'

Ashley edged along the aisle towards what looked like a living area and stood with her back to a fold-down table. The woman rested her arm on the edge of the kitchen sink.

'Two men came sniffing round the site about two or three weeks ago. They asked about Emily, which place was hers. I didn't tell them anything but one of the others here might have. That evening she knocked on my door. She was worried, I could tell. She told me she didn't know the men but she had a feeling they were up to no good. Anyway, they came back last week. It was dark, nearly ten in the evening. I saw them from my window. They were making a din, banging on Emily's door, shouting for her to come out. Then everything went quiet. I waited a bit then went over. I thought they would have gone on their way by then.' She curled the fingers of one hand into a fist. 'I saw them leaving – I was only a few feet away. Thank God, they didn't see me.'

'What did they look like?'

'I dunno.' The woman shrugged. 'It was dark by then. Both were white with dark hair. Could've been from East Europe somewhere.' Frowning, she glanced down at her hand, purple nailed. 'One had big shoulders and an oddly small face, delicate looking. He had silver rings on his fingers. The other one... I can't remember much. Bland face. Oh yes, his legs didn't look quite right. They weren't straight; you could see a gap between them.'

'Thanks, that's really helpful.' She considered getting her paper and pen out to note all this down but didn't in case it disrupted the flow of information.

'It's Dawn, by the way,' the woman said suddenly.

'Dawn, good to meet you,' Ashley belatedly replied. 'What happened after that?'

'They ran off into the woods. I knocked on Emily's door and asked if she was OK. She didn't want to let me in but I insisted. She said she was alright, they hadn't touched her but she looked absolutely terrified. I made her a strong cup of tea. She said the men told her they'd kick the door down if she didn't open up. When she let them in, they told her she was in trouble, and if she didn't stop what she was doing they'd come back and set her place alight, with her inside it.' Dawn looked down at her hand again, breathing noisily. 'I wish I'd gone over there sooner.' Her eyes examined Ashley's face. 'You're the first person I've told this to.'

'I appreciate it. Thanks for trusting me.'

'There's room to sit.' With her foot, Dawn nudged something stowed under the table.

'I'm happy to stand,' she replied with a confidence she didn't feel. 'The trouble she was in... did she tell you what it was?'

'I don't know anything about that.' Dawn moved her head decisively.

'Do you have any idea who those men were?'

'Not really, no.' The reply came late.

'You have some idea, though?'

Dawn's body stiffened.

'Why would they have threatened her like that? What was she doing that they didn't like?'

A twitch of the shoulders. 'As I said...'

'Neither of you went to the police?'

'I couldn't. Emily said...' A visible shudder passed through the woman, who crossed her arms tightly over her chest. 'She didn't want me to; she was scared of what those men might do. They told her if she told anyone they'd find out and come back. Anyway, the police never come this way if they can avoid it. They treat those of us here as pond scum, as bad as the travellers. Emily went to the police months ago about the...' Dawn rubbed her temple, '...about some things going on round here. They did nothing, showed no interest whatsoever. Which didn't surprise me one jot.'

'When did the two men visit Emily, exactly?'

'Three days before she was killed. The 7th of January. I worked it out after I read what happened. A woman found her body in the quarry...'

'That was me,' she said.

'Oh.' Silence. 'If that's all... I need to get myself some lunch.' Dawn opened a cupboard and began to open a tin of sardines.

'Do you think someone killed Emily?'

'What?' Dawn swivelled to face her. On her face, suspicion and fear.

'You said *three days before she was killed.*'

'It was nothing, I just thought...'

'Please, Dawn, I need to know. Since I found her... This has been eating away at me. I promise I won't pass anything you tell me on to the police, or anyone else.'

'Or anything I've told you already?' Dawn said eventually, her eyes fixed on her own.

'I promise.'

'OK. This is what I think, for what it's worth. I don't believe what people are saying about Emily killing herself. She would never have done that. She was worried about her illness, sure, after she stopped believing that Craig could cure her. The thought of having to have her liver and kidneys replaced, or having to sit beside a machine for hours at a time... It freaked her out. But she said she was going to enjoy life as much as possible, while she could still get around... She'd been saving up to go and see her mum and brother and granddad in Texas, and her nephews and nieces.' A rasp appeared in Dawn's voice. 'The last time I spoke to her, she was so excited. The beauty salon had paid her all the money they owed her. She'd been looking at flights to Dallas...'

'When was it you spoke to her?'

'It was that morning.'

'That morning?'

'The morning of the day you found her body.'

She didn't reply. The implication began to sink in.

'They did it, didn't they?' Dawn said. 'What they said they would.' She busied herself putting slices of bread into a toaster.

'Do you have no idea at all what might have been going on? Why those men were threatening her?'

'Look, I've said enough already.' Dawn studied her hand, dislodging some dirt from a nail. 'I don't want to get into trouble myself.'

'Please, Dawn. So, her death isn't for nothing.' She forced herself to say it.

'OK.' Dawn sucked in her lips so they disappeared. 'She was fixated with this idea that people were getting away with things. I didn't pay it much attention, to be honest. She was convinced that her garden of the place she lived in before had poisoned her. She was angry that the council didn't take it seriously. And she said she saw someone in the abandoned caravan.' She gestured towards the river. 'It's over there, in the woods. The council can't be arsed to move it. It's been there for years, locked up, the curtains shut. Several of us have complained but no one does anything.'

'She saw someone inside it? Who?'

'A man, Emily said.' Her tone became sceptical. 'She saw him through a gap in the curtains. She thought he had a black bag over his head.'

'You didn't believe her?'

Dawn's eyebrows lifted. 'She was a bit... How can I say? I went over with her early the next morning to check the van but there was no sign of anyone inside. I thought she must have been mistaken. Maybe the poison was affecting her brain. But now I'm not so sure. I've heard things at night from the woods, we all have.'

'What sort of sounds?' She felt a prickle of unease.

'The sounds of someone frightened. Shouts, cries. Muffled, like someone is trying to cry out but they have something over their mouth.'

Ashley stared. What was going on? She had an urge to get out into the sunshine, away from this place. Dawn stood motionless, holding onto a wooden spoon, her eyes seeming not to see.

At the mobile home entrance, Ashley put a hand on Dawn's shoulder and gave it a light squeeze.

'Thanks for talking to me.'

Dawn lowered her head.

'If you find out what happened to Emily, let me know. I hope you do. She deserves that, at least.'

Chapter 15
Bird Woman

1 February: 3.30am

The sounds of night seem louder than usual. There's the trumpetlike grunt of a Heffer on the organic farm. Everything is free range. The cows in particular seem to have a marvellous time. Then, an owl.

I have lain awake for an hour. A sudden sound had woken me, the origin of which I could not identify. It rang out clearly, making me think of a person in distress. What if someone is hurt? Shouldn't I go and investigate?

Something is going on in my wood, I am certain. Of late, I've seen men lurking here who aren't from the mobile homes or any houses in the vicinity. They are visitors, but not the usual kind. They have a tense, determined look, not the relaxed manner of someone out for a stroll.

I eat the last defrosted slice of the vicar's cake and start to layer up. There is no point doing anything hungry. Striding away from the cottage my confidence starts to erode. Though I know it well and I've brought a torch, the path is difficult to follow. Oaks sprout thickly, their gnarled boughs throwing monstrous shadows.

I crunch through leaves, stopping every so often to listen. With relief I spot the bat box attached to a tree. Instantly I know where I am.

The caravan sits in a clearing, almost hidden by the surrounding birches and weeping willows. Behind it, the river is invisible. The sound came from here, I have a hunch. I creep closer. Paint flakes off the door and windowsills. Rust marks the wheel arches. The curtains are drawn, a faded yellow. I go around to the other side, stumbling over an upturned stool. The curtains are closed on this side, too. There's a fingerprint inside the grimy window.

I go back around, push on the door. It doesn't budge. There's no sound from inside, no sign that anyone is here. But someone has been here, I would swear, very recently. The sharp tang of bodily fluids invades my nostrils. There's a metallic odour, too – blood? I shudder. On the ground by the lower step leading up to the door is a red patch. I bend down and touch. It is a little sticky. Despite an urge to flee, I pause. There's something small in the grass, catching the moonlight. I pick it up and stuff it into my pocket, then run in the direction of home.

Soon my panting must be audible to every creature in this wood. I lean over, hands on knees, gulping air. Close by an owl cries, making me start. I walk fast up the long incline towards the frog pond, taking care not to stray from the path. The moonlight is intermittent and my torch seems dimmer than on my way out. As I pass the algae-strewn pond, a sound stops me.

It is metallic, like the clank of metal against stone. I scan the trees for the source of the sound but see nothing except bare branches. I still my breath and listen. A distant voice, male. Authoritative with an edge of aggression, as if someone is giving orders. I can't make the words. I freeze, heart pumping madly, switch off my torch. Trying to locate the voice, I turn my head.

I am about to go on my way when I catch sight of two males in between the densely packed trees. They both wear dark clothing.

The Bad Women

I can't see much except their light faces and the reflective stripes on the trainers of the man standing still. The other's body is bent, his head lowered. He moves his arms rhythmically as if carrying out some task.

I step behind a thick tree trunk. Whatever these men are up to, I imagine they would not appreciate me watching. I observe for a little longer but can't make out any details of the figures, apart from one: the standing man's legs are bowed. Not a great deal but enough to notice.

The moon hides again. I make my escape, alternately walking and running. Once I've shut the front door safely behind me, I am so relieved I dance on the spot and let out a whoop.

Chapter 16
Ashley

The next day

Ashley set off to the Dolphin Clinic twenty minutes late, having spent fifteen deciding what to wear then another five considering whether she'd be better off staying at home. Ironically, given the workshop was about overcoming anxiety, her anticipation about attending had given way to a flurry of trepidation. What was she letting herself in for?

She arrived at Craig's place sweaty and stressed, parked and ran to reception, where a perfumed, impeccably presented blonde ticked her name off and accompanied her to the door of Studio 1.

Inside, Craig stood at the front of a large wood-floored room, talking to a group of people seated on yoga mats. He looked calmly confident, his sweatpants and sweatshirt showing off his trim physique.

'Ashley.' He seemed surprised to see her, in a good way.

'Sorry I'm late,' she said, feeling fifteen or so pairs of eyes scrutinise her.

'No problem, you're not in any trouble,' he replied lightly.

'Shoes and socks off please, belongings in the rack.' She dumped her things and headed to the free mat.

'Ashley,' Craig said. 'Would you like to share something about yourself, and what brought you here today?'

She wiped a sweaty palm on her leggings. 'I'm married with two grown-up kids. I work in publishing, graphic design – though I'm having a break now my mother's moved in. I'm here because I often feel anxious... like now, for example.'

Gentle laughter broke out around her.

Craig addressed the room. Anxiety was about fear. Often, the fear of being rejected or judged by others, or of failing to meet one's own rigid standards. The workshop would require active participation, he told them. Although they might find certain aspects difficult, it could be a vital step towards change.

They were asked to sit in a circle and share something they had done recently that they had misgivings about. Craig sat crossed-legged on the other side of the circle from Ashley, directing proceedings. His recent shave accentuated the small hollow on his chin.

What to share? She had changed her mind about coming here, she admitted, left home late and had been stressed on the way over.

Next, they had to tell the others about something they'd done that they found hard to talk about because others might judge them for it. This was disconcerting. Maybe she could make up something...

'I don't mind going first.' A woman with unkempt eyebrows tentatively raised her hand. 'I stole some money from my best friend,' she said. Others jumped in with stories of misconduct, selfishness and so on. Ashley felt her pulse quicken. What on earth was she going to admit?

'My mother moved in recently,' she told everyone. 'She fell badly a couple of times and was getting frail. I've had to make a lot of changes in the house and I've given up my job. But I wonder sometimes if I've made a big mistake. Sometimes I don't know how much longer I can cope... Once she made a comment about my cooking and I told her she should bloody well go and live somewhere else. I even googled a few care homes nearby.'

Clapping, and a flutter of supportive comments.

'We've all been there, Ashley.'

'That'll be me in a few years' time!'

They were asked to move around the room, then re-form the circle.

'Now, our last exercise before the break.' Craig looked around. 'Is there something you would be able to share that you haven't ever told anyone about? A secret you've been keeping? Something you feel guilt or shame around, which has become a burden? We're practicing overcoming fear here – but we're also freeing the mind of negative energy, which is essential for mind-body health.'

Silent glances between the participants. No one responded.

'Remember, nothing of what's said will be revealed to anyone outside this room.' Craig reminded them of the agreement they had signed, and grinned. 'No need to worry about confessing to any crimes you may have committed... I'll go first, then.' He looked down at the floor. 'When he was growing up, I was jealous of my younger brother. Everything he did was praised, everything I did was rubbish. My father never lost an opportunity to put me down. A huge amount of resentment built up inside me. I started lashing out at my brother. One time I hit him so hard he had to go to hospital. He needed an operation to save his sight in one eye. For years afterwards I was plagued with shame over what I'd done.' Craig exhaled audibly, then spoke in a lighter tone. 'Now, time for you guys. Anyone willing to take the plunge?'

One by one, they revealed their secrets. A pink-haired woman was the first to volunteer, followed by a bearded young man.

'Thank you, guys, for making yourselves vulnerable. Is there anyone who hasn't shared yet?' Craig's eyes rested on her. She was the only one who hadn't spoken this time.

The Bad Women

I helped to kill my next-door neighbour. The words formed in her head. *I was just going to talk to her but things got out of hand. Afterwards, I told the police I had nothing to do with her death. As a result, they investigated two innocent men.*

Had Craig's quip about confessing to their crimes set something loose? But her secret was too big to share.

'My best friend died when she was 20,' she blurted out. 'We were students at uni. The day she died, we had a stupid argument.' She felt her throat close. 'The last thing I said to her was... I'm sorry. I can't say the rest.'

Their last conversation was trapped inside her head. The two had been in the pub, the evening before the start of their finals. She had tackled her friend head on for a change, frustrated with Alison for announcing she was going to stay on for yet another drink.

Do you even want to get a degree? Spending the night here drinking isn't going to help you pass your exams.

I just need a few drinks to help me deal with the stress. I won't get through them otherwise.

You shouldn't have stopped going to the counsellor! You're throwing your life away, you know.

Ashley, don't be like this.

I'm fed up with you, Alison. Stay here if you want and drink yourself into a stupor, I'm going home!

With that, she'd left. Her usual tolerance had deserted her. She had been trying to help by saying what she thought Alison needed to hear. But she hadn't imagined in a million years that hours later her best friend would end up dead.

Craig dipped his head. 'Thank you, Ashley.'

'I'm sure your friend understands, wherever she is,' someone said.

Her emotions were so churned up, she couldn't take in the discussion that followed.

'Are you alright?' Craig approached her at the break, looking worried. 'I could see it was hard for you earlier.'

'I'll be OK, thanks. I just need a few minutes alone.' She attempted a smile.

'Take a stroll in the break, maybe. Opening yourself up like that can be painful. But letting go of toxic emotions is the route to a more authentic, contented self.'

She said nothing, suddenly annoyed with the man for his self-assured manner and his way of talking, and at how he'd got her to say way more than she'd intended.

As she left the room, Craig caught her eye.

'Ashley. Come and have a word before you leave this afternoon, would you?'

'Alright.'

Whether that was a good idea, she wasn't sure. Giving the others a wide berth, she took one of the coffees laid out in the reception area and gazed around the atrium. The place was impressive. Craig was lucky to have a friend as helpful as Steve, she thought.

After the break they were asked to move to music. Craig stood to one side, calling out instructions.

'Listen to whatever your body is telling you. Allow it to express your truest, deepest self...' She tried to follow the instructions despite feeling self-conscious and slightly sceptical. How was this going to help anyone's anxiety? 'There's no right or wrong way to move. Get in touch with your core self. Tune in to what it needs, right now.' She looked around at the others, wishing Elspeth was here. 'Let out any words or sounds you feel like making...'

The lights dimmed and the music became more percussive. She found herself swaying and lifting her feet, a trance-like state coming over her.

'We've reached the final part of the afternoon,' Craig announced once the music had finished. 'I will now guide you into a deep relaxation. You may find yourself feeling a little spaced out. This is a completely natural state.'

Ashley lay on a mat with her eyes closed as Craig had instructed them, focusing on his voice.

'Your breath is slowing. Letting go of any tension in your jaw, your shoulders, your hands... Letting go of any doubts or negative thoughts... As you listen to my voice, feel yourself relaxing, deeper. Your eyelids are heavy, your arms and legs are heavy. Feel yourself dropping down into your inner self, deeper and deeper... I am now talking directly with your subconscious.'

Something about his voice was compelling. Despite her doubts, her resistance was slipping away.

'Embrace the wisdom of your authentic self. Let go of anything that no longer serves you. Let go of any fears rooted in the past. Imagine them blowing away in a gentle breeze. However long they have been part of you, it is time to let them go...'

The rest of his words floated past. She lost track of time.

'...on the count of one you will be fully awake. Twenty, nineteen...'

As she came back to the room, a blissful sense of tranquility and wellbeing washed through her. She hadn't felt this good for ages. Craig had something, she had to admit.

'Wow, I feel incredible,' the bearded man said afterwards as they sipped cups of licorice root and aniseed herbal tea.

'Thank you, Craig,' said the pink-haired woman, her fingers moving through her hair. 'I feel ready to face up to my worst enemy!'

He dipped his head in acknowledgement.

Walking back to the car, she remembered Craig's request and hurried back.

'Hello? It's me, Ashley.' She knocked a second time on Craig's door, across the corridor from the studio.

Getting no response, she went inside.

The room was spacious and stylishly furnished: free-standing lamps, framed, abstract paintings and glossy plants. A leafy back-drop was visible through Venetian blinds. Craig was sitting in a high-backed leather chair, focused on his computer screen.

'Ah, Ashley. I hoped you'd come.' He held eye contact for longer than was comfortable. 'Welcome to my office. This is my second home these days.'

'It's a nice room. Did you furnish it yourself?'

'With Angie's help. Steve's wife.' He pulled his chair up to the coffee table and gestured to a matching chair opposite.

'Steve... The guy you were with at The Anglers?' She sank into the upholstery.

'That's right. He's been a mate since school. He invested in this place, helped me get the clinic up and running.' He gave her another long look. 'How did you find out about the workshop?'

'On the clinic's website.'

'I'm glad you decided to give it a go. I didn't think it would be your thing.'

'It isn't, really. Wasn't.' Again, she felt awkward.

'I haven't changed your mind?' He got up and went to a nearby coffee machine. 'Tea or coffee?'

'Just water, thanks.'

She scanned the bookcase. *Secrets of Shamanism; Healing with Indigenous Medicine; Inducing Deep Trance States; Hypnosis: Powerful applications to transform lives; Medicine Man: A journey from darkness to authenticity...*

'I wanted to make sure you were OK.' Craig sipped from his espresso cup. 'A lot came up for you, didn't it, when you were talking about your friend?'

'I realised how much guilt I felt for what happened to her.' She took the paper cup he offered. 'And I was annoyed with myself earlier for not being able to tell the story.'

He sat down. 'Do you want to tell me?'

Before she had decided even, words were tumbling from her mouth.

'Alison, my friend... She was found at the foot of an underpass on her way home. She'd fallen. Everyone told me she died because of her drink problem and it was nothing to do with me. But we'd argued just before. If I hadn't said what I did, if I hadn't left her to drink alone, maybe she wouldn't have died.'

She pictured Alison's body and the bag found beside it, its contents scattered over the pavement, among them the Murakami paperback Alison had been reading. It was the only thing of Alison's that she had wanted to take. Her chest began to heave. As she sobbed, she was aware of Craig standing beside her, his hand lightly pressing her back.

'There you go. Let it all out.'

'I'm sorry.'

'Don't be. I help people, Ashley. It's what I do.'

She mopped up her face with a tissue from a box he produced. What he said was true, maybe. Greater than her embarrassment at sobbing in front of Craig was less her relief at having unburdened herself. He was standing close enough for her to smell his fragrance... She tried to listen to what he was saying, something about the causes of her anxiety and how he might be able to help.

'If you can come back on Friday, I'd be happy to show you around and give you a taste of the therapies we offer.'

'I'm not sure. Thanks, though.'

'Your friend's death has obviously affected you very much. There's something else, too, isn't there?'

Her heart began to thump. She longed to tell him the truth.

'Something happened a few years ago. Something awful.'

'What happened, Ashley?'

'I... I did something.'

'What did you do?'

'I killed h—'

I killed her. She hadn't meant to say it aloud. His eyebrows knitted together and his expression became watchful. Had he guessed what she'd been going to say? Through the blinds, darkness. She checked her watch and got to her feet. She needed to get out of here.

'I'm so sorry, I'm taking up all your time.'

His chest moved as if heaving a sigh, and he stepped away from her.

'Oh, I meant to ask you something.' She hesitated. 'I understand Emily Hale was one of your clients. Did you know her well?'

'Yes, Emily was one of my clients.' He frowned. 'How did you know?'

'My neighbour told me, a Welsh woman. She used to see Emily here.'

'Ah, Rhianna. She was one of our first clients.'

He hadn't answered her second question, she was aware.

'Well, Ashley.' Craig walked to the door, then turned to her. 'I hope to see you again—'

'What about Emily? How well did you know her?' It came out too abruptly. The warm expression on Craig's face vanished.

'I didn't know her particularly well. She was clearly a troubled young woman who was suffering a great deal. I did my best to help her with her symptoms.' He cocked his head as if listening for some sub-audible signal. 'Many people come to me with conditions that conventional medicine can't treat. They don't want to accept that they may have a shortened lifespan and much pain and difficulty ahead; they're hoping for a miracle. Granted, some of my clients have proved their doctors wrong and lived way longer than they were supposed to, or recovered, sometimes– but only after they radically transformed their lifestyles and beliefs. When someone finds out I'm not offering a quick fix, they can be deeply disappointed.'

'As Emily was?'

'When she realised that I wasn't able to magically cure her, she became... difficult.' He blinked several times in quick succession. 'That's more than I should have said. Client confidentiality, I hope you understand. What made you ask me about Emily?'

'I found her body. I was walking my mother's dog near the quarry.'

He let go of the door handle, clearly taken aback. 'I see.'

Neither of them spoke.

'It got to me,' she explained, 'seeing her body like that, so damaged. Then, after Rhianna mentioned Emily used to come to your clinic...'

'You came to see what I was up to?'

Was he teasing her? 'I became curious about what you do here, that's all.'

His face broke into a grin. 'There's nothing wrong with curiosity, Ashley.' He held the office door open. 'I'd be more than pleased to show you what we get up to here.'

On the drive home, her head was full of Craig Matthews. She replayed his reaction after she'd mentioned Emily. He had been displeased, to say the least. Was there something he was hiding from her?

The other thing... she had nearly blown her secret to Craig. The workshop seemed to have unleashed an urge to confess everything. Or was it the attraction she felt towards the man, which showed no sign of abating? She had been a hair's breadth from revealing the truth about Tara's death and had said too much as it was. Craig's intuition was unsettling. What if he put two and two together, and realised what she'd been about to say?

Chapter 17
DC Peters

The same day

DI Lister's latest rant was directed at the whole team. Kate stood as far as possible from her boss.

'All of us need to gain the trust and respect of law-abiding local people,' the DI informed the detectives in the dingy office. 'As such, we need to convey a professional attitude. From now on I don't want anyone wearing clothing such as leggings, trainers and overly colourful shirts, irrespective of whether you are working in or out of the office. And unless permission has been granted in advance, there are to be no late arrivals on morning shifts, no matter how unreliable the local buses might be or how late one might have finished the night before.'

The rant went on but Kate was in no mood to listen. Clearly, DI Lister had never had the pleasure of travelling on the 380. As to the banning of leggings... Leggings were by far the most practical garment that a woman could wear. How could the DI – a fellow female, not yet middle-aged – possess such outmoded attitudes?

Afterwards, Kate hurried towards the coffee machine, alone as usual. Somehow, word had got around as to why she had resigned from her last job, going by the numerous questions recently concerning her resignation from the Met and her subsequent application to join a remote provincial Force. Someone – DI Lister, she had a hunch – wanted to make her transition into Elven's Serious Crimes Unit as difficult as possible.

The sergeant was already at the machine.

'Hey, sarge.' DS Renn usually stopped for a brief chat or gave her a nod and a friendly smile. But this time he retrieved his cup and turned away without acknowledgment.

Not him, too.

Back at her current desk, she began the latest task she'd been assigned, supposedly by 'the system': sifting through the database to shortlist all those who fitted the profile of so-called 'Moped Man'. For months, someone had been snatching phones, wallets and handbags from unsuspecting victims in broad daylight, sometimes waving an improvised weapon for good measure.

After an hour, she couldn't take it anymore. 'Fuck the lot of you,' she muttered, pulling a sheet of paper from her drawer. On it she'd written *Local persons of interest*. Below were two rows of names, lines connecting them:

Tara Sanderson – Ashley Khan – Elspeth Chambers – Clare Titchfield

Emily Hale – Ashley Khan – Brampton quarry

If only she had the time to try to make sense of it all. Ever since the sergeant's doubts and Ashley Khan's insistence that Emily Hale's death was not suicide, Kate had found herself leaning towards an alternative hypothesis.

DCI Hill and DI Lister still believed that Ms Hale, unable to tolerate the prospect of a rapid decline, had jumped into the quarry of her own volition. The coroner had gone along with the chief inspector's decision, concluding that Ms Hale's death was probable suicide. Although neither she nor DS Renn had seen the report (only a paper copy was available, which had been 'filed'), the pathologist must not have found anything substantial enough to justify further investigation. There was no adequate reason to devote 'scarce police resources' into investigating the matter any further, the DCI had conveyed via the DI. This was all very well, but Kate had been taken aback by DI Lister's response to her suggestion of looking into what might be going on at Brampton's former quarry. "Given there is no crime to investigate," the DI had snapped, "it would be a total waste of scarce resources." (DI Lister often parroted the chief inspector, Kate had noticed.)

Determined to demonstrate that her two bosses didn't know their arses from their elbows, Kate had begun her own surreptitious enquiries. This morning, thanks to her persistent phone calls to budget airlines, she had made a step forward. Just two days before her death, Ms Hale had booked a flight to Dallas, Texas. It had been scheduled to leave seven days later and the booking had not been cancelled. Surely, a woman about to kill herself wouldn't be planning a long plane journey. More solid facts were needed, though, and a motive for murder. Why, she asked herself yet again, would anyone want to end the life of an unfortunate young woman in rapidly declining health? And why were her superiors so averse to the possibility that Ms Hale's death might be murder?

Kate replaced two question marks on the third row with 'DCI H' and 'DI L', and drew a line connecting them, then she headed to the fire escape for a suck on her vape.

Chapter 18
Ashley

The next day

'We need to talk,' she said.

Zac took a shirt out of his weekend suitcase and laid it on the bed. He carried on unpacking, barely looking at her.

Downstairs, she made two coffees. On the worktop was a note from Diane.

Go ahead and eat without me. Bryce is picking me up.

That was considerate of her mother. At least Diane and the guy at number 11 were getting on well.

Zac came in and took the espresso cup she indicated.

'So, let's talk.'

'First, there's something you should know. A police officer came over here a week ago.' Zac wouldn't like it, but to not tell him, would create one more secret.

His brow furrowed. 'And? What did he want?'

'It's a she. DC Kate Peters. She said she was looking into Tara's death.'

'They've re-opened the investigation?' Zac got up from the table. His voice was uncomfortably loud.

'Seems like it. She wanted to know if I knew anything about a drawing that Clare did. I told her I knew nothing about it.'

'Clare?'

'Bird Woman, remember?'

'Ah, yes. The woman who saved you and Elspeth from going to prison.'

She explained about the drawing, the vicar seeing it and it going missing.

'I can't get my head around this.' Zac made himself another coffee, drank some and slapped the cup down on the worktop with a clunk. 'Why didn't you tell me before?'

'I thought it would be best to tell you in person.'

'So, now you're in their sights again. I thought all this shit had gone away once and for all.'

She stared at him, shocked at his despairing, hostile tone. How would she withstand another investigation? A thought struck her, one she hardly dared voice.

'What if I told the police what happened? I could explain that Tara's death was an accident, that no one meant to kill her. Things got out of hand, she slipped and banged her head.'

Zac stared at her open-mouthed, as if she'd said she was going to walk naked around Wilton Close.

'That's crazy—'

'Please, hear me out. I don't know if I can keep this secret anymore. It's affecting my health. I'm anxious, I don't sleep. I know we'd be punished for what we did. But if the jury believed it was an accident, the sentence might not too bad... I would happily take the blame. I could tell the police it was all my fault.'

'What if the jury didn't think it was an accident? None of you came clean at the time. Wouldn't they assume that you all deliberately killed her, or at least wanted to cause her serious harm? Even if a jury didn't find you guilty of murder or manslaughter, you'd still be guilty of misleading the police and withholding evidence. They could send you to prison for that.'

At the back of her mind, she registered the sound of the front door closing.

'I would tell them the truth,' she replied. 'That we argued about what to do afterwards. Some of us wanted to confess and others were afraid of what might happen—'

'Well, now two of you are dead, you can place the blame for the cover-up on them.'

'I wouldn't do that.' She hated his contemptuous tone.

'I understand what's going on.' Zac spoke in a low voice. 'You can't stomach the guilt of what you all did to her and what you agreed to do afterwards. So, you're prepared to tell the truth, irrespective of the harm it might do to anyone else. Elspeth is in her eighties. How is she going to cope with appearing in court at her age? And have you thought about the impact on us? If you confessed and the police charged you and Elspeth with murder, it would be all over the papers. What about me and the kids? We'd have no privacy left. Our faces would be all over Facebook, no matter what the result of the trial. You've made your bed, Ashley. Now you've got to lie in it.'

'I don't want you and the kids to be drawn into this, too.' If the secret came out, there would be repercussions for everyone. 'I wasn't thinking.'

'Like you weren't thinking when you volunteered to tell the police about the dead body you found?'

She felt the rush of blood to her skin.

'What if someone found *my* body? How would you feel about them walking on past?'

'That's ridiculous.'

'And for your information, I know it wasn't suicide, which is what the police believe.'

'How could you possibly know that?'

'The woman was about to visit her family in America. I spoke to her neighbour.'

'The last thing we need is for you to be digging around in something that doesn't concern you.'

'But it does concern me!'

His lips stretched into a smile. 'How, exactly?'

'Because...' Because Emily reminded her of Alison, who might not have died if she hadn't left her that night to carry on drinking. Because she wanted to make amends for what happened all those years ago. 'Because I saw her just before she died. She was running away from someone. Whoever it was, pushed her over the edge, I'm sure.'

'Look, Ashley. You saw what you wanted to see. Promise me you'll stop digging into things that don't concern you.'

'I'm not promising anything!'

She stomped out of the house. The first blossoms were out, but she hardly noticed.

Zac was probably right about Emily Hale, she grudgingly admitted. Whatever had or hadn't happened to the young woman, it didn't concern her, and attempting find out what really happened could bring unwelcome attention. What on earth could she do by herself, anyway?

If only she had stood her ground before. If she had resisted the pressure to cover up the truth about Tara's death, she wouldn't be in this situation now.

The next day

'Is everything alright, dear? I heard you and Zac arguing when I came in.'

Her mother's question came out of nowhere. She was driving Diane home from the dental surgery. They passed the Catholic church on the corner and entered The Wiltons, a tangle of streets at the top of Brampton.

'What did you hear?' She tried to interpret her mother's expression.

'I was in the kitchen making a cup of coffee,' Diane said, defensively. 'I could hear Zac shouting, so I went into my room and put some music on to drown it out... You two need your privacy. But you sounded very upset. If something's wrong... Well, you know you can always talk to me.'

Ashley gripped the steering wheel. She wasn't ready yet to tell anyone about her and Zac splitting up. Before he'd returned to Edinburgh, they had sat down and agreed to start divorce proceedings. The chasm between them was beyond repair, both agreed. She had also told him she'd try to avoid doing anything that might bring herself to the attention of the police, such as trying to solve the mystery of Emily's death.

'I wanted to say,' Diane continued as they turned into Wilton Close, 'I know I haven't always been the best of mothers. I'm sorry about that. And I know it isn't easy for you, squeezing me into your house, having to give up your job, running me around all over the place...'

Ashley nodded mutely as Diane unclasped her seat belt. The apology was unexpected. She couldn't think when her mother had last apologised about something – not since she'd moved in, at least.

Later, while unpacking the shopping, she realised that Diane hadn't actually said what she'd overheard. Oh, shit. What if her mother were to find out the truth about that night? Zac would go into meltdown. Then again, why should she stop her mother from learning the truth? There were only so many lies one could tell.

'Ashley.' Her mother looked up from her plate of yesterday's leftovers. 'I need to ask you something.'

'Go on.' She took a sip of water. This sounded serious.

'Did you and Elspeth do something to the woman who used to live next door? You didn't... You didn't really kill her, did you?'

The water went down the wrong way. She coughed and got up from the table, hoping that Diane wouldn't have noticed the rising colour in her cheeks, then returned to the table.

'Well?' Diane's eyebrows raised.

She had an urge to tell her the truth. How were they going to carry on living together without any honesty between them? After the police suspected herself and Elspeth of killing Tara, she had told Diane that neither herself nor Elspeth had had anything to do with Tara's death, the same as she'd told Sam and Layla. Every time she'd told Zac that she needed to tell them the truth, he had insisted that she keep quiet.

'Please, Mum. Let it go for now.' She trusted her mother not to pass on the secret intentionally. But Diane was a chatterbox. What if she let something slip?

'I wasn't born yesterday, Ashley. I know when someone's trying to pull wool over my eyes. Which is definitely what you're doing.'

'I promised Zac I wouldn't talk to anyone about what happened—'

'Not even your own mother? He has no right to make you promise not to talk to me.'

'You're right. But you don't know the whole picture.'

Her mother pressed on. 'I heard Zac say something.'

'What did you hear?'

Several long seconds passed. 'That a jury might find you and Elspeth guilty of murder.'

Her heart banged erratically. 'I've wanted to tell you for a long time, Mum, but I couldn't. Zac thinks we'll go to prison if the police find out what we did.'

'What did you do?' Diane's voice was firm. 'Tell me, Ashley. Whatever it is, I'm not going to sit in judgement. We all do bad things sometimes.'

'I killed her, Mum.' Tears clouded her vision. 'Tara. Not on purpose. I was so angry. I'd just found out what she'd done to my family. She tried to turn the whole village against us—'

'I'm not following.' Diane's brow furrowed. 'What happened between you two in the first place?'

Ashley explained as best she could what had happened – how Tara's jealousy of her friendship with Elspeth at the start of lockdown had escalated into a serious rift between Tara, herself and Elspeth.

'So you went over to have it out with her?'

'Elspeth and five others came with me. They were angry with her, too, for what she'd put me and Elspeth through. I threw an apple at Tara from the fruit bowl, the nearest thing to hand. Then we all started throwing fruit at her.'

Her mother was staring, her hand pressed over her lips.

'All of a sudden, she lost her balance. Her head hit the marble worktop.' The inside of her mouth was dry. 'She just lay on the floor, not moving...' She blinked the horrible image away.

'Oh, love.' Diane put her hand on hers. 'What an awful thing to have to go through, and to have to keep quiet about for all this time.'

She saw no judgement in her mother's eyes. A surge of emotion broke through.

'I don't think I can live with all these lies any longer, Mum. I'll have to face the consequences, I'm exhausted. But Zac thinks we'll all go to prison if I confess. That's why I promised I wouldn't say anything. Why I've become so paranoid in case the police realise the truth.'

'Darling, you must do what's right for you. No one else has the right to make a decision for you.'

She looked at her mother in surprise. Diane smiled.

'Whatever you decide to do, I'll be there for you. I promise not to say a word about this to anyone. Zac included.'

That evening, Ashley and Diane sat side by side on the sofa watching a reality TV show, sharing a Chinese takeaway and a bottle of wine. Suddenly, she felt comfortable with her mother. Maybe things really could work out.

A message pinged onto her phone. Craig. She scanned his message. She had texted him earlier, apologising for not being able to visit him at the clinic last Friday.

Why don't you come over tomorrow? 3pm is good

OK, she tapped out with a tingle of excitement. *See you at 3*

Chapter 19
Elspeth

Elspeth was en route to the community centre when she was waylaid by a stocky woman waving heartily from her front gate.

'Hello, Elspeth. Long time no see!' A toothy grin erupted on Rhianna's face. 'How have you been?'

Reluctantly, Elspeth came to a halt outside 28 Wilton Close. She was on time, just, for her weekly Pilates class. Any delay would mean scrabbling for a position at the back of the hall.

'Not so bad. Still trying to keep active, despite all the aches and pains.' She hesitated; with any encouragement Rhianna would go on about her ME for five minutes. 'How are you?'

'Can't complain. My new venture is going well. I've a spate of bookings coming up. One is for a new client; him and his wife are putting on a big bash. The Westons, you know? I've known her quite a while but this is my first job for them...' The woman gushed on, from time to time preening her hair.

'I'm afraid I've got to get a move on, my class—'

Rhianna butted in, oblivious.

'Did Ken speak to you about a ghost in his house?'

'Yes, he did. I think he's imagining things.'

'Really? Why do you say that?'

'He knows someone died there in mysterious circumstance, so—'

'In suspicious circumstances, don't you mean?' Rhianna looked at her with a knowing eyebrow lift. 'The police questioned you and Ashley about Tara's murder, didn't they?'

'Along with half the street.'

'It wasn't the same for you two, though. They brought Ashley into the station to question her. I saw her come out. She looked shaken.'

Elspeth gave her near neighbour a hard stare.

'They had us down as suspects for a while, that's true. But they soon realised they were barking up the wrong tree.'

Rhianna leaned onto her front gate, her head cocked. 'Why did they suspect you two in the first place, though?'

'I don't know, Rhianna.' Why couldn't the bisom mind her own business? She didn't need this. 'The police accused us of killing her with hardly a shred of evidence. We told them that Tara had fallen out with us, which they grasped at... It's true that we weren't on good terms with her. But the idea that we went next door and killed her is ludicrous.' Elspeth pointedly checked her watch. 'Thank God, eventually the police realised that, too,' she added to clarify matters.

Rhianna rubbed her cheek thoughtfully. 'Why did you fall out with Tara, by the way?'

'She fell out with us, is more accurate.'

'I never liked the woman, to be honest. She always saw me as an incomer, never said hello... But I thought you and her were good pals.'

'We were, till lockdown started. When Ashley started coming over to see me, Tara's nose was put out of joint, to say the least.'

'I heard that she did some really weird stuff,' Rhianna went on with an inquisitive sniff. 'Baking doctored cupcakes—'

'Brownies, not cupcakes. We think she put something inside them.'

Abruptly, Rhianna's head stopped nodding along. 'Poison you mean?'

'That was only our suspicion,' Elspeth said quickly. Flaming Nora, she'd put her clodding foot in it now. 'The police never found any.'

'But *you* thought Tara had tried to poison Ashley.' Rhianna frowned. 'I won't hold you up anymore, Elspeth. Don't you have a class to get to?'

Elspeth returned the brisk wave, turned on her heel and hurried away.

What a tricksy thing that Rhianna was, getting her to spill the beans like that! Typical of her. After Tara's death, beneath a veneer of friendliness Rhianna had seemed mistrustful of Elspeth, looking at her a little too long without speaking, as if she knew something was up. Now the woman knew just how far the relationship with Tara had broken down, her suspicions would redouble...

What a blunderbuss she'd been... she'd better not say anything to Ashley.

At Rhianna's shout, Elspeth sped up.

'If you ever need any catering done, be sure to keep me in mind!'

Chapter 20
Ashley

The next day

'Hey, Ashley.' Craig Matthews greeted her from the corridor outside his office. 'Glad you could make it.' He was in trousers and a snug-fitting white shirt highlighting his slim waist, open at the neck. 'Come on, I'll give you a tour of the place.'

She followed him into a room with white-painted walls bearing artworks and framed certificates. The centrepiece was a massage couch.

'Our therapists offer a range of complementary therapies: traditional ones with Asian roots such as reiki and reflexology, along with trendier ones that people read about on Instagram.'

He was standing an arm's length away. She nodded, trying to focus, aware of his faint scent of sandalwood. She was here to find out more about his connection to Emily.

'For those open to a more alternative approach, we do breath-work for healing early life and past life traumas.' He named several more therapies that she hadn't heard of or knew little about.

'This is the heart of the clinic.' He ushered her into a large sunny room with more artwork and framed certificates. Along one side of the wall were half a dozen flickering screens. In the corner, a black leather recliner. 'We have some of the latest diagnostic tools for the early detection of disease, which we can treat using a variety of methods. Please, come closer.'

He gestured to the first in the line-up of devices, a chunky electronic box attached to a screen.

'This is a diagnostic machine based on bio-resonance energetics. It scans the body for disease indicators and potential disruptors such as viruses and harmful bacteria.' He gestured to the screen. 'The repair function can be used on specific regions of the body to treat pain. In some cases it can restore an organ to pre-disease conditions.'

'Right.' She felt her scepticism return and followed him to the next device.

'This is the quantum biofeedback machine. It monitors stressors throughout the body and re-aligns them to restore optimum health.'

He seemed to passionately believe in this stuff, which sounded too good to be true – gobbledygook delivered in a way that might convince the gullible. But she would try to keep an open mind. Science didn't have all the answers, did it?

'Do you use these devices on a lot of your clients?' Had he used this sort of thing on Emily?

A beat. The background electronic whirr permeating the room grew louder.

'Not all.' A tiny frown on his brow disappeared. 'The techniques require a significant investment in time and money. But in some cases, we can achieve astounding results.'

She nodded. 'What sort of conditions can you treat?'

Craig sat down and gestured for her to take the other chair. His eyes were steady on her. Unexpectedly, she felt nervous. Did he see her as a potential client. Or was it something else?

'A wide range. Immune system conditions such as fibromyalgia, chronic pain and supposedly incurable diseases. I've had clients come to me in desperation, swearing they've tried everything, and leave healthy.'

She felt distinctly uneasy.

'But this isn't just about cures,' Craig went on quickly. 'It's about preventing illness. My expertise is in treating the impact of stress, trauma and repressed emotion on the mind-body axis, which are all ultimately expressed in the body as chronic disease. I take a holistic approach to health, looking at the client's mental state as well as their diet, lifestyle, et cetera. For example, I might use hypnotherapy and microdosing for treating trauma, along with somatic therapies. I also use hypnosis to treat phobias, anxiety, panic attacks and so on.'

'It sounds like you might be able to help me,' she said lightly.

'I'm sure I could, Ashley.'

That wouldn't be wise. She found herself staring, half mesmerised, into his eyes.

'You're very passionate about what you do,' she said, pulling herself together.

His face relaxed. 'I've been told I can be a bit too enthusiastic about my beliefs. Admittedly, I'd like to change the mindset of people who blindly follow conventional medicine—'

'Like me, you mean?'

'Maybe.' A grin transformed his face. He indicated one of the hi-tech machines. 'If you like, I can hook you up for a scan and you can see what it does for yourself.'

'I'd rather not, to be honest.'

'No pressure. I can see you're a little resistant to alternative approaches.'

'Thanks so much, Craig, for showing me around.' She glanced at her watch. 'I have to get going soon, I need to walk the dog.'

'I can sense something is locked in your psyche,' he said quietly, as if she hadn't spoken. 'A trauma of some sort. It's disturbing your system.'

'Really?' She felt her face flush.

'If you'd like to book a consultation with me... There'd be no charge. We could focus on the treatments which appeal to you most.'

'Thank you, I'll have a think.'

'I'll be on my way, then.' She was wondering if a handshake would be too formal when Craig reached for her hand and gave it a squeeze.

'Take care of yourself, Ashley. Remember, doctors often get it wrong.'

On her way out, she spotted a woman no older than herself walking unsteadily towards reception. She hurried towards her.

'Can I help you?'

The woman, out of breath, lurched to one side and flung an arm towards her, leaning on her while trying to straighten herself.

'Thanks, hun.' The woman spoke in a faint, raspy voice. 'I'm not normally as bad as this.'

'I'll walk with you to reception.' Ashley took hold of the woman's bag and her other arm and walked with her into the clinic to a line of plush chairs.

'I've been tottering around like an old lady,' the woman said. 'Can't seem to get my balance.'

'Hello, Mrs Carter.' The receptionist, generously perfumed and hair artfully arranged, approached them. 'Let's get you sitting down. How are you today?'

'I had to get a taxi here. I didn't like to drive—'

'I think that's a good idea. You shouldn't be driving anymore. Not until you get better, at any rate.'

Ashley hovered, curious, as the receptionist returned to the front desk and spoke into a phone.

'Nicki Carter's here. She's not in a good way.'

That evening, she kept picturing the frail woman. Mrs Carter was clearly very ill. Could Craig really be doing anything to help? Was he offering her complementary therapies to ease her symptoms, or something else that would supposedly cure her? Craig seemed to believe one hundred percent in his unconventional methods. But could he be inflicting serious harm on his clients through his distrust of doctors and an unwavering faith in the treatments he offered? And could he be linked somehow to Emily's death?

She closed her eyes and tried to visualise the certificates on the walls inside the clinic. A bachelor's degree in psychology and marketing from Aston University. An advanced diploma in hypnosis and hypnotherapy from a college with an American sounding name... Boston College of New and Evolving Medicine, that was it. There had been other certificates too, from the same institution... one in wellness coaching and the other in tribal medicine. Were they genuine qualifications?

She googled the degree in psychology and marketing. It looked genuine. However, she couldn't find the Boston College of New and Evolving Medicine. Had she had got its name wrong, or did it not exist?

Uneasy, she got up from the laptop. None of this proved anything, she reminded herself. It didn't necessarily mean that Craig Matthews was conning anyone, or anything like that.

Chapter 21
Elspeth

The next day

'I'm so glad to see you!' Ashley greeted her. 'So much has happened, I hardly know where to start.'

'Come in and tell me everything,' Elspeth said, closing her front door. 'I'll put the kettle on.'

'You've been hard at work.' Ashley paused to survey the spread.

'The Victoria sponge is from the bakery. Especially for Clare.' She had brought out her best china, which went nicely with the lavender tablecloth.

Ashley helped herself to a carrot stick. She had clearly taken trouble over her appearance. Unusually, she was wearing proper make-up and something other than jeans.

'That bright lipstick suits you,' Elspeth said. 'And a skirt... goodness.'

'I got fed up with my usual look.' Ashley gathered her hair behind an ear.

She placed the teapot on the living room table, set for three. 'What's happened, then? Sit down, let's make a start.'

'Zac and I have agreed to get a divorce.

'Oh, Lord. I'm so sorry, darling.' As a never-married woman, she was never sure what to say to her married friends when they had relationship issues, which they always seemed to, sooner or later.

'You don't need to be. It's been over between us for a long time. Ever since Tara... Nothing was the same after that.' Ashley looked at her with teary eyes. 'Also, I told him about the detective and the drawing. And how I wish I could go to the police and tell them what really happened. He took it badly.'

The teapot spout wobbled as Elspeth poured.

'You're not seriously thinking of confessing, are you?'

'Not in my saner moments.' Ashley bit on her lower lip. 'But I had to tell Mum. She overhead Zac and I arguing and put two and two together. She swears she won't tell anyone. The other thing... I talked to Craig after the workshop last week, and just about stopped myself from telling him the whole story. There's something quite... hypnotic about him.'

'Now wonder, he's a hypnotherapist! Or something like that. He mentioned it on his Instagram.'

'Yes, he was telling me about it when I went back to the clinic—'

'You went there again?'

'He showed me round. He thinks he can help me with my anxiety.'

'Did you say yes?'

Ashley toyed with her slice of cake. 'I don't think that would be a good idea.'

'You have a thing for him, don't you?'

'I wouldn't say that.'

'Come on, Ash, admit it. I can see it on your face.'

'Maybe a small thing.'

'I hope not, my dear.' She put down her teacup, unable to stop her laughter. Despite all of life's tragedies – or because of them – one had to laugh whenever possible.

'Elspeth!' Ashley dabbed at her eyes. 'Yes, I find him attractive. But nothing's going to happen. I'm not looking for a relationship, or anything else.'

'Never say never. What did he show you, then?'

'He's got a lot of fancy equipment.' Ashley rolled her eyes. 'Electronic, that is.'

'I'm seriously envious.'

'There's something that's been worrying me. As I was leaving, I saw a woman hobbling towards the clinic. She looked very unstable, very frail; I ran over and helped her.' A long pause. 'Do you think Craig could be taking advantage of his clients? Causing them serious harm, even?'

She felt a tug of irritation. 'Why would you say that?'

'What if vulnerable people are being harmed because they're so taken in by what he tells them, they get diagnosed late and don't get treated in time – or not at all?'

'Hold on, Ash. It's a free country, isn't it? People can believe whatever they want, even if it *is* totally wacky, according to you. Who knows, maybe his treatments do actually help some people. That woman has probably been to several doctors who've all told her she'll be dead in three months. If everything he did was mumbo-jumbo, he wouldn't have so many people clamouring to see him, would he? He said on Instagram that he personally had 27 clients last week, including online ones, and he's going to start a waiting list.' Elspeth paused for breath. 'Sorry, I didn't mean to go off on one. But you can be very judgmental.'

'I'd rather be judgmental than a total airhead!' Ashley lurched up from the table, tea spilling from cups in her haste.

Elspeth found Ashley at the sliding doors, staring into the back garden.

'Ashley, I'm sorry.'

No response. She tried again.

'We're so different in some ways. You're much more rational than I am. I admit I can be swayed easily and I didn't study much science at school. Please, can we agree to differ?'

Ashley turned to face her. 'OK, maybe we can meet halfway. You try not to be so woo-woo, and...'

'And you try to loosen up a bit.'

'Agreed.'

They hugged.

'I wonder what's happened to Clare?' Elspeth checked her watch again. 'It's coming up to three thirty; it's not like her to be late.'

'She could have gone off on one of her walks and forgotten the time, or...' Ashley's face scrunched with worry. 'What if something's happened to her?'

'It's more likely that she couldn't find her boots, or she's forgotten we agreed to meet up today.' Neither seemed particularly likely, she had to admit.

'If only we could phone her. I know she has a thing about mobile phones, but living in that remote spot... She ought to have a way of contacting us in an emergency.'

On cue, the doorbell rang. Elspeth went to get the door. Clare stood on the doorstep, breathing heavily, her face distinctly pink.

'Have you been running, my dear? There was no need. We weren't going to start on the cake until you got here.' She smiled broadly so Clare would know she was teasing.

Ashley appeared behind her. 'Clare, you made it!'

'Sorry for arriving so late.' Clare stepped inside. 'I didn't forget, I had a task to complete at home. I was mending my back fence and I noticed this morning some slats were broken. The job took longer than I expected. I didn't like to leave the house till it was secure.'

'Of course.' Elspeth helped Clare remove her coat. Underneath she wore trousers not designed for a solidly built woman of five foot ten inches. They were tight at the waistband and hung above her ankles, showing off polka-dot socks. 'What caused the damage, do you think?'

Clare looked troubled, and didn't reply.

'Well, come and have a cup of tea... Right, my dear,' Elspeth continued. There was a fresh pot of tea on the table and a slice of cake on each of their plates. 'Ashley and I have agreed that you need to get yourself a mobile. We know you don't like the idea much, but what if you need to contact us urgently, or we need to contact you? You're vulnerable, living alone next to that wood without anyone nearby.'

'Alright then.'

'You're agreeing?'

'Yes, you don't need to say any more.'

Ashley's brow furrowed. 'But you were dead against having a phone when we suggested getting a landline put in.'

Clare finished a large mouthful of cake.

'I've been... unsettled lately. It's occurred to me more than once that the cottage is in an out-of-the-way spot, and I've no next-door-neighbours to turn to. The out-of-the-way-ness is something I used to cherish, but now...' Clare scooted cake remains around her plate. 'A few days ago, I heard a scream in the middle of the night, from the wood. I couldn't get back to sleep, so I got up and went to see what it was.'

'On your own?' Elspeth and Ashley said at the same time. Clare ignored them.

'I had an instinct to look into the old caravan.'

'Well? What happened?' Elspeth tried to contain her impatience.

'It was locked and there was no sign of anyone inside. But there was blood near the door and an awful smell.' Clare wrinkled her nose.

'I'd have been out of there like a shot,' Ashley said.

So would I, Elspeth refrained from saying. 'Did you notice anything else?' She was rather enjoying this lurid tale.

'I found this on the ground.' Clare dug into her rucksack pocket and held out a bracelet made of silver and copper strands.

Ashley took the bracelet and inspected it. 'I wonder whose it is.'

'Take it, if you like.' Clare gulped down the contents of her cup. 'On my way back through the woods, I saw two men. One was standing. The other was bent down, doing something repetitive with his arms.'

'Digging a grave?' Elspeth felt the hairs on her arms rise. She rubbed her arms. 'This is getting seriously creepy.'

'That went through my mind, too. I went back the next morning, but I couldn't see any disturbed earth.'

Ashley dented her jaw with her fingertips. 'Have you told anyone else about this, Clare?'

I took the bus to Elven police station this morning. I had to wait a long time to speak to anyone; it was very understaffed in there. I told the officer at the desk what I noticed in the woods. I mentioned my fence being damaged, too. He didn't sound concerned. He suggested I install security cameras if I'm worried about my safety.'

'What a plonker!' Elspeth couldn't help exclaiming. 'Maybe DC Peters will be interested.'

'I doubt it,' Ashley said, 'given her reaction when I told her my suspicions about Emily. That blood you saw Clare could have been from anything – an animal, someone cutting themselves by accident... We have no idea what those two men were up to, unless you can describe them?' She raised an eyebrow at Clare, who sat up straight.

'Actually, I did notice something about one of them. He had bowlegs.'

'Bloody hell, Clare. Are you sure?'

Clare looked at Ashley, a wrinkle appearing on her forehead. 'I'd be willing to swear to it. Why?'

'They could be the same two men that Dawn told me about.'

'What men?'

Ashley fidgeted. 'I went to the mobile home site and spoke to this woman Dawn, Emily's near neighbour. Emily told Dawn that two men came to her mobile home and threatened to hurt her if she didn't stop what she was doing, whatever that was. Dawn said she didn't know. One of them had bowlegs, she said. This was just three days before Brillo and I found Emily's body.'

Silence.

'It does seem unlikely that there should be two bow-legged men in the vicinity of Brampton,' Clare said in a level voice.

'Yes, you don't see it much these days,' Elspeth said. 'Don't children with bowlegs normally get them straightened?'

'Maybe he's from a country without good healthcare,' Ashley added. 'Or his parents didn't get him operated on for some reason.'

Silence. Clare looked down at her plate, which still bore a small piece of Victoria sponge. Elspeth tried to remember the last time Clare hadn't swooped on her slice of cake and dispatched it within a few minutes.

'The wood has changed.' Clare spoke quietly, not looking up. 'Sounds that shouldn't be there, smells that shouldn't be there... people who shouldn't be there. I think something strange is going on in Brampton. Unnatural smells coming from certain fields. Grey vapours rising from the ground early in the morning. Around the quarry especially. Last summer I was bird-watching nearby and there was the most dreadful smell. I had to leave.'

Something arrived at the front of Elspeth's mind.

'They've been filling in the top quarry, haven't they? Maybe the smell is to do with that.'

'There's a fence around it now,' Clare said.

'They were burying bricks and soil there with huge bulldozers, when I last went.' Months ago, she had unintentionally driven to the site, thanks to her first and last satnav.

'Maybe they buried other things there as well.' Ashley

brushed crumbs off her top. 'Come to think of it, I noticed a bad smell at the quarry too, the day I found Emily's body.'

Something tugged at Elspeth's memory.

'I saw something on the Brampton Appreciation Society Facebook group the other day. Someone said they saw a lorry dumping waste on a field in the middle of the night.'

Ashley chewed her lower lip. 'I saw a pile of waste dumped in a field, on the way to the quarry.'

'There was a discussion about fly-tipping and people dumping their rubbish.' Elspeth dredged her brain about the post she'd seen. 'The librarian saw a rat coming out of a mound of rubbish left by the community centre – and someone accused someone else of secretly getting rid of industrial waste. A lot of it was probably gossip and exaggeration, as it usually is in that group. But maybe there's something going on that shouldn't be.'

'I don't know what the connection is with waste,' Ashley said, 'but there's definitely something disturbing going on around here. First, Emily is visited by Bowlegs and his friend, who insist she keep quiet about something. Next, I find her dead body in the quarry, and the police won't investigate it properly. Then Clare hears someone cry out in the middle of the night...'

'And sees something very ominous in the woods,' Elspeth finished, taking the cosy off the teapot.

'And now my fence has been broken.'

When Elspeth returned with fresh tea, Ashley was talking to Clare about her fence.

'When was it broken, do you know?'

'It must have happened last night, after I went to bed.' Clare grimaced, wrapping both hands around her cup. Her blue eyes were intense in the dimming afternoon light. 'I spotted two men tugging on it yesterday afternoon. There wasn't any damage then, but maybe... And I've seen figures near the cottage after dark, lately.'

'Figures?'

'It's too dark to see them properly.'

'But Clare.' Ashley's eyes looked huge in her small, pale face. 'What if those two men whom you saw in the woods that night saw *you*? They might have recognised you or followed you back to the cottage.'

'I know.' Clare dipped her head.

'I'm going to keep watch for any more peculiar things.' Ashley gripped her cup.

'Don't you think we should leave it to the police?'

'I need to do something, Elspeth.' Ashley sounded fierce. 'You said so yourself, the police are blind to the possibility of Emily being murdered. Dawn told me they never take any notice of anyone living in the mobile homes, no matter what concerns they raise. It's as if they don't care that something criminal might be going on.'

Elspeth rattled her cup onto the saucer. She understood Ashley's need to act. But how could this unlikely bunch of women hope to defeat whatever powerful forces they were up against?

'What if whoever it is, finds out what you're doing? Do you really want to get involved?'

'I'm already involved!' Ashley flung her palms onto the table. 'I know Emily didn't kill herself. She was running away from something – maybe Bowlegs and the other guy. What if the same two are watching Clare? She could be in danger. I can't just sit on my arse and do nothing.'

Clare raised her hand.

'I'll help, Ashley. I have good binoculars and an eye for detail.' She smiled. 'Humans are far easier to spot than birds, believe me.'

Ashley looked relieved. 'Thank you, lovely. If you're sure?'

'I'll start by visiting the quarry.'

'I'm on board, too.' Elspeth knew she was outnumbered. 'I'm not having you and Clare taking all the risks.'

'Are you sure?' Ashley looked doubtful.

No, she wasn't – but what the heck.

'It'll be a challenge,' she said. 'I may be getting more decrepit by the day, but I can still do things.' Exactly what things, she wasn't certain. Given her tendency to get tired by early evening, her no-longer-excellent eyesight and the increasing pain in her joints, they couldn't involve much more than moderate physical or mental exertion. 'I could snoop around and try to find useful information.'

'Thanks, Els.' Ashley dabbed at watery eyes.

'It'll be the three of us against the bad guys of Brampton.' Elspeth martialed her dormant dance-troupe leadership skills, reaching out to take Clare's and Ashley's hands. 'I hereby proclaim the three of us to be joined in...' What? 'A fight against the forces of darkness!'

Dropping hands, they broke into peals of laughter. Clare raised her cup.

'Bravo, Elspeth!'

'Group hug, chaps,' Elspeth said, reaching over to the other two.

She would do her utmost to support Ashley, she decided, despite the risks. God forbid, something bad should happen to any of them.

Chapter 22
Ashley

The next day

Her mother and the man from number 11 were sitting side by side on the sofa with Brillo between them, head on paws. Things were moving fast.

'Oh, hello there,' she greeted them.

'Hello, dear.'

'Hello, Ashley.' Bryce got to his feet, towering above her. 'I've seen you out with Brillo.' He had wide-set eyes and greying hair fastened in a straggly ponytail. He spoke in a loud drawl, not the local accent. 'Good to meet you properly.'

She took the oversized hand he extended. 'Good to meet you, too.'

'I'll take these.' Bryce stooped to pick up two empty mugs on the coffee table and left the room.

She joined him in the kitchen, she found a dozen brownish, roughly spherical objects on a plate.

'Cannabis crunch balls,' Bryce said from the sink. 'Made with peanuts and chocolate, and plenty of weed.'

'So, that's the smell.' The air was fragrant to say the least.

Her mother limped into the kitchen behind her walking frame.

'Bryce brought his stash of marijuana over. He thinks I should try some to see if it helps with my hip pain. We could try a few for dessert.' Diane winced as she lowered herself onto a chair. 'I asked Bryce to stay for dinner but he's busy later.'

'I'd love to have stayed, but I need to prepare for my meeting this evening.'

'Bryce is in the Residents Against 5G group,' Diane explained.

'I thought the mast was going ahead,' Ashley replied.

'It is.' Bryce spoke in a tight voice. 'Basically, telecoms companies can put up their towers wherever they want to. But some of us are keen to look at other things now.'

'Really?'

'They're worried about toxic chemicals in their gardens,' Bryce said through a yawn. 'The rest aren't interested, or they prefer not to cross our favourite developer.'

'He means Steve Weston,' Diane said. 'He has a hand in practically everything that goes on around here, by the sound of it—'

'I'd better be going, ladies.' Bryce cut across. 'Good to meet you properly, Ashley.' He flashed her a smile and stooped to pat Diane's upper arm. 'Look after yourself, hun.'

'A pity he couldn't stay for dinner,' Diane said after Bryce had left.

'Things seem to be progressing with you two.'

'We're only friends, Ashley. We're the same age, we have things in common. I'm not so interested in the physical side anymore.'

'Oh, I see. Is he OK with that?'

'He'll have to be.' Diane straightened in her chair.

'By the way, I had a chat to Ken yesterday. He waved at me as I was hobbling up to the front door. He seemed to want to unburden himself... I think the man's lonely, you know. Anyway, he's noticed a strange atmosphere in the house. He reckons it's to do with the previous owner.'

Not all that again.

'He'd just come across an old article from the *Herald*. It said that the police believed the owner of number 33 was killed during a violent assault, and they were questioning two people in connection with her murder. He said he was shocked rigid and he wished he'd never bought the blasted house in the first place. I felt sorry for the poor man. I said didn't he know before he bought the house that a woman had died there? He said the estate agent told him that the previous owner had died suddenly. But neither the agent nor Elspeth ever told him that Ms Sanderson was the victim of a violent attack.' Her mother looked down at her hand on the walking frame. Her talon-like nails were the colour of claret, courtesy of Curl Up and Die. 'Then he asked me what I knew about how she died.'

'What did you say?' She couldn't keep the alarm from her voice.

Diane gave her a pointed look.

'That it's as much a mystery to me as it is to you and Elspeth.'

With a surge of relief, she let out her breath. 'Mum, thank you! I owe you one.'

'In that case... Is something up? Ever since you came back from tea with Elspeth and Clare, you've been ruminating about something.'

She had better come clean, she thought. Her mother was as sharp as a tack.

'The woman Brillo found in the quarry; I think she was pushed on purpose.'

'By whom? Why would anyone do a thing like that?

'I don't know. But something is going on in Brampton. I've started looking into it... Elspeth and Clare are, too.'

Her mother's frown deepened.

'There's something else,' she said, before her mother could

object. 'Clare drew a picture of what happened the day Tara died, and someone's seen it.' She filled Diane in on the drawing and its repercussions. 'The police officer who came over is getting suspicious. If she happens to ask you anything, you'll be careful what you say, won't you?'

'Of course.'

She hesitated. 'You haven't mentioned any of this to Bryce, have you?'

Diane huffed, looking daggers. 'What do you take me for? I promised to say nothing to anyone. I'm not a complete See You Next Tuesday, despite what you seem to think.'

'Well, you two seem very pally all of a sudden.'

'While we're having this tete a tete,' Diane continued. 'I know this situation isn't ideal for you. I've been selfish, coming here and expecting you to turn your life upside down. I want you to know, you can go back to your job if you want. I'll cope by myself during the day. Bryce has offered to take me to the doctor or whatever.'

At the mention of Bryce, she bristled.

'I don't think you should be letting someone you hardly know into your life so quickly. Your new "friend" could disappear tomorrow.'

Her mother hauled herself to her feet, her face set.

'Once you're mobile, I intend to go back to my job,' Ashley said in a gentler tone. 'In the meantime, you're stuck with me.'

Neither spoke. Diane flicked through the newspaper while Ashley cleaned the sink.

'Did you see this in the *Herald*?' Diane held up the local paper. 'That woman is still missing.'

'Which woman?'

'The one from Brampton. It was in last week's paper.'

Ashley took the *Herald* to the table. The headline on page two was: Young Brampton Woman Still Missing: Mother Tells of Heartache. Below was a photo of an attractive young woman with shiny dark hair and a bright smile, followed by a short article:

The Bad Women

The mother of missing freelance journalist Cindra Patel, 23, has revealed her sorrow at their daughter's continuing absence.

'I am lost without her,' Mila Patel says. 'She has brought so much joy into our lives. It tears me apart to think what could have happened to her. She would never have gone off for all this time without telling us where she was.'

Cindra was living in Brampton with her parents when she went missing on 29th January.

Last year, she obtained a first-class honours degree in journalism from Bristol University. Her investigative pieces won university prizes two years in a row, says her father.

'Her passion for journalism and uncovering the truth inspired her fellow students. She wanted to dedicate her life to fighting injustice. From when she was small, she loved to watch the Panorama *programme on the BBC. She told us she was going to work on a programme like that one day.'*

Cindra's parents are concerned for her welfare. They urge the public not to forget about their daughter, and for anyone who knows of anything that might help to find her, to get in touch with the police immediately.

'Thanks, Mum. I'll keep this.'

'Do you think something bad has happened to her?' Diane made her way to the fridge, leaning heavily on her walking aid.

'Let's hope not.'

'After all this time, it's unlikely she's just going to turn up as right as rain.' Her mother opened a plastic container, sniffing its contents. 'What shall we have for dinner? There's some cauliflower cheese left.'

She didn't answer. Her head was filling with questions. Why would this young journalist have disappeared? Could it have anything to do with Emily? The date of her disappearance was interesting – more or less when Clare had made her nocturnal journey into the woods...

Ashley shivered. She wasn't hungry at all, now.

Chapter 23
Elspeth

The next day

'What did you want to show me?'

Elspeth passed the printout to Ashley, who was balancing her mug of tea on the arm of the chair.

'I found this on Craig's Instagram,' Elspeth explained. 'It's a comment from Emily389 made on his post last December about the Dolphin Clinic Detox Day. Her profile is still on Instagram. It's the same Emily, I'm fairly sure. The photo looks exactly like the one of Emily in the *Herald*. Biscuits are here, if you want one.'

She tipped digestive biscuits onto a plate. Oblivious to the biscuits, Ashley pored over the page and began to read aloud.

WARNING about Craig Matthews. Anyone thinking of going to see him for therapy at the Dolphin Clinic or on zoom – DON'T! He's put up dozens of success stories on here, making out that he is the ultimate healer. Yes, he has plenty of Insta followers who believe in him and some may have got good results. But that's not the full story. He took my money when I was sick - nearly six thou-

sand pounds - and gave me nothing back except 'treatments' that didn't work.

My doctors didn't know what was wrong with me at first but I knew I had something serious. Craig promised he could help me, said his methods have helped hundreds of people beat life-threatening illnesses. I wanted to believe him. I followed his advice to the letter but my symptoms didn't go away. Now I have liver and kidney disease, and constant poor health. I blame myself for being so gullible. Please everyone, protect yourselves from this man and help me spread this message far and wide. I hope my experience will stop others from making the same mistake.

With a long sigh, Ashley put down the paper. 'How terrible.'

'The poor girl seems to have put all her faith in Craig,' Elspeth replied.

'Have you seen any other comments like this?'

'Some negative ones, but nothing like this.'

They drank their tea in silence.

'You know,' Ashley began, looking into her mug, 'I can't help wondering if Craig might be involved in Emily's death.'

Elspeth spluttered and nearly dropped the remainder of her biscuit.

'Are you serious?' Flaming heck, Ashley *was* serious. Her eyes had that peculiar intensity they did when she was fixated on something. Elspeth tried to put her thoughts into words. 'He seemed so genuine to me... and caring. Of course, he would have been pissed off with this woman for accusing him of ripping her off. But would that really be enough for him to do her in, if that's what you're suggesting?'

Groaning, Ashley rubbed her forehead.

'I don't know. If Craig got angry at Emily and believed she was putting his livelihood at risk, and the reputation he's worked so hard to build... Who's to say what he might have done?'

'I doubt he's capable of murder.' Elspeth helped herself to another biscuit. 'You're not going to tell Craig what you think, are you?'

Ashley frowned. 'Not yet. But what if he did kill Emily?'

'Then he's got away with it, hasn't he? Like we did with Tara.' Something came back to her. 'I think Ken might suspect us, though. He was very strange with me yesterday.'

'Oh?'

'I knocked on the door and asked if he was alright. He's reacting quite badly to this article he found. And he seems to think Tara's ghost is haunting the house. He's asked me to pop over and give a second opinion.'

It was one of those damp, chilly, prematurely dark English afternoons that made one long to move to the Costa Brava, the Cornish Riviera or even Margate. Elspeth grabbed her keys and jacket.

Light from a TV flickered inside number 33's front window.

'Ah, Elspeth. I didn't expect to see you so soon.' Her neighbour stood before her in a grey jumper decorated with a splodge of tomato soup, grey jogging bottoms and slippers, and a grey expression.

'I hope I didn't disturb you.'

'No, thank you for coming over.' He looked at her from under straggly eyebrows, his shoulders drooping. She suppressed an impulse to correct his posture.

'Come in, come in.'

He led her into the living room. It was cooler there, even than her own house. An aroma of faded incense suffused the air. The clutter of old-fashioned, shabby furniture was incongruous in the smartly decorated room. Tara had always kept it nice, she remembered with sudden nostalgia. Keeping her jacket on, she took a seat on the brown velvet sofa opposite Ken's armchair.

Ken's expression had taken on a thunderous hue.

'I've only recently found out that the woman who used to live in my house was murdered—'

'She wasn't murdered. It was an accident, an unfortunate accident.' Too late, she realised her mistake.

'How would you know that?'

'I only meant... That's what I sensed, from the atmosphere in the house afterwards. I'm very sensitive to atmospheres. Once when I was here, getting the house ready to sell – Tara and I were friends for years, you know – I was standing right here in this room and her voice came through strongly. She said the police had got it wrong; she died in an accident, not murder.'

Ken raked his tongue over his teeth. The furrow between his eyebrows deepened.

'But the police thought you and Ashley were involved.'

'We were living closest to her, so naturally we bore the brunt of it.' She smiled her most alluring smile – as it had been in her heyday, anyway. 'I'm sorry I didn't mention any of this before. I know this situation has been difficult for you.'

'Did you sense anything else? When you came here, after she died?'

'No, that was the only time.'

Ken stroked his jaw. His grey complexion was gaining a pink flush.

'You kept quiet about how your neighbour really died. You told me she died suddenly but you said nothing about what a nasty end she had, with her head bleeding and bruises all over her body. I was left to read about it in the paper!'

'I'm truly sorry, Ken. I'm sure I did start to tell you but you didn't seem to want to know.' That was a little white lie. Elspeth crossed her fingers discreetly. Hopefully, Ken didn't have the memory of an elephant.

'Maybe I didn't want to know. I could see the house was a bargain and I really liked the area. But that isn't the point. You should have told me, Elspeth.' Ken walked to the window, then stood with his back to her.

'If you like,' she said with a beguiling smile, 'I'll have a look around the house, to see if I can sense anything.'

No response.

She was about to give up and leave him to whatever might be lurking when he turned around and beckoned to her. She followed him into the open plan kitchen, stopping at the central island worktop, just a few feet from where her former neighbour had come to a sticky end. Closing her eyes, she perched on a lone stool.

'I'm not picking anything up.'

'Are you sure?'

'It's on the chilly side in here, though. You need to turn your heating up.' Could the cold be a sign of something untoward? Surely not. 'Are you OK, dear? You look a bit peaky.'

Ken scratched the back of his neck. 'I don't know.'

'Sit down, I'll bring you a cup of tea. How do you take it?'

'Milk and one sugar. Strong.'

It took a few minutes to locate the teabags, sugar and a clean mug; the dishwasher was rammed with unwashed items. She added a second spoonful of sugar.

'Here you are, dear.' She placed the mug on the coffee table beside a grass-flecked sock and a depleted packet of crips, while Ken stared unhappily into the carpet. 'I'll pop upstairs in case I can sense anything there.'

The man gave a lackluster shrug. 'Knock yourself out.'

She climbed the stairs and made a quick tour. No sign of any apparitions. She opened the door onto the roof terrace. Daylight was fading. This was the first time she'd been up here in years, since she'd cleared the house of Tara's things. With a dart of remorse, she recalled how she and Tara had once danced up here in the spring sunshine. Could the woman's spirit really be lurking in this house? Maybe she ought to mention a few things.

'We didn't mean it, Tara,' she began, feeling foolish. 'We were angry with you for all the trouble you caused.' The air seemed to stir, as if something invisible had brushed against her arm. Or was it just the breeze? 'Tara.' Her voice came out in a little croak. 'Is that you?'

Nothing.

'I'm sorry for what happened,' she continued, glancing around in case anyone were to spot her talking to herself. 'I cared about you very much, and I still miss you. But much as I miss you, you can't stay here.' She paused, feeling even more foolish. 'Tara. If you're here, it's time to leave. We all need to move on. We've forgiven you for everything you did. Now you need to forgive us.'

A small cough from behind.

Her heart stopped. She spun around to see a dark figure looming in the doorway.

'Ken! What are you doing here? You nearly gave me a heart attack.' She glared at him. How long had he been listening?

'Sorry to startle you. I just came to say, the air is getting colder downstairs.' His tone was tense.

She joined him into the kitchen.

'Did you notice anything untoward up there?' A furrow formed between Ken's eyes.

'Nothing at all,' she replied firmly. 'I told Tara to move on, just in case. But honestly, I don't think you have anything to worry about, dear. The only spirits in this house are those bottles of whisky in your cupboard.' It was brimming with strong alcohol, she had noticed.

'Stay a little longer will you, just to be sure.' Ken removed a nearly empty bottle of Scotch from the cabinet. 'How about a wee dram to warm us while we wait?'

After a long, fruitless sit on an increasingly uncomfortable stool, Elspeth drained her second tumbler of whisky.

'Time is getting on. I'm going to have to go.'

'Oh, Elspeth, before you go.' Emotion flickered on Ken's face. 'Who killed her?'

'Who killed who?' She stared back at him.

'Who killed Tara?'

'I've no idea.'

He blinked twice behind his murky spectacles. 'None at all?'

'The police seem to have no idea who did it. After they gave up trying to pin the blame on us, their investigation went pear shaped.' Her bosom prickled with sweat. The man was like a rat up a drainpipe.

'But Tara was your close friend, your neighbour. You must have some idea who was responsible.'

Oh, dear Lord, what to say? She didn't want to cast aspersions, but it might look suspicious if she didn't suggest anyone.

'There's probably nothing in it, but...'

'Go on.' Ken was on his feet, leaning in. She smelt a stale curry tang on his breath.

'Tara didn't get on very well with Rhianna – the Welsh woman over the road. I did wonder if she could have done something. They had words over something horrible she found in her bin once, I remember.'

Ken's tongue worked inside his mouth.

'But that's very unlikely,' she added, already regretting her hasty words. 'You won't say anything to her, will you?'

He didn't reply. Elspeth crossed her fingers at her sides and hurried next door.

Chapter 24
Ashley

The next day

The large room was dominated by a huge stone fireplace. She sat at the table for two, gazing into the pile of logs, listening to the pops and crackles. After she'd texted Craig asking if he would be free for coffee, he had suggested lunch at the Barley Mow in Dinton instead. She'd agreed without hesitation – though a meal had overtones of a date, it would give her more chance to suss out the guy.

'Ashley.' In a few long strides, Craig approached the table. He wore a wool jacket over jeans and jumper, all in muted shades of green and grey, a look that wouldn't be out of place in a fashion magazine. In fact, she thought, he could pass for a model. 'Good to see you again.'

'Good to see you, too.' She meant it. Suddenly, the idea that this man might have been involved in Emily's death was ludicrous.

Craig peeled off his jumper. The close-fitting white shirt below revealed the tone in his upper body. He picked up a menu.

'You're looking great, by the way. You've changed your hair, haven't you?'

'I had it cut.' Plus, she'd had it properly blow-dried, which she never normally bothered with.

Over drinks – a small wine for her and a zero-alcohol beer for him – they settled into an easy conversation. Craig asked how she and her mother were getting on.

'We're still adjusting to each other,' she told him. 'How's the clinic going?'

He told her he was working hard trying to get funding to expand. He wanted to set up a branch in an urban location and extend the existing Dinton operation to offer retreats of various kinds.

'It sounds like it's all going well.'

'It is. We've only been going since last May and now we've almost got more clients than we can handle.'

'Does social media help get you clients? I think Elspeth has become addicted to your Instagram posts. She's always checking out what you're up to.'

He leaned onto his elbows, looking steadily into her eyes.

'To be honest, I have a fair few female fans, on Instagram especially.' The corners of his mouth lifted. 'Mostly down to Lydia's hard work. She's always badgering me to write stuff and take photos...'

'Lydia?'

'The young woman on the front desk. She helps me run the place... And she gives a good massage, for sure. He smiled again, disarmingly and she couldn't help back smile back. 'But that's as far as it goes.'

'Is that so?' Was he always as flirty as this, or was he coming on to her? Whatever, it was hard to resist his charm.

When their meals came, she tried to marshal her thoughts. To ask what she wanted to know risked upsetting the man, but she'd have to take that risk.

'Sorry, I'm eating like a ravenous beast.' Chewing enthusiastically, Craig looked up at her. 'I skipped breakfast this morning to get some socials out.'

'That can't be good for your health.' She smiled. 'Don't you have to set a good example to your clients?'

'You're right, I should practice what I preach.'

With the mention of Lydia and her massages, her curiosity about him had grown. She could hardly ask straight out, though.

'Have you ever been married, Craig?'

'No, I've never bought into marriage.' He put down his cutlery and leaned back in his chair. 'The whole thing is an outdated institution as far as I'm concerned. If people had relationships that suit them, many people's childhoods would be less toxic.' A corner of his mouth lifted. 'Sorry, it's one of the things I'm passionate about. A lot of my clients were damaged by their childhoods and have gotten ill as a result.'

'Is that what caused Emily's illness, do you think?' She sipped her wine to wet her dryness inside her mouth. Craig lowered his glass to the table with a clank.

'Emily didn't have issues like that to deal with. As far as I know, she had a happy childhood. After she first came to see me, her health went rapidly downhill. She told me there were poisons in the ground where she used to live. She was convinced they'd made her ill.'

'You weren't so sure?'

'I wasn't in a position to judge. Look, as I've said before, I can't talk about this—'

'Please, just one more question.'

He sighed heavily, folding his arms. 'Go on, then.'

'I know she got upset with you when she didn't get better—'

'I told her all along I couldn't guarantee I could help her.' His voice dropped. 'But she didn't take it on board. She said she had faith in me. Like lots of people with serious conditions, she was hoping for a miracle.'

'And then she started posting some negative things about you and the clinic on social media? You must have been angry with her.'

'How do you know about that?'

'Elspeth found Emily's comment on one of your Instagram posts,' she explained.

'Where are you going with this?' His voice was overloud and strained; Craig was certainly angry now. 'Are you asking me if I murdered Emily because she posted something critical about me on social media?'

The shock in his voice sounded genuine. Had she made a big mistake?

'You had nothing to do with her death?'

'I admit, I was pissed at her for spreading her views all over the place. She more or less accused me of being a charlatan, of taking people for a ride. I was concerned at what might come out and tried to limit the damage on social media. But no way could I have done anything to hurt her. She became my friend as well as my client. I was doing everything I could to help her. When I found out she'd tried to kill herself... I was devastated.'

'Craig, I'm sorry—'

'You really thought I could do something like that?' He whistled, scraping back his chair. 'I don't know you at all.' He picked up his jumper and jacket, took out a wallet and tossed some notes onto the table. 'That should cover most of it.'

'Please, don't go.'

She sprang up to go after him, then sat down; Craig was already out of sight. She picked up the bank notes.

A wave of dejection hit her. What had she done? Craig had told her the truth about Emily, she was sure. He had not had anything to do with her death.

The afternoon dragged. Ashley sat at her desk upstairs, staring out of the window. Dark grey clouds hugged the rooftops, reflecting her mood. Once again, she started to text Craig. She deleted the effort and pushed her phone across the desk, out of reach. It was too soon to contact him. In any case, he was unlikely to forgive her.

One question kept intruding into her thoughts. If Craig hadn't killed Emily, who had?

Bryce's boom of laughter came from downstairs. Irritation coursed through her. Yes, she was pleased her mother had a companion. But Bryce was around so often, lately. She wanted to veg out on the sofa.

Something else began to niggle. Craig had said Emily blamed her illness on poison in the ground where she used to live. What poison, where? Clare had mentioned waste being dumped where it shouldn't be, so had Elspeth. They needed to find out more. All of this was connected somehow, she had a feeling, and maybe it would lead them to Emily's killer.

She found Bryce and her mother sitting on the living room sofa, scrolling on their phones. On the TV, images of turtles.

'Hey.' Bryce raised his hand at her and sat up straighter. As usual, his grey hair was secured in a small ponytail. It looked ridiculous.

'Anything on TV?' She retrieved the remote from the sofa, resisting the temptation to sit down and start scrolling on her phone, too.

Diane looked up from her phone. 'Put on whatever you like, Ashley.' Her eyebrows lifted. 'How was your secret assignment?'

'It went well in one way, very badly in another.' She hadn't told her mother she was meeting Craig.

'That sounds very mysterious.'

'What's this?' Bryce looked at Ashley, then Diane.

'Ashley won't tell me who she met up with,' Diane replied. Both of them looked at her.

'I'm not five years old, Mum! I'd like a little privacy from time to time, if that's not too much to ask!'

She strode into the kitchen and made as much noise as possible, putting away pans. Having her mother here was stressful enough without Bryce. She rinsed some potatoes and began to peel and chop the carrots, vaguely aware of Bryce opening the kitchen door and settling himself against the worktop in the corner.

'Hun, I think we need to chat.'

Hun? Ignoring him, she set the potatoes on a rack in the microwave.

'Diane didn't mean to be intrusive,' Bryce continued. 'She isn't good at showing her softer side, that's all. She's only interested in what you're up to because she cares about you.'

'I know, you don't need to point it out.' She avoided meeting his gaze.

A knock at the door. Diane's voice. 'Are you two in the middle of something?'

'Come and join the party.' She turned to her mother. 'I've chopped some carrots for snacks.'

She caught Bryce's apologetic glance at Diane.

'How about I make us all a drink?' The man rubbed his hands together with a forced looking smile.

They were on their second round of margaritas. Ashley took another slug of the potent drink. She could get sloshed on this stuff, which was exactly what she needed to take her mind off Craig Matthews, Zac and DC Peters.

The 5G group had disbanded, Bryce was saying. At the final meeting some members had wanted to re-focus the group on the rubbish being illegally dumped in and around Brampton. The majority had voted against this, though.

'That's not to say illegally dumped waste isn't an issue. But people know what they're dealing with. Once you scratch the surface, worms start to appear.'

She was about to ask what he meant when Diane cleared her throat.

'How about getting the potatoes out of the oven, dear? If I drink any more of this, I'm going to be flat under the table.'

Ashley got up to rescue the baked potatoes, then caught Bryce's eye.

'What's that you were saying about illegal waste?'

Bryce stroked his moustache, his expression pensive.

'There's a lot rubbish being dumped where it shouldn't be, of uncertain origin. And there are rumours of toxic waste being buried.'

'Whereabouts?'

'The Summerfield estate, for one. It's a private estate on the outskirts of Brampton, built on a landfill that closed in the 1980s. Some of the residents blame it for their health issues. They say toxic chemicals are coming up through the soil – some are convinced they've got lakes of mercury underneath their back gardens.'

'How awful.' Diane regarded the remains of her potato with a dubious expression.

'I've never seen any evidence, myself,' Bryce continued. 'The site was declared safe and Brampton council gave the developer the go-ahead. But that doesn't stop the rumours of skullduggery.'

Ashley sat straight. Her heart began to race. 'The developer... Was it Steve Weston?'

'That's right. His company built the estate back in 2017, I think it was.' Bryce speared his potato.

'You don't think there's any truth in what the residents claim, then?'

'I'm not convinced there's anything poisoning them, put it like that. Though it's possible there are higher than usual levels of toxicity in the soil.' Bryce rubbed behind his neck, looking uncomfortable.

'What did you mean before about people not knowing what they're dealing with?'

Her question seemed to catch Bryce off guard. He wiped his mouth carefully with folded kitchen paper.

'It's a complicated situation, Ashley. A lot of people around Brampton support Steve Weston. They think that the people who complain about illegal waste are deluded.'

'I thought you didn't care much for him.'

Diane shot her a sharp glance. Bryce brushed crumbs off his sweatshirt.

'I'm not a huge fan. But nor do I wish to stoke fires. He's a rich man, a powerful man, and he has friends everywhere. The vicar at our local church, for example.'

'Liz Peaches?' The woman who Clare had accused of stealing her drawing, she recalled.

'Exactly. She was outraged once when I suggested – tongue firmly in cheek – that she only kept her job because Steve had persuaded the deacon to keep her on.'

'Why was she going to lose her job?'

Bryce shook his head.

'Where to start? She harangued one of the congregation who made a joke about women vicars during a church social. She lost her temper with a homeless man who always sips from a hip flask during her sermons. A few years ago, she had a run-in with a disabled man – the guy who used to zoom about in his electric thingie—'

'John Briars?'

'That's right. You know him?'

'He was in the local Covid support group with me, the year after Zac and I moved here. What was the run-in about?'

'He careened into her one evening on the path outside the church, so Liz told us. It was dark and the paving stones were very uneven. She fell, sprained her ankle and bruised her coccyx. Says she hasn't been able to walk without pain since.'

Another thing she hadn't known... Could John really have caused her such harm? Bryce certainly seemed plugged into all the local gossip – possibly one reason why her mother enjoyed being around him.

'John isn't her favourite person, I should think,' Diane said with a giggle.

Bryce was still focused on Ashley. 'If you're thinking about challenging Steve Weston, be careful.'

She didn't reply.

After Bryce left and Diane retreated to her room, she went to bed early. The more she found out about Steve Weston, the more uneasy she became. He seemed to be at the centre of a spidery web of connections in and around Brampton. And close by him, his friend Craig Matthews... Could Craig be playing a part in his friend's murky dealings? Maybe she shouldn't be too quick to find him innocent of any wrongdoing.

Chapter 25
DC Peters

The next day

'Hello, Miss Titchfield. I'm DC Kate Peters, if you remember. You reported some damage to your property?'

'That's right. I told an officer at the police station about my fence.'

Clare Titchfield kept hold of the cottage's front door, making no attempt to allow Kate inside. Intense, forget-me-not blue eyes were the saving grace of her heavy-jawed, rosy-cheeked face. Her substantial frame – five feet ten, at a guess – took up a good deal of the doorway.

'Could I come in and have a look?' At the unexpected silence, Kate felt a kick of irritation. Her stress levels had been rising all morning since she'd lurched out of bed and knocked over Mitzi's framed photo. 'We've met before, remember?' she pressed. 'I came here to ask you about your drawing.'

'I remember you very clearly, detective.'

Taken aback, Kate hardened her voice.

'Can you let me in, Clare? I'd rather not discuss this on the doorstep.' Strictly speaking, she was investigating the damaged fence that, she had just found out, was the subject of an incident report. But this was also an excuse for her to re-visit so-called Bird Woman.

'I was about to go out for a walk. You caught me just in time.'

The woman's eyes lingered on Kate's face. Was she planning a portrait? Abruptly, the door was flung open.

Kate followed the woman through the narrow gloomy living room, on into a galley kitchen. Its walls were lined with sketches and paintings of birds. She cast a glance around the paint-stained worktops.

'Has that drawing I asked you about showed up?'

'No, it's definitely gone.' Clare tossed her head. 'The vicar stole it.'

'Do you have any evidence for that?'

'Not that *you* would consider evidence. But she was the only person who could have taken it.'

'She denies possessing the drawing, Clare.' Another spike of irritation. One of the two women was lying. 'Could you show me the damage to the fence, please?'

Clare burrowed under a chair beside the back door, retrieved a pair of mud-caked Wellingtons and led the way through the back garden towards a vegetable patch as large as the cottage. Kate did her best to keep up with the woman's strides.

'This is it.' Clare pointed to a section of patched-up fence at the garden's rear. 'I put the timber in myself.'

The repair job looked thorough. The woods were adjacent to the back fence, Kate noticed.

'You told the officer you thought the damage was caused by someone trying to break into your property?'

'That's right.' Clare pulled a strand of creeper off the fence, from a large oak on the side of the wood.

'Why do you think that?' Kate retrieved her notebook from her rucksack.

'The day before I noticed the damage, I saw two men lurking

by the back fence. I was up on my observation post.' Clare pointed to a screened-off area on the kitchen roof. 'They didn't see me, as far as I could tell. I watched them for two or three minutes. They were tugging on the fence slats, trying to dislodge them.'

'What did they look like?'

'I couldn't tell. It was nearly dark and they had something hiding their faces, some kind of mask. I couldn't see anything below their shoulders.'

'Did you check the fence immediately after they left?'

'I did. There was no damage then. But the morning after, there was.'

'As far as you know, despite the damage to the fence, no one has actually broken into your property?'

'As far as I know.' Clare rubbed her upper arms. 'But I'm worried they might. I've taken extra security measures as the officer suggested. I've installed two bolts on my back door and posts to stop the sash windows opening properly.'

'Have you had any other unexpected visitors?'

'Only the vicar.' Clare pulled a rueful face. 'She's been over a lot lately.'

'You also reported a disturbance in Brampton wood. Can you tell me what happened?'

'It was five days before the fence was damaged...'

'The night of February the first?'

'That's right. I woke up about 3am after hearing a noise from the wood – a scream, it sounded like. As I couldn't get back to sleep afterwards, I decided to investigate. I found some blood beside the abandoned caravan.'

Kate looked at her notebook. The blood had been mentioned in the incident report. She had gone to look at the caravan herself yesterday and spotted a patch of dried blood on the steps leading to the door. The door had been locked – as it always was, according to the PC who had agreed to observe while she scraped samples into an evidence bag. There was no way of getting it approved for testing now, but perhaps later...

'Did you notice anything else?'

Clare gazed towards a jay splashing in the birdbath. 'I saw two men in the wood on my way home. One was standing, the other was doing some repetitive task. The standing one's legs were bowed. I think they might be the men who damaged my fence. I'm worried in case they saw me and followed me home.'

Kate made an effort to sound sympathetic. She had to admit, Clare didn't seem the type to imagine things that weren't there.

'I'm afraid that unless these two actually commit a crime, there's not much we can do. Being in the woods in the middle of the night isn't against the law.'

'I understand, detective.'

'Let me know if the men turn up again... or you're worried about anything else.' Kate put her notebook away and took out a business card. 'You can phone me on this number at any time.' She paused. 'You should be extra careful after dark. This house is in an isolated spot.'

Clare frowned, pocketing the business card.

'That's what Ashley and Elspeth say. They convinced me to get a mobile phone.'

'Your friends seem to be looking after you.'

'They do their best. Ashley pops in every week or so to check on me – and the three of us have afternoon tea quite often.'

'That sounds lovely.'

She felt a sudden affection for the woman. Plus, to be fair, Ashley and Elspeth did sound like good sorts – not the sort of women you'd expect to violently attack their neighbour and leave her dead on the kitchen floor. However, she wasn't going to let up in her mission to bring those women to justice. The worst criminals were often the most likeable people, her ex-boss had been fond of saying.

'Well, I'd better be heading back to the station.'

They squelched towards the cottage. Kate took off her mud-caked shoes. After tugging off her wellingtons, Clare looked up.

'Have you found out anything more about that missing journalist, Cindra someone? Ashley is worried that her body will be found in the quarry like that other woman's.'

'I'm afraid I can't discuss that. We're doing all we can to find Cindra Patel.'

'By the way, detective.' Clare got to her feet, her manly frame soaring above Kate. 'I've been visiting the quarry. It's a good spot for watching birds.'

A message flashed onto her phone: *BRIEFING 2.30PM.* Damn it.

'Sorry, what's your point?'

'I've found a lot of dead birds around there: crows, jays, magpies, robins... Someone or something has been killing them. I know it's not a proper crime – only one against the birds – but maybe you could look into it?'

'Dead birds are beyond our remit, I'm afraid. You should call the RSPB. Sorry, Clare, I have to go.'

On her return to Elven, Clare Titchfield's concern stayed with Kate. What was going on around Brampton Wood, and the site of those quarries? And where *was* that missing journalist? Could there be a link between her disappearance and Emily Hale's death?

Again, she wondered about Emily's killer, or killers. If Emily had been coerced to climb into the back of a van, been gagged and bound, driven to the quarry and pushed off the edge, it was a reasonable bet that more than one person was involved. Might the killers be the two men Clare Titchfield saw that night in Brampton Wood?

When she arrived back at the CID room, as old hands called it, the place was thrumming with busyness. Kate hurried to her computer to follow up a few ideas before the briefing started.

'Nice lunch?' DI Lister leaned on Kate's desk.

'I had to wait for a sandwich,' Kate lied, suppressing an urge to sink her teeth into DI Lister's hand.

'DCI Hill is giving a briefing in ten minutes, if you can find the time to put in an appearance.'

Her boss gone, Kate logged into the Force's incident reporting database. Could it contain information relating to Emily Hale's death? First, she typed 'Brampton Wood mobile homes', where Emily had lived.

Six incidents had been reported to police by mobile home residents within the past year. There were several complaints about excessive noise at night, for example, 'a dreadful commotion' and 'muffled cries coming from the river', and two incidents involving 'suspicious' adult males loitering in the wood after dark. Then something more interesting. Emily Hale had come into Elven station late last December, just two weeks before her body was found.

She claims her garden at Summerfield Estate has poisoned her. The local council should never have allowed homes to be built over that landfill. The company that built the estate knew perfectly well what was in that land.

A note was attached: *delusional woman?*

Kate blew loudly through her lips. It was likely that Ms Hale had been given short shrift by the duty sergeant; nothing appeared to have been done to follow up the report.

She switched to Google, typing in 'Summerfield Estate'.

A private affordable housing development in Mead Way, Brampton built in 2017 by S.G. Weston Construction Services.

Next, she googled S. G. Weston Construction Services. Incorporated in 2002, it employed 53 people in construction and waste disposal services. The owner and managing director was Steve Weston.

'Kate, the briefing's started.' DS Renn tapped her on the shoulder.

She logged out of the system, her mind ticking over. Steve Weston was the rich businessman who threw flamboyant parties at his 'castle' near Brampton. When he wasn't causing controversy, he did good deeds for the community. Soon after she had joined Serious Crimes, there had been a protest over the granting of a planning application.

She seated herself in the back row of the briefing room just in time. As usual, DI Lister sat straight-backed in the front row, notepad in hand. DS Renn, sitting two chairs away from Kate, gave her a conspiratorial smile. Thankfully, the coffee machine incident appeared to have been a one-off.

DCI Mark Hill cleared his throat and pointed at the screen with the remote device.

'This brazen robber is making a mockery of us all,' the DCI said in his nasal whine. Moped Man had attacked again, in a crowded street in Dinton, wearing a Batman mask and wielding what appeared to be a hand-gun, targeting a mother with a toddler who had just withdrawn £150 from a cash machine. This time he had made off on an electric bicycle. 'Souped up to go way faster than the speed limit', the DCI added, to scattered chuckles.

'The chief constable has been asking me why we're making such a pig's ear of solving these crimes. I need this man caught and brought to justice. From now on, everyone's priority will be Operation Nancy. All other enquiries go on the back burner.'

Kate let out a sigh. Operation Nancy was obviously more important to DCI Hill than her cold case, Emily Hale's death or an eccentric woman's concern about dead birds, or indeed, other brutal attacks taking place in the area. Those crimes always seemed to go unreported, however, and the DCI didn't seem overly concerned with bringing their perpetrators to justice.

By 8pm the office was deserted. Time for more digging.

From the Land Registry, she gleaned that Steve Weston's company owned the Brampton quarries site. The higher quarry had recently been filled in. Images on Google showed trucks arriving and soil being dumped, and the area as it was now, flat and grassy.

On Brampton parish council's website, she found a planning application titled 'Quarry Redevelopment Proposal'. It detailed plans for a sizeable housing estate to be built over the filled-in quarry with homes for 130 people, a play area, a car park and an improved access road. The proposal mentioned the council's support for brownfield housing projects. Three months earlier, a similar application had been declined; this modified application was awaiting a decision.

Interesting... Mr Weston was clearly benefiting from the council's intention to reuse land for housing. No doubt he stood to make a lot of money from this project, if it went ahead.

She searched for previous applications made by his company. Last year, S. G. Weston Construction Services had been given the green light to knock down tennis courts and a club house to build houses, despite numerous objections. Earlier that year, the company had re-submitted a proposal concerning Bourne Hall. The proposal, to convert various outbuildings into a wedding venue, required the closure of a footpath, long used as a shortcut by nearby residents. It had been approved despite many strongly worded objections.

Further back, she found the company's 2017 application to turn a former landfill on the outskirts of Brampton village into affordable housing. The plan had been approved despite concerns around the potential impact. 'Steve Weston should not be allowed to extend his empire at the expense of residents with legitimate concerns,' one resident had commented. Trawling through the minutes of Brampton parish council meetings, she found accusations of 'skullduggery' over important meetings being held at the last minute, or not sufficiently advertised in order to 'scupper the voices of local residents'.

At the very least, she thought, Weston had been lucky with his planning applications, but that wasn't a crime. So far, she had found no links to either Emily Hale or Cindra Patel.

Kate checked her watch. She would have to leave soon, or her extracurricular activity might attract suspicion. She googled Brampton quarry. Images showed the lower, unfilled former quarry. A fence studded with 'Keep Out' signs surrounded the site. She scrolled through a surprising number of images and videos. Kids messing about, ducking under fences and climbing down to the bottom of the quarry. Various objects found down there. Then a photograph of a human toe – a big toe, slightly mottled and cleanly severed. The caption below read: 'Look what I found in Brampton quarry.' The image was linked to a 2016 Reddit post.

A chill settled over her. Why was a severed toe inside the quarry?

She glanced at the time. If she didn't leave soon, she'd have to resort to a minicab. One quick check for any police records on Steve Weston, just in case.

As expected, the system showed Weston had no criminal record and no arrests. However, his employee had been reported missing in February of last year. Kyle Sutton's body had never been found; a brief investigation appeared to have petered out. Something else, too... Sutton's partner Finn O'Connor had contacted Elven police shortly after Kyle went missing and 'accused Steve Weston of making Kyle disappear'. There was no mention of any police follow-up.

Kate lurched forwards, nearly knocking over her unfinished

coffee. She was onto something big, she had the strongest feeling. Whatever it was, Mr Weston was involved. Questions buzzed around her head. How far would Steve Weston go to protect his business interests? Could he have killed his employee?

As she gathered her things, reality returned with a depressing thud. How was she going to investigate this man? He had money, power and influence, and a network of friends and associates to help him. She was a disgraced detective constable working mostly alone, stealing time to poke around unauthorised, who knew practically no one in this town besides staff at her local Sainsbury. No question, she should stop this before something went horribly wrong.

Chapter 26
Bird Woman

10 February

I set off on another trip to the quarry, DC Peters's blunt dismissal of what I told her was on my mind.

The detective is clearly no bird lover. She had zero interest in the unusual number of dead birds in the vicinity of the quarry. Nor did she appear to have any curiosity about the two men in the wood, or whether the men trying to enter my property might try to do so again. One small mercy, she seems to have given up pursuing that infernal drawing. For some reason, the vicar appears not to have shown it to the police. Perhaps it is hanging up in her bedroom? I hope it is being appreciated, wherever it is.

When I arrive, blue sky has given way to grey. Not wishing to repeat the experience of crawling under the fence, I climb the track to the upper quarry. Sadly, what was once a huge habitat for wildlife with countless nesting spots, is now a flat expanse of earth surrounded by a wire fence.

There is a splendid view from here though and the day is pleasantly mild. I squat behind a tree then find a mossy seat and train my binoculars on the lower quarry. The usual crows and magpies are present, along with several species I haven't spotted here before. I look them up in my worn pocket edition of the *Observer Book of British Birds*.

Lower down, two robins repeatedly fly away to a spot beyond the quarry's rim with something clasped in their beaks, and return. Forgetting my tea, I follow the back and forth of the birds. What is it they are carrying? Scraps of material? All manner of things have been dumped down there, I imagine.

Eventually I put down the binoculars. My eyes ache and I'm aware of how cold I am. I've stayed far longer than I meant to and have achieved nothing.

My walk home is brisk. As light begins to drain from the sky, my usual thoughts take hold. What if I see those men again? What if they return to my cottage? I give myself a mental shake. The detective constable didn't seem to think this scenario was very likely. In fact, she looked at me as if I were bonkers – which might not be so far from the truth.

I speed up as I approach the wood. Before now, I've never minded the dark. Living on my own on the fringes of a large wood with minimal chances of bumping into another human was ideal. But ever since that night-time trip to the caravan, I've been jumping at my own shadow. As usual I take the path into the wood and veer off at my front gate. A movement among the distant trees catches my eye, solidifying into a dark shape – the shape of a man.

Before I can be certain I've taken off like a startled horse, unlocking my front door as fast as I can manage. Inside, I press the door with my shoulder to make sure it's properly shut, draw the bolts top and bottom and secure the chain. I check that the back door is bolted top and bottom, and all the windows are locked and the curtains drawn. Thank goodness, the fence around the cottage is too high for anyone to be able to see in. Then, to distract myself from my fears, I turn on the kitchen radio and start preparing a mammoth meal.

Chapter 27
Ashley

The next day

'Hello, stranger!' She waved at John's image on her phone. His face was tanned rather than pale, as it had been before he left for Spain, and his expression lines were more pronounced.

'Ashley! Good to see you. It's been a long time.'

'It has. Too long.' She realised just how much she missed him. 'Am I interrupting anything?'

'No, you timed it well. I've just finished brunch by the pool... Ham and tomatoes, Spanish style.' John's background changed to reveal an outdoor pool, a dazzling blue.

'You're making me jealous. It's cold and damp here, as usual. How are you?'

'My bronchitis is back, unfortunately. Apart from that things are good. My friends are very hospitable, their cooking is incredible and my Spanish is coming on. How about you?'

She groaned. 'How long have you got?'

'As much time as you need. The only item on my calendar today is fifteen lengths of the pool. What's on your mind?'

'I found a woman's body in the quarry and contacted the

police. Zac went ballistic when I told him.' It all came spilling out, how they had agreed to divorce.

John looked at her a long time before speaking.

'Are you going to be alright?'

'I'll get through it.'

He gave her a quizzical look. 'Not quite what I asked.'

'I'm ready to be on my own, now. Though Mum's here with me for a while, so I won't be totally alone.'

'How's that going?'

'We're managing. My main issue is her new "friend". He's practically moved in with us.'

'What's he like?'

'He's friendly to me, and he does a lot for Mum. But I can't help wondering why he's with her. I don't want her to be hurt.'

'You think he might be after her money?'

'I do wonder, sometimes. Am I being cynical?'

'There's nothing wrong with a healthy dose of cynicism.'

They both laughed. Suddenly, she felt much better. John was the one person she could be totally open with and know that he'd be on her side.

'The other thing, a detective has been asking questions about Tara. She's had some information. She knows we were with her when she died.' Her heart started to race. 'Sorry, I'm getting panicky just thinking about it.'

'No rush. Take a few deep breaths and go slowly.'

She explained about the drawing and DC Peters's interest in the case.

'The thing is... Ken, the guy who moved in next door, is asking about what really happened to Tara. Elspeth and I are trying to fend him off but he won't give up. And Mum overhead me and Zac arguing. I've had to tell her everything.'

John picked up a piece of ham. 'Everything seems to be coming to a head.'

'I'll have to come clean about what we did soon, or...' Or she would break down under the strain of it all? She took a deep breath. 'How would you feel about me confessing everything to the police?'

He finished chewing, then rubbed his cheek thoughtfully.

'If that's what you wanted to do, I'd support you. It might mean some changes in our lives, especially if we all got put behind bars. I'd miss all the perks of being a retiree on a decent pension. I doubt the food is up to much inside – or the swimming facilities.' A dry chuckle. 'But the past is never really over, is it? We can't just bury it and expect no consequences. We did the wrong thing – maybe we should make amends.'

She breathed out in relief. 'You're the only one who's with me on this. Elspeth's not keen, and Ursula's dead against it, of course.'

'Of course. It was her idea to keep *shtum*, if I remember correctly.'

'The other thing I wanted to ask... Steve Weston. The more I find out about him, the more he seems to be connected to everything that's going on here.' She filled him in on her musings over who might be responsible for Emily's death. 'Do you know anything about him?'

'I met him at a Rotary Club do. He was effusive, charming... People took to him. A slick geezer, I thought. He's done well for himself, anyhow. He lives in a fake chateau bought with the proceeds of his business empire, much of it obtained from taking advantage of legal loopholes from what I've heard and encouraging people to act in his interests. He seems to have friends in all the right places.'

'Not a man to cross, then.'

'I certainly wouldn't.'

'Oh John, I nearly forgot. Were you and your scooter involved in an incident with the vicar a few years ago?'

'Ah, the incident.' He grinned, leaning back in his chair. 'My take on it is a little different from the vicar's. I was trundling along the path to the back entrance of the church, going slowly because of the uneven surface. She stepped out right in front of me without looking then stepped backwards to avoid me and lost her balance on a wonky paving stone. My scooter didn't touch her. But she insisted her fall was all my fault and told people I wasn't fit to be in charge of my machine.' He exhaled loudly.

'You're not the best of friends, then?'

'We never were friendly, but things got distinctly chilly after that. Liz Peaches is friendly with Steve Weston, did you know?'

'I've heard.'

'He made a large donation to the church repair fund. I heard rumours that he helped her keep her job after she pissed off some of her flock. Not me, I hasten to add.' Silence, save for the tapping of John's fingers. 'Do you really think he could have killed this girl? What would have been his motive? He may be an opportunistic, land-grabbing, power-hungry rogue, but it seems rather a leap to accuse him of murder.'

'I don't know his motive. I only know that no one wants to consider that Emily might have been murdered, not even the police.'

'He's probably friends with one of the local cops... Possibly more than one.'

'You could be right. Well, thanks for listening. I'll let you get back to the pool.'

'Let me know of any developments. Be careful, won't you?'

After dropping her mother at the dentist, she found a message from Dawn on her phone.

Just a thought, you could try knocking on Jude's door at the Summerfield estate. Number 51, I think. Emily used to live next door to him. They were close. He used to come here to see her here every day before she passed. He's a decent bloke. He might be able to tell you more about what happened to Emily.

On the spur of the moment, instead of going home she drove to the Summerfield housing estate. A large sign read:

Summerfield Village: Homes in Brampton at affordable prices

The houses were modern, compact brick boxes, all more or less the same. Number 51 was situated at a far corner of the estate, close to fields where cows grazed. She parked outside and pressed the doorbell.

Almost immediately, the front door was opened by a man in a furry blue hoodie, leggings and slippers. He was in his late thirties she guessed, slim with dreadlocks down his back and gentle eyes.

'Jude?'

'That's me.'

'My name's Ashley. Dawn told me you used to be close friends with Emily?'

'Who are you?'

She explained how she had found Emily's body and didn't believe that the woman's death was suicide as the police did. 'I spoke to Dawn at the mobile home park. She thought you might be able to tell me what really happened to Emily.'

He shrugged, his face stony, and finally spoke in a flat tone.

'Do you want to come in?'

She followed him into the house and down the hall.

'I'm really sorry about what happened to Emily,' she said when he came to a halt.

'So am I.' He gestured to the fridge. 'I'm having a beer, do you want one?'

He took two bottles of Heineken out of the fridge, handed her one and yawned.

'Excuse me, I was having a nap when you rang. I don't sleep much at night anymore.'

She took in the living area beyond the kitchen. A saxophone lay on a bare table. Not much furniture. No photos or ornaments.

'You're a musician?'

'Yup, when I'm not driving ambulances. The mortgage is pretty hefty given this place is built on a pile of poison.' He stayed standing, didn't offer her a seat. 'So, you found Emily's body?'

'With my dog's help.' She wondered at her use of 'my'. Undeniably, Brillo was starting to feel like *her* dog, not Diane's.

'And you don't think Emily topped herself.'

'No, I don't. I saw her running just before I saw her body. I thought she was running away from someone. I think she was pushed into the quarry by whoever was chasing her. Or she stumbled while trying to get away from them.'

'She didn't kill herself.' Jude's eyes locked onto hers. 'I know her, she would never have done that. The police latched onto suicide because they can't be arsed to find the bastard that killed her.' His jaw tightened. 'I'll never get over what they did to that girl. I can't get my mind round the fact that I'll never see her again, never again have a laugh with her...' His shoulders began to heave. He pressed a hand over his eyes. 'Sorry, don't mind me. Ask whatever you want to know. If I can help, I will.'

'When you and Emily were neighbours... was she living here on her own?'

'With her boyfriend, at first. It was his place. She moved in with him soon after my wife and I moved in. He didn't treat her well.' Jude cleared his throat. 'He got put away for drug dealing. She stayed on alone for a while, before they split. I looked out for her... we bonded, I guess. Both of us were worried about what was buried under our gardens.'

'Did you find anything?'

'Her dog used to dig up all sorts of stuff. You wouldn't believe what he found, bits of metal, oily cannisters, rat corpses, you name it. Emily tried to grow veg there at first, but everything seemed to wither. Once she found a puddle of silvery sludge. It was beyond disgusting. Eventually she was scared to set foot in her own garden. Hers was worse than mine, and that's saying something.'

'She didn't eat any of the veg?'

'The first crop of carrots, that's all. There didn't seem to be anything wrong with them.' He pulled a face. 'But in retrospect...'

'Did she complain to anyone?'

'She was always on at the council. So was I. Environmental health inspectors finally came round last year. Nothing came of it, surprise, surprise. The council should declare this place unfit for habitation. But it would cost the bastards too much to rehouse us.' He banged the beer bottle onto the worktop. 'Sorry, I'm going off on one.'

'No problem. I appreciate you being so open with me. So, Emily started getting ill...'

'She started getting terrible headaches; she'd never had one in her life before moving to the estate. The GP put her symptoms down to Lyme disease. No one believed her when she told them she was being poisoned by stuff buried in her garden. She moved out two years ago because of her health. She always did her best to be positive, did anything that might help her get well—'

'Like going to the Dolphin Clinic?'

'She had faith in the guy that runs it. I was sceptical, but she was determined to give it her best shot... All that treatment cost a bomb, though. She ended up in debt, maxed out on credit cards.' He heaved out a breath. 'I still can't believe she's gone, you know. was such a kind soul. Always thinking of what she could do for others.'

'It sounds like Emily was a lovely person.'

Jude nodded, turning away. He turned a key in the kitchen door and slid it open.

'I'll show you the garden. It's larger than most of the gardens on the estate. It's ironic, you know. When we first saw it, Jen said the house would be ideal for us to bring up kids.'

'You've got children?'

'Just the one. She's three now. Jen, my ex, moved out before she was born.' Jude put on a pair of boots left outside and held out a box. 'Shoe covers, make sure to take them off before you come back inside. We'll keep to the path, to be safe.'

Watching the ground carefully, she followed Jude to the shed at the end of the garden.

'Here's some of the stuff that was buried, from both our gardens.' He unlocked a padlock, opened the shed door and pointed to some shelves. Closest to her was a partly crushed, rusting cannister. 'Look inside.'

She stood on tiptoes, glimpsing a dark gunk inside. It smelled foul. She pinched her nostrils shut.

'What the hell's that?'

'I'm not sure. I suspect there's mercury and lead down here, leftover from the batteries they used to make, and possibly arsenic. We wondered if there could be PCBs, too. They can cause birth defects if they get into the food chain... as looks like happened here.'

He prised the lid off a plastic container. Inside was a partially decomposed rat or mouse with an oddly shaped head. She turned away, wanting to vomit.

'It looks like you've seen enough.' As Jude turned the key in the padlock, a thought struck her.

'What happened to Emily's dog, by the way?'

'Her sister took him in. He's still scampering about, digging holes. By some miracle he seems to be OK.'

Thank goodness, she thought, staring at several listless, black-tinged shrubs beside the fence.

'Is it as bad as this in the other gardens?'

A shrug.

'It's worse up in this corner.' Jude gestured towards the houses. 'Other houses are affected too, though. Lots of residents have complained about the smells that waft over, which can be seriously revolting. Some have found stuff in their gardens. As far as I know, no one else has got any serious health problems yet. Who knows, though.' He thumped the heels of his hands together. 'Some people say we're exaggerating about the health impact, the same ones who are shitting themselves in case house prices on the estate drop any lower and they can't sell up, the situation I'm in. I've lived in Summerfield for six years and that's six years too long. I can't stomach it anymore. But no one wants to buy this house with the history it's got, the same with next door – it's been empty since Emily left. The estate needs to be pulled down and the residents rehoused.' Jude glared at her. 'There's fuck all chance of that, though.'

He stomped towards the house.

Ashley waited a minute then followed.

Jude wasn't in the kitchen. She dumped her shoe covers in the bin using paper towels and washed her hands with plenty of soap and hot water. When she was finished, Jude was slumped against the kitchen door jamb.

'Sorry for losing my cool,' he said. She followed him into the other room, both of them standing. He didn't ask her to sit. 'It doesn't help anything.'

'I wouldn't be calm either, in your shoes. This situation is horrendous.'

'So you believe what I'm telling you, why Emily got ill?'

'I do. What I don't understand... How was this allowed to happen?'

Jude's eyes closed briefly, as if he was too weary to answer.

'How much do you know about this estate, Ashley?'

'Steve Weston bought this land a few years ago to turn it into housing. Before that it was a waste dump, basically.'

'Not just your typical residential waste, mattresses and what have you. They used to bury industrial waste here from the 1960s through to the mid-eighties. The land is rotten, stuffed full of God knows what. The council insists the landfill wasn't toxic but no one really knows, no one kept proper records of what went in there. The land was certified as safe to be re-used and the developer got planning permission to build on the site. There was supposed to be a waterproof layer built over the top. Someone was meant to check it was done properly. Obviously, they didn't bother to check it very carefully. Or maybe they were persuaded to come up with the right answers.' He shrugged. 'We'll never know. There's nothing we can do about it now, anyway.'

The weariness was back in Jude's voice. Her heart put on a spurt. Maybe there *was* something they could do.

'Can I ask you a few things about Emily?'

'Ask away.'

'When you last saw her, did she say anything about what she was doing, or give you any clue about what could have happened to her?'

'She was planning to see her family in Texas. She'd bought a return ticket. She was due to stay for three weeks. I dropped by to see her a couple of days before. She couldn't stop going on about this journalist she'd arranged to meet up with, someone who was taking what she said seriously. I told her to be careful, things happen to people who make trouble.'

'What do you mean?'

'There are people who know how to shut someone up, know what I mean? When someone is making trouble for them. They arrange for them to be taken to somewhere out of the way and have the shit kicked out of them – or worse.'

She shivered. 'Who are these people?'

'I've heard there's a couple of guys who work for someone high up in the criminal hierarchy. They do whatever they're told, no questions asked.'

'Did you tell the police about Emily talking to a journalist before she died?'

'There was no point. The police weren't interested. Emily had already gone to them and they told her they couldn't do anything.

She said going to them had been a waste of time. They're on the side of rich businessmen, not ordinary people.'

'When was this?'

'Last December, a week or so before she died. Just before New Year's Eve.'

'Do you know what she told the journalist, exactly?'

'She would have told her all the things she was angry about. The guy running the clinic she'd paid so much money to, because he said he could make her better. The developer for building over a waste dump and saying the land was safe when they knew it wasn't. The environmental health people for not believing poisons were coming out of our gardens... She hoped getting it into the media would help other people.'

'Have you got the journalist's details? I'd like to talk to her.'

A bark of laughter. 'Good luck with that. She's disappeared, I don't expect she'll be back.'

Oh, God. The young woman who'd wanted to work for the BBC.

'It was Cindra Patel?'

He nodded.

'Do you think Cindra was murdered?'

Another nod.

'By those two men you mentioned?'

'They probably did the dirty work.'

'Do you think they killed Emily, too?'

'I wouldn't be surprised.'

'Who would have wanted them killed, though?'

Jude grimaced. 'I don't know for sure. But most likely it was the men in charge of this place.'

'In charge of Brampton, you mean?'

'Brampton, Dinton, Cranleigh, Elven...' He named other local towns and villages. 'All around this place.'

She stared at him. 'Who are they, these men?'

'There's three of them, so I've heard. One's a cop, one's in organised crime, one's a businessman. Between them, they more or less have control what goes on around this place. They make decisions go their way, put a stop to anyone who's making too much trouble.'

'The businessman – is that Steve Weston?

His head dipped. 'He's ruthless – and clever. No one can touch him.'

She wiped her clammy palms on her jeans. Suddenly she wanted to be home.

'Thank you so much, Jude. You've been so helpful. I'll be on my way. All the best with everything.'

'Ashley.' Jude stood at the front door, looking at her steadily. 'If you can find out, I'd like to know what happened to Emily, how she really died. But don't put yourself in danger. It's not worth it. You can't change anything.'

For the rest of the day, she stewed on the conversation. If Jude was right about these powerful men causing both Emily's and Cindra's deaths, the three women stood next to no chance of doing anything about it. How could they hope to defeat such an adversary, and what might be the consequences of trying?

Part Two

Part Two

Chapter 28
Elspeth

Three days later

'Hello, Ken. How are things?'

'Hello, there.' For a change, Ken greeted her with a smile. He was thinner in the face lately, Elspeth noticed, and greyer. He wore baggy bottomed jogging trousers and his spectacles were as dirty as ever. She put down her shopping bags and stepped towards the fence between their front gardens.

'Lovely day, isn't it?' The recent rain had cleared, leaving a blue sky.

Ken had stopped smiling. 'Elspeth. Come in for a moment, will you?'

He led her into the kitchen. Above, sunlight poured through Tara's glass roof panels.

'Take a seat.'

The man might be lonely, she thought, settling onto the single stool. But he stood there leaning against the sink, without offering to make coffee. Something was definitely on Ken's mind, going by his concentrated expression and absence of speech.

'How is the ghost situation?' she said.

'I've not been troubled by that at all, lately. But something else has been troubling me a good deal.'

Oh, bloody hell. This was serious, she could tell. She crossed her fingers behind her back.

A vein pulsed in Ken's temple.

'Was it you and Ashley who killed her – the woman who used to live here?'

'What? No, of course not.' A tremor went through her arm.

'Tell me the truth, Elspeth.' He stepped up to her. 'You killed her, didn't you?' A fleck of spittle hopped onto his chin. 'You and Ashley killed her together. That's what people are saying. I'm living next door to a killer... Two killers!'

The man looked homicidal himself. Oh, flaming Nora.

'You're right,' she blurted out. 'We were involved. But it's not like you think.'

'I'm listening.' His face stayed close.

'It was an accident. She slipped and fell and hit her head. That's what killed her.' She felt her throat tighten, turning her voice to a raspy squeak. 'We went over to have it out with her, get things off our chests. But things got out of hand. Ashley threw an apple at her, then we were all joined in... We didn't mean to hurt her. Well, only a little.'

'Stop, I don't understand. You all threw apples at her? And who's "we"?'

She shook her head, aghast. What had she done?

'I can't say any more, I'm sorry. I've said too much already.'

'Elspeth. I need to know. I'm not going to tell anyone.'

Could she trust him? She had no choice.

'All I can tell you... Ashley and I were with Tara when she died. But it was an accident, not murder.'

'So why did you leave her dead on her kitchen floor and not tell anyone?'

'We decided not to tell them, in the end. Tara was dead, that was obvious. We didn't want to be accused of murdering her.'

'We?'

'The others with us. I can't say who.'

'I see.' Ken pressed his fingers into his stubbly jaw, glaring at her. 'You covered up what you did because you were afraid the police would accuse you of murder. Which they did, until a woman came forward and diverted their attention to two innocent men.'

She felt sweat breaking out on her brow.

'You won't tell the police, will you?'

With an irritated shake of his head, Ken moved away.

'This secret of yours has been hidden for all this time... I suppose a bit longer won't hurt.'

Unsteadily, she climbed off the stool. He'd caught her off-guard. What a blunderbuss she'd been. What would happen now? How likely was it that Ken would keep this to himself?

Chapter 29
DC Peters

The next day

Closing the door of DI Lister's office, Kate let out a whoop. The DI had agreed that the new lead concerning the death of Tara Sanderson warranted immediate action and asked her to proceed with further enquiries. The response was in stark contrast to the DI's distinctly chilly parting thrust: 'And Kate, please stop wasting time poking about in the affairs of respected members of the community.'

Someone had said something, or the DI had clocked her increasing out-of-hours use of the system.

Kate settled at her desk with the remains of her sarnie and leaned in to read the letter again. It had been printed in low resolution on a single page of A4, folded twice and placed inside a sealed envelope marked *FAO DC PETERS, Elven Police.*

Dear DC Peters,

I have some information that may be relevant to Tara Sanderson's murder.

The Bad Women

On the evening of 13th August 2020, I was walking past 33
Wilton Close when I spotted a small group of people waiting
outside Tara's front door. I recognised two of them, Ashley Khan
and Elspeth Chambers, who live on either side of number 33. I also
saw a man on a mobility scooter, who I believe was the disabled
man from 9 Wilton Avenue. A moment later Tara opened the door
and they all went inside. I carried on and thought no more of it.

This happened between 7.45pm and 8pm. I am certain of the time
as I was in the habit that summer of walking my dog after The
Archers at 7.15 and was always back in time for my Zoom fitness
class at 8pm.

I hope this is helpful. I would have come forward before now but
unfortunately, I missed the publicity asking for information. (I
have been preoccupied with my mother's ill health and often
needed to stay in Northumberland for long periods.)
This is a true account of the facts to the best of my recall.

Regards,

A concerned resident

An indecipherable signature ended the letter.

Kate stuffed the last piece of damp sandwich into her mouth. She had a strong hunch that the letter, hand-delivered to the duty sergeant that morning, originated from Ashley Khan's near neighbour, Rhianna Jones. Rhianna had insisted on preparing Kate a cappuccino during her informal interview at 28 Wilton Close and mentioned that her mother had recently passed away in a Northumberland care home.

The letter, being anonymous, might be of limited use in court. However, it was helpful in other ways. The time period indicated fitted nicely within the window for Ms Sanderson's time of death.

Also, the letter suggested that all four murder suspects had lied to the police during the initial investigation. Ashley claimed not to have seen the victim at any time after a visit next door for afternoon tea, ending at about 5.15pm. Elspeth claimed not to have had any contact with Ms Sanderson on the day in question, as had fellow Brampton residents Ursula Chalice and John Briars, the latter who was registered disabled, owned a mobility scooter and lived a stone's throw from Wilton Close at 9 Wilton Avenue, Kate had ascertained.

She would need to speak to all four at some point. First, a visit to Ashley Khan was in order.

Her heart quickened. It wouldn't be long before the net closed around Tara Sanderson's killers.

Chapter 30
Ashley

The next day

The chime of the doorbell woke her. Ashley checked the alarm clock: 8am. For God's sake.

'Oh, Rhianna, it's you.' The woman from number 28 was on the doorstep, neatly dressed and coiffed. No sign of Bat Ears. 'What is it? I was fast asleep.'

'Hello, Ashley.' Rhianna looked unrepentant. 'Sorry for the intrusion so early in the morning, but I'm going to be away for a while to deal with my deceased mother, and I wanted a word.'

'Go on, then.' She wondered if she should invite her inside.

'I wanted to say...' Rhianna pulled at a button on her cardigan then, with the ferocity of Bat Ears attacking a passing dog, let rip in a suddenly pronounced Welsh accent. 'I know you've been lying to the police, Ashley. I saw you and Elspeth go into Tara's house the evening the police were asking about – and the others, too. Don't pretend you don't know what I mean.'

No reply sensibly came, so she stayed silent.

'You and Elspeth need to tell the police exactly what it was you were doing there that evening. And for your information, I don't appreciate anyone casting aspersions in my direction.'

Aspersions?

'Ask Elspeth, she'll know what I mean.' With that, Rhianna turned on her heel.

Ashley stood staring at the now-empty path. Her heart seemed to be close to a coronary.

'Who was that?' Her mother appeared at the bottom of the stairs in her dressing gown.

'Nothing important, Mum.'

They ate breakfast in silence until the doorbell rang a second time.

Ashley put down her egg-laden fork.

'God's sake! Who's that now?' This morning, she felt every bit as irritable as her mother. Whoever it was, she had a strong desire to tell them to eff off.

But the figure through the spy hole was depressingly reminiscent of DC Peters.

'Good morning, Ashley!'

She frowned. DC Peters was dressed normally, in a jacket over a jumper and black trousers.

'Would you mind if I came inside? It's nippy out here.'

'My mother and I are still eating breakfast. You couldn't come back—'

'I'm afraid not.' The detective stepped decisively over the threshold. 'I'd be more than happy to join you both, though.'

She groaned, not quite silently, and led the way into the kitchen.

'Mum, this is DC Peters.' She did her best to inject a note of warning into her voice. 'You know, the detective I mentioned?' Diane's fork stopped midway to her mouth, her eyes widening. 'And this is Diane Crane.'

'Hello, DC Peters. I won't get up, I'm not so steady on my feet anymore.'

'Good to meet you, Mrs Crane. I'll let you both carry on with your breakfast. Don't mind me.' DC Peters pulled out a chair from the table and dumped her rucksack on it. Ashley met her mother's pointed look.

'Can I get you a coffee or anything?'

'No, thanks. I wouldn't mind using the toilet, though.'

'Down the hall, first door on your right.' Ashley sat back down to finish her eggs.

'I'll leave you to it.' Diane placed her fork down beside a half-eaten slice of toast. 'I must look a mess. I haven't washed yet, either. She should have told us she was coming.'

'The police never do, Mum.'

'Shush, here she is.'

DC Peters emerged from the bathroom, flicking her wrists. 'It doesn't flush easily, does it?'

'We don't usually have any issues,' Diane replied stiffly. She planted her feet behind the walking frame, her hands on the bar and pushed herself upright. 'I'll leave you to talk to my daughter, detective.'

DC Peters turned to Ashley. 'I'll sit here, shall I?' Not waiting for a reply, she picked up Diane's plate and empty mug and placed them in the sink, before seating herself in Diane's chair, opposite.

'So, Ashley. Do you know why I'm here?'

Her irritation with the younger woman's casual manner and continuing use of her first name, along with the stress and anxiety of the past few years, spilled over.

'You're determined to arrest me and Elspeth for Tara's murder. But you haven't got enough evidence, so you've been trying to wheedle information out of the neighbours. And you still haven't got enough evidence, so you thought you'd try and get me to confess.'

'Very good.' The young woman masked any surprise. She

relaxed back into her chair, her hands resting on the table. 'Do you want to confess?'

Her lungs felt as if they'd been squeezed into the size of a grape. Keep breathing, she told herself. But what to say? She so wanted to tell the truth. She'd had enough of this deception, ten times over. But what about Zac and the kids – and Elspeth, John and Ursula? And what about Emily, and the young journalist who'd gone missing, most likely murdered?

'I didn't kill Tara,' she said.

'I have evidence that suggests you did.'

'What would that be?'

The detective grinned, dimples showing, and leaned onto her elbows.

'You may think you're clever, Ashley, and that you've gotten away with murder. But let me assure you, you haven't. I'm only this far off from arresting you.' DC Peters made a tiny gap with her thumb and first finger. 'Very soon, I'll have all the evidence I need to charge you with Tara Sanderson's murder.' She leaned in further; Ashley could see every detail of her face: the concave nose, the acne scar on her chin and light blue eyes that flashed with passionate determination. 'If you're convicted, you could face many years in prison. Is that what you want?'

Ashley ran her tongue around the inside of her mouth. She was tempted to tell the truth. But was this a trick to get her to talk? DC Peters continued her onslaught.

'This is your chance to come clean Ashley and tell me what really happened. It'll be better for you in the long run if you tell me now what you did. If you cooperate, the judge will take that into consideration when it comes to sentencing.'

'OK.'

DC Peters blinked.

'I'll tell you everything soon, I swear. But first, there's something going on around here I think you should know about.'

DC Peters looked impatient and opened her mouth to speak. Ashley pressed on.

'I'm certain now that Emily Hale was murdered. I've been trying to find out what happened. I think I know who killed her and why.'

'Tell me, Ashley. Who do you think killed her?'

'Steve Weston.'

The DC's eyes widened. 'Why would he have killed Emily?'

'He killed her, or had her killed, for speaking out about a housing estate built on land contaminated by toxic waste. It was his company that built the estate.'

'Environmental crime – is that a reason to kill someone?'

'It's not about the environment. It's about people's health. Emily believed that the toxic waste buried in people's gardens was poisoning them. She was convinced that was what caused her illness. Shortly before she was killed, she contacted a journalist, Cindra Patel, who started looking into all of it.'

'The journalist who's disappeared.'

'Exactly.'

'Do you think he killed her, too?'

'It's possible, isn't it?

DC Peters was shaking her head. She seemed sceptical.

'Where have you got this information from, Ashley?'

'Someone who knew Emily. If you give me the chance, I'm sure I can find out more about what's going on. Maybe I can help you solve a much bigger crime than the so-called murder of Tara Sanderson.'

'So, what do you think is going on? What is this bigger crime?'

'Steve Weston is part of a ring of men who have taken the law into their own hands. They influence local decision-making using bribery and blackmail, and they use violence to stop people speaking out about them.'

'Anything else?'

'They have links to criminals, and possibly also...'

She stopped herself in time. What if DC Peters was herself involved?

'What were you going to say?'

'The police.' This officer might have a strange manner, but she seemed trustworthy.

The detective's hand made a sharp involuntary movement. 'Do you have any other details, or names?'

'No, I don't – not yet. Except...' She wondered if it was foolish to admit all she knew. But it might buy her time, and perhaps she could help the DC to save this place she'd grown to love from being taken over by rich, ruthless men. 'I've heard that they're called the Wise Men.'

A muscle at the corner of DC Peters's eye began to twitch.

'You've said these men use violence. Aren't you afraid they might try to hurt you, or one of your friends?'

'Of course I am. But I can't just stand by while women are being hurt and killed. I need to do something to help.' An image of Alison came. She pushed it away.

'I have to go,' Kate Peters announced abruptly, putting away her notebook and getting to her feet. 'I'll give some thought to what you've told me.' The DC picked up her rucksack.

Ashley shut the front door. She had an impulse to flee upstairs, to think. But her mother was coming out of her room, curiosity on her face.

'What was all that about?'

'I'll tell you later, Mum.'

'Please yourself.' Diane gave a hurt sniff and indicated the *Elven & District Herald* beside the food waste bin. 'Did you want to look at the local paper before I throw it away?'

She leafed through the pages, aware of the dull thud of Diane doing her mobility exercises. A picture of a farmer with a new-born goat; litter-pickers in front of a heap of rubbish-filled bags collected from Brampton Wood... A large photograph caught her eye – twenty or so people gathered behind a banner proclaiming, SAVE OUR HERITAGE, taken in the grounds of a building resembling a French chateau. The article below was about the closure of a footpath through the grounds of Bourne Hall, a property three miles from Brampton owned by 'local businessman and benefactor' Steve Weston. The footpath, which had been used as a shortcut 'for generations' according to the protest coordinator, had been closed to the public following the recent conversion of outbuildings into wedding venue facilities.

How interesting. Maybe she could find Bourne Hall and see it for herself.

Turning the pages, she spotted a short article on a charity event to raise money for the families of police officers facing hard-ship. Her eye lingered on a photo of a smiling, overweight man in a suit who looked very much like Steve Weston – tanned face, short greying hair, stub of nose – standing beside an older man in top brass police uniform. She read the caption. It *was* Steve Weston, with the police and crime commissioner. The man certainly was at the centre of local life.

Her mind wandered. Were she and DC Kate Peters on the same side, after all? Peters was also hiding something, she suspected, and neither were sure that they could trust the other. But their interests were the same, surely. Both wanted to defeat the real bad guys.

Chapter 31
Bird Woman

18 February

For a change, I take the path down to the pond. Since seeing those two men in the wood that night, I've avoided coming this way. But something at the back of my mind is insisting I return.

The wood is thick here with bare-branched hornbeams and occasional bursts of holly. Oak leaves coat the ground. Except for scatterings of crocuses and wood anemone, there are few signs of spring.

A bright green scum covers the pond. I take the path towards the abandoned caravan, walking faster, my hands deep into my pockets. Out of sight, a solitary woodpecker rattles. Although the sun is bright, a sense of gloominess pervades.

This part of the wood is a large bowl cut into the earth. It feels off from the rest and quieter, deader. Here and there, fallen trees, left to rot, and signs of humans – a shiny bangle tied to the branch of a hawthorn, a heart carved into an oak trunk, a footprint in waterlogged earth.

The path follows the Losle stream that flows into the river

further along. Beside the bank, a female blackbird is pecking at an object half hidden in the earth. I stop walking. If I'm not mistaken, this is close to the spot in which I saw those men doing whatever they were doing. When she flies away, I crouch beside the object, inside a disintegrating plastic bag. A fox has disturbed something buried here, most likely.

I push the bag with my foot, revealing a big toe. It is light brown, slender. The nail is painted with turquoise varnish. At the base of the toe is a little congealed blood. The cut itself is oddly precise. I stare at it, not fully believing my eyes. Why is someone's big toe here? Who does it belong to?

After some thought, I wrap the bag around the toe and stuff the package into my rucksack. What am I to do with this grisly find? I would have dropped it off at a police station, but the nearest is in Elven. In any case, I need to show this to Ashley.

Chapter 32
Bird Woman

19 February

Elspeth and Ashley arrive at bang on 3pm. Between them, they bring a chocolate cake, three pears and a large bag of roasted nuts. (Given my efforts to lose weight have stalled, I warned them not to bring too much.) I welcome them with a hug each. Once we are seated around my small table, I ask how things are going with Ken and the detective.

Elspeth's green eyes are despondent.

'Ken tricked me into telling him that Ashley and I were with Tara when she died. We're wondering if he might go to the police.' She glances glances at Ashley, who is clearly none too pleased with Elspeth's slip-up.

'I had another visit from DC Peters,' Ashley tells me. 'She said she had some new information, but didn't tell me what it was or who it was from.'

'Rhianna or Ken, probably,' Elspeth interrupts.

Ashley goes on. 'Then she tried to get me to confess to killing Tara'.

'She didn't of course.' Elspeth takes a large handful of nuts. I grab a handful, too, while there are some left.

'I told her what we've discovered about Emily,' Ashley goes on. 'And how Emily might have been killed by Steve Weston.'

'Craig's friend,' Elspeth says, in case I've forgotten.

'I hinted I might be able to help her with the investigation, if she doesn't arrest me, that is.' Ashley turns to Elspeth and smiles. 'I think it's worked.'

Elspeth stops crunching and beams at Ashley.

'That's bloody marvellous! Well done you. We're one up on Miss Columbo.'

Ashley makes a face as if she's embarrassed at the praise but secretly pleased.

'You don't think Craig killed Emily anymore, then,' I ask.

'No, I think I made a mistake.' She looks at the carpet and avoids my eye.

'But he's friendly with Steve so he might not be totally innocent,' Elspeth pipes up.

'We need to keep an open mind. I've been trying to get hold of him to apologise, but he won't take my calls.' Ashley looks from Elspeth to me. 'What is it, Clare?'

'I found something in the woods yesterday,' I tell them. 'Has everyone finished eating?'

Elspeth pulls a face. 'Don't keep us in suspense'.

'Back in a minute.' I dispense with my cake then put on my kitchen gloves, open the fridge (turned down to 4°C) and take out the plastic-wrapped toe, which I place at the centre of the table.

'Whatever is it?' Elspeth leans over as I the unwrap the object. 'Good God. That isn't...'

'Oh, Christ.' Ashley blanches. 'It's a toe.'

While they are recovering, I tell them how I came across the toe and where it was buried, near where I saw the two men.

'Flaming heck.' Elspeth pressed her fingers into her temples.

'That poor girl.' Ashley lowers her head. 'What if it's...'

'The journalist who went missing?' I supply.

Elspeth frowns at Ashley. 'You think someone cut off her toe, then killed her?'

'Hopefully, they killed her first.'

'Ash!' Elspeth grimaces. 'I've only just finished my cake.'

'She might not be dead,' I suggest.

Elspeth moans.

'I think she must be dead by now,' Ashley says somberly.

We discuss where the rest of the body might be. Nearby, is the consensus.

I get up, intending to put the toe back in the fridge.

'We can't leave a toe in your fridge.' Ashley frowns at me. 'We need to tell the police.'

I shrug. 'Wouldn't it be better for us to carry on looking into things ourselves? Given how useless the police have proved to be.'

Ashley pours more tea. 'Not just useless. Some of them could be involved in all this. If that's true, how can anything we do make a difference?'

Elspeth jiggles the large emerald on her finger. 'What if we end up like Emily – or this woman without her toe?'

I take a deep breath. Something is building inside me and I have to get it out.

'What the three of us are doing is important', I say. 'Something awful is going on, right under our noses. The police aren't doing anything to stop it – so we need to do something.'

They both look at me as if I've just laid an egg.

'Clare's right,' Elspeth says. 'OK, we're taking risks. But we're getting somewhere. I've started to feel I'm doing something worthwhile with my life, rather than just waiting for the end to come.'

Ashley rests her head in her hands. After nearly a minute she looks up.

'Alright, we'll carry on trying to find out what we can about Steve Weston and these so-called Wise Men. You keep your ear to the ground, Els. Maybe you can find out something useful about him.'

Elspeth smiles. 'Right you are, boss.'

'Clare, you keep an eye out in the woods and the quarry for anything else that's suspicious.'

I give Ashley a thumbs up.

We must look out for each other, Ashley tells us and not take unnecessary risks – we're to let each other know where we're going and text regular updates until we're safely home. She picks up her phone. 'Now I'm going to report this toe'.

5pm

DC Peters arrives with a male detective sergeant. They sit awkwardly on low stools at the table, now cleared, besides myself, Ashley and Elspeth.

DS Renn asks most of the questions, then DC Peters chips in with a few. She is determined to keep the upper hand, I sense. She asks if any of us have seen anything suspicious in the area recently.

'Nothing apart from what you already know', I reply. I remind her of the two men I glimpsed in the wood that night, and their attempt to break into my property, and the dead birds I found by the quarry.

DC Peters gives me an unfriendly look. 'Thank you, ladies,' the detective sergeant says cheerily, pushing himself up. 'Anything else you think of that might have a bearing, be sure to contact us.'

DC Peters puts her notebook away.

'How long do you think that toe was buried there?' I ask.

She starts to reply but DS Renn interrupts. 'We can't give you any information on that, I'm afraid.'

Ashley ignores him. 'We were wondering if the toe might belong to Cindra Patel. The missing journalist.'

'Come on, Kate,' DS Renn says with a sharp glance at DC Peters.

'That's a possibility,' DC Peters replies, giving her colleague a pointed glance.

When everyone has gone and the toe has been transferred into police custody, I add logs to the fireplace and make myself a mug of cocoa.

Staring into the flames, I dwell on our grisly finds of late. First a dead body, now a severed toe. What the heck will be next?

For once I'm in no hurry to eat supper. I'm glad of the fire's light and heat, and the reassuring presence of my little phone.

Chapter 33
Elspeth

Three days later

The Anglers was brimming, and noisier than her ears found comfortable. Fortunately, they had nabbed a table at the quieter, sunlit end of the lounge bar.

'How much money do you think Steve Weston makes from this place?'

Ashley shrugged. 'No idea.'

Elspeth sipped her wine and resumed watching the two men sitting at the bar, who were conversing in hostile tones, switching between heavily accented English and another language. The younger one was in designer gear, a gilet over his shirt and fashionably flared jeans. In contrast to his chunky upper body, he had a narrow, delicate face. The other looked more like a typical bloke. He kept glancing at his phone with cold eyes. You wouldn't want to meet either of them in a dark alley, she thought.

The two men were putting on their jackets. The older one drained his glass and stood up. With a jolt, as she saw that his legs bowed at the knees – not too badly, but enough to be noticeable.

'Look, over there, that man's legs,' she said into Ashley's ear. 'Do you think it's the man Clare saw in the woods?'

'Oh God. I see what you mean.'

They watched the men exit the pub, walk through the car park and climb into a silver-grey car, the younger man on the driver's side and the older beside him.

'Back in a min.'

She went off to find the loos. Several doors led off into smaller, low-ceilinged rooms. As she passed, a young man opened one door carrying a tray, and Elspeth glimpsed a table draped in a white tablecloth, where two men sat facing each other. She stopped with a jolt. One was Steve Weston – hefty frame, beer belly, stub of nose, shirt open at the neck – and a thin man in his sixties – gaunt face and severe, dated clothes. They sat in silence, occupied with their meal. The thin man's jacket didn't fit, she noticed, extra material folding at his back. Before either man could spot her, she hurried on.

On her way back, the door was closed.

'Guess who I've just seen?'

'Craig Matthews?' Ashley scoured her face.

'No, Steve Weston. He was having lunch with this chap. We should stay a bit longer, see if we can bump into him.'

'How are we going to do that?'

'I don't know. Let's order one of those desserts, they look delish.'

Elspeth studied the menu. When she looked up, a figure was walking through the car park – the thin man she'd seen earlier.

'There he is again. The man I saw with Steve Weston.'

Ashley followed her gaze. 'He looks ill.'

'He certainly could do with a new wardrobe.'

They watched in silence. The thin man passed the car that the two men from the bar were sitting in and carried on to an old-model Jaguar several cars along, which they climbed into. Within seconds of each other, both cars left.

'Hmm,' she said.

'He knows those two who were sitting at the bar, then.' Ashley sounded more interested now. 'I wonder who he is.'

As they were finishing their chocolate mousses, a solidly built man with short, grey-flecked hair began talking to the younger man behind the bar. Steve Weston. Elspeth tried to catch his eye, without success.

Finally, he noticed her. She gave him a friendly wave and her warmest smile.

'Hello ladies,' he said, approaching the table, a nearly empty wine glass in his hand. He had a soft Geordie accent. 'I've seen you two before somewhere, haven't I?'

'That's right,' she replied. 'Here, at your anniversary party. You've got a good memory.'

He looked from her to Ashley and back. 'Are you two ladies local?'

'We are.' Ashley coughed and gave her a stern look, which she ignored. 'We both live in Brampton, just up from the village.'

'I'm Steve.' Cautiously, he held out his hand. 'I own this pub, for my sins.'

'Oh, really?' She clasped his hand enthusiastically. 'Hello, Steve. Good to meet you. I'm Elspeth and this is Ashley... We're neighbours.' Ashley gave a half-hearted wave. 'Why don't you join us?'

Promptly, he pulled up a chair. 'Which street are you in, then?'

'Wilton Close,' she replied.

'Ah, I know it. You're on the hill, then. Do you have a good view?'

'Not bad. We're at the top, almost.' After Rhianna and a handful of other houses, anyway.

'How long have you lived in Brampton? If that's not a rude question.'

'It must be 25 years. My friend's a newbie, though.' She gave

Ashley, who was emanating chilly vibes, a pointed look. 'She's only been here since just before lockdown.'

The man chuckled. 'How do you like Brampton, Ashley?'

She tried to stay patient while Ashley came up with a reply.

'I like it very much, thanks. I feel at home here now – it took me a long time to settle in, though.'

'It was hard for me, too. I came down here from Teeside as a kid. At school everyone made fun of my accent.' Looking back at Elspeth, he said with a smile. 'People still do.'

'Something tells me you can handle it.'

'Fortunately, my wife is from here. Without her, I'd still be regarded as an incomer.'

'Does she help you run the pub?' Ashley's tone sounded frosty.

'Oh, I'm not hands on – I let my manager get on with that side of things.' He sipped his wine, looking back at Elspeth. 'Angie's in interior design – she's really put her mark on the property we bought a few years ago. It's big for just the two of us, but Angie fell in love with the place. It needed a huge amount of work to get it how we wanted... Getting permission for everything was excruciating. They've only just finished the renovations.'

'That must be a huge relief.' She beamed at him. 'Whereabouts is your place, Steve?'

'Three miles outside the village, heading south.'

She frowned, then nodded as if suddenly realising something.

'It's not that building that looks like a French chateau, by any chance?'

'That's right. Bourne Hall.'

'Really? I've always wanted to see inside it – haven't I, Ashley?' She gave Ashley a nudge in the ribs.

'Absolutely!' Ashley responded belatedly. 'My friend's quite the history buff – and she loves looking at other people's houses.'

'You might be in luck, then. We're putting on a big bash next

Saturday to celebrate the end of the renovations. If you two ladies would like to join us...'

'Thank you, Steve, that would be lovely.' She gave the man another full-beam smile. 'I don't get invited out so much, anymore.'

'Just plug Bourne Hall into Google, the address will pop up. Start time 7.30. Oh, and you'll need to dress up. Angie is very strict about guests making an effort.' He winked at her and got to his feet. 'Well ladies, I must get on. Lovely meeting you both.'

The man strode off. Ashley turned to her, jaw slack.

'How the hell did you manage that?'

'My natural charm, darling.' She took a glug of wine. 'I used to be quite popular with the opposite sex, back in the day.'

'I can believe it! You know who that was, don't you?'

'Of course, our friend Mr Weston. I was only pretending I didn't know him. I didn't think telling him that we suspected him of killing Emily was likely to go down well.'

'I still can't believe you managed to get us invited to his shindig. I wonder, though...' Ashley stroked her glass. 'Maybe he knew who we were all along and was only pretending he didn't. Someone could have told him about us asking questions.'

'I suppose.' It didn't seem very likely, she thought crankily. She turned to face her friend. 'What was all that about me liking looking at other people's houses? You made me sound like a nosey old bisom.'

'I was only trying to help you wangle an invite!'

They subsided into laughter.

Walked home, up the hill, Elspeth's hips and knees began to hurt. She thought of her beloved Triumph, now driven by a spotty chap in Doncaster. Not being able to drive was one of the worst things about being old.

'Have you heard anything from Craig yet?' she ventured.

'Not a peep!' Ashley gave a frustrated huff. 'I've called three times now but no answer.'

'Why don't you go round to his place?'

'He might shut the door in my face?'

'You could go over to the clinic again and sneak into his office.'

'I don't think so.'

'You're smitten with him, aren't you?'

'He's quite attractive, I suppose...'

'Ashley. You fancy the pants off him.'

'I wouldn't go that far.' Blobs of red had appeared on Ashley's cheeks. 'Anyway, I'm not available.'

'But you are now, aren't you?'

'I can't just leap from one man to the next.'

'Why not?' Elspeth began to giggle. 'It might help.'

Ashley snorted.

'Craig might be at this party,' she continued when both had recovered. 'You'll have a chance to talk to him then.'

'Do you reckon?' Ashley sounded unenthusiastic.

'Well, we've got less than a week to get ourselves ready. I'll have to look out something nice to wear.' She felt a tingle of excitement. 'Maybe we'll get some useful intel on Weston—'

'Intel? We're not spies, Elspeth.'

She rolled her eyes. 'Whatever, it'll be a chance to observe the man on his home turf, won't it?'

'Exactly. I've been dying to have a look at it, to be honest. But we need to be careful. He could be waiting for a chance to observe *us*.'

Back home, Elspeth pottered.

Which dress to wear, and which jewellery? Even more than the prospect of putting on her glad-rags, though, she couldn't wait to have a mosey inside the lord of the manor's chateau, fake or not.

Chapter 34
Bird Woman

24 February

A depressingly damp, cold day. I wonder haphazardly through the wood and end up on the bank of the Losle, keeping a good distance from the toe burial site. The light is dismal. The ground is mossy, uneven. I stumble.

My foot isn't caught on a root, but on what seems to be a decomposing animal under the earth. It's large for an animal, though. I make out a human leg. The flesh is mingled with what looks like clothing. The rest of the body is hidden by earth and leaf mold.

A sudden shift of my stomach contents makes me turn away and fold over at the hips. I take deep breaths and face the body again, ashamed of my squeamishness. I can't leave yet. What would Ashley say if I don't check the most obvious thing?

I kneel beside a shoeless foot, covered by a sock that shows signs of attack by sharp teeth. Carefully, I lift the sock using my handkerchief. Though the foot has significantly decomposed, its toenails are still visible. Turquoise varnish covers four nails. The big toe is missing.

After further stomach judders, I remove the phone from my inside pocket and ring the detective constable's number.

A harassed sounding voice answers. 'DC Peters.'

'I've found a dead body in the wood,' I say. She is immediately full of questions. I carefully describe the corpse and where it is, adding that one foot has no big toe, and that the remaining toes match the toe I found recently, in case the police should miss these salient facts.

When I get home, I locate the bottle of sherry that my brother gave me as a Christmas present in 2004 and fill my smallest glass. The resulting warmth in my belly is most enjoyable. After removing my jacket and boots, I pour some more.

Chapter 35
Elspeth

The next day

The three of them were gathered once again, this time at Ashley's. Although Clare described how she knew that the body she'd found belonged to missing journalist Cindra Patel, Elspeth inspected the teapot. While she liked Clare very much, she couldn't help being a little put out that Bird Woman had made a second discovery in barely a week.

'Are you OK, dear?' Ashley put down her mug and looked at Clare with concern.

'I don't know what's got into me. I'm not normally affected by dead bodies.'

'How many have you seen?' Elspeth asked.

'Four, including this one. My grandmother, a man at the bird sanctuary who had a heart attack – and Tara, if you count at a distance.' Clare's voice had a definite edge.

'I should think anyone who saw what Clare did yesterday would be affected by it.' Ashley's voice was sharp.

'When will they announce whose body it is?' Clare asked. She must be feeling bad, Elspeth noted; she had scarcely touched her cake.

'The police will have to contact her next of kin first. If it *is* Cindra Patel's.' Ashley's brow furrowed. 'Who could have done this?'

'A man,' Clare said. 'Or men.'

Mr Bowlegs and his pal, Elspeth thought.

What if the same happens to one of us?

The question was on her lips but there seemed no need to voice it. 'I'll refill the pot.' She got to her feet, relieved to have something to do.

'I need to say something,' Ashley began when Elspeth returned. 'This hasn't changed how I feel about trying to get some kind of justice for Emily – and for this woman, too – Cindra, it must be. But it's brought home just how dangerous it is to cross these men. I don't want either of you to join me with the idea that they might go easy on us because we're women, or we're not as young as we once were.'

The room was silent.

Clare spoke first.

'Ashley, I'm still on board. I know I'm vulnerable living at the edge of the wood. But all this is happening right on my doorstep. I can't just look away and hope the police will sort it out. From what I've seen of how they operate, they need all the help they can get.'

Determined not to be outdone, Elspeth cleared her throat.

'I may not have long left on this earth, and I'm definitely losing my sprightliness. But I'm damned if I'm going to let these blood-thirsty, brain-dead men get away with slaughtering inno-cent women. I want to go down fighting.' She met Ashley's gaze. 'If I don't make it, my will is with the solicitors on the High Street.'

'I hope there won't be any need for that.' Ashley wiped the corners of her eyes.

Elspeth chomped into her slice of cake. Despite her fighting talk, she wasn't quite ready to leave the planet. However, a violent end would be preferable to fading away with some incurable disease... She'd better start on her funeral plans. 'One more thing, ladies.' She put up her palm. 'I have some news.'

She waited until Clare had eaten her cake and Ashley had stopped scrolling on her phone.

'I've been thinking about what I could do to help our mission. The other day I went to the library and searched for all the mentions of Steve Weston in the local paper. His name came up dozens of times – his good deeds for Brampton, giving money to local good causes, construction work he's done, disputes about planning permission et cetera, et cetera. There was lots about Bourne Hall, too – that's his country pile that he's just finished renovating,' she added for Clare's benefit, 'the one me and Ashley are invited to. Anyway, it was about nearly seven and the library was about to shut... I came across an old article about an employee of Steve Weston's who went missing last February.'

Elspeth paused to build suspense and retrieve her notes.

'His name was Kyle Sutton. He worked at S. G. Weston Construction Services. Steve Weston is the company's managing director.' She held up a digital printout. 'The article was written a week after Kyle went missing. It has quotes from Kyle's partner, Finn O'Connor and a photo of both men. Finn says he's concerned about what might have happened to Kyle, it would be totally out of character for him to go off without saying where he was going. Also – Kyle used to work at the quarry. I'll read Finn's quote. Kyle was very stressed in the last few weeks, to do with issues at the quarry redevelopment site where he worked. "I am convinced that someone out there knows what happens to him and I plead with them to contact the police."'

She glanced at the others to check they were following. Both were rapt. Ashley sat upright. Clare was leant onto her forearms, chin pressed against steepled fingers.

'I couldn't find out any more about Kyle Sutton, and if he was ever found. But Finn obviously thought something dodgy was going on... I thought I'd try to track him down. Yesterday, I caught the bus to Winton, the village mentioned in the article where Finn and Kyle used to live. I took the photo of Finn and asked practically everyone I saw if they had any idea whether he still lived in the village. I finally struck gold with the newsagent – we got chatting about Winton entering the Tidy Village competition, about which he had a lot to say. Once he'd warmed to me, I popped out the article and gave him my spiel.'

'He knew Finn?' Ashley's eyes were wide.

'He was a friend! He gave me Finn's address – a mile down a local lane and very muddy – and offered to give me a lift! I was fit to drop by then. On the way, the man said he used to go drinking with Finn and Kyle – who never returned.' She retrieved the notes she'd made. 'So, I knocked on the door of the house and a chap looking like a Viking warrior appeared, except he had jet black hair. He was about six and half feet tall, with a big bushy beard. He didn't look much like his photo but I recognised his eyes – grey and piercing. I said I'd read about his partner's disappearance, did he have a few minutes? He obviously didn't want to talk to me so I said I'd kill to use his loo, I'd been traipsing around Winton for hours and hadn't spotted a single one. That did the trick. Inside was all low ceilings and beams. The place was in a dreadful state, you could hardly move for the stuff everywhere. Bottles of rum, old sewing machines, picture frames... The loo was full of cobwebs. I had to dust them away. There was nowhere to sit except one chair, which I had.'

She paused to drink her tea.

'I told him how you found Emily's body, Ash, but the police aren't investigating properly and we suspect it's all to do with this man Steve Weston. When I said the name, he got quite worked up. He and Kyle had been planning to marry – Kyle was operations manager in Steve's company and in charge of health and safety. He was working on a job to fill in the top quarry. Kyle told Finn about unauthorised waste he'd seen coming onto the site after hours, which Weston was dumping into the quarry by himself before leaving at night. He suspected Weston was making a profit from all the subterfuge. The day before he went missing, Kyle came home, properly upset. He said the waste was harmful to human health and needed to be properly disposed of, and he was going to report Weston. Steve had admitted he'd made a deal with a man he knew to accept some "dodgy industrial waste" from someone at Tilbury docks who needed to get rid of it quickly.' She added what she'd gleaned from the internet. 'That would be without going through the hoops that companies are meant to go through to protect the environment and public health, and without the huge extra cost. Landfill tax for harmless waste is two pounds something a tonne versus eighty-two pounds for hazardous waste—'

Ashley put up her hand. 'What was in this waste?'

'Kyle thought shredded bits of cars. Batteries, brake pads, et cetera. Something else, too.' She checked her notes. 'Oh yes, some of the waste may have come from old electrical transformers. The oil inside them used to be made of PCBs before they were banned everywhere. That's polychlorinated biphenyls—'

'I've heard of PCBs,' Clare interrupted. 'They're absolutely horrible chemicals, not biodegradable. They can enter the food chain. Woe betide any creature who ingests them – human, bird or anything else.'

'They're extremely toxic,' Elspeth said hurriedly, before her story was hijacked. 'Back to Steve Weston... According to Finn, he told Kyle to focus on doing his job and his loyalty would be rewarded. Kyle told Weston he wasn't going to let him ride roughshod over him anymore, he was going to report what he knew to the Environment Agency. Apparently, Weston went ballistic and told Kyle he'd be out of a job, if he did that. Finn thinks Kyle may have fought with Steve again the next day – the day he went missing – probably after everyone else had gone home. I wrote down what he said.' She stared at her handwriting. '"Kyle had a temper on him, like Steve but he kept a lid on it at work. If he'd lost his cool and the two of them had locked horns, God knows what might have happened. Kyle's body could be in a ditch somewhere – or inside that quarry, maybe."'

She glanced at the others' shocked faces.

'Finn said that he told Elven police his theory that Weston had something to do with Kyle's disappearance, but they didn't seem to take it seriously. He went to the local paper too but they said they couldn't print anything about Weston.'

'Worried about defamation, maybe,' Ashley said. 'Or they didn't want to ruffle Weston's feathers.'

'Hang on, let me finish! Finn's heart is broken,' she said, remembering the man's apology for his lack of hospitality. *Everything is different now. I've lost the love of my life. I hide myself away from the world, repairing leather jackets.* 'He was worried about what might happen to him if he caused trouble for Weston, so he stopped pressing the police to investigate what happened to Kyle. But he wants closure. He wants to see Kyle's body and lay him to rest.' She dabbed her tears.

'What Finn must be going through...' Ashley looked as if she was holding back tears, too. 'This is brilliant, Elspeth.'

'Thanks, sweetie, but that's not all – there's another link with Cindra the journalist, besides both her and Kyle going missing.'

'Go on.'

'Finn told me that shortly before Cindra went missing, she posted on the Brampton Appreciation Society Facebook group saying she was working on a story about toxic waste being secretly buried around Brampton and could anyone who had information contact her. He messaged her and they arranged to meet, but she never turned up. Because Weston had had her killed, I suppose.'

'Wow.' Ashley rubbed her brow. 'You can't blame Finn for being scared, can you? It looks as if Weston has been dumping

God knows what into that quarry and getting rich in the process. He killed Kyle first to stop people finding out what he was getting up to, and then Emily and Cindra, having found out they were about to spill the beans.' Ashley reached for her hand. 'Great work, Els. You've turned into a proper sleuth.'

She had to smile. Could this be her new role in life, one of the few areas where advanced age was arguably an asset?

'What is it, Ash?' Ashley was staring at her phone.

'It's her.'

'What's her?'

'The body that Clare found.' Ashley held up her phone. 'It's a news flash from the *Herald*. "The body found yesterday in Brampton Wood has been identified as belonging to Miss Cindra Patel, aged 22."'

'I was right.' Clare beamed at them. 'I told you, didn't I?'

Chapter 36
Ashley

Three days later

'Hell's bells!' Elspeth exclaimed on seeing her. 'You're a different woman!'

'I made an effort,' Ashley replied. The dress had been worn once, at a cousin's wedding. Her strappy heels were low enough to walk in, just. She had pushed the boat out with the rest, too – hair up, glitzy jewellery and more make-up than she'd worn in years. 'You don't look so bad yourself.'

Elspeth wore a rose silk dress that floated down to her ankles with a thick rope of pearls and a leather jacket. The look was effortlessly chic.

Just before 7.30pm, they drove through an imposing set of gates. They peered through the windscreen. Ahead, Bourne Hall loomed, dark against the fading sky.

'So, this is it.' Elspeth read from her phone. 'It was built in the 19th century, styled on a 17th-century chateau in the Dordogne.'

They parked and set off on foot. Other guests were arriving, too, in smart frocks and formal black and white. A path led under an arch and through a herb garden to a flight of steps. Elspeth gazed up at the house.

'Impressive, isn't it?'

'I don't think I should have worn these sandals,' she replied, anxiety fluttering inside her at the prospect of having to mingle with a crowd of strangers. She wasn't overly fond of social occasions, let alone one as grand as this. They followed two couples into a formal hall decorated with stuffed boar heads, tapestries and framed oil paintings, and she gave up trying not to be impressed.

'That must be Angie,' Elspeth hissed in her ear.

A slender woman dripping with diamonds in a figure-hugging gown was greeting guests. Copper hair rippled down her bare back. She looked to be in her late forties. Her slender face and widely spaced green eyes gave her a feline aspect. As they approached, her smile abruptly turned to puzzlement.

Elspeth stepped forward. 'I'm Elspeth Chambers, and this is my friend Ashley Khan.'

'Hello, Elspeth, Ashley, so pleased to meet you!' She took hold of Elspeth's hand. 'I'm Angie Weston. Welcome to Bourne Hall!' Her voice dripped like warm honey.

Ashley gave Angie a smile and walked on into an even bigger room, hung with chandeliers. There must have been a hundred people in there, among them Craig. Another horde of butterflies took off inside her. Overnight, she had gone from desperately wanting to talk to the man to desperately not wanting to be anywhere near him. Then there was the prospect of being in the vicinity of Steve Weston for the entire evening.

'All good?' Elspeth glanced at her enquiringly.

She groaned. 'Is it too early to go home?'

'You'll feel better soon. Come on, let's get a drink.'

They approached a table where two dapper young men were serving champagne. Ashley's heart sped up; their host was standing nearby, chatting with newly arrived guests.

'Hello ladies. We meet again.'

'Steve!' Elspeth responded immediately with a full beam smile and submitted to a kiss on the cheek.

'Hello, Steve.' She forced a smile, clocking his gaudy bow-tie and alert eyes. His northern accent had disappeared. 'What a stunning home you have.'

The corners of his eyes crinkled. For a moment he seemed a harmless, likeable chap.

'It's such a treat to be here,' Elspeth said. 'We're so glad you invited us.'

'Not at all.' He spoke warmly. 'I'm glad to have the company of two such well-dressed ladies.'

He had the gift of the gab. You'd never think that underneath lay such a despicable person. She sipped nervously from her flute as Weston talked to Elspeth about the history of the property.

Angie appeared at Weston's side, the stones on her fingers twinkling. He turned to her.

'I'm glad we got another delivery of champagne. I'm getting through a truck-full here... Ashley, have you met my wife? Angie has been planning this bash for months.'

With relief, she turned to Angie, who happily listed the many changes to the house, not least the newly installed jacuzzi.

'I enjoy the finer things in life, I don't mind admitting. There's nothing I like better than a glass of red while soft music plays in the background and the jacuzzi bubbles around me.' Angie gave her a searching look and glanced at her ring finger. 'Are you married, Ashley?'

'We've separated.'

'These things happen,' Angie said. 'I was married twice before I hooked up with Steve.' She placed her hand on her chest. 'He's not an angel, I know. But his heart's in the right place. He'll help anyone who needs his help.'

No comment seemed to be required.

'I understand you've met our wellness guru.' Angie smiled. 'That's what we call Craig, whenever he gets too serious about his health crusade. He can get intense, you know.'

'I've noticed.' She felt unsettled. Had Craig talked about her to this woman, or her husband? What else might they know about her?

'Well, it was lovely to meet you.' Angie's eyes flicked to an approaching couple.

Ashley looked around for Elspeth; she wasn't with Steve Weston anymore. Then she saw Craig standing in the middle of the room opposite a talkative attractive woman. Craig listened, nodding occasionally. Unlike most of the male guests he was casually dressed, in a shirt, black jeans and the blazer he'd worn at their disastrous lunch.

Despite herself, she felt a stab of envy, which was clearly ridiculous. She and Craig weren't seeing each other, and now they weren't even friends. No doubt he had dozens of females he could turn to for companionship, and more. She needed to put him out of her mind.

Ashley hurried towards a table bearing a platter of finger food and scooped up a handful of nuts, the healthiest option. Five minutes later, Weston approached Craig and greeted him with a backslap. The two men walked off, their heads close, laughing.

'You're Ashley Khan, aren't you?'

She turned to see a familiar woman holding a snack-laden plate. A frizz of greying hair was pulled off her face with slides. Her outfit was old-fashioned: a high-necked blouse decorated with bows and a calf-length pleated skirt.

'That's right.'

'I'm Liz Peaches. The vicar at St John's church.' The woman's small dark eyes fixed on Ashley's. She wasn't wearing a clerical collar.

'Pleased to meet you, vicar.' Ashley started to raise her hand, but let it fall to her side. Liz Peaches was eying her with unalloyed hostility.

'I know what you've done,' the vicar said abruptly, putting her plate down.

'What are you talking about?' She knew already, though.

'You killed her, didn't you?' The words were emitted in a fierce hiss. 'Your neighbour, Tara. You and your friends killed her. You were lucky. No one liked her so no one minded too much what happened to her.' The vicar's lips pressed into a thin, tight line.

'That's not true,' Ashley replied, with a glance behind. No one was within hearing range, thank God.

'Everyone knows it's true. I saw the drawing Bird Woman did. It shows you all bombarding that woman with fruit, as clear as eggs are eggs. You, the old woman who used to take dance classes, surly Ursula, always complaining about the church being too cold for her rehearsals... And that awful man who ran into me at 90 miles an hour in his blasted disabled contraption. My leg still hasn't healed properly.'

Ashley stared. The hostility behind the words shocked her almost as much as the words themselves.

'If you don't mind me saying,' she said, feeling wonderfully reckless, 'you don't sound very Christian. I thought vicars were meant to embody Christian values like kindness and forgiveness.'

The vicar's jaw slumped and her expression reset to a stony glare, with no trace of either kindness or forgiveness.

'How dare you? Excuse me. I'm not standing here and listening to this!'

Once the vicar was out of sight, Ashley leaned on the table. Her heart was beating hard and rather erratically. Liz Peaches was onto them. Soon, the whole of Brampton would know about that effing drawing. Bird Woman would be forced to confess what she really saw and the police would arrest them all, leaving the Wise Men free to run amok.

'Her bark's worse than her bite, I think you'll find.' She heard a plummy, assured male voice, from a man with a greying goatee and a scarlet bow tie close by. Had he heard any of their conversation? The man's eyes wandered to her cleavage. 'Graham Braithwaite, by the way.'

'Ashley Khan.' Reluctantly, she took his offered hand. 'What do you do, Graham?'

'I used to be in shipping. But my duties for Brampton parish council have taken over life somewhat.'

'That sounds like hard work.'

'It certainly is. Trying to get everyone to work together without acrimony, judging contentious issues fairly...' He heaved a sigh. 'Then there's the effort of stopping women from taking over our meetings. They always want to talk for twice as long as they're allowed.'

'The other female councillors, you mean?'

'That's right. Fortunately, there's only two.'

She gasped and grasped for a suitable reply, to no avail.

'I'll be off, then. Good to meet you.' With a stilted wave, the man departed. She turned to Elspeth now beside her.

'Prejudiced old goat,' she muttered. Had the man used his position to block other women from joining the council? No doubt he was another pal of Steve Weston's.

'Having fun?'

Ashley tugged Elspeth's arm. 'Thank God you're back. Come on, let's explore the house. I don't think I can bear to talk to anyone else.'

She led the way up a marble staircase, past more tapestries and portraits. Elspeth stopped halfway up, a grimace on her face.

'My knee... What are we looking for?'

'I've no idea. Let's just keep our eyes open, in case we spot something of interest.' Their host's dark secrets would be carefully stowed away, she thought gloomily.

They headed along the first-floor landing, peeping around a

door that wasn't shut to find sloping ceilings, deep eaves, shutters and a Juliet balcony.

'What's that?' Elspeth stopped, cocking her head. 'Someone's coming.'

Footsteps from below, echoing on the marble, and voices, indistinct.

'Let's go!'

Ashley grabbed Elspeth's hand and ran out of the room, away from the staircase. She tugged on the handle of the first door they came to and went inside. The room contained an old-fashioned toilet with a long flush chain and overhead cistern, and a chipped handbasin. It was barely large enough for them both. While Elspeth sat on the toilet seat, Ashley drew the bolt across, as quietly as possible.

The footsteps grew louder, as did the voices – male voices – until the men seemed to be practically outside.

'Don't be fucking stupid,' one man said in a high-pitched nasal voice. 'I don't care what TM says. If I did that, I'd be hounded out of my job. Everyone has orders to crack down on organised crime. It's the PCC's latest hobby horse. Tory voters won't stand for ordinary people getting hurt—'

'I don't care what your orders are. You've got no choice, Mark. TM will throw us to the dogs if you don't call your men off – including that little upstart constable who can't keep her nose out of the trough.' At first, she didn't recognise this voice, either. It was deep, with a strong accent – from Teeside, Hull or around there. With a tingle of horror, she realised the voice belonged to Steve Weston. 'Word is she's been sniffing about where she isn't wanted, asking questions about my business, who I'm associating with... She's been asking about the Hale woman, too. We need to shut her up before she finds out something that will put both us away for a long time. Not that we'd last long in the slammer. Most likely I'd wake up one day with a slit throat – and we both know what happens to bent chief inspectors with a taste for underage boys.'

224

'She doesn't know anything. My DI is keeping tabs on her.' The nasal voice was now threaded with anxiety. 'The situation's under control.'

'It's not just Peters,' Weston replied. 'Three birds from Brampton are dipping their beaks in, too, so I hear. Two of them are here tonight, Ashley Khan and Elspeth Chambers.'

At the mention of her name, her heart began to thump painfully hard. Anger filtered through her fear. How dare he speak like that about her and her two brave friends? The foul, hypocritical man, going about pretending he was God's gift to the local community when all the while he was in league with criminals.

'She's been mouthing off about someone murdering the Hale woman,' Weston continued. 'We need to give them all something to think about... Right, we'll do our business in here. You've got the full whack, this time?'

A rap on the door. The handle moved up and down violently. Ashley shrank back from the door.

'Jesus! Someone's in the crapper.'

'I'll be a while, darling!' Elspeth called out in her posh old woman voice. 'You might want to find another loo, perhaps, if you are in a hurry?'

Ashley clamped her hand over her mouth, stifling her laughter. The voices continued, quieter.

'Let's go to the bedroom.'

'What about Angie?'

'She's too busy flouncing about trying to be fuckin' lady of the manor.'

Sounds of a door opening and closing.

Ashley eased the bolt back, cracked open the door. The landing was empty. She turned to Elspeth. 'Quick, let's go. Follow me!'

At the end the hall, as she'd hoped, there was another, less grand staircase.

'Slow down!' Elspeth sounded tired.

The staircase emerged onto a gallery. Panting, Ashley leaned over the balustrade and waited for Elspeth. Below was the hall. Leading off it, yet more rooms. Further along, another staircase. They hurried down, passing mounted swords and fake arrow slits. Back on the ground floor they walked side by side in silence past spacious rooms with herringbone parquet floors and antique furniture. Inside one was a Beckstein grand piano, its lid raised. Behind it, glass doors gave onto an empty terrace.

'I need some fresh air,' Ashley said.

'I need the loo,' Elspeth replied. 'See you by the downstairs one.'

Ashley slid open the door and went to the guardrail. Below, the curving hillside led down to a distant river, lit by a three-quarter moon. She watched its silver reflection appear and disappear. Voices drifted on the breeze.

She shivered. The night was cold and her dress was thin. The earlier adrenalin had gone, replaced by a sick sensation. The conversation they'd overheard upstairs... though she wasn't sure what all of it meant, clearly, she was in danger, as were Elspeth, Clare and DC Peters. Weston and the other man – a police officer, by the sound of it – were in something crooked together, along with 'TM', whoever he was. Thin Man?

'I've been looking for you.'

She started at the familiar voice. A few feet away from her, Craig leaned over the railing. His eyes glinted in the moonlight.

'I'm surprised you've found me.'

'I persisted.' Craig turned towards her. 'The view's quite something, isn't it?'

'It is,' she replied. 'Your friends are lucky to live here.'

'I wanted to say...' He stepped closer to her. 'You're beautiful.'

His scent drifted towards her – light, notes of sandalwood. She imagined kissing him, then was afraid that she wouldn't be able to stop herself.

'Ashley.' He touched her upper arm.

The kiss happened before she could think any better. She tasted the salt spice of his mouth and felt the warmth of his hand through her dress.

For a few seconds, silence.

'I wasn't sure how you felt about me.' His eyes stayed on her face. She couldn't read his expression. 'I mean, apart from thinking I'm an unethical bastard who might be a killer.' He laughed, a tight, angry sound.

'I'm sorry about what I said before. I don't really believe you could kill someone.'

He mock-wiped his brow. 'Oh, that's a relief.'

Craig touched her skin above her neckline. He glanced to the lit room beyond the terrace and stepped away, extending his hand. They walked together towards the house, past planters spilling over with early tulips, then she stopped. Keeping her hand in his, he closed the gap between them and kissed her. His hand, on her lower back, pressed her body into his. She couldn't remember wanting someone so much.

'Shall we go inside? Somewhere no one will find us.' Craig.

She wanted to say yes, let her desire take over. Then she remembered Steve Weston.

'Steve. You're close to him, aren't you?'

Craig let go of her hand. His breathing became quiet. The gap between them reopened.

'He was my best mate. I know him better than almost anyone. We were friends at secondary school in Elven. Both of us were from outside of the area, which kind of bonded us. I got picked on for my Stoke accent... He helped me to stand up to them for me. They stopped after that.'

He hadn't answered her question, she realised. 'You're still good friends with him, aren't you?'

'We'll always be close. It's not just what happened at school. Later, when I really needed someone, he was there.'

'Go on,' she said.

'Ten, twelve years ago, I had a kind of crisis. I was selling stuff online – beauty products, health supplements... Sales took off and I made a lot of money. People would give all their money to a three-headed goblin for a chance to look young again.' He looked into her eyes. 'But the success didn't mean anything. I stopped feeling good about myself. I moved to Thailand, pushed the self-destruct button. I did extreme sports, partied, spent huge amounts on drink and drugs. Steve rescued me. He threw out the booze and the drugs and moved in until I was clean. I owe him my life.' He looked beyond her. 'People see his success and think he's a scheming bastard. But that's not who he is – not all he is. Under-neath, he's a good guy.'

She thought of Angie's plea. Could they be right about Steve Weston?

'How did you get into health, then?'

He spent two years in an Ashram, he explained, chanting, meditating and studying Indian spirituality. Wanting to help people change, he developed his own brand of healing using hypnosis combined with traditional eastern methods. As Craig talked something ticked over in her mind. Was there still a chance that he'd been involved in the murders of the two women?

'What is it?'

'Nothing.' The breeze stirred, bringing a gabble of voices.

'You still have doubts about me, don't you?'

She rubbed her arms. 'I didn't say that.'

'You didn't have to.' His gaze seemed to pierce her skin. 'Are you just pretending to like me? Do you really just want to find out more about Steve?'

'Of course not!'

'How do I know you're not just saying that?'

'Because I wouldn't.' Anger spilled from her voice. The icky sensation was back. She took a step away from Craig. She didn't want to stay here, trying to second guess this man. 'I'm not feeling that great, actually. I think I'll go home.'

'Alright. Goodnight, then.'

Craig looked as if he didn't believe her. Fine, he could believe what he liked. She went inside, leaving him on the terrace.

Chapter 37
DC Peters

Three days later

Kate toyed with her sad excuse for a sarnie. She considered whether to finish it or take a brisk walk. Neither option appealed.

The office was quiet. Many officers, including DI Lister, were at a Cindra Patel murder enquiry briefing to which she was not invited, not being on the team. This would be a good opportunity to make inroads into her unofficial investigation into Elven's dark side.

According to rumours circulating in Serious Crimes and tidbits gleaned from a local source, the Wise Men consisted of a tightly knit group – three in number. One, known as Thin Man was believed to be high up in a regional organised crime group that supposedly dealt in the illegal disposal of hazardous waste. Kate suspected that Steve Weston was one of the Wise Men. Indeed, the trio could have evolved to protect him from unwanted interference. Extortion was apparently Weston's speciality. She had recently received an anonymous voice message from someone claiming to be a local farmer, not far from the site of Brampton's former quarries. He accused Weston of dumping waste on his land at night as payback for him objecting to Weston's proposal to build over the reclaimed quarry. Weston had threatened 'to come for' him if he made any more trouble, such as reporting 'black gunk' leaching off his land, or anything else to suggest that the quarry job hadn't been carried out to the highest standards.

On her own, though, and with DI Lister breathing down her neck, making further inroads into the dark side would be difficult. Alternatively, Kate mused, she could visit Brampton and spend more time pestering the residents of Wilton Close.

But the thought of traipsing through the rain knocking on unopened doors made her feel even more depressed. The supposed drawing of the murder scene remained elusive. Both the bird woman and the vicar denied any knowledge of its where-abouts, and Clare Titchfield refused to admit that she had seen anyone in Ms Sanderson's kitchen that August evening, other than the men she had originally identified. Kate needed more evidence than that anonymous letter to arrest Ashley and Elspeth for murdering their neighbour.

Admittedly, the prospect of arresting anyone for Ms Sander-son's murder was complicated by Ashley's recent information – and insights, it had to be said – concerning the dark side. To arrest Ashley now would mean losing both an ally, albeit one on the other side of the divide, and an increasingly valuable source of information. The waters had gone from crystal clear to distinctly muddy.

Just as Kate had decided to stay at her desk and wade through more potential Moped Man CCTV footage, her mobile rang.

'Hello, Kate. I have something to tell you. Quite a few things, actually.' It was Ashley Khan.

'Go on.'

'It's to do with what we talked about before.' Ashley sounded cagey. 'Could you come over?'

'I'll be with you in half an hour.'

It would be an excuse to get out of the office. The car keys were hanging up in the DI's office, and no one was around to make a competing claim. She'd allocate the time to the Tara Sanderson case and no one would be the wiser.

Fortunately for her stress levels, the traffic was light. While struggling with the squeaky, ineffective windscreen wipers, she wondered if Ashley's information would be about Cindra Patel. Frustratingly, she didn't have access to information on the enquiry. So far, going by the downcast faces emerging from briefings, they hadn't made any breakthroughs. The killer or killers were likely to be linked to the victim, DCI Hill had said at the first press conference. There was no evidence they had struck before.

Kate parked and walked through heavy rain, arriving damp and bedraggled at number 32 Wilton Close. A spate of furious barking from behind the door stopped abruptly.

'Brillo, stop! Hello, detective, come in.'

The dog nuzzled her leg. Kate bent down and offered the terrier a hand. It was nice to be greeted with such passion. She wondered how Mitzi was doing.

'Can I get you anything?' Ashley's hair was untidy, and her cardigan had a button missing.

'Coffee, thanks.' She needed to be alert for the journey back to town; driving in rain wasn't her forté. She peeled off her damp top. 'Would you mind if I dried this on the radiator?'

The kitchen was a mess. Plates lined the sink. Ashley swore under her breath as she rummaged in the dishwasher. Kate pulled up a chair at the table, which needed a wipe.

'Is your mother around today?'

'She's in hospital. She had a fall.'

'Sorry to hear that. What happened?'

A loud exhale. 'She slipped while taking out the food bin. She went without her walker so she could use both hands. Unfortunately, there was a frosty patch on the path that she didn't see.'

'Ouch! Is she badly hurt?'

'She's fractured her hip and bruised some vertebrae. They want her to stay in hospital for a few weeks.' Ashley frowned. 'The reason I phoned, detective... A few things have happened, I think you ought to know about.'

'I'm all ears.' Kate got out her notebook and sat down. She would have registered Ashley Khan as an intelligence source, only DI Lister or DCI Hill might have asked unwelcome questions. Instead, she would take copious notes.

Ashley placed a cup of coffee in front of Kate and told a story about Mr Weston's former employee, Kyle Sutton, going missing after a dispute over Weston allowing toxic waste to be illegally buried at Brampton quarry. The crux of it was, Sutton's former partner, Finn O'Connor, suspected Weston had killed Sutton to shut him up.

'I'm sorry, Ashley,' Kate said. 'This is all very well, but seeing that Kyle Sutton's body hasn't been found, speculating about a possible murder is premature.' It was all extremely interesting, however.

'I see.' Ashley looked peeved. 'Well, maybe you could bear it in mind if a body is ever found.'

'What was the other thing?'

'Elspeth and I overheard something at the party on Saturday night.'

'The party?'

'Steve Weston's party. It was quite upsetting. I think it might relate to the men Elspeth and I saw in the pub recently. I'm sorry, I'm not making much sense. So much has happened, lately.'

'Start at the beginning. You saw some men in a pub?'

'About ten days ago, Elspeth and I were in The Anglers having a drink. Two men were sat at the bar opposite us. They drove away from the pub together. One definitely had bowed legs, like the man Clare saw in the woods.'

'I see,' Kate said. 'Tell me more.'

'The bigger one wore trendy clothes, lots of rings. He was in his late twenties, early thirties. The bow legged one was older, average build with cold eyes.'

'Did you hear anything they said?'

'Yes, but they spoke in a foreign language.'

Could they be the same pair that Clare Titchfield had sighted loitering outside her property, and up to something in nearby woods? Since the bird woman had reported her concerns, Kate had been trawling the system trying to identify the two men. Among the possibles were a Croatian pair with addresses in Elven. They had been interviewed on suspicion of GBH, but they were never charged.

Ashley also mentioned a 'thin man in out-of-date clothes' dining alone with Steve Weston, whom Elspeth had seen. Kate's ears pricked up. As far as she knew, Thin Man's identity was unknown to the police. He had left just before the other two men, Ashley said. He had looked grey in the face and was in his late fifties, they guessed.

'What about the cars these men drove? Did you notice the makes, colours, number plates?'

'The thin man drove a black Jaguar. Neither of us remember the number plate. We're not sure about the other car.'

With an anxious qualm, Kate checked her watch. The drive back to the office through the heavy traffic in the pouring rain would be hellish.

'What was the other thing? You overheard something at Steve Weston's party?'

Ashley didn't reply immediately.

'Elspeth and I were wandering around upstairs. We heard voices on the stairs and ran into the toilet to hide. Two men started talking outside. One was Steve Weston.' Ashley pressed her top teeth into her finger. 'From the conversation, it sounded like the other was a police officer based at Elven. That's where you work, isn't it?'

'Did you get his name?'

'Only his first name – Mark. But we're certain that Steve Weston referred to him as a chief inspector.'

Kate felt herself jolt. DCI Mark Hill was the head of Serious Crimes and a detective chief inspector, the only one based at Elven.

'It sounded like Steve Weston was blackmailing this guy,' Ashley continued. 'What he actually said was, "We both know what happens to bent chief inspectors with a taste for underage boys".'

Kate stared at Ashley, a surge of emotion interfering with her ability to speak. Was the DCI one of the Wise Men?

'What else do you remember?'

'Someone they called "TM" was mentioned several times. Could that be the Thin Man?' Ashley produced a piece of paper. 'I've written down what we can remember. The man called Mark said he had orders to crack down on local organised crime, and something about not being able to turn a blind eye or he'd lose his job. Steve argued with him, said Mark had no choice, if he didn't call his men off, TM would...' Ashley made air quotes, '"throw them both to the dogs".'

Her mind raced. Was the DCI being pressured by Thin Man not to disrupt certain sorts of crime, thus putting him in conflict with the demands of top brass? Could that be why the Cindra Patel murder enquiry wasn't getting anywhere?

'Steve Weston mentioned you, too.' Absorbed in her startling thoughts, Kate only half registered what Ashley said.

'What did you say? He mentioned me by name?'

Ashley fidgeted. 'Actually, he said "that little upstart constable". He said he knew you were looking into the Wise Men and Emily Hale's death, and they needed to shut you up before you found out something that would put the two of them in prison for a long time.'

'Oh.' She looked down to see the ground sloping up towards her.

'Are you alright?' Ashley sounded alarmed. 'DC Peters?'

Kate opened her eyes, willing her heart to quieten. This was a threat to life, surely?

'Kate?' Ashley touched her arm. 'Here's a glass of water.'

'Thanks. I had a dizzy spell, that's all. What else did they say?'

'Steve Weston mentioned me, too.' Ashley looked pale. 'And Elspeth and Clare. He said we were "sticking our beaks" into things that didn't concern us, and this Mark guy needed to keep an eye on us.' Ashley's voice was strained.

'Well, they can fuck right off,' Kate muttered, before she could stop herself.

'They're dangerous, aren't they, these men? They could hurt us.'

'Yes, they are. You three need to be careful. From now on, don't try to investigate on your own without my say so. I mean it, Ashley.'

On her way out, Kate gave Brillo a back rub.

Now she knew who the third Wise Man was. She also knew that not only was she in danger, but Ashley and her two friends.

Another thought cut through. These men weren't going to get away with what they were up to. Kate touched the door frame. Somehow, touch wood, she was going to end their dominance over this town – without herself or the three women getting hurt.

Chapter 38
DC Peters

The same day

S he was still grappling with the insane possibility that DCI Hill was the third of the Wise Men. Weston and Thin Man must have something on the DCI that had persuaded him to turn a blind eye to whatever they were up to, risking years in prison. Was DI Lister in on this, too? Who else might be?

Kate hung up the car keys in the DI's office – thankfully Lister was in a meeting – and went up to DS Renn's desk.

'Rob. Do you have a minute?' Whether he liked it or not, she was going to have it out with him.

'What can I do you for?' DS Renn was in a blue-and-grey checked shirt today. His brown eyes were friendly.

'Let's go outside.' She led him to the top of the fire stairs. The rain had turned into a thin drizzle. No vapers or smokers yet. 'Why were you standing by my desk yesterday, when I wasn't there? Were you looking for something?'

He pulled hair off his brow. 'The boss asked me to check up on you. She was worried about you working on your own. She asked me to find out if you were doing anything outside of what you're meant to be working on.'

Nothing would surprise her about this place, anymore. But DS Renn... She had trusted him.

'What did you tell her?'

The sergeant spoke softly. 'I didn't tell her anything, Kate – and I'm not going to.'

'So what were you doing at my desk?'

'The boss was watching me. I thought I'd pretend to have a quick look, so she thinks I'm on her side.'

Kate wiped rain off her face. 'How do I know that you aren't?'

'There's a couple of things I haven't told you.' He glanced at the fire door. 'I'll meet you at Macy's in ten minutes. We'll get soaked if we stay here.'

From all the mopping and wiping, Macy's was about to close. It was a cheerless little place, the closest café to the office.

DS Renn sat at a table at the back, hands wrapped around a cup. Kate ordered from an unsmiling woman at the counter and pulled up a chair.

Rob placed his palms on the table. The lines on his brow looked deeper, and he hadn't shaved recently.

'OK, Emily Hale. I was on duty at the scene that night, after her body was called in. I had a wander up to the access road, where the SOCOs had been taking photos. The lights were still on. Near the tyre mark I spotted some tape stuck to a bush. One of the SOCOs saw me looking, came over and picked it up.'

'Kelvin?'

'Yes. He was turned away from me so I couldn't see him what he did with it. I went back down to the body, assuming he'd bagged it as evidence. But when I checked the exhibit list next morning the tape wasn't on there. DI Lister seemed to think I was mistaken. I said no, I'm certain. She got aggressive, asked if I was accusing someone.' With a long exhale, DS Renn sat back.

Kate's coffee came. She gulped it down, grateful for the caffeine.

'You think Kelvin got rid of the tape?'

'There's no other explanation. He could have squirreled it up the sleeve of his forensic suit.'

'But why bother to hide a piece of tape? Anyone could have dropped it.'

'I doubt it, given what else I found.'

Her heart put on a spurt. 'Are you going to tell me?'

'Last week, the boss left her office in a hurry – she didn't lock the door. I had a sneaky rummage around her desk. The pathologist's report on Emily Hale was there. I had a gander. It mentioned traces of adhesive around Emily Hale's mouth. Some hairs near the upper lip had been pulled out... consistent with a gag being applied and removed.'

She heard the suck of her breath. The sergeant's eyes locked onto hers.

'Emily Hale was held against her will, then pushed off that ledge. I'd put money on it.'

'This stuff was in the report the whole time, and no one said anything. DI Lister must have seen it.' It was all coming together, now.

'Exactly. DCI Hill, too, most likely.'

'And without the tape there wasn't enough evidence to conclude that she'd been gagged, as opposed to doing some home beauty treatment. There was nothing to outweigh the evidence pointing to her suicide.'

'And the coroner went along with the DCI, and no one was the wiser.'

Kate swilled the froth of her cappuccino. 'So, Kelvin got rid of crucial evidence, because the DCI asked him to, or DI Lister on his behalf.'

'Agreed.'

'Emily could have been picked up by the killer or killers some time after she left her mobile home to go for a walk. She was probably forced into the back of a van, gagged and cuffed and driven to the quarry – by which time she'd managed to free her wrists. When they opened the van doors, she surprised them and made a run for it, dropping the gag or ripping it off as she ran.'

'But the killer caught up with her.' The sergeant took over. 'He forced her off the ledge then went down to the body to check she was dead.'

Their eyes met. DS Renn was on her side after all.

'What I'm not getting,' Kate said, 'is why the DCI would want to make Emily's death look like suicide rather than murder.'

'I've no idea.' He steepled his hands, pressing his forehead against them.

'I've got one,' Kate replied.

He lowered his hands to the table, his eyes scanning her face.

'Sorry, guys,' the waitress interrupted in a voice lacking any hint of regret. 'We're closing.'

DS Renn pushed himself upright with a sigh. 'We'd better be getting back anyway. The boss might get suspicious.'

They walked back towards the office. The rain had stopped. A brisk wind scudded litter across the pavement.

'What were you going to say?' The sergeant stopped and turned to her.

It's to do with the Wise Men, she'd been about to say.

'I don't know for sure. Someone's got to him, someone he can't say no to.' If he could be cagey about revealing everything he knew, so could she.

'Hey, wait. Do you think the boss is involved in whatever this is?'

'I do.' She turned to him. 'For a start, she asked you to check on me—'

'That could be because she thinks *you're* dodgy'.

'It's not just that. It's the timing.'

'What do you mean?' The sergeant watched her face closely.

'Yesterday, when she called you in asked you to check up on me... It was just a few days after...' She stopped herself. *After Steve Weston's party*, she'd almost said. But should she tell him about the conversation Ashley had overheard? If there was the smallest chance he might go blabbing to the DI – or the DCI, even – she was done for. 'Listen, let's talk again in a few days, once I've thought all this over.'

'Sure,' DS Renn said.

They resumed walking. In the distance, a PC emerged from the police station side of the building.

'Oh, Rob.' She glanced up at him. 'That time I said hello to you at the coffee machine, did you ignore me on purpose?'

'Sorry?' He blinked, his brow creasing. 'No, no, I didn't mean to ignore you – I didn't hear you, Kate. I must've had my earbuds in.'

The 380 bus put on a spurt and made it through the lights. Kate closed her notebook and put away her pen, picturing the car she would buy if by some miracle she was ever made sergeant.

Her phone pinged. It was DS Renn's email. The subject line: *Taken with my phone*. Attached were photographs of pages in the pathologist's report. She clicked the first. Rob had highlighted a paragraph.

Traces of adhesive were found around the mouth and several hairs

*in the region of the upper lip had been removed, both of which are
consistent with the placing and removal of strong adhesive tape
around the victim's mouth.*

The next photograph contained a highlighted section.

*The abrasions and bruising on the wrists and lower arms suggest
that the victim may have been restrained prior to her death.*

So, Emily Hale's death had been suspicious all along. Both DI
and DCI had insisted it wasn't and arranged for the removal of
evidence suggesting otherwise, effectively ending the investigation. But why had Emily Hale been killed in the first place? Had
she obtained information that threatened the Wise Men –
evidence of their criminality, or the exposure of their identities?
Had she planned to give Cindra Patel this information, hoping it
would be made public?

In the turmoil of her thoughts, she didn't see her stop.

'Driver!' Kate stabbed at the overhead bell.

She stood on the wet pavement, suddenly deflated. What was
she doing in this godforsaken place without anyone in her life, not
even her beloved Mitzi? Why not resign, go back to London and
become a teacher, a bus driver, anything but a police officer? But
to give up now... If the criminals were to win, what would happen
to those three women? She had an ally in the sergeant. Perhaps,
with the women's help, she and the sergeant could defeat the men
intent on undermining this place.

Chapter 39
Ashley

The next day

A shley opened the driver's car door and climbed in, grateful that the latest visit to see her poorly mother was over and that hospital parking fees go up after an hour, providing her with a handy excuse to leave.

She slipped her debit card into the slot, put the car into gear and drove towards home.

It had been her third visit to Diane. There'd been no sign of her mother's previous post surgery euphoria, just a heady mixture of frustration, resentment and depression. When Ashley had foolishly remarked it was as well that the hip scheduled for replacement had been fractured rather than the good one, she'd taken a blast from both barrels.

'That's all very well for you to say! I'm in constant pain, I can't sit up or walk. On top of that I'm going to be stuck in this place for the next two to three weeks. And once I get home, it's going to take me months before I can walk properly.'

She had tried not to be drawn into an argument about the

reason for Bryce only visiting once, which Diane had plainly thought was inadequate.

'He'll come again,' she'd said, 'unless you were as grumpy and bad tempered with him as you are with me.'

'That's got nothing to do with it! He was probably put off coming again by the rumours going around about you.'

'What rumours?'

'That Tara died because you and Elspeth and those others in the Covid group attacked her. Have you not heard them? I've been asked three times whether they're true! First by Ken next door, then by the Welsh woman across the green, and yesterday by one of the nurses here, who then had the temerity to ask me if I've seen the drawing that the police are looking for!'

Ashley tried to focus on the road. Sleet was falling from plump, silver-grey clouds. By now, everyone in Brampton had probably heard the rumours, too, if her mother's account was true. But she was almost past the point of caring. What was the point of worrying about something she couldn't change? As long as the police had nothing solid against them, and that blasted drawing didn't come out of the woodwork...

She looked forward to spending the evening home alone – apart from Brillo – cosying up with an unhealthy ready meal. Of course, this sudden serious injury was a big setback for her mother, and the thought of coexisting with a depressed, immobile woman for months on end wasn't cheering. But they would manage, with luck. The house was already set up for Diane's hip replacement recovery: grab-bars installed beside the toilet, inside and outside the shower, bright lighting downstairs and any objects that she might trip on removed. Her mother just had to remember to use the effing walking frame.

She settled down in front of *Traitors* with a microwave spinach and ricotta ravioli. Before long, her thoughts moved from the reality show. She had not heard anything from Craig since the party, not even a brief text to say sorry for upsetting her. She couldn't decide if she was relieved or disappointed. Surely, he didn't expect *her* to apologise? That certainly wasn't going to happen.

Her thoughts turned to the detective's recent visit. Kate Peters had definitely been interested in the conversation between Weston and the police officer, Mark whatever-his-name-was. In fact, it was surprising just how much she'd been affected. If this Mark was her boss, she would presumably be in a difficult position. Would she report him, or bide her time until...

The brisk chime of the door-bell made her start. Elspeth? She checked her watch. Just gone 9.30pm – Elspeth would be having her bath. Who else would visit at this time?

'Hello, Ashley.'

The voice was syrup smooth, without warmth. She took in the bulk of Steve Weston – the hands in pockets, the polished leather shoes, the slope of his belly visible under his coat. The whisky on his breath.

'Steve, it's you. I wasn't expecting anyone so late. Do you want to come in?' The chill air sliced through her clothing.

His lips stretched into a lifeless smile. 'No need, this won't take long.'

He was a threat, her body knew. She folded her arms tightly across her chest.

'I invited you to my home in the spirit of friendship,' he said. 'With the hope that we could come to a mutual understanding. I hoped you might realise that there are some people who should not be... fucked around with, put it like that. Instead, I find out you've been snooping around – and not just inside my house.'

She opened her mouth to speak. He carried on.

'I think you know what I'm talking about, Ashley. I know you and your lady friends have been poking your noses into my affairs. You may think you're smart enough to get the better of me, but let me assure you, I have many friends who have my back.' He smiled, showing his teeth, and brought a phone out of his pocket. 'One happens to be the local vicar. She showed me this.'

He shoved his phone in front of her face. The screen showed a drawing of people with shocked and angry faces – Clare's drawing. Her heart stopped for a second.

'It shows you and your friends in the process of killing your neighbour Tara Sanderson, if I'm not mistaken.' He put the phone away. 'I'm sure an intelligent woman such as yourself will understand its significance. Once it's in police hands, they won't hesitate to charge you.' He paused, rolling his lips in an ugly motion. 'Are you looking forward to going to prison, Ashley? Do you know what it's like inside, away from your family and friends, sitting inside a bleak cell for hours on end, having to put up with crap food and constant noise, at the mercy of everyone around you?'

'You can try to frighten me but it won't work.' Her voice was barely audible to her own ears. The man carried on.

'Do you know what it's like to be spat at, assaulted and tormented by vicious hags who think nice middle-class women like you are fair game?'

She shuddered, not from the cold.

'But I'm not absolutely heartless, Ashley. If you decide to call off your misguided campaign against me, I will destroy this crucial evidence and do what I can to ensure the matter goes no further.'

She wanted to spit in his face. How dare he come here and threaten her?

'Are you trying to blackmail me?' Her words came out in a thin, nervous-sounding dribble.

'You don't need to say anything right now, my dear.' Another cheerless smile. 'Think it over, that's all I ask.' He rubbed his palms together briskly. 'A bit parky, isn't it? I'll leave you to enjoy your nice warm home. Just so you know, if you ignore my offer, you'll soon be wishing you hadn't. There are even worse things than prison, you know.'

She watched Weston climb into his Mercedes. Ten minutes later, her heart was still hammering in her chest.

The palpitations continued that night. Her sleep was interrupted by ominous, fear-filled dreams. When she wasn't asleep, she ruminated on her visitor's words. It was blatant blackmail. The hateful man had made no attempt to hide that. But around here, what was legal hardly seemed to matter.

She caught herself. Reap what you sow... She too had committed a serious crime. She had disregarded the law and lied to the police; what right had she to get upset over others doing the same?

As the darkness dispersed, she thought of Craig, that night at the party. She let the memories come back. His electric pull on her, their kiss. How she had wanted to go with him, more than anything...

She groaned and shut her eyes. Had Craig told Steve about Ashley 'snooping around'? If he was miffed with her, perhaps. He was likely to be loyal to Steve. Could he know that his friend was responsible for the deaths of three people – and that she herself was at risk of being harmed?

Chapter 40
Ashley

The next day

Confronting her reflected face in the mirror, Ashley moaned. A thick mass of wavy auburn hair framed her heart-shaped face. Her remaining looks, marred by deep half-moons under her eyes. She had never felt so tired, or so vulnerable.

While towelling herself dry from her shower, the doorbell rang. She was tempted to ignore it, in case it was Steve Weston. But he wouldn't contact her so soon, would he? Finally, she pulled on her dressing gown and slippers and went downstairs.

'Hello, darling. Aren't you up yet?'

'Elspeth! Thank goodness it's you.' Never had she been so glad to see her neighbour's stylish figure.

'Who did you think it would be?'

'Oh, I don't know...' Before telling Elspeth about Weston's blackmail attempt, she needed to decide what she was going to do in response. 'Anyway, how are you?'

'I've just had a text from Ursula. She wants to meet us at the Green Goddess café in half an hour.'

Ashley groaned. 'What for?'

'She didn't say. She says it's urgent.'

'I don't fancy going anywhere right now.'

'You don't look so good. Is everything alright?'

'I slept badly.'

'Has something happened?' Elspeth's large green eyes roamed her face.

'Something happened last night,' she admitted. 'I'll tell you everything later.'

'Shall I put her off, then?'

'No, let's get it over with.'

A woman in her sixties with short hair and spectacles rugged up in a coat and beany was sitting at an outside table. She had a cup and saucer in front of her.

'Hello Elspeth, Ashley,' Ursula made the slightest of gestures, which could have been a wave. 'I'm sorry for all the urgency but I thought we needed to talk.'

Ashley headed to the counter with Elspeth. She badly needed some coffee inside her before facing Ursula. The woman could have thanked them for coming, at least.

'What's on your mind?' Elspeth said as they sat down. Ursula's face twisted as if she was in pain. She glanced along the row of empty tables and at pedestrians passing by on Brampton High Street before replying in a low voice.

'Have you heard the rumours going round the village?'

Ashley busied herself sipping her cappuccino. Elspeth bit into her croissant. Ursula shook her head, obviously irritated.

'Well?'

'What rumours, Ursula?' She would play dumb, she decided.

If she mentioned Saturday's confrontation with the vicar, Ursula would probably have a heart attack.

'People are saying that someone's made a drawing of Tara's killers. Mrs Gale at the post office asked me this morning if I'd seen it, and last night one of the choir asked me how well I knew Tara.' The woman made an unpleasant guttural sound. 'I overheard two altos whispering behind my back, too. I think someone must have seen this drawing and recognised me.'

The vicar, perhaps? Ashley looked sideways at Elspeth.

'Rumours aren't evidence,' she said with more assurance than she felt. 'They can't charge us unless they have evidence to prove we killed her.'

'Well, if they get their hands on this drawing...' Ursula glared at her. 'I've been talking to a friend who used to be a defence barrister. If we're charged with murder or manslaughter, we could have to go to prison until the case goes to court. I made out it was a hypothetical situation, of course, and she's nowhere near Brampton.'

Elspeth sighed ran her fingers through her immaculately cut blonde hair.

'I understand you're upset Ursula. But I'm not sure what any of us can do about this. People will get bored soon and find something else to talk about, with any luck. I think we should try to ride it out.'

'Ride it out?!' Ursula's voice shot up half an octave.

Elspeth put a finger to her lips and stage whispered. 'Hush! That woman over there is watching us like a hawk.'

The three glanced in unison at a woman now installed at the far table, peering over the screen of her laptop.

'If police question any of us again,' Ursula continued, 'we mustn't give anything away. God knows how long we could be in prison for, given the cover-up—'

'—which was your idea,' Ashley interrupted. 'If we hadn't agreed to it, we could have come clean. We might have got off with community service or whatever and we wouldn't be in such an impossible position.'

'I beg your pardon.' Ursula glared at her. 'Please, don't rewrite history. And keep your voice down.'

'Ashley's right,' hissed Elspeth. 'Hiding the truth has made it all so much worse. It's made us look like we're guilty of murder.'

'What's done is done.' Ursula folded her arms, her chin tilted up, making little effort to curtail her full voice. 'There's no point in squabbling among ourselves. We need to agree on a way forward.'

'Could you keep your voices down, please? I came here to work on my novel.' The woman from the other table had come over.

Elspeth apologised while Ursula muttered something. The three split the bill, then Ursula left with a cursory goodbye.

'Ursula really gets my goat, sometimes,' Ashley said as she and Elspeth walked home. 'No, most of the time.'

'She's scared, that's all.'

'So am I.'

Elspeth glanced at her in surprise.

'All this is way more complicated than Ursula realises,' she explained. 'I had a visit from Steve Weston last night. He tried to blackmail me.'

'What?'

'He has Clare's drawing and he's threatening to go to the police.' She described what had happened.

'That takes the biscuit! What a mangy, low down, prick-for-brains! Picking on a defenceless woman like that... What did you say to him?'

'Not a lot. I was too stunned.'

'So, what are you going to do?' Elspeth asked as they walked home.

'I don't know. I'm damned if I'm going to just do what he wants. But I'm worried what might happen if I don't.'

'Have you told the detective that he's tried to blackmail you?'

'I don't know if that's a good idea. What proof do I have? It would be my word against his. And if he found out...'

'Oh Lord.' Elspeth frowned, massaging her brow. 'What an unholy mess.'

She steeled herself. 'I haven't told you everything. I promised DC Peters I'd tell her the truth about how Tara died... if she held off arresting us.'

'Are you serious?' Elspeth's green eyes fixed on her.

'I can't live with this lie any more. It's been eating away at me. I was thinking... If we can help DC Peters get the evidence she needs to charge Steve Weston with Emily and Cindra's murders, then she might be willing to put in a good word for us – if and when we're sentenced for what we did to Tara.'

'If we're not bumped off first, that is.'

'I know, it's risky. Too risky.'

Elspeth stopped walking and fiddled with her ring.

'I know all this has been a weight on your shoulders, Ash. I suppose I've got used to the sword of Damocles hanging over my head, but I'm a lot older than you are. Who knows how long I've got left.'

'A long time, I hope.'

Ashley looked sternly at Elspeth. They carried on walking in silence.

'Last night Steve said it was the vicar who'd given him the drawing,' she said as they arrived at number 32. 'I wouldn't be surprised if she's been going around the village telling everyone exactly what she thinks happened to Tara.'

Elspeth tittered. 'She clearly thinks you and I are bad women who've got away with murder. It's not just her, either.'

'Who else – Ken?'

'I'm not sure about Ken. I'm certain Rhianna knows something, though. I didn't get a chance to tell you earlier and I wasn't going to say it in front of Ursula... She stopped in front of my gate yesterday afternoon, would you believe, and asked if I had any theories about who killed Tara.'

'No! What did you say?'

'I just said, some people should mind their own business, which she didn't like one jot. She gave me the evil eye and rushed off.'

'I'm not surprised! We should be careful what we say to her from now on. She's friendly with Craig – and probably the Westons, too, given she did the catering for their party.'

'While you were snogging Craig, I saw her having a chinwag with Angie. They looked pretty pally to me.' Elspeth sighed and massaged the back of her neck. 'About your plan to save Brampton, Ashley. I'm with you one hundred per cent. So will Clare be, I'm sure. I'm not standing by while that See You Next Tuesday tries to blackmail you. We're going to fight these criminals – the ones in the police, too.'

Tears pricked at the back of her eyes. What would she do without Elspeth's passion and loyalty?

'Thanks for the support, love. It means a lot. But please, be careful.'

Chapter 41
Bird Woman

7 March: 7.45am

I am ashamed to admit that I've been too frightened to walk in the wood of late. Since coming across the young woman's body and Ashley being threatened by the Weston man, not to mention all their warnings to be extra vigilant, I can't go anywhere without constantly expecting men to leap out at me from behind a bush.

I've stayed home for the past two days, making sure everywhere is locked before I go out and turn in at night, and that the phone is always charged. This morning, I woke up and realised I've become a prisoner in my own home. So I've challenged myself to go out and do something useful to contribute to the efforts of our unlikely trio.

I'm as capable as many men, I keep telling myself. Admittedly, though, I was apprehensive while preparing my rucksack for the day ahead.

I haven't told the others about my fears, in case they see me as the weakest link. I don't want to let them down, I believe in what we're doing. We are ordinary women who have taken on powerful men, the most powerful men we know. That is something I must hold on to.

10.20am

I stride out briskly, my gloves, beany and rucksack on. It's cold again today. Frost coats the grass and my breath forms little white clouds. I follow the path upwards through woodland, away from the Elven Road. As I near the fence around the filled-in quarry, an off-kilter smell invades my nostrils – acidic with a hint of organic foulness. Grey fumes float off the grassed-over soil that have no obvious origin. From up here I can see for miles around, and there is no mist anywhere.

I follow the track down towards the lower quarry. I'm glad of my thick boots. Here and there, a black liquid pools between clumps of grass. It has a familiar unpleasant smell. Whatever is it? Did those dead birds drink from here? Near the edge of the huge hole, I stop to drink tea from my flask and text Elspeth my location. Then I squeeze under the broken fence via a tunnel in an old badger sett. I can't see any walkers today, fortunately.

Inside the depths of the old quarry among a hotchpotch of rocks and concrete slabs, I dig into the debris. The phone is in my pocket, switched on, at maximum volume. I wear my toughest gardening gloves. Occasionally I use my trowel but most of the time I only need my hands. The shade is dense, and I have to work fast to keep warm.

At a quarter past one, I climb up to the rim and sit down in a sunny patch to eat lunch. (With great will power, I managed to avoid bringing a chocolate brownie.) It's a relief to be in the sunlight. So far, I've found all sorts of interesting bits and pieces, though nothing significant: a nest built inside a discarded tyre, a squashed Trilby, a broken office chair oozing out its stuffing and a dozen other household objects. Also, there are cans of paint, rusty wire fencing, rolls of mildewed, insect-eaten material and an old-fashioned pram that was common in the 1960s.

The older stuff is buried lower. I feel like an archaeologist. A small collection of objects is accumulating in my rucksack: compact mirror, a set of weights for a kitchen scales without the scales and a horseshoe.

2.30pm

I've found something.

A bulging polythene bag, the kind that is used for rubbish, is wedged deep into the gap between a hunk of concrete and an ancient television set, where no one could accidentally come across it. Someone put it here on purpose.

I clamber up with the bag, untie the wire ties and take out the contents.

A pair of black leather men's gloves with a tear in the left-hand middle finger. An empty glasses case. A tub of still-edible miniature chocolate bars. (I tested one.) A green mug with *Feck Off You Feckin Eejit* around it. A battered photograph, 5x8 inches.

The photograph has pieces of Blu Tack stuck to the back. It shows a sandy-haired middle-aged man in steel-rimmed spectacles with his arm around the shoulders of another man, who's broad-shouldered with dark hair, a generous moustache and a beard. Both are smiling as if they were caught laughing at a joke. Are they still together, I wonder, and do these objects belong to one of them? Or did a relative or friend discard them after the men died? But it seems odd that anyone would want to hide such things.

I haul my rucksack home.

On the way I text Elspeth to say I've found something. She phones immediately and asks what it is. I list each object and its salient features. When I describe the photograph, Elspeth gasps like a dying fish.

'Clear tomorrow's schedule,' she tells me, 'we're going to visit someone.'

Chapter 42
Elspeth

The next day

While Finn made coffee and Clare repeatedly flushed the downstairs toilet, Elspeth examined the rural scenes framed on the walls of the gloomy, low-ceilinged room. The trip to 3 Stokes Lane had taken an hour by bus. Finn had collected them from Winton's post office and driven them in his old Land Rover to the house at the end of the lane.

A sense of dread was collecting inside her. Was this how police officers felt when they had to tell someone their partner or relative had died? Perhaps she should have handed the bag over to the young detective. She brushed the thought swiftly aside. Like Clare, she had considerably more confidence in their trio than in Elven's detectives.

Finn entered, stooping under the doorway, and placed the tray on the only space left on the table that dominated the room. After handing out the mugs he perched on an upturned crate. Elspeth and Clare took the two stools opposite. Finn's warrior-like figure seemed to crowd the narrow space. There was no room for a fourth person, she thought; it was just as well Ashley needed to be elsewhere.

'What did you want to show me?' Finn wiped his mouth with his hand and set down his mug.

'I found these at Brampton quarry yesterday.'

Clare propped her rucksack on the floor in front of Finn, withdrew the gloves, mug, glasses case and a somewhat depleted bag of assorted chocolate bars and placed them on the floor in front of Finn. The man reached forward and picked up the gloves, running his fingers over the leather fingers and flexing them. He put a glove to his face, shut his eyes and took a long breath in.

'And there was this,' Elspeth said, taking the photograph from Clare. They had mended the tear with sellotape. Finn let go of the glove and took it.

'It's him,' he said, still looking at the photo.

'I'm sorry, Finn.' Elspeth glanced at Clare, willing her not to say anything tactless. 'Would you like us to leave you alone for a few minutes?'

'No, stay where you are.' Finn said, examining the glove again. 'It's not a surprise. I've been waiting for this day for over a year.' He indicated a tear in his middle finger. 'This is where a spaniel nipped him. He loved dogs. People, not so much.'

Clare sipped her coffee. Elspeth dabbed her eyes with her handkerchief. Finn picked up the empty spectacles case from the floor and looked inside.

'He never went anywhere without his glasses.'

The room was quiet except for clicks as Finn clenched and straightened his fingers.

'Maybe he had all this inside his locker,' he said, picking up the photo again. 'In the site hut.'

'Yes, maybe,' Elspeth replied. 'Presumably he was wearing his glasses when he went missing.'

'He was killed, Elspeth, I already told you.' Finn's blue eyes fixed on hers. 'The company claimed Kyle went missing after leaving work. He left at six thirty, supposedly – that's what Weston told the police, anyway. But he was never seen leaving by anyone else, and he left his car in the car park. When I told the cops about the car, they said he might have decided to go for a walk, or to walk home for a change – three and a half miles! That's when I knew they were on Weston's side.'

Clare chewed the cud, as she did when deep in thought.

'You said you knew where Kyle's body might be buried?' Elspeth looked daggers at her. Trust Clare to go rushing in like a bull in a china shop. 'We need to find the body,' Clare went on, ignoring her. 'So we can prove that Steve Weston killed Kyle.'

Elspeth cleared her throat loudly, trying to catch Clare's eye.

Finn left the room and returned with a shoe-sized box. He placed each of the recovered items inside it, then lowered himself back onto the crate.

'Elspeth told us you thought Kyle's body might be buried somewhere,' Clare continued, a question mark in her voice.

'It's in the quarry,' Finn said in a flat voice. 'The one Weston's covered over.'

Elspeth cut in. 'How can you be so certain, Finn?'

The muscles at Finn's jaw tensed. 'It's where I would have put it, if I'd just killed my employee and didn't want anyone to find his body.'

'He would've had to hide it so the other employees wouldn't find it the next day,' Clare said.

'Exactly. I reckon he could have done it himself. He had all the machinery he needed right there on site.' Finn spoke as if he had carefully thought this through. 'He could have used a forklift to move the body, or the backhoe. Kyle said he knew how to operate it. He used it himself when the operator was off sick, even though Kyle told him he shouldn't without a certificate.'

'Sorry, I'm not following.' Clare leaned forwards, hands on

knees, a deep groove appearing above her nose. 'What's a backhoe?'

'It's a JCB – an articulated digging machine that someone sits inside. The front end digs and the back end scoops up soil or whatever. He'd have had to get Kyle's body into the bucket, somehow. Or he could've used a bulldozer—'

Clare was following intently. 'But what if he killed Kyle inside, in the hut? How did he get the body outside?'

'He dragged it out or rolled it, maybe. He's strong enough. Maybe he called for help. Three men would have made light work of it. They could have taken the body into the quarry, dumped a load of soil over it, and no one would have been any the wiser.'

Clare's head cocked to one side. 'I see, more or less.'

'I told all this to the police. They gave me the brush-off, looked at me like I was some sad sod with addled brains. Said, "No body, no crime."'

'Could you help us find Kyle's body, Mr O'Connor?'

She looked at Clare in surprise.

'There was a lot of information on his laptop.' Finn frowned. 'Lorries arrived at the site waived through without their contents being inspected. Times and dates of suspicious deliveries... Where in the quarry the waste went to, and so forth. The police never returned it. Fortunately, I moved all the files to mine before they took it away. I didn't trust them to investigate it properly.'

Elspeth got in her question. 'You think there might be something useful among the information?'

'I don't know. I've not looked at it since that time. I would have, but that man Weston...' Finn growled from deep in his throat. 'If he knew I was helping you find Kyle's body...'

'How would he find out?'

'He would, believe me. He has friends everywhere, including in the police. All this time I haven't told anyone what was on Kyle's laptop. I knew if I did, it would get back to Weston.'

'We're working with a detective,' Elspeth countered. 'She's on our side.'

A caustic laugh.

'You don't understand, Elspeth. People have been hurt, people who did nothing wrong except resist the pressure Weston put on them. That man is in bed with the vilest of criminals. They won't think twice about punishing anyone who gets in their way. Last year, a farmer was tied to a chair by two men who broke into his property because he'd confronted Weston about his animals getting sick after drinking black water leaching from the ground. They threatened to hack off his right foot if he caused any more trouble. He was on my darts team, a nicer bloke you couldn't ask for. And years ago, a local councillor was thrown off a railway bridge because he wouldn't let Weston walk all over him whenever he wanted to.' Finn's voice began to tremble. 'Both those men were too scared to go anywhere near the cops. They knew they would do nothing to stop those men, quite the opposite, in fact.' He looked from Elspeth to Clare. 'I admire you women for your guts. But you don't know what you're up against.'

'Someone has to do something, don't they?' Clare replied, without hesitation. 'It may as well be us.'

Elspeth wanted to clap her hands and hug Clare but made do with an appreciative nod. Finn stared at the floor. In the lengthening silence, she removed the newspaper photos of Emily Hale and Cindra Patel from her bag and propped them against a nearby sewing machine.

'These young women were murdered, too, Finn. Emily got ill, we think, from the toxins buried in her garden, probably thanks to Steve Weston building houses over land poisoned by toxic waste. After she started speaking out, Weston decided to get rid of her. Then he had Cindra Patel killed. She was collecting information about Weston and his illegal activities for an article, we understand. And now you tell us there are others he's done God knows what to. Surely, you want him stopped? How long can we accept what's going on and do nothing about it?'

Eventually, Finn spoke.

'More than anything else in the world, Elspeth, I want to find Kyle and lay his body to rest. Yes, I want Weston stopped. I appreciate what you women are trying to do. It's brave, beyond measure. But I'm an ordinary man. I'm not sure I can do any more.'

Chapter 43
DC Peters

The same day

'I thought we should talk,' DS Renn said.

It had been nearly a week since their confrontation. They were standing on the fire stairs in chilly early morning sunshine.

Kate sucked on her vape. Her stress levels were mounting. Finding out the DCI had gone rogue, these secretive meetings with DS Renn, and now items supposedly belonging to Weston's former employee found hidden in the old quarry, which in Ashley's words 'show that Kyle really was murdered'. Ashley had even asked for Ms Patel's parents' address because the enquiry team 'might have missed something'.

Turning one's principal suspect in a murder investigation into one's principal informant on a separate murder investigation that one was not actually part of, then supplying said person with information to enable them to conduct their own unofficial investigation, was obviously not standard practice. But how did you proceed when you suspected your boss's boss to be part of an underground criminal network, actively seeking to prevent its crimes being investigated, going so far as to cover up murders it was responsible for? Especially now the DCI knew that she and Rob were onto him. Her training had said nothing about how to cope with such a situation.

The sergeant held a vape to his lips. He looked uncomfortable.

Kate smiled at him. 'How did the Cindra Patel briefing go?'

'Nowhere, as usual.' DS Renn brought the vape to his mouth and coughed. 'The main lines of enquiry look like dead ends. We found CCTV footage of two men getting into a car parked close to Brampton Wood. It led us to two elderly blokes having a stroll. They were miffed about being questioned, accused us of being homophobic. Now the DCI has latched onto Jason Bell, the last known person to see Cindra alive. He lives in one of the mobile homes. Says he was working out by the river and saw Cindra walk by.'

'You don't think it's him?'

'He's an obvious suspect: 48 years old, unemployed, unkempt, hardly speaks to anyone. But we've got nothing on him, and he's denied having anything to do with her death. Specifically, coshing her on the head with one of his free weights, giving it a quick rinse in the river then lugging the body deep into the woods and burying it, all by himself.'

'No murder weapon yet?'

'Nope. A good part of the wood has been searched. I suggested trying to identify the two men Clare Titchfield spotted in the woods that night and looking at your Croatian pair. But the DCI stomped on that idea, said it was too tenuous a connection.' He made an exasperated face. 'It's as if he doesn't want to find her killer.'

'He doesn't.'

Kate met the sergeant's raised eyebrow. It was time for her to lay her cards on the table. She had not yet revealed Ashley's information about DCI Hill, just in case she had been mistaken about the sergeant. But unless he knew what she knew, they had no chance of getting anywhere.

'I have an informant, and what she's given me explains a lot. Why the DCI is always dragging his heels, why he hid the evidence indicating Emily Hale's death wasn't suicide...'

'Go on.'

'She overheard him talking at Steve Weston's party, the weekend before last. You know, the businessman and benefactor—'

'What did she hear?'

'Weston and the DCI were discussing a criminal network, one that both of them are in. DCI Hill is in it up to his neck.'

'Which criminal network?'

'You've heard of the Wise Men?'

'Of course. They're responsible for most of the serious violence and extortion going on for miles around. They punish anyone who steps on their toes or shows any sign of having a free will.' He frowned. 'Are you serious, the DCI is one of them?'

'Him, Weston and another man they called TM – probably Thin Man.'

DS Renn whistled. 'Thin Man... No one has been able to identify him, as far as I know. Word is, he repairs expensive watches as a front. What else did you find out?'

She told him the rest.

'Why didn't you tell me any of this before?' DS Renn pulled at his collar. 'You knew all this when we last talked, didn't you?'

'I did. But I wanted to wait a bit.'

'To make sure I wasn't on the wrong side?' His cheeks flushed. 'How do I know *you're* not on the wrong side?'

'I'd hardly be telling you all this if I was, would I?' She flung her vape into the bucket. Honestly, what was the matter with him?

'It works both ways, Kate. If you want me to trust you, you need to open up. You've told me nothing about yourself or what you're doing here. Why did you leave your last job? All I know is the rumours going round—'

'Which are?'

'That you're either selfish or cowardly, or both.'

'It's true.'

He blinked. 'It is?'

'I was on a job that went wrong. I was still in uniform, had just finished detective training. My partner was wounded by a man we tried to arrest. Suddenly he got out a knife. I panicked and ran upstairs to hide, leaving my partner bleeding. It took me four minutes to call for help. He had to be resuscitated. By some miracle he survived.'

Remembering, she felt queasy. While her colleague lay bleeding on the carpet, she had tried to save herself.

'The investigation said I wasn't at fault, I was temporarily incapacitated, blah blah. I had to take sick leave. To get back in, I had to convince the panel that I wasn't a basket case. Finally, I got a DC job in south London. My past followed me, though. I tried to stick it out but in the end...'

'You tried to start over, out here.' DS Renn clasped her arm. 'If I was suddenly faced with a knife-wielding maniac, I'd probably have run, too. So would a good number of us. You need to let go of the guilt and focus on doing your job and stop giving a fuck what others think.'

'Thanks, Rob.' Relief washed through her. 'You head back, I need a minute.'

Chapter 44
Ashley

The same day

The house was quieter than ever. The TV was off and Brillo lay asleep, emitting the occasional snore, on the living room floor. From outside the house, nothing.

Ashley drank the splash of cognac in her glass, then broke off another square of chocolate. The curtains were drawn against the chill and the standard lamp glowed in the corner. It was only ten o'clock, too early to go to bed. Without Diane around she felt less frustration and stress, for sure. But she had got used to her mother's presence, she realised. For all her faults, Diane had provided an unspoken female solidarity.

She wasn't in the mood for reading or watching TV, and scrolling on her phone wouldn't help with this bout of insomnia. With a sigh, she re-read the latest message from DC Peters, in reply to her request for Cindra's parents' address. Kate had given Mila Patel's mobile number, followed by: *So far, I understand the enquiry team has found nothing of significance in the house. I don't expect that you will be able to find anything either.*

The cryptic remark seemed to provide something bordering

on acceptance of the unofficial visit she had in mind. Well, that was good enough.

With a smile, she re-read Layla's message.

Can't believe you and dad are splitting up. Yes, we should defo talk. Can it wait a week? Life here is crazy busy right now. Hugs, L xxx

The response was typical of her daughter; getting hold of her was often next to impossible.

At the loud ring of her phone, still in her hand, she nearly jolted out of her seat. The ringer was set to maximum in case Elspeth or Clare should urgently need to contact her.

'Hello?' For a horrible moment she imagined Steve Weston at the other end.

'Mum. It's me.'

'Sam! I thought it might be someone else. You saw my message, then?'

Her son hadn't realised just how bad they were. She answered all his questions, stressing that they would both always be his parents, there for him no matter what.

'Better go, Mum,' he said twenty minutes later. 'I'm on duty at the helpline soon.'

'Before you go, Sam...'

'Yeah?'

'Remember the woman next door who died suddenly, a few years ago?' She had an impulse to admit the truth, there and then. But this wasn't a good time. 'I'll tell you another time.'

'Tell me what?'

'I promise to tell you and Layla everything, as soon as I can.'

'Keep safe, Mum.'

She wondered if she should have told him about how she was helping DC Peters, but that too could wait.

After the conversation, her anxious thoughts took over. How long did she have before Steve Weston carried out his threat and handed over the drawing? Would he try other tactics to persuade her to do what he wanted? Should she tell DC Peters about Steve Weston's blackmail attempt? Maybe Kate could do something to protect the three of them.

But what could DC Peters do to protect them when, so far as she could tell, the Wise Men were no closer to being caught? With the help of this Thin Man and his two thugs, Steve Weston remained free to threaten whoever got in his way. The chief inspector had presumably not yet been unmasked as one of the Wise Men. No wonder, with him in charge, the police were so ineffective at solving these murders.

She heard a sharp, dry sound from the back of the house. Her heart beat faster. She waited. There, again. It was from outside. A fox barking, that was all. She got up and inspected the house, which seemed emptier than ever. Brillo carried on snoring, all four paws up, oblivious.

She thought of the bag of Kyle Sutton's things, hidden at the bottom of the quarry. Had Kyle had been another victim of Steve Weston? If the trio could hold out a little longer and somehow manage to find Kyle's body, could that lead to Steve Weston being arrested?

The spurt of excitement faded. They had no means of digging up the quarry and no authority to do so. If the police weren't willing to investigate and not even Kyle's former partner was willing to help because he was too scared of the possible repercussions...

Ashley shivered. She would tuck herself up in bed and try to get some sleep.

The Bad Women

The alarm clock showed 2.40am. She lay in bed, adrenalin coursing, her heart skittering, ears straining. A noise had woken her. What was it?

A minute or so of silence, then a loud thump from downstairs. Someone was trying to break in, or...?

She needed to get help. Zac? The unoccupied mattress stretched beside her. Elspeth? She would be alarmed by her phone ringing in the middle of the night. She found Kate Peters's number on her phone.

Another loud thump. Brillo turning over on the hall floor. What was wrong with her?

As she was dozing off, the fox barked again.

God's sake... Then another noise, one she couldn't place, like a gentle scraping. After a while it stopped. Her heart was still pounding away, though and her cortisol levels must have reached a new high. It was no use, she had to go and check or she'd never get back to sleep.

She put on her dressing gown and slippers and moved the bedroom curtain aside. All looked normal. She picked up a three-kilo neoprene hand weight. Keeping the lights off, she padded downstairs and peeped through the front door spy-hole. No one there. Still clasping the weight, Ashley stood to one side of the glass doors and peered into the garden. Then she opened the doors looking outside until she was satisfied there was no one lurking.

You're overreacting, she told herself, putting down the weight. She placed a slice of bread in the toaster, feeling foolish. Weston hadn't threatened to kill her if she didn't comply, as far as she could remember.

The slice burst out of the toaster, once again setting off her internal alarm. She buttered the toast, trying to remember Weston's exact words.

No, how stupid could someone be? Weston didn't need to threaten to kill her. He'd already killed Kyle, Emily and Cindra.

What was to stop him from killing her, too? He wasn't afraid of the police. He wasn't afraid of anyone.

Ashley bit off a corner of toast, scarcely noticing the slippery crunch. This threat was bigger than any she had known in her life. What if she never saw Sam and Layla again? Elspeth and Clare were in danger, too. But she knew deep in her heart that she couldn't give up, not until she'd done one last thing, anyway. If it came to nothing, she swore to herself, she would admit defeat and confess everything to Kate Peters.

She retrieved her phone and found Cindra's mother's mobile number, then keyed in a message.

Hello Mila, this is Ashley Khan. I got your number from DC Peters. I am helping her find out who is responsible for killing your daughter. Would you be willing to speak to me?

Chapter 45
Ashley

The next day

S he was alone on a vast hillside while lightning flashed. All around, shrubs and trees ignited as they were struck, one by one, their black skeletons visible through the yellow flames leaping into a yellow sky. It was her turn next. There was nowhere to run, no safe place. A crack of lightning zigzagged down from the sky...

With a yell, Ashley jolted out of sleep. A sluggish grey morning crept in from behind the curtains. She was in bed, looking at the bedroom in all its ordinariness.

Well, she'd survived the night, that was one thing. But pain throbbed in her temples and the inside of her mouth was as dry as a pile of cinders. She felt as refreshed as a burnt-out log.

Beside the bed, her phone lit up with a notification. A message from Mila Patel.

Can you come to see me this morning at 11? I've got a shift at the hospital this afternoon. Address is below. Thank you.

She shoved herself upright and grabbed the alarm clock. It

was just gone ten. The address was in Cranleigh; she'd have to hurry to be there on time.

At 11.05am she arrived, only five minutes late, at a newish semi on a quiet, tree-lined road. The door opened within moments of her ringing the bell. A large, handsome woman in bright layers and oversized, black-rimmed glasses greeted her.

'Ashley?'

'Yes, Ashley Khan. You're Mila?'

Light brown hands cupped hers, ushered her inside a large room brimming with arty looking objects. Though cheerful, it was dusty and untidy.

'Ashley, thank you for coming to see me. I'm so grateful to you. Ravi's at work so it's just me. I'll put on some coffee.'

'Great, thank you for getting back to me so quickly. I didn't expect—'

'It'll be easier to talk without Ravi here.' Mila smiled confidingly. 'He can be very headstrong and impulsive. If you were to tell us about...' Her face lost its brightness, and the woman seemed to grope for her bearings.

'I'm very sorry about what happened to Cindra. It must be a terrible time for you. I thought about contacting you before, but I wanted to give you some space after the news.' Ashley removed the bracelet from her bag – a simple wrap-around band, made from a thin sheet of silver. 'Do you recognise this, by any chance?'

'It's hers.' Mila clamped her hand over her mouth then reached out to take the bracelet. Her eyes glittered with tears. 'Where did you find it?'

'Not far from the river.' She couldn't admit that it was found beside a locked caravan. That suggested something worse, somehow.

'Do you know who killed my daughter?' Behind her spectacles, Mila's eyes became huge.

'I don't know for certain. But I think the killer – the man who ordered her death, anyhow – was someone she'd been researching for an article—'

'She was working on that story day and night,' Mila interrupted, a hand pressed to her sternum. 'It seemed to be centred on this one man who trampled over everyone. She wouldn't tell us who it was, in case...' Her voice faltered. 'In case it got us into trouble.'

She wouldn't reveal Weston's name, she decided; that might compromise the police investigation, such as it was, not to mention her own one.

'Do you know anything else about the story she was working on?'

'It was all about people getting away with things they shouldn't. Injustice, that was her big thing at uni. This project was important to her. She was always on her phone. She was so excited when people wanted to talk to her. Emily, especially.' Mila's hands absently touched the top of an armchair. 'She blamed herself for Emily's death, you know. Sometimes she went to the jetty where she and Emily had planned to meet.' She took off the spectacles and dabbed the corner of her eye, then seemed to remember her thread. 'Ravi worried that she might upset the wrong people. She said the story needed to be told. She sent an outline to lots of newspapers and magazines. But no one wanted to touch it.'

'Why not?'

'I think it was the legal aspects; they didn't want to be sued. She was pinning her hopes on someone at the BBC taking it on.' Mila looked away, her voice fading.

'Have the police said anything to you about who they think the killer is?'

'No. They came here and rifled through Cindra's room. DCI Hill assured me he would do everything he could to find Cindra's killer, but we have heard nothing since except platitudes and excuses.' Mila looked directly at her. 'Please help us, Ashley. What has happened... it is beyond words. This killer, he must be punished. He has taken the jewel in our lives. To go on without her, to be reminded every day she is gone... It is a living death.'

Ashley hesitated. Her mouth felt dry, suddenly.

'I'll help you find him,' she said. 'But please, don't tell anyone else I said that. There are bad people in Elven – inside the police, too.'

'I understand. Cindra said something like that.'

'I need to find out what Cindra knew. Is there a copy of the story she was working on?' She closed her eyes and offered up a silent prayer. This was what she needed most of all.

'It was on her laptop. But the police have already searched her room. They couldn't find her laptop or phone. They said they were probably with her when she was...' Mila took off her glasses and wiped her eyes. 'She carried her laptop everywhere in those last weeks. She said she needed it for her story.' A sliver of a smile. 'I was so proud of her accomplishments. Ravi thought she was naïve, but I always had faith in her. At university she won a prize for the best article. Her tutor said she would go on to do great things.'

'Was there anything else she might have used, apart from the laptop? A PC, a notebook device, an actual notebook?'

Mila's brow wrinkled. 'I don't know of anything else, though there was a tape recorder. Digital recorder, I mean. She read into it sometimes. The police didn't find that, either.'

'Do you know where she kept it?'

'In her desk drawer. I'll take you upstairs and show you.'

She followed Mila up two flights of stairs. The paintwork on the walls and skirting boards was chipped and grubby in places. Mila opened a door to a simply furnished room painted in turquoise containing a single bed, dominated by a heavy desk.

'It's not here.' Mila sifted through the contents of the top drawer. Ashley stood beside her, observing what she could. Batteries, stationery, sticky notes, glue, highlighters. A stack of business cards with *Cindra Patel, Freelance Journalist* printed on thick card. 'Nor here.' She opened and closed the remaining drawers, revealing nothing of interest.

'Could she have hidden it somewhere?' Cindra might have been concerned about someone trying to get hold of the story before it was published.

'You are welcome to look. Anywhere you like, go ahead.'

'Thanks.'

She opened the first drawer of the chest of drawers. It was still filled with an assortment of small items: knickers, bras, camisole, scarf, gloves, socks... She pushed the drawer shut and opened the next. This felt ghoulish, and being watched made it even worse.

A thought struck her. 'What about back-ups?'

'She used to back up religiously. She was very security conscious.'

'Using what? Disk drives, memory sticks?'

'A memory stick. The police asked about that. too. They searched in here for a long time but they couldn't find any.' Mila stood in the doorway. 'I will leave you to look, dear.'

She gestured her thanks.

After searching the bedside cabinet, the shelves inside the wardrobe and a jewellery box, she started on less obvious places. She picked up a small wooden box and opened the lid to a tangle of hair bands and a wrapped-up piece of Blu Tack. Then, a pencil case containing felt-tips; a tin of birthday cards, theatre tickets and tram tickets; and a mug filled with foreign coins. Gloom quashed her cautious optimism. This would turn out to be a waste of time. She had lifted the woman's hopes for nothing.

Beside a thick, nearly melted-away candle lay a box of matches. She picked that up too and slid it open – only matches. Disappointment snagged in her throat.

There was nowhere left to look. Only a vase sitting on its own on a shelf. She stood on a chair, reached up and slipped a couple of fingers inside the rim. Soft, brittle flakes met her touch.

Oh fuck, it was someone's ashes. She was about to put the vase back when her fingertips touched a hard object, deep down. She drew out a metal keyring.

What? She nudged the inner section. The keyring unfolded, revealing a rectangular metal tongue. A memory stick.

Chapter 46
DC Peters

The same day

K ate sat opposite the bundle of printed paper and began to read. At the other end of the kitchen table, Ashley sat watching as each page was picked up, read and put down.

The Two Faces of Steve Weston
By Cindra Patel

Steve Weston is a well-known, widely liked businessman and benefactor with strong links to the local community. He has owned the Brampton pub The Anglers since 2021. Among his many contributions to local organisations, he has donated £10,000 to the St John the Baptist church restoration fund and £12,000 to Elven Foodbank. The construction company he founded in 2002, S. G. Weston Construction Services, employs 53 people and has built many homes and offices in the region, often on 'brownfield' sites. His personal portfolio of properties includes his grade II-listed 'castle', Bourne Hall. However, there is another, less well-known side to this man. While researching this article, I heard many times that Weston is part of a secretive criminal ring who have effectively gained control over aspects of local life.

I first heard of the Wise Men when I overheard a conversation at a funeral in a Brampton church. (Two days earlier a local councillor had been found dead under a railway bridge.) Understandably, people are reluctant to speak openly about them. I began to look into Weston and his affairs, and rumours suggesting he is one of the Wise Men.

This article contains allegations that Weston has committed range of crimes, from illegally disposing of toxic waste to extortion and conspiracy to murder. Due to their concerns about safety, my sources wish to remain anonymous. I myself have been threatened by Weston, as was Brampton resident, Emily Hale, now dead in suspicious circumstances.

Emily Hale's death and Summerfield estate

- Emily Hale's body was found on 10 January in a former quarry owned by Weston. Emily phoned me shortly before her death. Says her ill health was from exposure to toxins buried in her garden on Summerfield estate. Our planned meeting never happened. Despite my statement to police her death was treated as suicide.
- 120 people living on Summerfield estate, built in 2018 on site of a landfill dating from 1972; Weston claimed site has been remediated.
- Phone call with Emily: Weston to blame for her ill health as she stated this in her post to Brampton's public Facebook group [taken down by admin within hours].

- Emily sent me 56 photos of objects/materials from estate gardens and results of soil tests from gardens of 5 residents at their own expense – 'well above allowable concentrations of mercury, arsenic, lead and other toxins and significant levels of PCPs' [polycarbonatephenols].
- Council: 'Independent soil testing is underway to assess if any action needed. Before permission to build was granted, measurements were made to ensure no toxic substances present in concentrations harmful to human health.'

Toxic waste disposal at Brampton Quarry

In 2020, the Environment Agency gave Weston a license to reclaim the upper quarry; works completed last year. The stated aim of returning the land to its natural state has changed to building homes on the site. This is legal, but evidence that SW used the quarry works to illegally dispose of toxic waste, making a substantial profit:

- Log from S2 of vehicles with hazardous waste markings entering the site (7.45pm to 9pm when no one on site except Weston) and photos of loads being removed. S2 told by one lorry driver that the loads were old electrical transformer cores and shredded cannisters of oil, which filled the cores [oil is rich in highly toxic chemicals e.g., PCPs].
- S3: While drunk Weston boasted he was paid large sums into his Swiss bank account to receive 'not strictly speaking kosher waste, difficult to get rid of legally' at the quarry works. He said this came from 'legit businesses' and 'a local kingpin' set up regular deliveries 'for a cut'.

- S1 says he was victim of repeated intimidation by 'two bastards who did Weston's dirty work' and 'I am not the only one'. He suspects Weston used coercion/bribery to get site inspector to falsify his measurements. He and other councillors were coerced by SW to 'smooth the way' for the Quarry Homes Development Proposal; Wise Men protect Weston from 'the wrong sort of attention'; Weston has a 'top cop feeding out of his hand' and paid a PI to find 'skeletons in the closet' of local planning officials.
- S2 was told all his animals would be killed unless he stopped his complaints re. impact of the quarry works on his animals/land. He suggested Weston bribed Environment Agency officials to overlook concerns that he was dumping toxic waste in secret.

End: Have we come full circle?

In 2017, Weston built housing on land which he knew was, or was likely to be contaminated with toxic chemicals, despite the potential health hazards. Seven years later, despite evidence of the health impact on Summerfield estate's residents and of Weston being responsible for the illegal burial of toxic waste within Brampton's supposedly reclaimed upper quarry, alongside allegations of serious criminality, Weston has not been charged with any offence. At the time of writing, he is awaiting permission to build 140 homes on the 'reclaimed' quarry.

As she was reading the draft article, a horrible sense of irony struck her. Cindra Patel was dead too, now. Killed for trying to make Emily Hale's death count for something.

'Where did you find this?' Kate picked up the memory stick and inserted it into her rucksack pocket. A warmth began to spread from deep in her midriff. She wanted to kick the table leg.

The Bad Women

'In a vase in Cindra's room. It was on a shelf, high up. The log mentioned in the article is on the stick. So is this. It's Emily's Facebook post.' Ashley pushed a sheet of paper towards her, showing a screenshot.

Hello Brampton people.

I think a lot of you will want to know what's been going on in our village and how the houses on Summerfield were built on poisoned land. I lived on the estate for 5 years before I had to get out due to my health.

When we moved in, I used to go in the garden all the time. But from the start we noticed things. A foul smell in the mornings. I started getting headaches, which I'd never had in my life before. My health went downhill, I couldn't do things I'd always done, like cycling to the shops.

The doctors didn't know what was wrong with me at first. I spent all my savings on remedies from alternative practitioners and treatments that didn't work – the Dolphin Clinic, mainly. Our dog used to dig up weird stuff in the garden. Metal coils, rubbery bits, God knows what. By the time we twigged it could be affecting our health, it was too late. I now have liver and kidney disease and countless things wrong with me. Sometimes I feel like an old lady, though I'm only 24.

One doctor told me he thought I'd been poisoned by arsenic and heavy metals. Then it all started to make sense.

I blame Steve Weston for what happened to me. His company built the estate over a toxic dump. He knew the health risks but making money was more important to him. Lots of people say I'm wrong because they like Steve, he's such a generous guy, so caring, how

could he do something like this. I say, look at the evidence then
make up your mind.

I don't care anymore what might happen to me as a result of this.
It's time to do something. We need to get the estate declared unsafe
for human habitation and get justice for Steve Weston's victims.
Most importantly we need to stop anything like this from
happening again. Anyone willing to join me to take action against
this man, please message me.

Emily

Kate took a tissue from the box Ashley pushed towards her,
patted her eyes then blew her nose.

'Is any of this going to help your investigation into Steve Weston?' Ashley gestured to the pages in front of Kate.

'I think so,' she said, glad to have something concrete to focus
on. 'It shows he had a motive to kill both Emily and Cindra – and
there's information here we can use to investigate Weston further.'

Ashley frowned. 'But not enough to arrest him?'

Kate paused before replying. This conversation was bizarre.
She was effectively collaborating with the main suspect in a
murder case.

'I don't think so,' she replied, honestly. 'To charge him with
Emily and Cindra's murders, we'd need stronger evidence. Physical evidence.' There was no point arresting Weston only for him
to call his lawyer and be released. That would only alert the DCI,
putting both her and the sergeant in danger, not to mention
Ashley et al.

The corners of Ashley's mouth dropped.

'You did well to get hold of this, Ashley,' Kate said. 'You're
making better progress investigating Cindra Patel than our team.'

'If you can't arrest him... What if he tries to hurt my friends –
or me?'

'Has he threatened you directly?'

'He's got Clare's drawing.' Ashley went to the sliding doors and looked into the back garden, bare except for a bush of fiery red camelias. 'He warned me to stop interfering in his affairs, or he'd send it to the police.'

'Well, it seems to have turned up.' The package had been hand-delivered to the station an hour ago, addressed to: *The detectives on the Tara Sanderson case*. Kate had collected the cylinder-shaped item.

'What?' Ashley's eyes nearly popped out.

'I haven't opened it yet. Depending on what I find, I may have to arrest you on suspicion of murdering your ex-neighbour. If we charge you, you'll probably be detained for a few days until you go before the local magistrate.'

'So, I have until when to find something else on Steve Weston? Tomorrow? The day after?'

'Is there something in particular you have in mind?' Kate couldn't help smiling. This woman had balls, she had to admit.

Ashley leaned onto her forearms. 'If someone came to you saying they knew where a body was buried – someone who Steve Weston had killed – would you be able to search for it?'

'Who does the body belong to?'

'Kyle Sutton.'

'And the someone is Finn O'Connor?'

A nod.

'It would depend where the body was,' Kate replied, 'and how difficult the search was. If it was on private property, we'd need authorisation. With the way things are, I wouldn't be able to go to my boss.'

Ashley frowned.

'Her boss is the chief inspector you told me about,' Kate explained. Given how far she had gone down this unusual, no doubt reckless path, she may as well go all out. 'Where does Finn think the body is?'

'Inside the filled-in quarry.'

'It's unlikely then. We'd need to show reasonable grounds to get a warrant.'

There was zero chance of getting permission to search that quarry, not while it belonged to Steve Weston, anyway.

Kate found DS Renn at his desk in a quiet corner of Room 3. It was a crisp, sunny day; most of their colleagues were probably 'pursing enquiries' outside.

Ashley Khan had found a memory stick in a vase in Cindra Patel's former bedroom, she told the sergeant.

'She found the stick in a vase?'

She smiled. 'It was under Cindra's gran's ashes.'

'Good for her. I doubt I'd have looked there.'

'Ashley gave me this.' Kate held up a bracelet inside an evidence bag. 'Clare Titchfield found it outside the locked caravan on the 29th of January, the night she saw two men up to something in the woods. Cindra's mother has confirmed it belonged to Cindra.'

'I don't believe it.' He rolled his eyes. 'Those women are putting us to shame.'

'Was Cindra killed inside that abandoned caravan, do you think?'

'I should think. But the DCI doesn't want us to break into private property unless we have evidence.'

'That's a pathetic excuse.'

'I know. Presumably someone still has the keys to that caravan, but we can't find any record of who owns it. The registration plate vanished long ago.'

'I honestly can't see how Jason Bell could have killed her then lugged the body, unless he's going for the world strong man record. How would one man have moved a body into the middle of the woods on his own?'

'Agreed. It makes no sense that he's a suspect. Unless the DCI is trying to stop the real killer from being arrested.'

'By the way, a package came for me. I think it's the drawing I've been looking for.'

'The one meant to show Tara Sanderson being pelted with fruit?' The corners of his eyes crinkled. 'I need to see this. Where is it?'

'In my locker.'

'Why didn't you just open it?'

She hesitated. She needed to tell the sergeant everything, now.

'Because if it clearly shows the woman being attacked, we'd have to arrest her.'

The sergeant's frown deepened. 'Why would arresting her be a problem?'

'Because I've promised to delay her arrest, to give her a chance to get more evidence against Weston.'

DS Renn's eyebrows shot up. 'Excuse me?'

'I know it's not standard procedure.'

'It fucking isn't.'

'She's smart, Rob. She could find something to help us.'

With an exaggerated groan, the sergeant pushed himself to his feet. 'Let's have a look at this drawing, then.'

The basement locker area was empty. Cautiously, Kate removed the cylindrical package from her locker. DS Renn took it and slid out a roll of thick white paper, which he unrolled onto a nearby bench.

'Looks like you have your drawing, Kate. It definitely shows a woman being attacked with fruit. And no way is this anyone's imagination.'

Kate looked down at the drawing. The fury in the faces united the small group positioned around a fruit bowl. They were pelting a woman crouching nearby, in front of a fridge, her hands warding off blows. It was precisely detailed, so vivid she could have been at the scene herself.

'This is Elspeth.' Kate pointed to the elderly woman with chunky earrings who was selecting a large, round fruit. 'And here's Ashley.' She pointed to the petite woman with a heart-shaped face and wavy hair.

'I remember interviewing them.' Rob squatted down beside her. 'That looks like an apple she's about to toss.' He pointed at Ashley. 'The guy on the disabled scooter... John someone?'

'John Briars.' She indicated the older woman with short hair and glasses. 'That must be Ursula Chalice. What's that she's holding?'

Rob took out a pair of reading glasses. He put them on and peered at the drawing.

'Sheet music.'

'It's her! She's in a choir.'

'Bloody hell, Kate. They're going down for this.'

They stared at the drawing in silence. Whoever did this was a talented and experienced artist, which Clare undoubtedly was, with her years of drawing birds and an exhibition at a local gallery.

DS Renn pushed himself to his feet, grimacing. 'What's Clare's last name again?'

'Titchfield'.

'Look, her initials are in the corner. C. T.'

'So, she did lie about seeing two men in Tara Sanderson's kitchen. It was all a fabrication to protect her friends.' Kate lowered herself to the bench. This was hard evidence, even if Clare carried on maintaining the drawing was from imagination. A jury would see it for what it was, a depiction of a concerted attack.

There was no note inside the cylinder. She re-wrapped the drawing and locked it away.

Kate and the sergeant walked in silence to the café, wind bending clumps of daffodils.

It was good to know that she was no longer alone against the dark side, and that DS Renn was at her side. He had a solid build; if he needed to physically defend himself, he would likely make a decent go of it.

At their usual table, Kate toyed with her cappuccino. Two women with fractious children ensured they weren't overheard.

'We've got to bring them in soon, haven't we?' She looked up at DS Renn. 'Clare, Ashley and Elspeth, at least.'

'We'll bring in Clare first. We need her to say that the drawing is real and confess to fabricating that story.'

'What about Ashley? I promised her a couple of days.'

'We'll wait and see what Clare says. There's no point cutting off our noses.'

'What about the DI? Are we running any of this past her?'

'We need to be careful. If she's in on what the DCI's up to...' Rob massaged his temple. 'I saw her with him again this morning.'

'And?'

'Something's up. She saw me as she left his office and looked at me like I was a turd on legs.' He downed his espresso. 'I looked in as I went past; I overheard the DCI talking to someone on his mobile.'

'What did he say?' She wondered how good his hearing was. The door wouldn't have been open, surely?

'"I agree, mate. We have to stop them before they bring us all down."'

'The DCI was having a chinwag with Weston?'

DS Renn shrugged.

'Who did he mean by "them", do you think? Ashley and her friends?' Kate stared at him, recognition dawning. 'Us?'

He pushed away his espresso cup.

'Maybe he meant just us two,' she said. 'Or us *and* those three.'

'Hill said something else, too.' He sighed, looking at the table. '"I'll do what I can from my end."'

'Fuck, that sounds ominous.'

The fear she had blocked rushed in. They were two low-ranking cops trying to take on their senior officer along with a secret criminal ring that the whole town was afraid of... What were they thinking? Three people had lost their lives already.

'I'm sorry, Kate. I didn't mean to scare you. Are you alright?'

'I'm fine.' She fished out the remains of her sandwich and took a bite. Carbs always helped when she felt like this. 'How will we ever get enough on the Wise Men to charge them, let alone the DCI?'

DS Renn was slow to reply.

'We need to corroborate the claims from Cindra Patel. If we can track down her sources and get them to make a statement...'

'That's a big if.' Clearly, they had been too scared to give their names, why would they do so now?

'I know. We'll need something solid on the DCI, too.'

'We could ask for help from outside – the anti-corruption lot or regional organised crime, is it now?'

The sergeant shook his head emphatically. 'If we go to them half-cocked, we'll look like idiots, and word might reach the wrong people.'

'Could we go to the chief super?' Detective Chief Superintendent Snow, the DCI's boss, didn't exactly inspire confidence. She had seen him in a video on the Force website. He'd come across as old-fashioned and opinionated.

'No, we need to involve as few people as possible until we have evidence that can't be dismissed. Then we'll either call for help or arrest the DCI ourselves, and the rest of those bastards. Sorry, Kate. We're on our own.'

'What if they try to kill us in the meantime? How are we going to protect ourselves?' Her voice sounded shrill to her ears. 'I don't think pepper spray is going to cut it.' The danger was what she feared most about being a police officer. But she had never expected the enemy to be a fellow officer.

The sergeant didn't reply.

'And what about Ashley and the others? We can't protect them either, can we?'

'No, we can't.'

The noisy children and their mothers had left, deepening the silence. Kate put on her coat and got up to pay. As the sergeant joined her, hands in his jacket pockets, she wondered how long it would take to regret what she was about to say.

'One thing is puzzling me, Rob. How did you overhear the DCI talking on the phone? I mean, if the door was shut...'

A second. Two seconds.

'I read his lips.'

'Oh, when did you learn that? Not that anyone shouldn't, it must be useful—'

'I'm going deaf, Kate.'

'Shit. I had no idea.'

'It's a genetic thing. Runs in my family. I learnt to lip-read years ago. The hearing loss is manageable, for now. I can hear most of what's going on. I'm not going to be as deaf as a post overnight.'

'Do they know? I mean the DI, anyone in HR?'

'No, and I'm not telling anyone till I have to. They'd kick me out of the Force.'

'I'll not say a word. Anything I can do to help, just ask.'

They walked back to the station.

'There's one thing you can do,' DS Renn said as they were about to separate. 'Come back with me, tonight.'

She gave him a quizzical look. 'I'm not into men, you know. Or women, anymore.'

'Purely as a sensible precaution. My place is a ten-minute drive, not a long bus ride. There's a sofa-bed. I'd sleep a lot better if I didn't have to spend the night worrying about something happening to you.'

It made total sense, she had to agree.

'Do you have a spare toothbrush?'

He gave a thumbs up and bounded up the stairs. Kate headed into the bathroom, smiling.

Chapter 47
Ashley

The same day

The lack of sleep showed in her face, reflected in the mirror. Today, she felt every one of her 55 years. She dragged the brush through her hair and put on makeup. She needed to be presentable. There was no time to waste. If she was on the verge of being arrested and possibly locked up for months, she needed to do this while there was still an opportunity.

She grabbed her mobile and called Finn's number. Phone to ear, she hunted for her car keys and her trainers.

'Please, Finn,' she urged. 'Pick up!'

She was prepared to believe in anything right now, including telepathy. A voice message cut into the ring tone, inviting her to call back or leave a message. Then a real time voice broke in – rough at the edges, diffident.

'Who is it?'

'Finn, it's Ashley. Elspeth's friend.'

'I know who you are. Elspeth mentioned you.' He sounded weary, not to mention wary.

'I need to speak to you, urgently. Are you at home now? I'll drive straight over.'

An exhalation at the other end. 'I'm not dressed. I don't have anything more to say. You'd be wasting your time—'

'Please, Finn.'

A long pause. The sound of knuckles cracking. 'You're a stubborn one. Alright then, give me half an hour.'

Chapter 48
Bird Woman

9 March: 2.30pm

Chewing the remains of my sandwich, which takes longer than I expect, I tie my boot laces. If I don't get a move on, it'll be getting dark before I'm back home. I double-check the back door is locked and bolted top and bottom, and all the windows are shut and locked. Satisfied that my abode is as safe as I can make it without installing steel bars in the windows, I drop an apple into my pocket and set off.

The cottage is starting to feel like a prison. Sometimes I dread returning to another long sojourn indoors, all because some men have no idea how to behave.

I follow the back roads towards the river rather than cut across the wood. I have a mental image of the young journalist's killers as the two men I spotted lurking behind my back fence. They deserve to have their balls stabbed with a darning needle. I doubt I'd ever have the balls to do this, but imagining it is rather pleasant.

All seems quiet on the police investigation front of late. There have been no more reporters in the wood talking to cameras.

The police seem to have forgotten about the other dead, quite possibly murdered woman. Maybe the detective is doing something behind the scenes. Ashley seems to have faith in her. I just hope she doesn't show up here to interrogate me again. Now she's got her hands on my drawing – if what she told Ashley is to be trusted – she might be planning to arrest me for wasting police time and goodness knows what other crimes I've committed to keep my friends out of trouble. I wish I had never drawn the godforsaken thing. If I ever happen to stumble upon another crime scene, I shall most certainly avert my eyes and hurry on.

The wind, a brisk northerly, picks up as I approach the river. I speed up, wishing I had worn my coat. The river has that slightly off smell that it sometimes has, a signal that something is not right.

I've told Ashley we should contact the environment people and report Weston for dumping toxic waste in the quarry and building homes over land that is killing people. She wants to wait until we know for sure he's committed or arranged the three murders, so he can be arrested and hopefully sent to prison – otherwise he'll know we've been squealing and send those two creepy men after us.

Will they try to scare us into submission by chopping off our toes, I wonder? Or have we managed to make these vile men so angry that they'll kill us and be done with it? On balance I'd rather come face to face with these men and have it out with them, rather than constantly peering into the shadows wondering if this will be my last day.

5.50pm

Have been sitting in my chair for the past twenty minutes, trying to recover my equilibrium.

I heard a noise outside the cottage – a creak then a sound like a laugh – and opened the front door and peered into the darkness. But no lurking men, only the distant stir of branches and the wind's soft moan. I was about to close the door when I made out something propped against the gate. Aided by the light-sensitive lamp I've installed over my front door, I went down the path to see what it was – a doll, dressed in modern clothing with a plume of shiny platinum blonde hair and a smiling red mouth. The sort of doll any small girl might have.

At first, I didn't notice anything strange, except that it was on my side of the gate, facing the wrong way – inwards, towards the cottage. Assuming someone must have found the doll lying nearby and placed it here, I bent down and picked it up, intending to display it more prominently. Then I saw that the feet were missing – cut off below the ankles. I dropped the doll as if it had scalded me and ran inside.

I'm going to make a mug of cocoa now and settle down with my blanket and the radio. I don't want to have to think about that butchered thing but I know it's going to niggle at me for the rest of the evening. Who left it there, and why?

The answer seems straightforward enough. Someone is trying to frighten me into changing back into what I used to be, a harmless eccentric with zero interest in the ways of other humans. I admit, right now, I am tempted.

Chapter 49
Ashley

The same day

'Ashley,' Finn said in a dull voice. 'You'd better come in.' He was broad and towered over her. A black, grey-tinged beard encroached onto his cheeks, hiding his lips. In the poor light it seemed to merge with his dark grey jumper.

'Hello, Finn. Pleased to meet you.'

The only reply was a faint noise that contained no element of welcome. She followed the man into a large room dominated by a table. Woodsmoke lingered. Heavy curtains, half drawn, blocked most of the daylight.

Finn didn't sit or offer her a seat. He listened impassively as she described her visit to Cindra's mother and her discovery of the memory stick, then took the printed draft article she handed him.

Leaning over the table, he read without speaking. When he'd placed the last page on the pile, he stood there, head down as if deep in thought. Suddenly he turned away, his hands over his face and his shoulders heaving.

She slipped out of the room.

Nearly half an hour later, Finn came into the kitchen, where she was sitting with the cup of tea she'd made.

'I've changed my mind,' he said gruffly. 'We need to find Kyle's body.' He was holding an A4 graph pad. The words *SITE ACTIVITY* were written in capitals on the cover. 'I've had another look at the stuff on his laptop. Like I thought, he was logging the spots in the quarry where suspicious loads were dumped. He also made sketches of the site.'

He opened the pad. Ashley bent over the drawing. It was a quarry from above, she realised, in outline – a somewhat lopsided circle. Superimposed on the outline was a grid of squares and part squares, marked in pencil. Each contained a number from one to twenty-seven.

'They divided up the quarry with a grid system,' Finn explained. 'They filled it from the bottom to the top, layer by layer, starting at layer one, square one at the western edge of the most southerly row, filling to the eastern edge of that row on square three. Then they filled the squares in the second row, filling in the other direction from east to west. And so on, row by row, layer by layer, till they'd filled in the whole thing.'

'How big are the squares?'

'They're forty by forty metres.'

'OK... What about those circles?' Superimposed on the grid were three much smaller circles, shaded inside.

'They could be boreholes. Kyle mentioned liquid waste coming in, too – all of illegal.'

Finn turned the pages and pointed to a drawing of two squares labelled '11' and '12'.

'The key thing is,' he continued in a slightly more animated tone, 'we know from this where they stopped work at the end of day that Kyle disappeared. It was a Monday. They'd reached the boundary of squares eleven and twelve – that's forty-four metres from the eastern edge of the quarry and thirty-eight metres from the southern edge. According to this diagram, the top of the layer they were filling was two metres below the surface. The layers were always one metre deep, as far as I can see.'

'Is that important?'

'It means they'd finished filling square eleven and the next day would have gone on to fill square twelve. So, the body is likely to be buried somewhere on that boundary, between two and three metres down – which means we don't have to search the whole square. The other thing... At the end of each day Kyle recorded the readings of the bulldozer's GPS. Here.' He flipped to another page and back again. 'We know the exact position on that boundary in decimal latitude and longitude where they stopped work that Monday – this lower left corner.' He pointed to a spot on the drawing. 'Which would be the obvious place to start searching.'

'OK. But I don't get why you think the body is going to be on the boundary. How can we be sure that whoever killed Kyle dumped his body there? They had the whole of the quarry to choose from.'

'Because that's where there would have been a change in the level.' He sounded frustrated. 'Of course, I can't say for sure. The body could be anywhere in that quarry – or anywhere else.'

She said nothing, still at a loss.

'I'll try to explain.' He cleared his throat and fixed his eyes on her, his expression tense with concentration. 'Let's say they had an altercation after the others had left that ended up with Weston killing Kyle. Most likely they would have been inside the site hut, but that isn't important. It was February, so it would be dark by five. Weston would have the cover of darkness and no one around to question what he was doing. The quarry would have been the perfect grave. By then it was nearly full, so access would have been easier. He would've had to make sure that the burial site didn't attract attention, though; he needed to bury the body somewhere deep enough for it not to be spotted as it decomposed.'

Finn took a long breath, his fingers tapping the worktop.

'Inside the quarry there would have been two levels – the top layer, two metres down and the layer below, a metre below that. They were mostly using reclaimed soil as filler, Kyle said, along with the toxic stuff, which was probably chopped or shredded. The filler would have been compacted by vehicles repeatedly going over the surface, meaning the surface of those layers would have been fairly flat. So, yes, in theory he could have moved the body from the hut to anywhere inside that quarry, with someone else's help or using a forklift, say. But he would've needed to dig a hole big enough for the body, moving heavy machinery back into the quarry to do so unless he had some men to help him dig a grave by hand. Then he'd have had to dump the body, fill in the hole and smooth it over so it didn't stand out; making sure nothing was visible that someone might notice after a while – it could have been days or weeks before they got around to filling that spot over.'

Finn's cheeks were flushed. His voice became more animated.

'Whereas dumping the body on the boundary would have been much easier and quicker. He could've just dropped the body onto the lower level and covered it over by hand using whatever soil was around with a shovel or whatever. He wouldn't have needed that much. There could well have been soil piled up nearby to use the next day, or he could've just shoved some over from the higher side. Next day they'd have carried on with the operation, dumping more soil over the body, not even guessing it was there.' Finn dipped his head. 'Actually, I heard from Sandy the bloke he worked with. That next day it was business as usual. When Kyle didn't turn up, they shuffled the jobs round until they could get another ops manager in. No mention of anything untoward.' A bitter laugh. 'Of course there wasn't.'

'I get it now – I think.' She met Finn's eyes. 'But even if we assume the body is somewhere on the boundary, if it's two or three metres down, wouldn't we need one of those mechanical diggers? That's assuming we could get inside the site, even. Clare says there's an eight-foot wire fence around it now. And could we definitely find the position of these squares, now the quarry has been covered over?'

'It would be tricky, for sure.' Finn pulled pensively on his beard. 'As you say, we'd need an excavator, a small one anyway. To get into the site we'd need bolt cutters. To avoid detection, you'd have to go in at night, presuming there's no cameras or alarms. And to have any chance of spotting the body, we'd need a good set of lights. By now it would be seriously decomposed, so probably not much left apart from the skeleton, and that could quite easily be chopped into bits with the machinery. Also, we'd want to take heavy duty gloves and maybe masks in case we came into contact with asbestos or cyanides, or whatever... But marking out the boundary of those two grid squares on the ground shouldn't be too hard. We've got the coordinates right here in latitude and longitude.' He tapped the notebook. 'You could use any portable GPS or a phone with Google Maps.'

Ashley stood and poured herself a glass of water. Her body was all over the place lately from lack of sleep, shivery one minute, too hot the next. And now it felt as if another, weirdly fearless, woman had stepped into her body.

'We're going to do this, then?'

Finn cocked his head, his eyes narrowing. 'The cops are the ones who should be doing this, not us.'

'They're not going to.' She stood facing him. 'I've already asked the detective who's helping us, the one we're helping, rather. She can't get permission to search the quarry. Not to mention, one of her bosses might be on Weston's side.'

'You want me to risk a conviction for trespass and criminal damage and whatever else on the slim chance we might be able to find Kyle's body in there?'

He was right, this whole idea was incredibly risky. But it was her last chance to make things right. Maybe they could even save Brampton.

'If you don't, who else will? His body's down there some-where, isn't it?'

Finn stroked his beard for a long time, then shrugged. 'It'll be one hell of a job. But I know someone who might be able to help us.'

Ashley drove home on a high. She'd done it, had got what she'd come for.

But to find Kyle's body in a hole over one hundred metres across... The more she thought about it, the more difficult the task seemed. What if the earth had shifted since the burial and they missed the body? What if they accidentally broke the body into pieces? What if it wasn't in the quarry at all?

All she wanted to do, was have a cup of tea, a bath and a long nap. First though, Brillo needed a walk.

The terrier made a big fuss of her when she got home and was clearly ready for a walk. She wolfed down a hunk of bread and cheese, attached his lead to his collar and set off to the lake.

Clouds scudded across the sky. She kicked through the carpet of oak leaves, grateful for the quietness of the place. In a flash of anger, Craig came to mind. Had he told Steve anything about her he shouldn't have?

Her heart leapt at her phone's ring.

'Hello?'

'It's DC Peters. Given the situation I advise you, Elspeth and Clare to stick together as much as possible from now on, especially after dark. Could you find somewhere to stay for a while, the three of you?'

'For how long?'

'For the next few days, at least.' Voices in the background.

'Sorry, I have to go. Call me if you find anything significant, or in an emergency.'

She called Brillo and set off for home, mulling over the conversation. Once inside the front gate she let the dog off the lead as usual. Instead of waiting for her to open the door, he pushed his head into the base of the hedge.

'Get away from that!' He was chewing on something there.

She yanked the dog away by his torso, unlocked the front door and shooed him inside, then crouched down by the hedge. Someone had left red meat there. She scooped the two uneaten chunks into a doggy bag.

'Hello there. Is anything the matter?'

Ken. He peered over the front fence, clad in a beanie, quilted jacket and jogging bottoms.

'I found these pieces of meat under my hedge.' Ashley held up the doggy bag. 'The dog's just eaten one. Someone must have put it there on purpose.'

'How awful. Some dog-hating people put poisoned meat down, you know.'

She shook her head, irritated by the man. 'You haven't seen anyone do anything like that, have you?'

'No, 'fraid not.' Ken stood there, looking mystified.

'Oh, by the way.' She recalled DC Peters's advice. 'You don't know any local places to stay, do you? Airbnbs, holiday cottages...'

'My niece has an Airbnb but she's in Carlisle. You'd probably want somewhere closer.'

'Ideally.'

'Are you taking a holiday, then?'

'Sort of. Me and a couple of friends.' She managed a smile. 'It's a bit last minute. We need somewhere from tonight.' Ken didn't reply, rubbing his cheek. 'I've got to get Brillo to the vet.'

Under the bright kitchen lights, she examined one of the chunks. Something was inside. Brillo sat at her feet, eyes trained on the meat, clearly hoping another piece might come his way.

With a kitchen knife she dug out a grey pellet and stared at it, her stomach flipping.

Was it a slug pellet? Or rat poison, or...? She inspected the other piece. It, too, had a pellet inserted. Her heart began to gallop. A cold sweat broke out. How long would it take for whatever was in that pellet to work? She rang the vet's number. The line was busy. She put the meat back in the doggy bag and called Brillo.

On the way to the vet's, she phoned Elspeth.

'Hi, it's me. I've just had a call from DC Peters – she wants the three of us to stay together from now on. We need to find somewhere to stay, from tonight, a B&B or something. Do you know anywhere? Somewhere close enough that we can get back here quickly if we need to.'

'I've always fancied going to The Spinney,' Elspeth said. 'It's expensive, though. I'll have a look on the internet for some others. Dog friendly, I presume?'

'Yes, good point.' She glanced behind her. Brillo was tugging at his harness. 'I'll tell Clare to go over to yours. I'll phone once I'm back from the vet. I've got an emergency with the dog.'

'What's the matter with him?'

'He ate some poisoned meat.'

'Flaming heck. What See You Next Tuesdays some people are.'

She rang Clare's number but Clare didn't pick up. Ashley left a message.

'Clare, it's Ash. The three of us need to stay somewhere for a while. Can you get over to Elspeth's place straight away? Bring your undies and toothbrush. Oh, and please call Elspeth as soon as you get this message.'

In the vet's waiting room, Brillo lay at her feet. He was definitely showing signs of something now. A woman sat opposite gripping a cage with a cat inside. For once, instead of trying to jump on the cage, Brillo showed no interest. She ruffled his fur, murmuring words of reassurance. As the minutes passed, impatience spilled into anger.

'Please, can a vet see my dog soon? He's been poisoned.'

He could die if he wasn't treated quickly... Never again would she complain about the inconvenience of having a dog. The terrier might technically belong to her mother, but he had nestled his way into her heart.

The vet confirmed that the dog had symptoms of poisoning – mild, fortunately – and expected Brillo to make a full recovery.

'Oh, thank God.' The tension in her neck and shoulders lifted and the heaviness around her heart.

'He was lucky not to have ingested any more of the pellets,' the vet added. 'That could have been fatal.'

On the way home she phoned Elspeth.

'Is Clare with you yet?'

'Not yet. She rang me earlier and said she'd come over as soon as she'd finished her meal. I rang just now but there's no answer.'

'That's weird.'

'I know. Hopefully she's just got the radio on loud or something. How's the pooch?'

'He's going to be OK, thank God. Any news on somewhere to stay?'

Elspeth had found a cheaper place with vacancies that took dogs but it was thirty-five miles away. All nearer accommodation, including The Spinney, was either unavailable or didn't take dogs, she explained, so she would keep looking.

Next Ashley called her mother and explained what had happened to Brillio. Predictably, Diane was horrified.

'Who could have done such a thing?'

'Some horrible, selfish person who doesn't care about hurting others?'

Diane's question stayed with her as she drove through dark streets. She had avoided Diane's question so as not to worry her. However, she had no doubt as to who had left that meat: the thugs that Steve Weston called on when he needed to intimidate someone.

Her stomach growled. She was hungry, despite that chilling thought – and where the hell were the three of them going to spend the night?

By the time Ashley arrived home, it was gone 7.30pm.

While Brillo was settling into his basket, before she'd had chance to make the tea even, the doorbell rang. She exhaled in irritation.

Ken stood on the doorstep.

'I heard you come in,' he began, looking past her. 'How's Brillo?'

'He's going to be alright.'

Ken's face broke into a rare smile, exposing several uneven teeth. 'That's good news. Er... have you found a place to stay yet?'

'Not yet.'

'You're welcome to stop at mine for a bit if you don't mind roughing it. I've a spare room with two beds that never get used. And I wouldn't charge you a penny.'

She thought quickly. So far, this was the only reasonable option. It would be convenient and hopefully Ken's presence would deter anyone from bothering them.

'That's kind of you. If you're sure it's no trouble?'

'None at all.' He fidgeted, seeming uncomfortable. 'I'll go and sort the beds, then. Come over whenever you're ready.'

'Great, thank you. We'll be with you soon with any luck.'

Before setting off again, she looked longingly at her mug containing a tea bag.

Ashley parked opposite the path leading to the woods and

walked to Clare's cottage. A light shone behind the thin leaded windows on either side of the front door, which probably meant Clare hadn't left yet; she turned the hall lights off if she wasn't in to save on electricity.

She rang the doorbell, waited, then rang again.

'Clare! Can you come to the door?!' Nothing. She banged with the knocker, loudly enough to wake the heaviest sleeper. 'Clare! Can you hear me?'

A noise from inside. The thud of feet coming towards her. Through the narrow window, a man loomed. Her brain did a double take. Why was a man opening the door? Had he killed Clare? She waited, ready to turn and flee, her heart going berserk.

But it was definitely Clare standing in the doorway, all five foot ten inches of her hefty frame, the expression on her long face caught between fear and confusion.

'Ashley! I'm so glad it's you.' Clare yawned and rubbed her eyes. Her bright blue eyes darted towards the wood.

'Who else would it be?' Ashley stepped into the hall, breathing in a savoury smelling fug. 'Have you been asleep? I tried to call earlier but there was no answer.'

'I'm sorry. I found a doll propped by the gate earlier – a sinister looking thing.' Clare screwed up her face. 'Someone had chopped off its feet, would you believe.'

Her stomach lurched. Again, she had no doubt who had been responsible.

'You didn't see those two men, I take it?'

'No, only in my imagination. I decided to cook a hearty meal to distract myself, probably too much for one person. Just as I meant to leave the house I sat down in the armchair for a minute and nodded off. I didn't hear the phone ring; I'd left it in my rucksack by the front door.'

'OK, Clare.' She got to her feet, eager to be gone. 'Let's get going.'

Chapter 50
Elspeth

That evening

'This is very nice, isn't it?' Elspeth glanced around Ken's spacious spare room. A double bed, a single pulled out sofa-bed and a scattering of new-looking modern furniture fitted in easily. Both beds had been prepared with sheets and blankets. 'It's been recently decorated, by the looks of it.'

'Only two beds, though.' Ashley looked from herself to Clare. 'Who's going to sleep downstairs on the futon, then?'

Clare squeezed past Elspeth, plonked herself on the double bed and bounced up and down.

'I'm the biggest,' she declared. 'Bagsy this one. I doubt I could fit on that.' She looked disdainfully at the single bed.

Elspeth bit her lip. She ought to be magnanimous, she thought, given Ashley's harrowing experience with her dog and a suspicion that Clare might snore, as overweight people often did.

'You take the other bed, Ashley. I don't mind sleeping downstairs.'

Ashley placed her small suitcase on the sofa-bed smiled at Elspeth.

'Fine with me. But what if Tara's ghost makes an appearance?'

'Oh, shut up Ash.'

'Well, you'll have Brillo down there to protect you.'

She didn't reply, a tad irritated. Being by far the eldest of the three, she could have laid claim to the best bed. And what if any other unwanted visitors arrived? She glanced at the closed curtains.

'Do you think we're safe here?'

'I was checking the rearview mirror on the way back from Clare's.' Ashley removed her toilet bag from her wheely suitcase. 'I didn't notice anyone following us, or anyone in any of the cars outside.' She opened the bedroom door. 'I'm going to brush my teeth.'

Elspeth went downstairs, leaving Clare to do her nightly exercises. Brillo, on his back on a makeshift bed in the hall with his paws in the air, didn't stir as she passed. She found her neighbour watching TV.

'Hello Ken. Thanks again for being so hospitable.'

'Don't mention it.' He muted the TV. 'I hope you all enjoy your... little holiday.'

'We decided to have a break,' she started. 'It was a spur of the moment thing. I know it sounds odd but we have good reasons for wanting to be away from home.'

'I'm sure you do, Elspeth. I'm not one to pry.' He beamed at her through uneven teeth. 'Do you fancy a nightcap?'

'No thank you,' she replied hastily. 'I was just getting some water.'

'I've left out three glasses. The futon is over there, for whoever's going to sleep on it.' He indicated a spot not far from the kitchen. 'I'll be heading up myself shortly.'

'Thanks, Ken. Goodnight, then.'

'Goodnight, Elspeth. See you in the morning.'

She lingered in the kitchen for a few moments, regarding the futon. The thought of sleeping down here, next to where Tara had died so horribly gave her goosebumps.

'I'm going to sleep up here, too,' she said to the other two once she was upstairs, depositing the futon on the floor and three glasses on the dressing table. 'I'll squeeze into this corner.'

There was just enough room under the window.

'Do you think we'll find Kyle's body tomorrow?' Clare said after the three had put on their nightwear and made repeated trips to the bathroom.

'I don't know,' Ashley took her suitcase off the bed. 'Finn seems to think we have a decent chance.'

Ashley had told them that Finn had found someone willing to lend him a JCB. Finn's mate would let him have the machine tomorrow night. The three women had agreed it would be prudent to search for Kyle's body at the earliest opportunity, in case the detective was planning to arrest them.

Elspeth put down her hairbrush and turned away from the mirror. 'I've ordered something from Amazon that might help... If it turns up on time.'

'What did you order?' Clare stopped examining her toenails and looked up.

'A metal detector,' she replied.

'Excellent idea,' Ashley said.

'It can be tuned to specific metals like gold or silver. So if he has a belt with a metal buckle, say, or any jewellery with metal...' She had spent hours reading up on metal detectors.

'How far down does it work?' Clare looked sceptical. 'My nephew had one, years ago. It didn't pick up much except old pennies and bottle tops.'

'It can detect objects buried up to thirty metres underground, so it says.'

She was interrupted by Ashley's phone, an owl hooting.

'It's John,' Ashley said. 'Can I put us on video?'

'If you must. I've taken off all my makeup.'

'I don't mind.' Clare was climbing into bed. 'But I'll be asleep soon.'

John's tanned, craggy face filled the screen, along with his bass voice, sounding somewhat hoarse.

'You're with all three of us. We're all staying with a neighbour; the detective said we should keep together.' Ashley panned the camera. Clare waved and disappeared under the duvet.

'Good evening, ladies! Is this a convenient time?'

'It's fine,' Ashley replied.

'Hello John.' Elspeth sat down on the bed beside Ashley. 'How are you keeping? You sound wheezy.'

'Actually, I'm not so good. The doctor has diagnosed me with pneumonia and told me not to travel.' He took a laboured breath. 'Which is infuriating, because I'd already booked a flight home. I wanted to do my bit to support the three of you. I don't like the idea of you facing danger on your own. But fate seems to have intervened.'

Ashley replied. 'Rest up and come over when you're better, John. We can manage by ourselves.'

'You can still help, though.' Elspeth nudged the phone her way. 'Did you read what Ashley sent? We'd welcome your thoughts on our plan to find Kyle's body.'

'I did, Elspeth. You guys seem to have thought it all through. The plan sounds risky, though. What if someone hears the digger and comes to see what's going on? Word could get out to these men. If Mr Weston finds out you were trying to unearth the body of someone he'd killed, he'd be...'

'Shitting himself,' Elspeth finished for him.

'Turning purple, I was going to say. But that fits.'

'The quarry is in an isolated spot, John.' Ashley sounded worried now. 'I doubt anyone will be there late at night.'

'But sound carries more at night.'

'We'll have to take the risk. It's a small excavator – one and a half tons. It shouldn't make that much noise...'

Impatient, Elspeth cut in. 'Do you think we have a chance of finding this body, John?'

'A finite one, put like that. You'll need luck on your side... Please, be careful.'

'I get that you're worried,' Ashley said. 'So am I. But this is a chance to do something for the people who've lost someone important to them – Emily's friend, Cindra's parents, Finn.'

Elspeth swallowed to clear the lump in her throat.

'And everyone who's been hurt trying to stand up to those men,' she added.

'It's not just that.' Ashley's shoulders heaved. 'If we did find Kyle's body, that would be solid evidence against Steve Weston. If we confess what we did to Tara, and the police ever decide to arrest Weston, the judge might treat us more leniently.' Ashley looked sternly at Elspeth. 'But Finn and I can search alone. You and Clare don't need to risk your lives, too. You've both done plenty already.'

'Well, I insist on being part of this, too,' she retorted.

'So do I!' Clare's head popped up from the bedclothes. 'You're not going to do this on your own.'

'Sounds like a plan. What's happening with the drawing? The police have it now, you said?'

'I'm going to admit that the scene is real,' Clare called out, 'and I made up what I said about seeing two men in Tara's kitchen. It's time I got it off my chest.'

'What about Ursula? Does she agree to all this?'

'We aren't going to ask her,' Elspeth replied.

'Poetic justice, I suppose.' John gave a dry chuckle. 'She got us into this mess, didn't she?' He yawned. 'Well, ladies, good luck for tomorrow.'

The three wished each other goodnight. She noticed Ashley wipe the corners of her eyes.

'You miss John, don't you?'

'Yes, more than I thought. I hope he gets better soon.'

'He'll be fine Ash, I'm sure.' She lay down on the futon. 'Well, we've got a big day tomorrow...'

'It's stuffy in here, isn't it?' Clare was fiddling with the window mechanism. 'I think we need some air.'

Oh, flaming Nora. This was the last straw.

'I don't want cold air on me all night,' Elspeth said, as reasonably as she could manage.

'Stop arguing, you two!'

'Just a crack, then.' Clare pulled the window about a quarter of an inch in.

Elspeth woke with a start. The room was black, except for a whitish shape in the doorway. A person-shaped shape. The ghost?

She stared at it, waiting for it to move. A scream began to build. She needed to turn on the light. She lurched in the direction of the nearest lamp – from memory, one had stood on the dressing table.

From a foot away, sounded a honk that could have come from a small elephant. She let out a gasp, thrust out her hand to grab the lamp.

'Get off me!'

Light flooded the room from the lamp beside Clare's bed. Elspeth's hand gripped Clare's left foot.

Clare blinked at her. 'What are you doing?'

Ashley groaned and opened her eyes. 'What's going on?'

Elspeth let go of Clare's foot. The door was closed, she saw now, as it had been when they'd turned out the lights. Attached to a hook, a large white dressing gown was draped over other garments. It resembled a headless figure.

'Your snoring woke me,' she said to Clare, feeling foolish. 'I was trying to find a light switch. Sorry to wake you up.'

While Clare was in the toilet Elspeth gently shut the window, re-covered herself with the duvet, pushed her ear plugs firmly in and fell asleep almost immediately.

Chapter 51
Bird Woman

10 March: Breakfast

I wake up for the fourth or fifth time. This time it's not Elspeth complaining about my snoring or soothing voices from Ashley's pillow. It's a rat-tat-tat, too loud. I burrow under the duvet.

'Oh my Lord, it's the detective!'

Elspeth's at the window.

Feet thumping downstairs. Voices below. Ken's, Ashley's and Elspeth's. And DC Peters, too. I burrow deeper.

Feet coming upstairs, fast. Heavy breathing.

I force my eyes open. Elspeth stands over me, face flushed.

'DC Peters is waiting for you downstairs! Hurry up, get dressed. She'll get even crosser if you keep her waiting.'

When I eventually manage to get myself downstairs, DC Peters is tucking into croissants with Ashley and Elspeth. They are chatting with the polite stilted manner of residents breakfasting in a small guest house. Ken, bringing two mugs to the table, raises his eyebrows at me.

'Ah, here she is.'

'Morning, Clare.' Ashley gives me a probing look, at odds with her cheery tone. Her hair is messier than usual. She pulls out the chair beside her, opposite DC Peters. 'Have a seat.'

'You're just in time for a croissant,' Elspeth says. She is neatly coiffed, kitted out in vividly coloured knitwear.

'Good morning, Clare' DC Peters says pointedly as I'm about to grab one of the croissants, temptingly close. Her mouth is downturned, lip gloss smudged at one corner where golden specks fleck her lip.

'Morning Kate.' I automatically use her first name. Her scowl deepens.

'Tea or coffee, Clare?' Ken glances at DC Peters as if seeking confirmation that this is acceptable.

'Tea please' I reply before anyone can object. Ken puts a mug of steaming tea in front of me and scurries away. A tense silence falls.

I drink in the warm croissant smell. Ashley pulls hers apart and spreads one piece with marmalade. DC Peters pops one into her mouth. After a brief chew she pulls hair behind an ear.

'I need to ask you some questions about your drawing, Clare' she says stiffly. 'At the station.'

'Of course, no problem. Er – can I have my breakfast first?'

DC Peters makes a show of looking at her watch.

'We need to leave in five minutes. I'm running late. It took me an hour to find you here.'

I grab a croissant, tear off a piece and stuff it into my mouth.

'Do you two have any plans for the rest of the day?' DC Peters asks, looking at Ashley.

'Um, no, not exactly,' Ashley says, glancing at Elspeth.

'A bit of shopping maybe,' Elspeth says.

'I would rather you both stayed put here for the foreseeable,' DC Peters says. 'I don't want you exposed to any danger.' She scrapes her chair back. 'Clare, are you ready?'

At the police station

I'm trapped in a drab little room. The only reason I know time hasn't stopped is because I can see a clock on the wall. With a sense of doom, I watch the minute hand's intermittent jerks towards the hour.

'I shouldn't have done it,' I say. 'I'm sorry.'

DC Peters sits opposite me. An older male officer, DS Renn, sits beside her in a colourful lumberjack shirt. Beside me, my 'duty solicitor' makes a note in her pad. Despite a long wait for her to arrive, she seems crisply capable.

DC Peters started by reading me the caution about not relying on things that you don't say in court, or something similar. Then she placed my drawing on the table between us. I admitted that it was mine, drawn from the scene I witnessed on the evening of the 13th of August 2020, when I was walking along Wilton Close after a spell of birdwatching and happened to see a woman in her kitchen fending off a volley of fruit. This brought on an onslaught of questions: what exactly I saw, why I lied to police, when I drew the scene, and so on. Throughout, the DC's expression ranged from sceptical to fierce.

'You've spun us a web of lies, haven't you, Clare,' DC Peters says. It seems not to be a question. 'All to conceal the fact that you witnessed your friends Ashley and Elspeth attacking their neighbour.'

She sounds more like a police officer now and looks more like one. She has wiped away her lip crumbs and re-applied lipstick.

'I did lie,' I admit. 'My friends thought they might be arrested for murdering their neighbour. But they didn't murder her.'

'How do you know?'

The irritating buzz of the overhead lights gets louder. I crave to be outside, away from these relentless questions. I've been watered and fed (a listless sandwich) and have been to the bathroom twice (accompanied by a uniformed female). The solicitor has tried to limit what I say, often urging me not to answer. But I know I must tell the truth now.

'I saw them all throwing fruit at a woman,' I repeat. 'The woman who lived at number 33. I looked through my binoculars to get a better view. She put her hands up to defend herself, then appeared to stumble... I carried on walking. I didn't see a murder taking place.'

DC Peters scrunches her brow.

'How long were you watching?'

'About a minute. Two possibly.' I resist my urge for sarcasm.

'What made you draw this scene in the first place?'

'I couldn't stop thinking about it.' I explain as best I can that it's not every day you see a woman being pelted with apples. The group's physical exertion combined with their intense emotions had struck me. It had also been a chance to practice drawing hands and faces, I add.

The detectives look at each other.

'Thank you, Clare,' says DS Renn. He tells the recorder we are stopping for a break. As both officers stand, a wave of panic threatens. How long are we going to continue? I am an outdoors woman. I need the birds, the trees and the sky. This room hasn't even got a window.

'Will I be able to go home soon?' I ask. 'To Ken's house, I mean.' It seems ironic that the house is the very one where this supposed murder took place.

'I'm afraid not, Clare. You have admitted lying to the police about a crime you witnessed, part of a murder enquiry. As a result, officers were misdirected away from their two principal suspects. This is a serious offence.'

DC Peters' stern voice and furrowed brow amply convey the seriousness.

I try to ignore my latest pang of hunger.

Chapter 52
Ashley

Later that morning

Gripping a saucepan in one hand and a tea towel in the other, Ken approached the table where she and Elspeth were clearing the remains of breakfast.

'Would someone mind telling me what's going on? I was more than happy to offer you a way out of a tight spot, having accepted what you said at face value. But it appears that you took advantage of my generosity to try to evade the police.'

Ken's eyes, magnified behind his thick-lensed glasses, darted from her to Elspeth and back.

'No, no, that's not how it is,' Elspeth said, her face aghast. 'You've got the wrong end of the stick, Ken.'

'We weren't trying to evade the police.' Ashley adopted what she hoped was a calm, authoritative tone. Beneath her neutral expression, her nerves were pulled taut. 'We're trying to evade the men who want to hurt us.'

'The men who want to hurt you?'

'Exactly.' Elspeth smiled at Ken. 'And Clare was intending to go to the police anyway to confess to lying about what she saw, only the detective turned up here first.'

'I don't understand. Clare saw you both attacking the woman who used to live here, or murdering her, should I say?' Ken took half a step back, raising the saucepan as if preparing to defend himself.

Ashley sat down at the table and motioned Elspeth to sit, too.

'We didn't murder her,' she told Ken. 'Sit down, I'll explain everything.' Their neighbour stayed standing, looking uncertainly from one woman to the other.

'He's gone out of his way to help us,' she whispered into Elspeth's ear. 'He has a right to know why we're here.'

'So, what happened to her, this woman who used to live here?' Their neighbour wiped his nose with a withered piece of tissue. 'I've waited long enough to get an honest answer to a simple question.'

'It's a long story,' she began. 'During the pandemic, Elspeth and I fell out with her—'

'She fell out with *us*, is more accurate—'

'It started soon after the first lockdown began. Tara resented me for becoming friendly with Elspeth.' She did her best to explain about Tara blaming her for all manner of things, and the woman's increasingly bizarre behaviour.

'She seemed to lose all sense of reality.' Elspeth rolled her eyes and sighed. 'It was horrendous.'

Ken's eyes widened.

'Anyway,' Ashley continued, 'it all came to a head when she overheard us in the garden and thought we were laughing at her.'

Elspeth leaned in and spoke in a low voice. 'We think she tried to poison Ashley.'

'I went over there – here – to have it out with her. Elspeth came to back me up. So did John, Ursula and another two, no longer with us. Long story short, I lost it and threw an apple at her, and everyone joined in. She slipped, fell and hit her head. We could see she was dead. Some of us started to panic, thinking we'd be accused of her murder.'

'Ursula, in particular.'

'We all got roped into covering up the truth,' Ashley carried on. 'But we've decided enough is enough. We're going to confess everything, just as soon as...' At Elspeth's nudge, she broke off. 'DC Peters has been on our tails for months, and now someone has given her Clare's picture of what she really saw through Tara's kitchen window.'

'Which is why the officer wanted to speak to Clare?' Ken frowned at her. 'But if you aren't hiding from the police, who *are* you hiding from?'

'There are some bad men after us,' she said. 'Connected with the man who owns The Anglers.'

'I don't know who you mean – I'm not one for pubs.' Ken's brow furrowed again. He rubbed at a stain on the knee of his joggers. 'Why are these men after you?'

'Back in January,' Elspeth began, 'Ashley found a body. Emily Hale. She was murdered because she blew the whistle on Steve Weston for building over poisoned land, which included her back garden.'

'The man from The Anglers,' Ashley explained. 'His company supposedly reclaimed the quarry. But he buried a load of toxic chemicals there as well, with the help of his criminal friends. They threaten anyone who tries to expose them.'

Ken looked down at his dirty trainers, then shrugged.

'Wouldn't you be better off letting the police deal with all this?'

'The problem is,' she replied, 'one of the men involved with these criminals is a senior police officer.'

'Does DC Peters know what's going on?'

'She's trying to get these bastards, too,' Elspeth's green eyes flashed. 'But she's only a detective constable.'

'So, you're in my house hiding from these men who want to hurt you.' Ken's cheeks began to redden.

Ashley glanced at Elspeth. They had acted too hastily, she thought.

'I understand if you're angry, Ken,' she said. 'We should have told you all that in the first place.'

'It was the detective's idea,' Elspeth added. 'She told us we needed to find somewhere to stay right away. But no one wanted to put up three women and a dog.'

'Except gubbins here.' Ken rubbed his palms on his joggers.

'I'm sorry, Ken. If you're in danger, too... We'll find somewhere else to stay.'

'You don't need to leave.' Ken looked from her to Elspeth and back. 'Just tell me the truth. What else haven't you told me?'

She described the plan to search for Kyle's body.

'Well?' she prompted when Ken hadn't spoken for ages.

The man leaned back in his chair, his lips stretching into a lopsided smile.

'Not bad! I'll lend a hand, if you like.'

That afternoon

Ashley placed the Victoria sponge on Ken's coffee table. Afternoon tea had been her idea, because who knew how long it might be before they could do this again.

The cake that Ken had bought from the village bakery, together with her sandwiches, were enough for three very hungry people. She was still hoping that Clare would be released in time to join them, but so far there was no word from either Clare or DC Peters. Maybe, she thought, Clare was being charged for lying to the police...

They might all be appearing in court soon. With the help of Ken's computer, she and Elspeth had spent the morning painstakingly composing separate confessions detailing their involvement in Tara's death. John had written one, too. The only person who hadn't confessed was Ursula, who'd ranted down the phone at her about the path they'd chosen being madness.

'Are you joining us for a cup of tea, Ken?'

Her neighbour lowered several tatty carrier bags onto the hall floor, took off his glasses and gave them a rub with his sweater.

'I won't, thanks. I'm getting ready for tonight.' He indicated the bags. 'I've found some things in the shed.'

'Excellent, thank you. Oh, by the way, you didn't notice anything suspicious when you went out?'

'No men sitting in cars or hiding behind bushes, no.' He chuckled. 'But Rhianna was walking past with her dog. She wanted to know if I'd seen you or Elspeth lately.'

'What did you say?' Elspeth stood in the kitchen doorway.

'I said I hadn't seen either of you for a few days. I thought that might be wise, in the circumstances.'

'Good man.' Elspeth nodded. 'We don't want any tittle-tattle going around before Operation Quarry gets under way.'

'That's what I thought.' Ken headed into the kitchen.

Ashley settled on the sofa and nibbled the corner of a sandwich. She had stressed to Ken that tonight's plan was top secret; no one must know, especially Rhianna.

'I wonder why Rhianna asked Ken if he'd seen us,' she said.

'The bisom is probably wondering if we've been arrested yet,' Elspeth replied with vehemence, sitting down beside her.

'Maybe she's hoping to pass on to Steve where we are.' The thought sent a shiver down her spine. Elspeth rubbed her arms, cocooned in emerald green wool. 'We'd better be careful she doesn't spot us when we leave this evening.'

They were getting paranoid, she thought, but better safe than sorry. Earlier, they had discussed whether to tell DC Peters about Operation Quarry. They had decided not to in case she tried to stop them going. Breaking into the site and digging around for a body would no doubt be illegal as well as risky. However, they would phone her asap should they find anything or at the first hint of danger.

Between them, they had tried to think of everything. Finn had checked the quarry that morning; the surrounding fence was still there, studded with *Keep Out* signs. He hadn't spotted any security cameras or alarms. Entry was via a pair of padlocked gates. Ashley – with Elspeth if the metal detector had arrived by then – would drive to Finn's after dark and wait for Finn to pick up the excavator from his mate. She and Elspeth would then drive to the quarry with Finn, excavator in tow, arriving late enough for there to be no walkers or joggers around.

'I'll check the porch again,' Elspeth said, getting up.

'No sign of it yet?'

'Zilch. It was meant to be next-day delivery.' Elspeth looked exasperated. 'It should have bloody well come by now.'

'Nothing,' Elspeth said on her return. The two sat in silence, watching intermittent chinks of sunlight breaking through cloud. Ashley ate another sliver of sandwich while Elspeth picked at the cake's icing. Both women were thinking about Clare, she guessed.

From the kitchen, footsteps.

'Look what I found!' Ken brandished two garden spades, propped them against a nearby armchair, then returned with a bulging bag. 'Industrial masks and gloves, in case of any toxic materials. I'll see if there's anything else.'

Her phone rang, making her start. It was Diane.

'Oh, hello Mum. How are you getting on?'

'The pain is getting more manageable. Is everything alright? You sound strange.'

'I'm OK. Things are a bit difficult right now, though.'

'What things?'

'I can't say too much—'

'Too much? You haven't told me anything at all! You've been very secretive lately. I know something is going on that you're not telling me.'

'We've something planned for later tonight. It's a bit risky.'

'What's a bit risky?' Diane's voice teetered upwards.

She hesitated. 'We're going to search for a body, if you must know.'

'What? A dead one?'

God's sake, she should have kept her mouth shut. 'Sorry Mum, I can't say any more—'

'You'll tell me later, I know. Oh, by the way Ashley. Bryce tells me you're not at home.' This had an accusatory ring.

'How does he know that?'

'He rang on the door and there was no answer. He wanted to have a word with you about something.'

'Really? What would he want to talk to me about?'

A click of the tongue down the line. 'I've no idea! He popped over to see me with some flowers and we had a nice long chat. The point is, where are you if you're not at home?'

'I'm staying somewhere else for a short time, to be on the safe side.'

'Why would you not be safe?'

'Because of the men I told you about. DC Peters suggested it.'

'You didn't think to mention it to me?'

'Sorry, Mum. I have to go.'

The plan for tonight was stressful enough without having to deal with her mother's frustration. It was odd about Bryce. He would have to wait.

They both started as the doorbell rang. They were sitting in silence, the scarcely touched afternoon tea spread out in front of them. They heard Ken's footsteps to the door. Moments later a tall, ruddy-cheeked woman entered the room.

'Hello, stranger.' Elspeth beamed at Clare. 'We thought you'd never turn up. We're having a last supper. Ashley's idea.'

'They let me go pending further enquiries.' Clare plonked herself into the vacant armchair. 'For now, I'm a free woman.'

Ashley passed Clare the plate of sandwiches. 'You must be knackered, and hungry.'

'You can say that again! I had one measly sandwich and a cup of tea the whole time I was there.'

'Tuck in. We haven't started on the cake.'

Chapter 53
DC Peters

That evening

'Are you getting anywhere?' The sergeant hovered by her desk.

'I may have something here,' Kate replied. The office was almost empty. An IT guy tapped into his keyboard. 'Do you know anything about the councillor who jumped from a railway bridge in 2016?'

'That was before my time.' DS Renn checked his watch. 'I'll make a start on that interview strategy or the DI will be suspicious.'

DI Lister had agreed to release Clare after Rob argued that they should focus their resources on arresting and charging the four suspected of murdering Tara Sanderson. Kate had breathed a sigh of relief – their interviews with Clare Titchfield had left her uneasy, like a child after probing the shell of some harmless crab. But instead of bringing in Ashley, Elspeth, Ursula and John, she and DS Renn had searched for further evidence that DCI Mark Hill had acted illegally. Fortunately, DI Lister had left at five.

They already had evidence of Hill's suspicious behaviour in

relation to Emily Hale and Cindra Patel. The DCI had steered the murder investigation away from obvious links between the two women, such as Emily Hale's death the day before Cindra Patel had arranged to meet her. The links were amply demonstrated by documents stored on Ms Patel's memory stick, which to her mind indicated Mr Weston's involvement in the women's deaths. But Hill had dismissed the memory stick evidence. Jason Bell was still the only official suspect for Ms Patel's murder, despite the lack of evidence pointing to him.

Kate took a slurp of coffee and shoved the cup down. Cold, the brew was even less palatable. She clicked away from Councillor Black onto the Google image of the toe found at Brampton quarry in 2016, then onto Weston's development proposal for Summerfield. There was a connection between the three things, she was sure.

About forty minutes later, DS Renn reappeared at her desk.

'If you still haven't found anything Kate, we'll have to give up on Hill.'

'Give me five minutes. I'm onto something.'

'It's gone eight. I don't want us to be the only ones in the building.'

She stared at the screen, trying to block the sergeant's nervous vibes. While they had enough evidence to justify arresting Steve Weston and Thin Man, Rob believed, arresting DCI Hill, a senior police officer, was another thing altogether. They couldn't risk seeking outside help, which left the option of arresting Hill themselves, at the same time as the other two Wise Men.

She checked the system again for anything else relating to Councillor Black. Documents on his death had been stored all over the place, as if to stop them being found. At last, the pathologist's report on Black's death... She skimmed through it for what she wanted. A photo of his foot.

'I've got it!' She sat up straight, nearly knocking over the coffee. 'Remember that photo of a toe I found on Google? I know who it belonged to.'

'Tell me.' Rob didn't sound enthusiastic.

'Graham Black. He was on Elven Town Council's planning committee when he died – on the 13th of November 2016. That was a month after the first Summerfield housing proposal was rejected—'

'Summerfield? The estate Weston built?'

'Yes, where Emily Hale used to live. Black's body was found underneath a railway bridge. The death was declared to be suicide by the Coroner after Hill decided there were no suspicious circumstances. But there were, and they were ignored.'

'Go on.' Rob moved beside her, looking down at her screen.

'I found a witness statement from a passerby. She saw two men in dark clothing lurking behind bushes on the old railway path, about fifty yards from the bridge. She couldn't see their faces; she thinks they were covered. That was fifteen minutes before Black's body was found. A man matching Black's description was seen half a mile from the bridge, ten minutes' earlier. It looks like he went out for a walk and was grabbed.' Kate paused for breath. 'I've just found the pathologist's report. Black's left big toe was missing.' Kate pointed to the screen. 'There's a photo of his foot and a note that there were signs of the wound healing. The toe was likely severed weeks before death.'

'So, despite this witness statement and the missing toe, Hill didn't pursue the investigation.' Rob took a piece of licorice from his pocket and began to chew. 'Which means this is another suspicious death linked to Steve Weston that Hill didn't investigate properly.' Rob massaged his shoulder, grimacing. 'Why would Weston have wanted Black killed, though?'

'Black was being pressured by Weston to approve his housing project, but he refused?' Kate clicked onto the council's planning portal. 'Summerfield wasn't approved until 2017, after the development proposal was modified. The first proposal was rejected by the committee in September 2016. The two men seen by the railway bridge might have been our Croatian friends. Maybe they visited Black before the vote on the first proposal to apply some extra pressure.'

'Lopping off his toe for good measure.' DS Renn puffed air through his lips. 'Nice blokes we're dealing with.'

'Then, when it was apparent that Black hadn't done what they'd asked for – persuading the committee to approve the proposal, maybe – they killed him to send a signal to the other committee members. The second development proposal was approved six months later.'

'Maybe Black knew about the toxic waste buried there.' Rob glanced around, frowning. 'Everyone's gone – let's get out of here. Have you got screen shots?'

'All done, Sarge. Do you think it's enough for us to act on?'

They hurried down to the basement, DS Renn ahead.

'We now have clear evidence pointing to Hill conspiring to further Weston's interests. But say you arrested him first thing tomorrow while I tried to nab the other two... They aren't going to come like lambs. And what about the men in black? If there were more than two of us it would be an option, but as things stand...'

They walked quickly towards the Renault hatchback, the sergeant almost breaking into a run. Kate said nothing. She was looking forward to another evening at his flat sharing a takeaway and a bottle of wine. The elation of her detective work was ebbing, her nerves becoming tauter by the minute. She was relieved when the engine started without a hitch and they were through the barrier without anyone emerging from the shadows.

Chapter 54
Ashley

That evening

T he car was taking forever. Behind, the trailer and its load of machinery thudded with every bump in the road.

The tension in the car was palpable. No one spoke. Finn drove. Ashley sat in the back seat beside Clare. She needed to be there now, inside the quarry. Her fingers cradled the phone in her lap. No message yet from Elspeth. No metal detector, then.

Here and there, the distant lights of houses. Widely spaced streetlights did little to pierce the darkness. Suddenly they turned onto a narrow, unmarked road. It curved upwards, skirting the remaining quarry's maw. Finn pulled up under a small tree and they climbed out into the night. Above, a curl of moon against the black.

The powerful beam of Finn's head torch picked out a wire fence, enclosing a huge empty space. They walked towards the gates.

'Clare, are you OK?'

Clare gave a thumbs up and a wan smile. She looked done in, but she'd insisted on coming.

While Finn tackled the padlock on the gate with a bolt-cutter, Ashley unloaded the boot with Clare. She put on her beanie, glad of Finn's thick jacket. Inside of the fence, she made out a low, rectangular building, the former Portakabin on Kyle's map. Moonlight glinted off a small window. In this vast space, she felt tiny. Fingers crossed, no one else would venture out here tonight.

Ahead, Finn struggled with the padlock securing the gates.

'Fuck it,' she heard above the grind of metal against metal. Finn's face strained with exertion. A snap of metal.

Finn pushed the gates open and returned.

'We'll leave the digger where it is for now. Best to avoid unnecessary noise. We'll mark out the dig zone first.' He hauled on a rucksack, then held out a spray can of paint and a portable satnav. 'Ashley, take these and follow me. Clare, stay here and keep watch. If anyone comes, give us a shout or phone me.'

Ashley half ran over the gritty soil to keep up with him.

'Here,' he said eventually, after stopping several times and poring over the drawings and the satnav in turn. He sprayed a large white dot on the ground then removed a set square, compass and metal tape measure from his rucksack. 'Hold this end. I'll mark off the line.'

Ten minutes later, he returned. A thick white line stretched into the distance.

'All done.' They returned to Clare.

'Cheer up, lass.' Finn patted Clare's arm. 'You two get your gear on while I get this thing going.' They watched him climb into the cabin behind a huge articulated metal arm, bright orange. After several attempts, he coaxed the digging machine off the trailer and through the gates. She and Clare set off in their industrial masks, protective gloves and layers of warm clothing. The digger stood at the start of the white line, its metal bucket raised. Finn clamboured down from the cabin.

'Right, ladies. We're going to tackle this thing methodically, OK? No rushing, no panicking if anything goes wrong. We won't

333

be able to talk to each other while the machinery's on. If you need me to stop for any reason – you've found something or there's an emergency – give me this signal.' He held his arm vertically and swung it down.

They gave him a thumbs up.

'Let's go.'

Ashley walked silently beside Clare behind the excavator, carrying her shovel, watching the Kubota's caterpillar tracks inching over the earth. The engine's heavy thrum drowned out any other sounds. She watched the hydraulic arm lower its scoop, the engine noise a thick roar as the machine broke the soil and dumped it effortlessly aside. A deep trench began to replace the line, which carried on into the distance, glinting in the moonlight. How long was this going to take?

Once the digger had advanced, they turned on their head torches and began sifting with spades through the piles of earth discarded by the digger, on either side of a deep gorge in the soil. Hopefully, any human bones here would be easy to spot.

She and Clare worked on either side of the trench. At first her movements were awkward, but she started to feel the blade cutting deeper through the loose, chalky soil. The torch beam was powerful enough to spot plenty of objects in its path – stones, cigarette butts, small pieces of metal and plastic. But nothing remotely like a bone.

Ahead, the excavator stopped, its bucket raised as its engine extinguished, leaving a merciful silence. Ashley put down her spade. It was only an hour since they'd started digging but it felt like three. She needed a break; her arms ached and the cold seemed to slice through her clothing. She peeled off her mask and gloves with relief and went to get the thermos of tea.

Clare joined her at the start of the dig zone. She looked knackered, too, sweat pooling on her brow. They took turns sipping from the plastic cup. The tea, hot and strong, was reviving.

'Alright, Finn?' Ashley indicated the flask. 'Cup of tea?'

'Thanks, but I've a tot of whisky with me.' Finn retrieved a silver hip flask from his rucksack.

Ashley checked her phone again, wondering if Elspeth had called. Earlier, only one or two bars had shown on her phone. In this spot, the signal was down to zero.

'Are we on track with digging?'

The digging was taking longer than he'd hoped, Finn told them. The Kubota had reached the 10-metre mark; at this rate it would take four or five more hours to reach the end of the dig zone. The soil lower down was mixed with 'all sorts of stuff', he explained – chopped or shredded materials, too tough to cut through.

'We'd better get back to it, then,' she said. After what seemed like hours later, there was a tap on her back accompanied by a yell outside her left ear. She spun around, spade raised ready.

But it was Elspeth.

'Bloody hell, woman! What are you doing, creeping up on me like that?' She hadn't bothered to put her mask back on as there didn't seem to be any noxious fumes yet.

'Sorry to startle you. But I've been yelling at you both for the past ten minutes.'

Behind Elspeth, she saw Ken walking along slowly, headphones over his ears and elbows held at his sides, holding out a strange cylindrical metallic device like a radar gun. Smaller tubes stuck out from the main tube. As he walked, he moved the device slowly to and fro in an arc.

'It came, then,' Ashley said.

'The delivery man left it with Susan and Ron; I finally

thought to go over and ask.' Elspeth rolled her eyes. 'Ken spent ages setting up the thing. It's way more complicated than I thought.' Elspeth hugged herself, gazing across the vast space. 'It's desolate here, isn't it? I'll get a spade.'

Ken trudged beside the long mound of dug-up earth, ahead of the three women, slowly swinging the detector tube from side to side. Suddenly, he took off his headphones and shouted.

'Down there! Something's giving off a strong signal.' He pointed to the deep pit in the soil.

All three ran over and began to dig. Twenty minutes later, they unearthed a squashed beer can.

'All that work for nothing!' Elspeth let out a wail of anguish.

Ashley said nothing. She wasn't at all hopeful anymore that they would achieve their goal. Ken stooped over the device, fiddling with the controls on the small backlit screen.

'I've adjusted the setting. The detector is sensitive to anything metallic, so it's going to pick up a lot of stuff apart from what we actually want.'

'Which is?' It was an obvious question, so she thought.

Elspeth answered, somewhat tersely. 'Belt buckles, watches, jewellery – anything made of metal that Kyle might have been wearing when he was killed.'

'Wouldn't they have taken anything like that off him?'

'Not necessarily. Not if they were in a hurry.' Elspeth clasped gloved hands together and stamped her boots. 'Chaps, let's carry on. It's too cold to be out here yakking.'

They carried on sifting. Ken walked ahead, swinging the detector. Further signals resulted in further spates of frantic digging, only to turn up coins, ring-pulls and other metallic rubbish. Finally, Finn stopped the digger and spoke with Ken, both men casting worried glances over the detector. Spades downed, the three women stood by.

'Shall we swap roles?' Clare called out mischievously. 'You two dig and we women will do the clever stuff?'

Ken scowled and Finn ignored her. Ashley wiggled her fingers. Their tips were going numb. She took off her gloves and saw the blisters on her hands. No wonder digging had become so painful. The thought of going back to work filled her with gloom. But she was the one who'd suggested this in the first place, she told herself. Somehow, she had to see it through.

She removed the snack bar from her pocket and took a bite of nutty chocolate. It tasted heavenly.

'Over here! Ashley, Clare, Ken!'

It was Elspeth, calling them over for about the sixth time. She had taken over detecting from Ken, and the objects they'd unearthed with the device were getting larger – pieces of metal in various forms and sizes. No sign yet of a body, though.

Ashley stopped mid-action, about to lift a spadeful of soil, or more accurately, 'this toxic shit', as Elspeth referred to it. The consistency of whatever was underfoot had become denser and chewier, making it even harder to make headway. Would they be able to spot human remains amongst all this? Her spade felt heavier than ever, her back ached and her right palm hurt from blisters. She had no idea what time it was – some time after 2am, when they'd last downed tools, and before daylight was due to creep back, at around 5.30am. So far, the only positive thing about Operation Quarry was that no one had tried to interfere with what they were doing. No one else was in the vicinity so it seemed, though with the thick blanket of darkness beyond reach of their torches and the near-constant drone of the digger, it was hard to be certain.

Her gaze fell on the narrow makeshift building in the distance. Was the Portakabin where Weston had killed Kyle? She shivered. Reluctantly, she picked up her spade and carried it towards Ken and Clare.

Chapter 55
DC Peters

That evening: 8.30pm

While DS Renn drove, Kate closed her eyes and tried to relax. Her shoulders ached. Despite DS Renn's soothing jazz piano playlist, a headache was coming on. The stress of the past few days was catching up with her. What would those three ruthless men do to two cops who threatened to remove them from their perches and deliver them into incarceration? The fact that one headed the Serious Crimes Unit only added to her anxiety. As an ex-cop in prison, Hill would face worse than most, as he would be well aware.

'Sorry.' DS Renn swung the wheel hard.

Kate opened her eyes, trying to stop her side from thumping into the passenger door.

'What the hell?'

Rob glanced at the rear view. Kate turned and looked through the rear window. Directly behind them, a black saloon.

'Is that car following us?'

'Hold on.' Rob accelerated towards the mini-roundabout, bumping over the raised section. Scarcely slowing, he swerved the car onto the left turn-off. She braced herself again. Tyres squealed, the car veered close to the roadside then overcorrected into the oncoming lane. They were now on a twisty B road bordered with trees, without street lighting.

'You've taken your advanced driving course, then,' she said when she had recovered sufficiently.

Rob's mouth was set in a grim line. Kate glanced behind again. The black saloon was still there, close enough now for her to see a burly man at the wheel and another slumped beside him. It was low-slung, clearly designed to go fast. She removed her phone and snapped the car and its registration plate.

'Shall I get a registration check?'

'Go ahead. I reckon that's Thin Man's F-type Jag. Looks like he's let his pals borrow it.'

Around them, dark fields. Not much traffic, fortunately. They were on the edge of town, well past Rob's flat. Where was he taking them?

Before she could ask, Rob put his foot down again. She gripped the door handle, her eyes trained on the road. The engine whined, struggling with the slope. Her colleague was clearly no stranger to fast driving, but this hatchback wasn't up to the job. The other car was closing. It was going to ram them.

'Watch out!'

The jolt juddered through the car, forcing her body forwards then back against the seat.

'Shit!' She twisted to look behind. The black car was closing again. 'Are they trying to kill us?'

'Fuck.' Rob's voice was low.

A tractor came around the bend ahead, over the central line. The car was going too fast... Rob yanked on the steering wheel, propelling the car to avoid the tractor. A tree loomed in front of the windscreen. Automatically Kate pressed her body over her legs, bracing her head with her arms.

Somehow, Rob managed to get the car back on course. They

rounded the bend without incident onto a stretch of straight road. She barely registered the screech of tyres behind, followed by a loud thud.

'Sounds like they've come off the road. What a pity.' Rob's mouth twisted into a grin. He glanced at Kate. 'Sorry about that, kiddo. Are you alright?'

'Still alive, thanks. I'll open the window in case I throw up.'

No way was she getting into a car with this man again, she vowed, gulping fresh air. The road was narrow and potholed but wonderfully straight. Rob kept up their speed, too fast for her liking, glancing repeatedly in the rear view.

'We're not safe, are we?'

'Don't worry. We're going to be OK.' DS Renn turned on the navigation. 'Tap in a postcode for me, will you?' She did as he asked. 'My brother lives this way. He'll put us up.'

'You think someone will find us if we go to yours?'

Rob shrugged. 'The DI has my home address, so safe to assume Hill has it, too. Neither of them knows where my brother lives.'

Chapter 56
Ashley

Later that night: 3.45am

The long thigh bone leading off the pelvis was starkly white in the torchlight.

'We've found him,' Clare said in a tone of disbelief. 'Those bones are definitely human.'

They stood at the base of the trench, crowding around the section of skeleton protruding from the soil. It had taken half an hour for the five to dig down after Elspeth alerted them.

'At last.' Elspeth flung down her spade. 'I'm shattered. I'm ready to join this guy down there.'

'Is it him?' Ken looked at Finn, as if the man would be able to recognise Kyle from these bones.

'He would have been wearing a gold ring when he died,' Finn said, his voice unsteady. 'It didn't come off easily. I gave it to him when we got engaged.'

Ashley took out her phone and held it high. A single bar. She tapped out a message to DC Peters.

We're at the top quarry looking for Kyle's body. Please get over here quickly. We've found something

Ken and Finn were on their haunches, peering at the bones – a torso, she realised.

'Look.' Ken pointed to something resting on a lower rib, glinting silver.

'It's his belt. I recognise the buckle.' Finn fell onto his knees and reached out to touch the round of silver, attached to a piece of disintegrating leather. Tears tracked down his cheeks. 'He bought it in the Rocky Mountains. We went there on holiday together.'

Finn pushed himself to his feet and stumbled away.

Ashley turned her head. There had been a sound just now, towards the gates, she could have sworn. She climbed out of the trench and stared into the darkness.

'What is it?' Elspeth frowned at her.

'I thought I heard something.'

'There's no one else here,' Ken swept an arm across the black expanse.

'We should go,' she said. Someone might have heard the machinery and come to see what was going on. If the Wise Men were to find out where they were...

'I'll take this.' Ken picked up the metal detector and headed towards the gates.

'Thank you all for doing this,' Finn said in a low voice, wiping his face with a sleeve. He looked at her. 'I didn't really believe this could happen.' He hauled his rucksack over a shoulder. 'I'll get the machine back on the trailer.'

Ashley photographed the human remains and hurried towards the gate. The sooner they were away from here, the better.

'Come on you two, hurry up!'

Elspeth mock saluted. 'Alright, sergeant major!'

The excavator spluttered into life. Far ahead, she could see Ken nearing his Vauxhall. She phoned DC Peters's number but there was no answer. Where was the woman? Noticing the time on the screen – nearly 3am – her heart sank. She tried again, swearing as an automatic reply kicked in.

'Kate, this is Ashley. We're at the top quarry. We've found Kyle's body. Come over as quickly as you can...'

A sharp cry, beyond the gate. Heart leaping, she ended the call. There was no sign of Ken now; a white van had pulled up beside his car. She turned to Elspeth and Clare.

The rest happened before she could even think to call 999.

Two men were running towards them. One of them carried a hammer.

She froze as the man with bowed legs approached her, hammer raised above his head. One side of his face was swollen and discoloured. She swerved away from him. But the second, more powerfully built man grabbed her arms and forced them behind her body.

If you can, run. If you can't... She kicked backwards like crazy, trying to hit his shin. But still he gripped her arms. Close by, Elspeth was sprawled face down on the ground. Short blonde hair poked out from her beany. Bowlegs crouched beside her, fastened her wrists. His foot covered Elspeth's head. The hammer was on the ground beside him.

She heard someone grunt behind her. The man holding her loosened his grip to rub his knee, screaming profanities. She recognised him as the second man at the pub. Gloves hid his rings but his thin, childlike face was uncovered.

Bowlegs grabbed the hammer and walked towards Clare, speaking in a mocking, high-pitched voice as he raised the hammer then struck the back of her head. Clare staggered and fell.

Ashley ran. She needed to get help before they were all killed. Her legs pumped furiously. The gates, she was through...

Suddenly the air was knocked from her. A heavy weight pinned her, pushing her face down into the soil. Once again, her arms were forced behind her back. This time bindings were pulled tight around her wrists, cutting into her skin. Everything went black. There was something covering her head. Something was pushed into her mouth. For a moment she couldn't breathe. She tried to scream. Only a muffled squeal emerged. Fear clawed at her. Her mind began to blur. She could let go of this body, not come back.

From nowhere, a torrent of anger. She struck out with her heel again. A moan of pain from behind. This time the man didn't let go. Somewhere in her mind she registered the digger engine cutting out, then distant shouts.

A sharp pain in her shoulder. Her arm was being tugged – she had to move. Her feet couldn't keep up, began to drag. Panic surged. She felt herself go limp.

Suddenly she was shoved hard from behind. With a stab of pain, her wrist met a hard surface. A floor. She was inside the Portakabin. The air was different – warmer, stale. Close by, she felt and heard two loud thumps each followed by a muffled cry of pain – Elspeth and Clare?

The door slammed. A lock turned.

For a long moment, nothing. Then an outbreak of thuds, moans, muffled shouts and other desperate noises.

Minutes passed. Their sounds dwindled. Then the lock turned and footsteps approached. A male voice rang out, sending a chill through her.

Steve Weston.

'Welcome, ladies. You've found out my secret, I see. Very enterprising of you all, I must say.' The voice became coarser, suffused with menace. 'But you're going to suffer the consequences now. You're going to wish to God you hadn't gone to all that trouble.'

Chapter 57
DC Peters

Earlier that night: 10pm

The house exuded normality. In the living room, three boys squabbled over the background of a TV reality show. Here in the kitchen with DS Renn, it was almost impossible to believe that someone might want to harm them.

Rob's brother and his wife had insisted they stay the night. After plying them with hot soup, they left the two of them alone.

'Do you think they were hurt, those two?'

Rob shrugged. 'Minor injuries, at least. I doubt they were going fast enough to kill themselves, more's the pity.'

'Maybe we should have called it in. What if they were badly hurt?'

'We needed to get the hell away.' Rob carried on massaging his knees. He looked exhausted. 'The way they came at us... That wasn't meant to scare us off. The Wise Men want us out of the way, permanently.'

Kate stared into her no-longer-hot chocolate.

'What are we going to do next? Now we've got a name and address for Thin Man, we could bring in all three in one fell swoop, I suppose.' But she'd had her share of excitement for one day.

In the past hour they had identified Thin Man via the registered keeper of the Jaguar – Lazar Bilbija. The same name was registered with an electricity provider at an address 33 miles from Elven, Rob had discovered. Kate's internet search had identified Bilbija as the managing director of a firm that imported watches and antique clocks. The guy had been hiding in plain sight for years, they realised.

Rob downed the rest of his beer.

'I need a decent kip and so do you. Let's see how the land lies in the morning. Also...' He lowered his voice. 'Someone who knows Weston has given me some useful intel. If I can get him to make a statement, it'll add to our ammunition.'

'Let's hope so. I'm off to bed, I'm bloody knackered.' It wasn't even ten thirty but already her brain was powering down.

'Night, Kate. Sleep well.'

She opened the door of her allocated room, to find a forest of furniture and household objects surrounding a single bed. She navigated through to the window and peeked through the curtains – fields. This place felt safe. With any luck, she would have a good night. She checked the notifications on her phone – nothing urgent, nothing from Ashley – and hunted for somewhere to recharge the device.

Chapter 58
Bird Woman

11 March: about 3am

When I came to, my first thought was: *No, I refuse to die here.*

My second: *I'm going to die here and no one will remember that I always did my best for the birds.*

I'm lying on my side on a cold, extremely uncomfortable surface. My hip and ribs are sore. My shoulders ache from the positions of my arms, fastened behind my back, and something sharp digs into my wrists. My head hurts the most. It aches with surprising ferocity. For good measure, strange patterns stream under my eyelids. Thick material covers my head so I can't see a thing. Are Ashley and Elspeth still here with me? I start to call their names but there's something jammed in my mouth.

I'm trapped. My heart flutters. I can't get enough air in.

I make myself relax. Suddenly, I recall how the two men attacked us. The hammer in Mr Bowlegs hand, and the coldness of his eyes, the fresh cuts on his face, the blood caked on his brow. My attempt to escape, a black wall coming down...

We found the body of the man that Steve Weston killed and

assumed would remain hidden from the world. He's going to kill us, isn't he? How will we get out of this? If we are all hooded, gagged and trussed at the wrists...

Stop panicking, I tell myself. Think, Clare.

I moan three times, one short one long and one short. From one side of me comes a noise like a startled bee – Ashley? From my other side, three short mews like a disgruntled Siamese, which puts me in mind of Elspeth. Despite tears wetting my eyes, I almost giggle at this attempt at conversation.

After an age I manage to raise my top half into a sitting position, then wriggle backwards on my bottom until I make contact with a wall.

The walls are thin, admitting sounds from outside. I hear two male voices, harsh and fast, speaking in a foreign language. Another voice joins, in English, controlled and steely. The first voice speaks in poor English. After a few minutes, the voices recede.

My thoughts scramble in all directions. Will someone rescue us? Maybe Ken got away after he was attacked. Maybe Finn managed to raise the alarm. Maybe the detective will pick up Ashley's message and come to get us.

But what if no one comes? We have to escape before something even worse happens to us. How, though? Our rucksacks and phones will no doubt have been taken. We can't speak to each other, can't move our hands, can't see a thing.

Then I remember what I packed into the front of my knickers before leaving this evening, just in case. I can feel the items nestled in against my skin. With a supreme effort, I pull my hands as far as they can go towards them, stretching my fingers.

But I can't reach that far. I know one thing, though, I'm not going to let this pathetic bunch of knob-ends get the better of me.

Chapter 59
DC Peters

K ate sat up in bed with a start. It was dark, still. In her dream, bells had been ringing.

She tried to remember why she was in this cluttered little room. It all came rushing back. They were hiding from violent criminals, and DCI Hill was one of them.

And what about the three women? She'd forgotten to check in with Ashley last night. Were they staying put as she'd told them?

She groped her way between the massed objects to the wall socket, where her phone was wedged between a velvet pouffe and a pile of curtain material. The screen showed a missed call from Ashley at 2.50am, over half an hour ago. She played the voice message.

Kate, this is Ashley. We're at the top quarry. We've found Kyle's body. Come over as quickly as you can.

There was urgency in Ashley's voice. The message ended abruptly. She played it again to make sure. Yes, there was a shout in the background. Something was wrong.

If Ashley and her friends had really found Kyle Sutton's body in Weston's quarry, it could change everything. But the women were in danger. She had to get to them before the Wise Men could...

She pulled on her sweater and leggings and ran to wake the sergeant.

Chapter 60
Bird Woman

11 March

I have no idea how long it took me to communicate to Ashley and Elspeth that I wanted one or both of them to extract the items that were inside my underwear. The three of us were gagged, hooded and trussed at the wrists. Eventually I managed to guide their hands to the unusual bulge below my belly, whereupon they seemed to twig what was required.

We tried various permutations of people and methods, ending up with Elspeth (who has the longest and nimblest fingers, I ascertained) on her knees with her back to myself (also on my knees) while her fingers groped the waistband of my trousers then inside my large M&S pants. After many unsuccessful attempts, the items were liberated.

Elspeth whooped as the Swiss army knife followed by the small glass jar toppled onto the floor. Kneeling in front of me so her fastened hands were directly in front of mine, she trapped my wrist with her thumb and first finger and set to work on the bindings.

I yelped through my gag and the sawing slowed.

Footsteps, getting closer. Raised voices from outside. I went to where the jar had clattered, collected it and pressed my hands behind my back. The lock turned. Swish of cold air.

'Good, you are still here.' A male voice in heavily accented English, accompanied by an unkind laugh. I squatted lower, praying my bottom was hiding the jar and the knife was out of sight.

A second voice. 'We come back for you soon. Enjoy your last minutes alive.' A laugh as they left the room.

I was scared beyond measure. Also, I was desperate to wee but determined to salvage some dignity and not do it in my knickers.

From outside, a deep voice. An Englishman.

'Is that him? There's not much left of the bugger, is there? Good work, guys. Put him in the van with the other two, then finish off the three biddies. We'll shove 'em all off the side of the boat. The cops'll never find them.'

The words set off a mad rage inside me. We were going to free ourselves.

Elspeth's sawing continued. In minutes, my arms dropped to my sides. I rubbed my sore wrists, removed my head covering and gag and stood blinking. The lights were off in the room but an electric glow leaked in through a small window.

Quickly, I cut the other's bindings. While they removed their hoods and gags, I unscrewed the jar of chilli jam. (I bought it by mistake, not noticing the 'extra hot' on the label. A tiny speck turned my mouth into a furnace of pain.)

'Hurry, dip your fingers in here,' I told them. 'It's very spicy, be careful. When the men come back, we'll poke our fingers into their eyes.'

They looked at me in surprise.

'I'm not sure I can put a finger inside someone's eye,' Elspeth said, dipping her fingers. 'But I could spread this over their little plonkers, no problem.'

Outside, voices again.

'Quick, behind the door!'

The voices passed easily through the wall. This is what I heard, as accurately as I remember.

First, the native Englishman who had first spoken to us, who I presumed was Steve Weston.

'You aren't in fuckin' charge here, Mark, I am. We're gonna finish off those bitches. Karma for trying to bring me down. Or do you want me to get them to finish you off, too?'

A reply came in a harsh nasal voice, who I presumed was DCI Hills.

'Mate, don't threaten me! You're losing it. No way we can kill five people and get away with it – not with Fat Kate about to expose us and Rambo Rob helping. We'll all be nicked for murder. Let's get the fuck out of here before they find us.'

'You're out of your mind. We're not leaving anyone behind to blab. We'll dump the bodies off the boat, minus teeth and fingers, far enough out that they won't be found till anything recognisable has long since been washed away. We're all going to take a little holiday till all this blows over.'

The nasal voice.

'How do you think you're going to get away with that? We need to get out of here before the shitshow arrives and nicks us all. You know what they do to cops in prison. I'll be dead meat.'

'You make your bed...'

Further inaudible exchanges.

Weston: 'Now shut the fuck up. Craig's in Whitstable waiting for us. Let's do this before we're rumbled.'

'No you effing aren't,' Elspeth says beside me under her breath. The three of us are standing shoulder to shoulder along the wall beside the door.

The door swings inwards. A light flicks on. A man with bowed legs steps inside the room.

I raise my arm, two right middle fingers extended.

'Get the other one!' I shout, thrusting into the man's gelatinous pockets, ignoring his screams. My left hand grips his belt. I swing my knee up into his groin. He rears back, bellowing like a birthing cow and staggers to the floor.

His burly mate is fighting off Ashley and Elspeth's combined onslaught until Elspeth rams her hand down the front of his jeans. He bucks and bellows, hate in his eyes, fists swinging. One almost reaches Ashley but she neatly sidesteps, grabs an ear and smears chilli jam into his eyes.

I refuel my fingers and offer the jar to the others.

'What the fuck's going on?'

It's Weston, outside. I motion the others to join me by the wall beside the door.

'Ashley, you grab his hands. Elspeth, get his gonads. I'll do the eyes.'

A tall, broad shouldered man strides into the room. Seeing the two men writhing on the floor, Weston stops short and swears.

'Now!'

Fear takes away any qualms. I launch my fingers at his eyes. He roars and grabs at my hair. He's on top of me, tears streaming down his cheeks. His fingers tighten around my neck. My vision fades.

The room comes back. My body drags in a huge breath. The hands have gone. Weston is on his back, spluttering and swearing, his face covered with red gunk. Ashley pulls me to my feet and shepherds Elspeth out of the room. Quickly, she locks the door behind us and pockets the key.

'Where's Ken and Finn?'

There's no sign of either. I also look around for Nasal Man and Thin Man.

'In the van!' Elspeth points to the white van beside Ken's car.

Ashley opens the rear doors. Inside, two men lie with bags over their heads, their arms forced behind their backs. Ken moans and lifts his head. The other man doesn't move. I recognise Finn's jacket.

I lean over my knees and take in air. I am exhausted.

A hatchback pulls up behind Ken's car. Before its occupants can get out, two men appear from the shadows and run towards us. The one with grey hair opens the van door on the driver's side and slides into the front seat. The other is thin with a grey face and holds a hammer.

The sight chills me. How can we fight off a man with a hammer?

I shout a warning as he comes up behind Elspeth. Elspeth tries to cover her head with her hands. Ashley throws herself at Thin Man's feet. He topples but is still grasping the hammer.

DC Kate Peters emerges from the hatchback's passenger side and runs towards Thin Man holding an aerosol can in front of her. Simultaneously, the middle-aged, checked-shirt detective emerges from the driver's side, runs to the van's rear and jumps inside.

Thin Man gets to his feet and raises the hammer above Ashley's head. His expression is oddly impassive. Before he can lower the implement, DC Peters pushes her can close to his face. Thin Man staggers back, dropping the hammer. Ashley grabs his arm and twists the shoulder – out of its socket, judging by the man's wailing. Elspeth helps to hold his arms while the DC handcuffs him.

The van starts to drive away, back doors flapping.

A shout from inside. The van swerves. It's about to careen into a tree, I think. But it jerks to a halt. Checked Shirt jumps down from the passenger side, runs across to the driver, pushes Grey Hair against the van and handcuffs him.

'Fuck you' Grey Hair yells. I recognise his voice from earlier – Nasal Man.

'The Portakabin!' I shout, gesturing. 'Weston and the other two are locked inside!'

Checked Shirt sprints away. Against the yellow streaked eastern sky, the dark, lonely form of the digging machine. I run past the van to a clump of trees and do my business.

On my return I see DC Peters tending Ken and Finn at the back of the van. Finn's face is swollen and badly cut. His eyes are shut. Ken is coughing and trying to sit up. He doesn't see me.

Police cars and ambulances arrive, lights flashing and sirens blaring. Two paramedics run towards the van and two to the Portakabin. Two uniformed police officers help DC Peters get Thin Man into a police car.

Steve Weston, Bowlegs and his burly mate are led out of the Portakabin in handcuffs. All look dreadful. Blotchy faces and red-rimmed eyes.

I join Ashley and Elspeth, who are hugging and crying. They make way for me, and the three of us hug and cry together.

A short time later, following my revival with a mug of tea and two chocolate muffins, I conveyed the gist of the aforementioned events to detectives at Elven police station.

Chapter 61
DC Peters

6am

'Thank God, we did it!' Kate looked at DS Renn. The ambulances and squad cars had left, and the SOCOs were arriving.

The sergeant smiled.

'Hill's face was a picture when I read out the caution.' He nodded at the three women, still comforting each other. 'I think we've left them long enough. Do you want to...?'

'Sure.'

She tried not to think of the severely decomposed human remains inside a black refuse sack at the back of the van that DCI Hill had attempted to drive away. With any luck, the remains would prove to belong to Kyle Sutton. That would strengthen the case against the arrested men – whom they now knew to be Lazar Bilbija aka Thin Man and his strong men, Zoran Injac and Milan Kovic, along with Steve Weston and DCI Hill.

Kate went over to the trio. Reluctant to disturb the moment, she coughed loudly. The women looked at her with damp faces.

'Kate,' Ashley said in a flat voice.

'Hello, Ashley… Elspeth, Clare. Sorry to disturb you. Would you mind telling me what you witnessed earlier?'

She took notes while Ashley and Elspeth explained how they had dug up Kyle Sutton's body – identified by Finn O'Connor from his belt buckle.

'We heard Ken shout out as we left,' Ashley said. 'Then Bowlegs and his friend came towards us.' Clare had been hit on the head with a hammer, and the women locked in the Portakabin.

'Steve Weston threatened to kill us.' Elspeth broke in. 'But Clare had a knife stowed in her underwear.' She turned to Clare. 'You saved us, my dear.'

Kate put down her pencil. 'You've done an extraordinary thing, the three of you. We'll need to get detailed witness statements now.'

Elspeth frowned. 'Of course. But could we get some sleep first? We've been up all night. I'm desperate for a kip.'

The three women had risked their lives in order to bring down the Wise Men; it seemed wrong to put them through another ordeal. But she couldn't put this off any longer.

'I'm afraid I'm going to have to ask you to accompany me to the station, Elspeth. You, too, Ashley. Would you both step aside, please?'

'We're going to cooperate fully.' Ashley spoke firmly. 'We've printed out our statements describing what happened the night our neighbour died.'

'Thanks for that.' Kate cleared her throat and placed her hand on Ashley's upper arm. 'Ashley Khan, I'm arresting you on suspicion of murdering Tara Sanderson on the night of the 13th of August 2020…'

After reading out the caution, she arrested Elspeth.

9.30am

She and DS Renn were sitting side by side in an interview room, across from Ashley Khan and her solicitor. Kate was asking the questions; Rob had insisted she have the satisfaction of steering the case through to its conclusion. Only now, ironically, that wasn't what she wanted at all.

'To be clear, Ashley. You are now admitting that you were with Tara Sanderson when she died, which contradicts what you told police on several occasions in August 2020, when you denied returning to Ms Sanderson's house?'

'I lied.' Ashley closed her eyes, biting down on her lower lip. 'I was there when Tara died, so were the others. But we didn't intend to kill her.'

DS Renn tapped his fingers on the table.

'The others being Elspeth Chambers, John Briars, Ursula Chalice, Greg Sutherland and Ferne Wood?'

'That's right.'

'Why did you confront Tara?' Kate asked.

'I was angry with her. I'd gone there to have it out with her. The others came with me for moral support.'

'What had made you angry with her?'

'There were a series of incidents. Tara was jealous of my friendship with Elspeth. I found out that she'd deliberately spread lies about my family. My daughter got hurt as a result. She could have died.' Ashley pressed her teeth into a finger. 'I couldn't forgive Tara for that.'

She must stay professional, not let this affect her. Her throat was tight, though. Rob, now looking at her, nodded and addressed the petite woman across the table.

'What happened when you confronted Tara, Ashley?'

'I said what I needed to say. Then I noticed the fruit bowl.' Ashley spoke in a quiet voice, just audible. 'I was so angry, I threw an apple at her. The others joined in.'

'What was the effect on Tara?'

'She got angry and upset. She pleaded with us to stop.'

'Where did the fruit hit her?'

'On her arms, chest, stomach... All of a sudden, she slipped. Her head hit the worktop as she fell.'

Ashley tried to sip from her cup of water. Her hands were shaking so much she couldn't bring the cup to her mouth.

'Let's take a break,' Kate said, about to stop the recorder. She didn't want to torment this poor woman any longer.

'I'll carry on.'

Rob glanced questioningly at Kate. She nodded.

'What happened after that?'

'We took her pulse and checked for breathing. We were sure she was dead.' Ashley's face paled. 'Some of us wanted to call 999. But others said we should clean up the fruit marks and leave, so no one would know it was us.'

Kate paused. 'Was that what you wanted to do? Clean up and leave?'

'I wanted to tell the truth.'

'But you didn't call 999?'

'No, it was decided not to get the police involved. I didn't have the strength to go against the others.' Ashley gave a sad smile. 'I've wished so many times since that day that I'd found the courage to do what I should have done. Maybe that's why I risked so much to help you with the other thing.'

'Thank you, Ashley.' Kate stopped the recorder.

The hope she'd been clinging to – that they would be able to avoid charging Ashley Khan and Elspeth Chambers with any crime connected with Tara Sanderson – was withering. Another irony. Only weeks ago, she'd wanted nothing more than to see the pair convicted for Ms Sanderson's murder.

10pm

Kate yawned, wondering if she could slip away. A gaggle of her colleagues had gathered around DS Renn's desk, the pub clearly on their minds. Now would be a good time to leave. The last 380 would leave in ten minutes.

'Coming for a drink, Kate? I think we deserve one after today.' Rob stood beside her, shrugging on his jacket.

'Ha, you can say that again! And not just today. I haven't forgotten that car journey from hell.'

'I know, I know. Sorry about that.'

She grinned at his repentant expression.

'Next time you feel an urge to go fast, just warn me in advance, OK? I'll make sure to hop out beforehand.'

Rob made a goofy face. 'So, are you coming?'

'I know we should celebrate, but I'm shattered.'

It had been a big day.

DI Lister and several other officers had been relieved from duty pending investigation, the detective superintendent had announced on a visit from Force headquarters.

Kate and Rob had been questioned about the events at daybreak, then congratulated by the acting DCI, hastily brought in from another part of the Force – they had done 'a grand job' and she would be recommending both for promotion. Then, overseen by the acting DCI, they had helped members of a regional unit compile the evidence needed to charge the arrested men.

In a stroke of luck, the sole of a Timberland boot found in Bowlegs's wardrobe, imprinted with a piece of chewing gum, had matched the footprint found at the quarry. DNA samples taken from the caravan where Ms Patel had been held had matched those of Thin Man and his henchmen. Tests on the blood she'd taken from the caravan step showed it had come from Ms Patel.

To Kate's relief, fifteen minutes earlier the Crown Prosecution

Service had given the go ahead for all of the arrested men to be charged.

The Croatian pair were down for the murder of Cindra Patel and Emily Hale, plus the kidnap and attempted murder of Ashley Khan, Elspeth Chambers and Clare Titchfield. Weston and Thin Man would be charged with the attempted murder of the three women, and conspiracy to murder Cindra Patel and Emily Hale. Weston was also down for Kyle Sutton's murder. To cap it all, both men would be charged with conspiring to pervert the course of justice, along with DCI Hills. It was one of the gravest offences in the book, especially for a senior officer.

A loose end had been tied up, too.

To Kate's surprise, a Dawn Elms from the mobile homes had come in that evening saying she had information about Emily Hale's and Cindra Patel's deaths. Along with a large number of locals, she had heard about the morning's arrests and wanted to help police.

'I saw two men threaten Emily,' Dawn began. 'A few days before her body was found.' Her descriptions matched those of the Croatians. Kate asked why she hadn't said anything before. Dawn had been scared of the Wise Men and hadn't trusted the police to investigate. 'I really wish I had.' Dawn then admitted to seeing the same pair standing on a path near the jetty bordering Brampton Wood on the day Ms Patel went missing. Her voice became almost inaudible. 'Someone must have known that she used to walk there,' Dawn said. 'They must have ambushed her.'

'If you're not coming to the pub, I'm giving you a lift home.' Rob gave Kate an appraising glance. 'I'm not having you wait for a bloody bus.'

'If you promise to drive carefully.'

They walked down the corridor together.

'You went above and beyond today, Kate. The guts you showed tackling Thin Man... He could have killed you.'

'I was just doing my job,' she insisted. Inside though, she was glowing.

'You probably saved Ashley's life, too, you know.'

'And Clare saved all three of their lives by taking control of the situation like she did.'

DS Renn turned to face her. 'It doesn't take away from what you did, though.'

Her uneasiness returned.

'It doesn't feel right that we've charged Ashley and Elspeth with manslaughter, after all they've done to help us. If Ashley hadn't insisted that we'd got it wrong about Emily Hale's death being suicide, the Wise Men would still be at large.'

'I'm with you. Unfortunately, the new DCI wants to play by the book.'

Chapter 62
Ashley

Four days later

Ashley lay slumped against a pile of pillows, her tea growing cool beside the bed.

It was past ten but she felt too lethargic to get up. Being held and questioned then charged with manslaughter after that horrific night had taken its toll. Almost as bad as the experience of pleading guilty at Elven magistrates' court to the manslaughter of Tara Sanderson. Despite all this – and the pinpricks of dread she felt whenever she thought about her upcoming court appearance for sentencing – she could not begin to describe her relief at having finally fessed up. She had done what should have done years ago.

And, thank God, the trio's efforts seemed to be leading towards justice for the Wise Men. Weston, Thin Man and the two thugs were expected to get life sentences if convicted, which given the strength of the evidence they almost certainly would be, according to DC Peters.

Justice appeared to be underway as far as the environment

was concerned, too. The *Herald* had been pressing for action to be taken.

Slowly, Ashley pushed herself to her feet.

Thankfully, her solicitor had accepted her decision to plead guilty of manslaughter; a jury might have found them all guilty. Although Tara's death had been unintentional, the actions of herself and the others had set up a chain of events leading to the fatal fall; it could be argued that the possibility of causing serious harm ought to have been foreseen. More importantly, the solicitor stressed, an immediate guilty plea would lead to a reduced punishment.

Ashley's future now hung in the balance, though, and those of her two friends. Elspeth had pleaded guilty to the manslaughter charge, too, and so had John, who had sent a written plea; although he was recovering well, he'd been advised not to travel. To their great surprise, so had Ursula. She had probably felt obliged to confess given the rest of them had, Elspeth thought. Since their court appearance, Ursula wasn't returning calls. All four had been given bail, which was lucky according to the solicitor. They could have been held on remand until sentencing, set to take place at Elven Crown Court in three weeks. Clare had not been charged with anything after all, which she had a hunch was down to Kate's intervention.

It wouldn't be long until she knew what fate had in store. Prison was a definite possibility. The prospect was hard to comprehend. How would she get through years behind bars? She ought to take advantage of her freedom while she had it, she told herself, and she needed to prepare the house for her mother's return from hospital. Diane's rehabilitation would be a challenge for them both.

They'd get through it though, she had a feeling, if she wasn't locked up by then, of course. Her mother had listened to her worries about being faced with a long prison term and provided unexpected support. *You did all that you did knowing you could have been killed. I know you're a good person, love, whatever that judge said. I'm very proud of you.*

The nagging question, which she'd pushed to the back of her mind, hit her with force. What about Craig Matthews?

She had checked with the other two; Elspeth wasn't certain but Clare had also heard DCI Hills say something like: 'Craig will be waiting for us in Whitstable.' She hadn't yet mentioned this to DC Peters.

The doorbell rang. Ashley pulled on a dressing gown and slippers and hurried downstairs.

'Morning, sleepyhead. What are you doing in bed still?' Elspeth held up a copy of the *Elven & District Herald*. 'We're mentioned on the front page!'

She ushered Elspeth inside and put the kettle on. Elspeth spread the newspaper over the kitchen table.

'It's a statement from Elven Police.' Elspeth read aloud.

'"The trial of Steve Weston and the others accused of involvement in a criminal network is expected to be held at Elven Crown Court later this year. We believe they were members of a trio known as 'The Wise Men', which has been the scourge of our community for many years, using blackmail, threats of violence and corrupt police officers to evade justice.

'We acclaim the sustained effort and extraordinary courage of the three women who helped us to arrest and charge these men: Ashley Khan, Elspeth Chambers and Clare Titchfield. The women's discovery of Kyle Sutton's body in a reclaimed quarry owned by Steve Weston's company, S. G. Construction Services has helped our case immeasurably.

'Lastly, I wish to reassure local people that we will do everything in our power to transform Elven Police into an operation fit for the twenty-first century.'"

Elspeth turned to Ashley. 'What do you think of that?'

'Blimey. I'm lost for words.' She set down two plates of buttered toast. The three women had been warned to expect their names to be mentioned in a police statement. But this went a lot further than she'd expected.

'Good for the Herald.' Elspeth wiped an eye. 'That's made me go all weepy. There's something else about us, too. Have a look at the last paragraphs of the Editorial.'

Ashley read as instructed.

'"The trio's unselfish actions in catching the sinister ring have rightly been commended, as they will surely be by most of the community. We hope that the apprehension of these criminals will mark the end of their sway over Elven and its surrounds, and allow us to build a new, invigorated town.

'Furthermore, we at the Herald sincerely hope that the actions of Ashley Khan and Elspeth Chambers will be taken into consideration when they are sentenced for the manslaughter of former Brampton resident, Tara Sanderson. In the Herald's view, these women have acquitted themselves of their past crimes by their brave deeds, and do not deserve to be sent to prison."'

She smiled at Elspeth. 'Who'd have thought? The Herald standing up for us instead of the mighty Steve Weston.'

Elspeth turned the page of the newspaper.

'Ah, this is interesting. "Weston's alleged environmental crimes is being investigated by the Environment Agency. Work is due to start next week. A team has started taking soil samples from the reclaimed former quarry, which indicate a heavy presence of toxic materials, many of which are hazardous to health, harmful to the environment or both."'

'There's more about the inspection of Summerfield. They've found a thick oily substance, now banned... and the council has agreed to rehouse the estate's occupants.'

That was definitely a result. She watched Elspeth turn the pages with gusto.

'Flaming Nora. Look, Ash. I didn't see this... What a hoot! People have been dumping their rubbish outside Weston's place.'

The Bad Women

Elspeth pointed at a photograph of a huge mound of rubbish, stretching out into the distance.

They leaned over the article.

ENOUGH IS ENOUGH: RUBBISH PROTEST AROUND WESTON'S 'CASTLE'

Jake Turbin, environment reporter

Locals have been dumping their rubbish onto the grounds of Bourne Hall, six miles from Brampton, a grand Grade II-listed property owned by businessman and property developer, Steve Weston.

Since news of Mr Weston's arrest broke earlier this week (see page 1), a stream of vans, lorries, cars and people arriving on foot have dumped a variety of waste outside Bourne Hall. The impressive pile of refuse stretches around the property like a smelly moat: household items, grass cuttings, rotten food, etc. It is a protest against Mr Weston's treatment of local people according to Helen Tucker, one of the women who arrived today carrying boxes of eggs.

'It's time that man got his comeuppance,' she says. 'He likes to make out he's on our side, shelling out for this or that good cause. But for years he's been lording it over us. Closing down paths we used to walk our dogs, pressuring us to agree to his plans, using our precious countryside to get rid of toxic waste... and those poor people living on poisoned land... He deserves everything that's coming to him. I hope he gets a long stretch in prison.'

Farmer Tom Goodall says of Mr Weston: 'He's been illegally dumping God knows what in our fields for years. When I heard about him being arrested, me and my mates were at the pub celebrating.'

*Brampton parish council member, Barbara Elkington comments:
'Steve Weston always got away with his abuse of power because
most of us were scared to stand up to him. Well, that's all changed.
Look around you. This is the voice of the people.'*

Elspeth folded the newspaper. 'I'm going to frame this. Shall
we go over there and toss a few eggs?'

Before she could answer, her phone bleeped with a message.
Layla had seen the article online.

*Mum, you're famous! I'm so proud of you. Sam and I have
added our names to a petition to stop you going to prison. L xxx*

Ashley wiped the tears from her eyes. Support from the local
paper, a petition... There was hope that they might be saved from
prison. Plus, she had to admit, she was desperately proud of what
the three women had achieved.

When Elspeth had left, she rang Kate Peters. Time to get it
over with.

'Hello Kate, it's Ashley. I have something else to tell you about
that night at the quarry. It's to do with Craig Matthews.'

There was a noticeable delay before the DC responded.
'Go on.'

'When the men outside the Portakabin were talking about
escaping in a boat, I heard one say: "Craig's in Whitstable waiting
for us." As in Craig had a boat waiting there, something like that. I
think the Craig must be Craig Matthews, Steve Weston's friend. I
really didn't think he was involved in all this. But thinking about
it... I know he's been close to Steve for a long time...' She trailed
off.

'Thanks for letting me know.' The DC paused again before
speaking. 'I think you should talk to Mr Matthews directly about
this.'

'I don't understand.'

'I'm afraid I can't say any more.'

God's sake, what was going on?

'Before you go, Ashley. I want you to know I appreciate all you've done to help us. I'm doing everything I can to stop you being sent to prison. I can't promise anything, but we've written to the judge who'll be sentencing you. The same applies to Elspeth.' A brisk sigh the other end. 'I probably shouldn't have told you that. Please don't mention it to anyone.'

Ashley smiled. An overwhelming sense of gratitude filled her for the undetective-like detective.

'My lips are sealed.'

Ashley stood in the kitchen looking at Craig's number on her phone screen, her finger poised above the green phone icon.

For an hour she had puzzled over what DC Peters had told her about Craig Matthews. Was Craig involved with the wise men? Or had those men been talking about another Craig? Despite Craig being a long-time friend of Steve Weston, it was hard to believe he would have knowingly helped such a man escape justice.

Don't bother with him anymore, part of her insisted. He could be dangerous, and he was unlikely to tell her the truth.

But she had to speak to him. If Craig really had been willing to help these despicable men, she wanted to know.

'Hello, Ashley. Good to hear from you.' At his voice she felt a joyful leap of her heart, as if the organ was entirely divorced from her brain. 'I've been reading about you in the *Herald*. I was about to call and wish you well—'

'Please, stop. I need to ask you something.' She hesitated. 'Are you... Did you... You didn't offer to help Steve Weston and his buddies escape, did you, the night they tried to kill me and Elspeth?'

'What the fuck? Of course I didn't. Why are you asking me this?'

He sounded genuinely shocked.

'You've been friends with Steve for years, you told me yourself. He helped you set up the clinic, and you owe him.'

'Ashley, stop. I've never been part of that, I swear.'

'Did you know that he came to my house and blackmailed me? Threatened to hurt me if I didn't do what he wanted?'

'No, I didn't know.'

'Did you know he had me, Elspeth and Clare gagged and hooded, and shoved into a room for hours?' She squeezed her eyes shut. 'Then he came in and told us he was going to kill us?'

A long silence.

'I didn't know. I'm sorry you had to go through that, Ashley. I knew Steve was up to some bad stuff. But I didn't know how bad it was till recently.'

'So you weren't intending to help him escape, with the rest of those bastards?'

'No, I wasn't. Ashley, let me explain—'

She interrupted, unable to stem the anger welling up. 'So why did I hear Steve say, "Craig is in Whitstable, waiting for us?" I'd really like to know.'

The call cut off.

Starting to cry, she ran out of the house into a thin drizzle. She still didn't know the truth. He could still be innocent, couldn't he? But how likely was that? He was a fraud, wasn't he? He convinced people to buy treatments that didn't work. How many more women like Emily had there been? How much money had he made out of people's misery?

When she had walked until her feet hurt, she came home.

Craig was waiting. He was slumped against the porch, head down, hands in pockets. His eyes were shadowed and his face etched with worry.

'What are you doing here?'

He straightened. 'I need to tell you something.'

She folded her arms. 'Tell me.' After what she'd been through lately, she wasn't going to risk him doing anything to hurt her.

Craig glanced around. 'Can I come inside?'

'I'd rather we talked out here.'

'Alright then.' He shrugged, his Adam's apple bobbing. 'It's true I've been friends with Steve for a long time. He saved my life, I couldn't forget that. For years, I knew he was breaking rules, cutting corners. He told me things over the years, let things slip. I tried to put them aside, not let them affect our friendship.' He ran his fingers through his hair and looked away. 'I was wrong. I admit that.'

Craig's tongue was working inside his cheek.

'A couple of weeks ago, I heard him say something... I knew I had to do something. Steve met with Lazar at my place a few times – the guy they call Thin Man. When they couldn't meet at The Anglers, or somewhere else.'

Just hearing the name made her feel sick.

'What I heard... Steve told Lazar that he might have to kill you, before you "brought them all down".'

She froze. 'Kill me?'

'That's right. I've been helping the police ever since – DS Rob Renn. I told him everything I knew. He asked me to pretend I was on their side. He told me not to tell anyone, not even you. The night you all went to the quarry, Steve phoned me in the early hours. He kept saying "She's found the body" and "I thought I'd buried him deep enough". I had no idea what he was talking about but he sounded desperate. He said the cops were onto him, he needed to disappear for a while and he wanted me to help him. I wanted nothing to do with it but I made out I was going along with him, so the police would have a chance of finding him. I made up a story about knowing a guy in Whitstable with a boat, who owed me a favour and could help them get away – Steve and Lazar and the cop who worked for them.' Craig's head moved slowly side to side. 'Christ, that was hard. I thought he was going to see through me. But he believed me. I told him the time and coordinates of where I would meet him. Then I phoned DS Renn and told him exactly what I'd agreed to do.' He let go of a long breath.

'You did all that... Why?'

Craig spread his arms.

'The information I gave Rob was another nail in Steve's coffin. I helped to get him charged with Kyle's murder – and conspiracy to murder those two women, among other things. I couldn't live with myself anymore, knowing what I knew. The other reason was you. Knowing he wanted to hurt you...'

A storm of shock coursed through her.

'It must have been scary,' she said, 'turning against him like that.' They were standing within touching distance.

'Yep.' He blew out through his lips. 'If Steve ever twigs what I've done, I've no doubt he'll try to kill me, or get someone to do it for him.'

'I'm sorry I doubted you, Craig.' She stepped closer to him. The enormity of what this man had done was sinking in. 'I didn't really believe you were on his side. But I...'

'You needed to check, just in case.'

She felt her face warm. 'I should have known I could trust you.'

'Yeah, you should have.' He leaned in, kissed her lightly on the mouth. 'We could have been friends – more than friends. But that's how it goes, I guess.' Craig looked sad, then met her gaze, his expression harder. 'If you could keep this to yourself, I'd be grateful. I don't want anyone to shoot me in the back just yet.' His mouth turned up at the corner, not quite a smile. 'If you have to tell anyone, at least wait till tomorrow night and I'm out of the country.'

'You're leaving?'

'It's time to re-group. I'll always be a healer, but I'm closing the clinic and stopping the socials for a while. I'm going to a place a long way from here – a long way from anywhere.'

'Oh.' She felt the words ready in her mouth. *Please, don't go!* 'I hope it works out for you,' she said.

On the other side of the gate, Craig turned back and waved.

'Bye, Ashley. See you around.'

Chapter 63
DC Peters

Three days later

The two of them were sitting together, apart from the others. She was on soft drinks after too many glasses of lager.

'How's the investigation going?' The sergeant had been helping with the enquiry into DCI Hill's illicit activities, and other officers suspected of facilitating them.

'It might be coming to a close soon. The guy I mentioned before... He's given us a statement about Weston that can be read out in court. The judge will keep his name confidential.'

'That's great. What's he said, then?'

'It's sensitive, so keep this to yourself.'

'Of course.'

'In essence...' Rob put down his glass of wine and lowered his voice. 'He overheard Weston talking about "the cop and the boy". He understood this referred to a police officer. Weston had found out that this cop had been up to all sorts in his spare time. No prizes for guessing who.'

'DCI Hill, I take it?'

'Weston more or less stated outright that the officer had

promised to divert police attention away from Steve Weston's illegal activities in return for Weston promising not to expose his secret, i.e., sadistic criminal acts he committed as a serving officer involving an underage boy. The boy had been persuaded not to report anything, so it seems.'

Kate nodded. 'Is there anything else that I "might like to know"?'

'People have been coming forward with evidence of Hill's involvement with the wise men.'

'People?'

'An ex-partner, a retired cop... It's looking like Hill has been turning a blind eye to some very nasty goings on facilitated by Thin Man – videos of males of various ages sold on the dark web, for one.'

'What a scumbag.'

DS Renn heaved a sigh. 'Most were trafficked, some in care. Hill let Thin Man to operate without restraint in return for Thin Man keeping his secret.'

'He gets no sympathy from me.'

'Nor me. It looks like he'll be inside for quite a while.'

'What about DI Lister?'

DS Renn nibbled a crisp.

'It looks like she might get time, too.'

'I can't say I'm particularly unhappy to hear that.'

'I didn't think you would be.' The corners of his eyes creased. 'Well done, partner. We got them in the end.'

Before she could think better of it, Kate leaned in and gave the sergeant an awkward side hug.

'Thanks, Rob.'

'What for?'

'Everything.'

Chapter 64
Ashley

Ten days later

'I need to tell you something,' her mother said abruptly, looking up from her Kindle. Diane lay in her bed propped up by pillows, surrounded by mobility paraphernalia, kneading one hand with the fingers of the other, not meeting Ashley's eyes. Since being discharged from hospital, her mother had set about the physiotherapist's exercises with surprising resoluteness.

Ashley turned away from the pot plant she was watering. 'Well?'

'I think Bryce was talking to Steve Weston all along.'

'What do you mean, talking to him?' She put down the measuring jug.

'Telling him things. Supplying information to him. Trying to, anyhow.'

The back of her scalp prickled. 'I don't understand. How do you know this?'

'That afternoon, before you went to the quarry... After I phoned you, I phoned Bryce. I mentioned how mysterious and secretive you were being, and I thought you might be in some sort of danger... Also, I—' Diane met her eyes briefly. 'I said you were planning to go somewhere. He asked where – I said I didn't know but you were going to look for someone's body.'

She stared at her mother, stunned. Was it possible? Was that how Steve Weston had found out that the three of them were at the quarry that night? She had wondered how he'd known.

'I never thought he would...' Diane looked stricken. 'That he might be passing things onto Steve. But he's disappeared, hasn't sent a single message since that phone call. And I've started to remember... Just before my accident, he let slip something about staying at "Steve's villa in Marbella". I said, "How come? I didn't think you two were friends. I didn't think you liked him." He looked at me in an odd way and went, "No, no, we aren't friends, that was ages ago, Steve was a friend of a friend, a group of us went", blah blah. It was like he'd been caught out and he was trying to hide it. I was going to mention it to you but with everything else going on I forgot.' Diane pressed the heel of her hand into her brow. 'That's not all. Once or twice, he asked me things that seemed a bit off.'

Ashley waited. The prickly sensation crept along the back of her head.

'What sort of things?'

'He asked things like, "Do you know what those three are getting up to?" He told me he thought you'd all be better off minding your own business. Also, he asked me if you'd been talking to a Dawn Elms from the mobile home site. I gave him short shrift, said I didn't have a clue. Oh yes, and he wanted to know how Clare had found that journalist's body, how she knew where to look... He always sounded so casual when he asked, as if he was naturally curious. I didn't think anything of it.'

She went closer to her mother. The last pieces of the puzzle were fitting together. It was hard to believe this man had duped them both with such ease.

'You didn't tell Bryce that the three of us were planning to go to the quarry later that night?'

'No, how could I? You didn't tell me. But he must have guessed – or maybe Steve Weston did. Ashley, I'm so sorry. It was my fault that man found you. If I hadn't said anything to Bryce...' Diane buried face her in her hands. 'You could have been killed.'

'Mum, it's OK. You didn't know, nor did I. You can't blame yourself.'

'I should have guessed. That was the entire reason he was with me, wasn't it? He was helping that evil man all along. That was all he wanted from me – information about you and what you were doing. He didn't care about me at all.'

'No, I think he did care about you, Mum. He seemed to genuinely like you. Maybe he didn't start out to deceive you, but later, when Steve found out that you and Bryce were friends and realised I was onto him...'

'He persuaded Bryce to spy on you, using me to do it?'

Ashley nodded.

'I'd like to wring Bryce's neck,' Diane said. 'Very slowly. But fat chance of that... I finally got through to his sister on the land-line. She's looking after his son, so it seems. Bryce is away on a fishing trip in New Zealand and won't be back for three weeks, and he doesn't want to hear from me anymore.

'Oh, Mum.'

She didn't know what else to say, so she put her arms around her mother as she sobbed.

Three days later

'More tea, darlings? Or shall I open Rhianna's champagne?'

Elspeth stood up, teapot in hand. She looked especially glam today in emerald jewellery that set off her green eyes, cigarette pants and a purple poncho. Her short blonde hair was set in waves.

Clare put up her hand. 'Champagne! I've never had it.'

'I agree. Let's open the fizz and celebrate properly.'

The three women were seated on Elspeth's roof terrace.

Ashley sat back, enjoying the warm sunshine on her skin. For the first time in ages, she felt no worry about the future. The sheer relief of the judge handing her a suspended sentence this morning – 12 months – had lifted her into a state of near bliss. She wouldn't have to go to prison! Elspeth had been given the same sentence, as had John – he was back living in Brampton and had attended the hearing in person. The only one of the four to be sent to prison was Ursula, who'd been given six months, though hopefully she would serve only three.

. Clare, in the courtroom viewing gallery, had cheered as the judge handed down her sentence.

The judge had mentioned a string of mitigating circumstances for herself. Her 'campaign to save Brampton from organised crime' and her 'previous exemplary character' – personal statements had been sent in by nearly fifty people – along with the fact that she was now Diane's sole carer. Regarding both herself and Elspeth, the judge had noted their lack of dangerousness and evident remorse, and that both women had 'risked their lives for the public good'.

'We're bloody lucky, you know,' she said when Elspeth returned with the *Tattinger* and three champagne flutes. 'We could be behind bars now eating stodgy stew and cabbage.'

'Poor Ursula.' Clare brushed sandwich crumbs off her new black trousers, bought for the visit to court. 'I wonder what she's thinking right now?'

'Nothing we'd want to know, I should think,' Ashley replied.

Elspeth clasped the bottle between her thighs. As foam spilled down the sides of the bottle, the cork flew high and disappeared over the terrace railing.

'I hope Tara's happy now we've all confessed.' Ashley looked at Elspeth with a smile. Elspeth rolled her eyes, filled three glasses and handed them out.

'To us,' Ashley said with feeling.

'To us!' Elspeth and Clare cried out in unison.

'Ken hasn't seen the ghost again, anyway.' Elspeth lifted her flute. 'To Tara. May she rest in peace.'

Ashley glanced at her phone. A message from John. He was back at home, just around the corner from Wilton Close.

Fancy coming over for coffee tomorrow?

Without hesitation, she typed in a reply. *Absolutely, can't wait!*

When the bottle was empty, the three walked side by side towards the green at the centre of Wilton Close, where a sizeable number of people had gathered by trestle tables bearing plates and cups, decorated with bunting. She recognised some as residents of nearby streets. Rhianna and Ken, who had hurriedly organised a party to celebrate the trio's freedom, were deep in conversation. To her relief, Bryce was nowhere in sight, nor was the vicar.

'Goodness! Look at that.'

Ashley looked to where Elspeth was pointing. A banner had been erected across the street. In large letters was the message:

THANK YOU
ASHLEY ELSPETH & CLARE

She blinked back tears. Elspeth took her hand and squeezed it.

'Come on, you two.' Clare sped towards plates of sandwiches and a Victoria Sponge. 'There's cake!'

Acknowledgments

My thanks to Brian Price for his forensic expertise and to Graham Bartlett for his police procedural advice (any departures from 'reality' are of my own making).

I received invaluable help from certain people while researching this book, especially with aspects of the construction industry and the criminal justice system. I won't name anyone here, but you know who you are!

Thanks to Imma Boada for her accounts of village life, and in particular, what some councillors are getting up to behind the scenes.

Thanks to all those who have read my books, or are intending to do so. I am truly grateful for your support.

Lastly, my thanks to my English teacher, Mrs Kidd, for installing a belief that I could write, back when I was a disobedient teenager who spent much of the day outside the headteacher's office.

Jennie Ensor

About the Author

Jennie Ensor, a Londoner with Irish heritage, writes a range of fiction but her speciality is cosy crime with a twist of dark humour and psychological suspense.

Jennie began her writing career as a freelance journalist, writing investigative pieces on environmental crimes before turning to fiction. As well as novels, she writes poetry. Her prose poem 'Lost Connection' placed second in its category in the 2020 Fish Lockdown Prize. Aside from her passion for reading, she is a keen classical singer, and she loves mountain trekking and wild swimming.

Find out more about Jennie on social media and her website https://jennieensor.com.

Also by Jennie Ensor

Published by Hobeck Books and available in ebook or paperback:

Silenced

The Bad Neighbour

Other titles by Jennie:

The Girl in His Eyes

Not Having It All

Blind Side

Hobeck Books – the home of great stories

We hope you've enjoyed reading this novel by Jennie Ensor. To keep up to date on Jennie's fiction writing please do follow her on social media.

Hobeck Books offers a number of short stories and novellas, including *Saviour* by Jennie Ensor, free for subscribers, in the compilation *Crime Bites*.

Also please visit the Hobeck Books website for details of our other superb authors and their books, and if you would like to get in touch, we would love to hear from you.

Hobeck Books also presents a weekly podcast, the Hobcast, where founders Adrian Hobart and Rebecca Collins discuss all things book related, key issues from each week, including the ups and downs of running a creative business. Each episode includes an interview with one of the people who make Hobeck possible: the editors, the authors, the cover designers. These are the people who help Hobeck bring great stories to life. Without them, Hobeck wouldn't exist. The Hobcast can be listened to from all the usual platforms but it can also be found on the Hobeck website: **www.hobeck.net/hobcast**.